Praise

Pillar
First Book i...

"Bishop only adds luster to her reputation for fine fantasy."
—*Booklist*

"Reads like a beautiful ballad. . . . Fans of romance and fantasy will delight in this engaging tale."   —BookBrowser

"Provides plenty of thrills, faerie magic, human nastiness, and romance."   —*Locus*

The Invisible Ring

"Entertaining otherworlds fantasy adventure. Fresh and interesting."   —*Science Fiction Chronicle*

"A weird, but highly diverting and oddly heartwarming mix."   —*Locus*

"A formidable talent, Ms. Bishop weaves another intense, emotional tale that sparkles with powerful and imaginative magic."   —*Romantic Times*

"Plenty of adventure, romance, dazzling wizardly pyrotechnics, and [a] unique and fascinating hierarchical magic system. The author's overall sublime skill [blends] the darkly macabre with spine-tingling emotional intensity, mesmerizing magic, lush sensuality, and exciting action, all set in a thoroughly detailed, invented world of cultures in conflict. . . . It and its predecessors are genuine gems of fantasy much to be prized."   —*SF Site*

continued . . .

Praise for Anne Bishop

Queen of the Darkness

"As engaging, as strongly characterized, and as fully conceived as its predecessors . . . a perfect—and very moving—conclusion."
—*SF Site*

"A storyteller of stunning intensity, Ms. Bishop has a knack for appealing but complex characterization realized in a richly drawn, imaginative ambience." —*Romantic Times*

"A powerful finale for this fascinating, uniquely dark trilogy."
—*Locus*

Heir to the Shadows

"A rich and fascinatingly different dark fantasy, a series definitely worth checking out." —*Locus*

"Features a fascinating world consisting of three realms amply peopled with interesting . . . characters. Events are set in motion which will be resolved in one of the most eagerly awaited conclusions to a trilogy."
—*The Romance Reader*

Daughter of the Blood

"Anne Bishop has scored a hit with *Daughter of the Blood*. Her poignant storytelling skills are surpassed only by her . . . deft characterization. A talented author." —*Affaire de Coeur*

"A fabulous new talent . . . a uniquely realized fantasy filled with vibrant colors and rich textures. A wonderful new voice, Ms. Bishop holds us spellbound from the very first page."
　　　　　　　　　　　—*Romantic Times* (four and a half stars)

"Lavishly sensual . . . a richly detailed world based on a reversal of standard genre clichés."　　　　　—*Library Journal*

"Mystical, sensual, glittering with dark magic, Anne Bishop's debut novel brings a strong new voice to the fantasy field."　　　　　　　—Terri Windling, coeditor of
　　　　　　　　　　　The Year's Best Fantasy and Horror

SHADOWS
AND
LIGHT

Anne Bishop

A ROC BOOK

ROC
Published by New American Library, a division of
Penguin Group (USA) Inc., 375 Hudson Street,
New York, New York 10014, USA
Penguin Group (Canada), 90 Eglinton Avenue East, Suite 700, Toronto,
Ontario M4P 2Y3, Canada (a division of Pearson Penguin Canada Inc.)
Penguin Books Ltd., 80 Strand, London WC2R 0RL, England
Penguin Ireland, 25 St. Stephen's Green, Dublin 2,
Ireland (a division of Penguin Books Ltd.)
Penguin Group (Australia), 250 Camberwell Road, Camberwell, Victoria 3124,
Australia (a division of Pearson Australia Group Pty. Ltd.)
Penguin Books India Pvt. Ltd., 11 Community Centre, Panchsheel Park,
New Delhi - 110 017, India
Penguin Group (NZ), 67 Apollo Drive, Rosedale, North Shore 0632,
New Zealand (a division of Pearson New Zealand Ltd.)
Penguin Books (South Africa) (Pty.) Ltd., 24 Sturdee Avenue,
Rosebank, Johannesburg 2196, South Africa

Penguin Books Ltd., Registered Offices:
80 Strand, London WC2R 0RL, England

First published by Roc, an imprint of New American Library,
a division of Penguin Group (USA) Inc.

First Printing, October 2002
20 19 18 17 16 15 14 13 12

Copyright © Anne Bishop, 2002
All rights reserved

[Roc] REGISTERED TRADEMARK—MARCA REGISTRADA

Printed in the United States of America

Without limiting the rights under copyright reserved above, no part of this
publication may be reproduced, stored in or introduced into a retrieval system, or transmitted, in any form, or by any means (electronic, mechanical,
photocopying, recording, or otherwise), without the prior written permission
of both the copyright owner and the above publisher of this book.

PUBLISHER'S NOTE
This is a work of fiction. Names, characters, places, and incidents either are
the product of the author's imagination or are used fictitiously, and any resem-
blance to actual persons, living or dead, business establishments, events, or
locales is entirely coincidental.
   The publisher does not have any control over and does not assume any
responsibility for author or third-party Web sites or their content.

If you purchased this book without a cover you should be aware that this
book is stolen property. It was reported as "unsold and destroyed" to the
publisher and neither the author nor the publisher has received any payment
for this "stripped book."

The scanning, uploading, and distribution of this book via the Internet or via
any other means without the permission of the publisher is illegal and punish-
able by law. Please purchase only authorized electronic editions, and do not
participate in or encourage electronic piracy of copyrighted materials. Your
support of the author's rights is appreciated.

For
Kandra

ACKNOWLEDGMENTS

My thanks to Blair Boone for continuing to be my first reader, to Jenny Wegrzyn for telling me all the things hawks don't do so that I could justify why mine did them, to Kandra for her continued work on the Web site, and to Pat and Bill Feidner, just because.

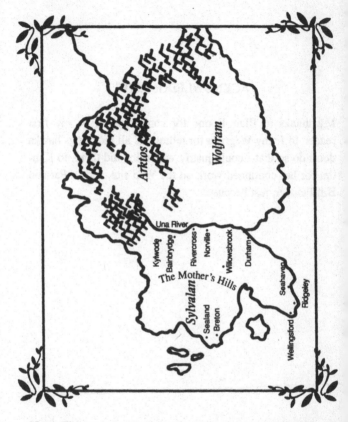

The following place names appear on the map:

Wolfram

Arktos

Una River

Kynwode
Bainbrydge
Rivercross
Norville
Willowsbrook
Durham

The Mother's Hills

Sylvalan

Seahaven

Ridgeley

Sealand
Breton

Wellingsford

Note: This map was created by a geographically challenged author. All distances are whimsical and subject to change without notice.

Chapter One

Sitting cross-legged in the middle of the bed's sagging, lumpy mattress, Lyrra brushed her dark red hair and studied the small room she was sharing with Aiden.

At least it was clean. The floor was swept, the sparse furniture dusted and polished. And the tavern owner's wife had proudly claimed that she always put fresh sheets on the bed, even if a guest spent only one night.

Despite the mattress, this room was luxurious compared with the one they'd been in two weeks ago. There, a bold little mouse had run across her foot while she was washing herself in the chipped basin that was as close to a bath as that particular tavern offered. Her shriek had woken Aiden from a sound sleep, lifting him out of bed in a tangle of covers. At least he'd landed on the bed—mostly—and didn't hit his face on the floor.

He wrote a song about it that made men roar with laughter and women give her sympathetic smiles.

The wretch.

A burst of male laughter rose from the tavern below.

Lyrra wrinkled her nose, then smiled. Aiden must have reached the point in the evening's entertainment where he was singing a few of the bawdy songs he knew. And the Bard knew plenty of them.

But there were some bawdy songs he didn't sing anymore. Whenever someone asked for one of those songs, he'd say he didn't know it. Which was a lie, of course. Aiden was the Fae Lord of Song. It was part of his particular gift of being *the* Bard that he knew the words of every song, could play any tune he'd heard.

She could guess when he'd stopped singing the more . . . blatant . . . songs about men and women because of the one song he *did* sing at every tavern or inn they stopped at for food and lodging.

"I gave her kindness, courtesy, respect, and loyalty," Lyrra sang softly. "I strung them on the strands of love. 'These are the jewels for me. These are the jewels for me.'"

The song was called "Love's Jewels." The Fae had called it "The Lover's Lament," and most still did. But Aiden now sang it with the extra verses he'd learned last summer. Learned from a young witch who had tilted their understanding of the world and had left some of them scrambling to set things right again.

That hadn't been Ari's fault. She hadn't asked for the Fae to intrude in her life. But they had, and in doing so learned more than they had bargained for.

Sighing, Lyrra set her brush on the wobbly table beside the bed. She closed her eyes and sat quietly for a moment. If she reached out with her gift, if she let it drift through this small village and the surrounding farms until it touched an open, willing heart, what would that person receive from the Muse tonight? A poem, a play, a story? It could be any of those things. But it would be a poem, a play, a story about sorrow and regrets. These people already seemed to have their share of that. When Aiden had sung his song that was a warning against the Black Coats, she'd seen the way the men's faces had turned grim—and she'd seen the tears, and the fear, in the women's eyes. This place hadn't been touched by the Inquisitors, but villages just to the east of here had suffered. After that, she and Aiden had kept the songs and stories funny or romantic, things that would lift the spirit or nurture the heart.

Since nothing she could send tonight would lift the spirit, she kept her gift to herself. But withholding it made her sad, and she wondered if a story filled with tears was better than no story at all.

She shook off the feeling when she heard the footsteps outside the room's door. By the time the door opened, she'd worked on presenting a smile of greeting.

That smile faded when the black-haired, blue-eyed man stepped into the room. His harp case was slung over his shoulder by one of its straps. In his hands, he held a steaming mug and a small plate containing two slices of buttered bread and a piece of cake.

"I thought you might like a cup of tea and a bit of a nibble," Aiden said, pushing the door closed with his foot before taking the couple of steps that brought him close enough to the bed to hand over his offering.

He looked tired, Lyrra thought as she accepted the cup and plate. Well, they were both tired, and she'd been traveling with him only for the past few weeks, ever since he'd come back to Brightwood to find out why she hadn't met him as planned. But he'd been traveling since last summer, singing songs in the human villages to warn people about the Black Coats, the Inquisitors—and traveling up the shining roads to tell the Fae Clans that the witches who lived in the Old Places were the descendants of the House of Gaian, and their deaths by the Inquisitors' hands were the reason pieces of Tir Alainn were disappearing. It was physically wearing to stay in the human world and travel from place to place day after day, singing the songs and telling the stories. It was emotionally wearing to pass through the Veil that separated the human world from Tir Alainn to visit the Fae Clans and see the stubborn faces and hear the dismissive remarks when she and Aiden tried to tell them the witches needed the Fae's protection.

"Drink your tea while it's still warm," Aiden said. He bolted the door, then crossed the small room to carefully set his harp beside the table and two chairs placed beneath the window. He undressed with his back to her, leaving his shirt on until he got into bed beside her and was covered below the waist.

Disturbed by this new modesty of his, Lyrra sipped her tea and ate a slice of buttered bread. They had been lovers on and off for several years, whenever they were both staying with the same Clan in Tir Alainn and during the times when they'd made brief journeys together in Sylvalan. Then, he'd been brash, arrogant, sure of his welcome as a lover. And he hadn't thought twice about undressing in front of her.

She handed him the cup to share the tea and insisted he have the other slice of bread and half the cake. She was hungry enough to eat it all, but so was he, despite a hearty dinner they'd been given as part of the fee for their performance. There had been too many lean meals lately.

When they finished, she put the cup and plate on the bedside table, next to her brush and the candle she'd lit when she'd come up to the room—and decided it was time to find out what had been preying on his mind lately. It was something more than the loss of another piece of Tir Alainn, something more than the loss of another Daughter from the House of Gaian.

"Aiden, what's been troubling you these past few days?"

He stripped off his shirt, tossed it on one of the chairs, then lay back. He tucked one arm under his head. The other lay across his belly. "What isn't troubling me these days? I've spent almost a year talking and talking and talking—and no one has listened. The Old Places are still unprotected, the witches are still unprotected, and the Fae sit above it all in Tir

Alainn, expecting everything to go on as it has for so long without making any effort to make sure it *does* go on. The foul thoughts and feelings the Inquisitors brought with them from Wolfram last year haven't been cleansed from people's hearts and minds. If anything, those thoughts are spreading, slowly seeping into other parts of Sylvalan. Those words are still poisoning men's hearts against the Great Mother, women in general, and the witches in particular."

"That's been true for months," Lyrra said softly. "But there's more now."

"It's nothing."

"Yes," she said dryly, "and pigs can fly."

He gave her a shadow of one of his old smiles. "Perhaps they can in some far-off land beyond the sea."

Lyrra stiffened, recognizing it was her heart more than her pride that was stung. She had asked a serious question, and had, by the asking, offered to share whatever troubled him. And he was going to brush that offer aside as if it were whimsy. Very well, then.

She leaned over to blow out the candle when he said, "It wears on a man when fear is his constant companion."

She turned to look at him. "You've been afraid you might meet up with the Inquisitors?"

"No. I've been afraid you would."

She didn't know what to say. Pleasure at hearing he cared lifted her heart. Fear of the things she'd heard Inquisitors did to women accused of being witches churned in her belly, making her feel a little sick.

"Late last summer, I visited a Clan about half a day's ride east of here," Aiden said, not looking at her. "They wouldn't listen to me. There were two witches living in a small cottage in the Old Place that anchored that Clan's territory to the human world, and the Fae wouldn't listen to me when I explained the danger that had crept into Sylvalan because of the

Inquisitors. When I came back this way on my way to Bright-wood, men were in the Old Place cutting down the trees. The witches were gone, the shining road was gone—and another piece of Tir Alainn was gone with it.

"I thought of you, Lyrra. If you'd left Brightwood to meet up with me as we'd originally planned, you might have stopped at that Clan's house to rest. If you'd stopped there at the wrong time, you might have disappeared with the rest of the Fae who had lived there, and there would have been nothing I could have done."

"Someone else with the gift of story would have ascended to become the Muse," Lyrra murmured.

"She wouldn't have been you," Aiden said quietly. He took a deep breath, then let it out slowly. "A few days before I reached Brightwood, I passed through a human village and saw a little girl with red hair. And I thought . . . if you had a child, that's what she would look like—a darling little red-haired girl with a sweet smile that would grow sassy in a few years." He swallowed, the muscles in his throat working with the effort of it. "And I thought if I was the man who had sired your child, I wouldn't be content with knowing your male relatives would help you raise her. I'd want to be the one to rock her to sleep at night and teach her the songs and kiss the scraped elbow or skinned knee. I'd want to be her father instead of just her sire."

"That's not the way the Fae live," Lyrra said. She felt tears sting her eyes and wasn't even sure why she wanted to cry.

"That may be, but the ways of the Fae may not suit *all* of the Fae," he replied a little sharply.

"There are good reasons for our living the way we do," she said, her own voice taking a sharper edge. "The main one being that Fae males aren't capable of keeping themselves to one lover."

A long pause. "I haven't been in as many beds as you

seem to think," Aiden said, turning his head to look at her. "And I always came back."

"To dance with the Muse."

"To be with you, Lyrra. And you haven't been without lovers when I wasn't there." An unspoken question shimmered in his eyes.

"I—" Something was happening here. Something between a man and a woman, not between the Bard and the Muse. "I haven't invited as many men to my bed as you seem to think."

He sang quietly, "I gave her kindness, courtesy, respect, and loyalty. I strung them on the strands of love."

"These are the jewels for me," she finished just as quietly, unsettled enough to feel dizzy.

"Would they be enough?" he asked, a strange, strained note in his voice. "If they were offered each day, would they be enough?"

"They would be precious," she murmured. "Priceless." She bent her head so that her hair would fall forward, hiding her face from him. Her heart beat oddly. She couldn't seem to draw in enough air to breathe properly. She felt as if Aiden were holding a treasure she craved just out of her reach.

"Would they be enough for you to accept one man as a friend and lover? As an . . . exclusive mate?"

Pushing her hair aside, she studied his face, baffled by the uncertainty in his eyes. "Are you asking if I'd be willing to accept you as an exclusive mate? As a—" What did the humans call it? She knew the word as well as she knew her own name. But she couldn't remember either at the moment.

"As a husband," Aiden said softly. "Yes. That's what I'm asking."

Tears stung her eyes. She pressed a hand against her mouth, not sure if she was going to laugh or cry. There were too many feelings spinning through her.

She drew her hand away from her mouth, let it rest on her throat, and felt her pulse beating wildly. "The rest of the Fae will say we've been contaminated by spending so much time in the human world."

"These are our lives and our choice," he said, sitting up so they were eye to eye. "Do you really care what the rest of the Fae will say or think?"

Lyrra shook her head, reached for him.

He pulled her into his arms and held her tight.

"Yes," she whispered in his ear. "Yes, I'll take the jewels of love that you offer, and, giving them back in turn, I'll accept you as friend, lover, and husband."

When he tried to kiss her, she pressed her head against his shoulder and wept.

"Lyrra," he said, alarmed. He shifted her until she was sitting on his lap and rocked her. "Why are crying? If you want this as much as I do, why are you crying?"

She made an effort to hold back the tears, since they were making it impossible to speak. "When I was at Brightwood over the winter, I read the journals the women in Ari's family had left behind. This is what they wanted. This is what they *had* once and wanted to have again. This is what Ari never would have gotten from Lucian. I met her only that one time, but I liked her. It seems so unfair that, because we met her, I've gotten my own heart's wish and she—" She swallowed the tears. "And she got nothing more than whatever kindness Morag gives to the spirits the Gatherer takes to the Shadowed Veil."

Aiden rocked her for another minute. The storm of emotions that had battered her was fading now, leaving her limp and exhausted. Comforted by the movement and the feel of his arms around her, she began to drift toward sleep.

"We all have secrets," he said quietly. "Things we know that we don't share for one reason or another. We all have the right to have thoughts that are private. But I've noticed that, among humans, it usually is not considered breaking a confidence when something is shared between a husband and a wife."

"That's part of love," she replied.

He took a deep breath, let it out slowly. "Lyrra, sometimes words can lie even when they tell the truth."

"I'm aware of that," she said, a little prickly. "After all, I *am* the Muse."

"Ari is gone."

She felt the tears sting her eyes again. He didn't need to tell her the obvious. Wasn't that what she'd been talking about a minute ago? Ari had been captured by the Inquisitors, and Morag had told Dianna and Lucian—

She sat up slowly.

Sometimes words can lie even when they tell the truth.

"Ari is gone," she said, watching Aiden's eyes, seeing the silent message in them: there was something under the words being spoken that she needed to pay attention to. Over the past few weeks, they'd gotten very good at giving each other these silent messages as they sang and told stories and listened to what the villagers and farm folk said—and didn't say.

"Morag told Dianna and Lucian that Ari was gone," she continued. Truth and lies. "And because Morag is the Gatherer, they assumed Ari was dead. But she never actually *said* that. She just said Ari was gone."

"Yes," Aiden agreed, "that's all she ever said."

Lyrra thought a moment, then shook her head. "She *did* take two spirits up to the Shadowed Veil."

"Yes, she did."

"Then—" Lyrra paused. Ahern, the Lord of the Horse, had been killed in the confrontation with the Inquisitors when they came to Ridgeley—and Brightwood—last summer. Had there been someone else at Brightwood? Someone none of the Fae but Morag had known about? "What happened to the young man Ari was going to wed? What was his name? Neall. Yes, Neall. Morag . . . said he was gone."

"He gave her kindness, courtesy, respect, and loyalty," Aiden sang softly.

Unable to sit still, Lyrra scrambled off the bed to pace the width of the small room.

You're the Muse. He's the Bard. He expects you to be able to hear what isn't being said. Just as Morag had expected him *to understand what* she *hadn't said.*

He'd gone to see Morag one last time before she left Ahern's farm. Why would she have told him anything? Because he had grieved Ari's death—and the loss of a Daughter of the House of Gaian.

"He got her away from them," Lyrra said, more to hear the words spoken than to speak to Aiden. "Somehow, Neall got Ari away from the Inquisitors. And then took her away from Brightwood, as well." She pressed her hands against her face. "If the Lightbringer and the Huntress ever learn that the last witch from Brightwood still lives . . ."

"They would search for her until they found her, and they would bring her back to Brightwood, regardless of what Ari wants," Aiden replied. "Dianna would bring her back so that *she* wouldn't have to stay in the human world and be the anchor that keeps the shining road open and her Clan's piece of Tir Alainn intact. And Lucian would bring her back to have Ari as his mistress because he lost her before he tired of her—and because his pride wouldn't tolerate the truth that she'd chosen a human male over him." He paused. "But that is merely speculation. Morag said Ari is gone, and the Gatherer would know that better than the rest of us."

"Mother's mercy, Aiden." Lyrra sank down on the end of the bed. "Let's hope they never realize that what Morag said wasn't what they assumed she meant." Then she turned and gave him a brilliant smile. "Ari is gone. Isn't that wonderful?"

Answering her smile with his own, he held out a hand. When she took it, he tugged her toward him, lying back so that she was stretched out on top of him.

He played with her hair and said, "When humans wed, there are speeches and customs that are observed to seal the bargain. We've spoken words to pledge ourselves to each other, so there's just one other thing to do to seal the bargain."

He looked at her with eyes full of lust and laughter.

She gave him a soft kiss, then wiggled her body just enough to get a hard response from his.

"Vixen," he said, wrapping his arms around her.

"I am not!" She paused. "Well, yes, I am. Some of the time."

Laughing, he rolled until she was under him. "Come, wife. Let's seal the bargain."

This time, when they gave each other their bodies, they also gave much more.

Aiden stared at the ceiling. Lyrra slept peacefully beside him.

Yes, husbands and wives kept secrets, but there were some secrets he *had* to tell her now, for her own protection. If something happened to him, she had to know where to run—and what places to avoid at any cost. It wasn't safe for a woman to travel alone anymore along the eastern border. In some places, it wasn't safe to *be* a woman, now that the Inquisitors had come to Sylvalan and somehow convinced the eastern barons—and through them, other men—that women were lesser creatures who had no purpose, and no value, ex-

cept to provide men with comfortable homes, sex, and offspring.

Aiden rolled over and tucked himself around Lyrra, needing the closeness.

He'd missed her over the past year with a fierceness that
had made him ache. And even though he'd worried at times
that the Inquisitors might come back to Brightwood, he'd
been grateful she'd stayed there—until he'd returned to see
her and discovered Lyrra hadn't stayed by her own choice.
Then the anger and frustration he'd been feeling toward his
own kind had turned on Dianna, who was the Lady of the
Moon, the Huntress, the female leader of the Fae. She and
Lyrra were the only Fae at Brightwood who had some aspect
of power in them that made it possible for them to anchor the
magic in the Old Place and, with enough other Fae present,
keep the shining road to Tir Alainn open.

Last summer, after part of the Clan had come down to the
human world, Dianna had asked Lyrra to remain at Brightwood a few more days while she went to Tir Alainn and took
care of a few things before coming back to live in the cottage
that had belonged to Ari's family. Dianna returned to Tir
Alainn—and stayed there, leaving Lyrra with the choice of
remaining to anchor the shining road or putting an entire
Clan at risk if she left.

It was only when he'd returned that Lyrra had sent a warning through another of the Fae that she was leaving. *That*
brought Dianna back to Brightwood. Lyrra refused to tell
him what had been said before she left, but he imagined it
hadn't been a pleasant leave-taking. And the cold courtesy
with which they were greeted whenever they went up a shining road to a Clan house in Tir Alainn told him that Dianna
had been spewing her bitterness over having to remain in the
human world to anyone who would listen. He and Lyrra were

being blamed for putting Dianna's Clan at risk and leaving *her* "exiled" at Brightwood.

The fact that no Lady of the Moon from another Clan had offered to come to Brightwood and try to be the anchor for the magic in the Old Place was telling. Perhaps that was just the self-interest that came naturally to most of the Fae—or perhaps, despite being willing to condemn Lyrra for her decision, no one trusted Dianna enough to offer, not after she'd broken her promise to the Muse.

He could fight the Clans' cold courtesy with sharp words, but he couldn't fight what was happening in Sylvalan. What he'd seen in some of the villages he'd passed through last summer and autumn had chilled him. Women wearing something called a scold's bridle that deprived them of the ability to speak. A woman being strapped in the public square, while the men witnessing the punishment hadn't been able to tell him what she'd done to be treated so badly, only that it was necessary to teach a woman modesty and pleasing behavior.

Those things had been bad enough. But something else had come across the river from Wolfram over the winter, something that made the men so uneasy they wouldn't talk about it. Something that the eastern barons were ordering done to make sure women remained in what was now considered their proper place in society. A "procedure," the men had muttered, to rid a woman of unhealthy feelings.

Shivering, Aiden snuggled closer to Lyrra.

He hadn't been able to find out what this new danger was, but the fear of it was one of the things that had sent him galloping back to Brightwood.

Whatever was wrong in the human villages in Sylvalan was spreading. Even a village like this one, where nothing seemed out of place, made him uneasy. More so now, when the desire to protect Lyrra was stronger than his desire to survive.

Tomorrow they would head for villages closer to the Mother's Hills, places farther away from the eastern border of Sylvalan. Maybe they would come to an Old Place and take the shining road back to Tir Alainn and rest for a few days. And try, once again, to convince the Fae that the human world was no longer a place where they could amuse themselves when they chose and ignore it the rest of the time.

Because if the Fae didn't act soon to protect the witches and help the humans protect themselves from what the Inquisitors were doing to the people of Sylvalan, none of them—the humans, the witches, the Small Folk who lived in the Old Places, or the Fae—would survive.

Chapter Two

Standing in front of the morning room door, Liam smoothed back his dark brown hair and resisted the urge to give the tops of his boots a quick polish on the back of his trouser legs. His mother knew he'd already been out working, had requested this appointment during the time when he usually came in to spend an hour going over accounts and correspondence and, lately, to reply to the black-edged notes of condolence. She wouldn't expect him to look like anything but what he was—a man who tended the land that belonged to him and looked after the people who worked for him. The fact that he was now the Baron of Willowsbrook didn't change anything. He'd been riding over the land for twenty years now, had started visiting the tenant farms on his beloved sorrel pony when he was barely seven years old. She wouldn't criticize him for being dressed in clothes that were a bit sweaty and smelled of animals.

Maybe it was because she *wouldn't* criticize his appearance that he had the urge to run upstairs and put on a fresh shirt before stepping into a room that was bright, feminine, and soothing.

Giving the door a light rap with his knuckles, Liam walked into the room. His mother, Elinore, stood at the glass door that opened onto a small terrace, no doubt watching the birds that gathered to drink and bathe in the stone basin that was scrubbed and filled with fresh water every morning. The sunlight made the strands of gray in her light brown hair shine like silver. She was a small, slim woman with an inner strength that had weathered all the emotional storms of her marriage.

He may have inherited his father's looks—the dark hair, a face handsome enough to catch a woman's eye, height that was a little above average—but he was glad he'd inherited his mother's hazel eyes. Woodland eyes, she called them, because they were a brown-flecked green. Sometimes he wondered if, when she looked at him, she saw only a younger version of his father. At least when she looked at his eyes, she had to know there was a part of her in him, as well.

"Good morning, Mother," Liam said. He glanced at the tray on the table near the sofa and instantly became wary. The tea, thin sandwiches, and pastries weren't unusual fare for a midmorning chat, but the decanter of whiskey was definitely out of place. Elinore didn't approve of indulging in strong drink, especially so early in the day. That she'd arranged for the decanter to be here meant she thought one of them would need something more potent than tea to get through this conversation.

Turning away from the window, Elinore offered him a hesitant smile. "Good morning, Liam. Thank you for taking time out of your day to meet with me."

Heat washed through his body, a sure sign that his temper was rising. Making an effort to keep his voice calm, he replied, "Thanks aren't necessary. You're my mother. My being the baron now doesn't change that." At least, he hoped it didn't.

"No, but . . . it does change some things." She walked over to the sofa, sat down, and offered another hesitant smile. "Please sit down. There are some things I need to say to you."

Reluctantly, he sat on the other end of the sofa. Then

something occurred to him that had him leaning toward her, tense. "Brooke's all right, isn't she?"

"Brooke?"

The surprise in Elinore's eyes, warming to amusement, made him feel limp with relief. His ten-year-old sister was a delightful child, but she did tend to get into scrapes.

"Brooke is fine," Elinore said, pouring tea for both of them. "A bit sulky since it's a lovely day and she's stuck doing lessons instead of working with the new pony a certain someone recently gave her for her birthday."

Taking the cup of tea she offered him, Liam gave her a bland stare. "I seem to recall another someone slipping money to that certain someone with the instructions to purchase new tack for the new pony."

"Is that what you recall?" Elinore asked innocently. "Do you also recall that certain someone telling Brooke she could skip her lessons this morning so that he could take her for a long ride so the pony wouldn't get bored working in the confines of the training ring?"

Liam choked on the tea he just swallowed. "I said maybe. After the midday meal."

" 'Maybe' means yes."

"Since when?"

She just looked at him until he wanted to squirm. That was the problem with trying to argue with his mother, even playfully. She knew him too well and remembered far too many things from his own childhood.

"After the midday meal, if she has her lessons done, I'll take her for a ride and we'll put the pony through his paces," Liam said.

"Listening to the two of you determine the definition of 'done' should be quite entertaining," Elinore said placidly.

"I—" Liam leaned back, feeling a bit sulky himself. He wasn't going to win this round. Brooke was his little sister.

His baby sister. He'd already been away at school when she was born, and her first years were odd flashes of memory for him. A baby who drooled and giggled when he made funny faces at her. An infant who had learned to crawl between one visit home and the next, and had sent him into a panic when he'd put her on the carpet and turned his back for what he swore had been no more than a minute, only to have her disappear on him. The toddler who giggled and ran through the gardens as fast as her chubby little legs could take her. The bright little girl who chattered about anything and everything to the point where he'd nicknamed her Squirrel. The silent, wary child she became whenever his father was around.

As the male head of the family, he'd do his best to be firm about getting the lessons done, but the minute she turned those big blue eyes of hers on him, he'd cave. He remembered too well how it felt to be stuck indoors laboring over sums when the land beckoned.

"Liam." Elinore sipped her tea and didn't look at him. "Did you mortgage the estate?"

It didn't surprise him that she'd known his father had intended to take a mortgage out on the estate. No doubt the old baron had taken cruel delight in telling her he was stripping the land for everything it was worth.

When his father's man of business had gone over the accounts with him, he'd been appalled at the amount his father had intended to wring from the already foundering estate. And he'd felt an obscene kind of gratitude that the old baron had choked to death while dining with his current mistress before the papers had been signed.

"Yes, I took out a mortgage," Liam said, gulping down the rest of the tea. "A small one." Enough to pay off the tradesmen his father owed and give himself some money to honor his own bills for the next year or so. Elinore had provided him with a generous quarterly allowance ever since he'd first gone away to school, and he'd been grateful for it, but now that the estate was his, he didn't want to live off her money. With proper care and management, the land should be able to provide him and his family with a good living.

"I see." Elinore set her cup down, then folded her hands in her lap. She focused her gaze on the terrace door. "I'll make the same bargain with you that I made with your father."

Don't treat me like I've become him just because I hold the title, Liam thought fiercely.

"I'll pay the servants' wages and the household expenses," Elinore continued, her eyes still focused on the terrace door. "And I'll assist in paying any bills for the upkeep of the tenants' cottages. But I won't pay any bills for the upkeep of the town house in Durham, nor will I pay for any of your . . . personal . . . expenses."

Meaning, if he took a mistress as his father had done, he'd have to pay for his own pleasure. Not that he thought much pleasure could be had from a mercenary creature like the woman his father had been bedding when he died. On the other hand, he couldn't blame her for being mercenary. It had showed she'd had a better understanding of his father than the other women the old baron had enjoyed.

"It's a generous offer," he said. It stung that he had to accept it, but he was practical enough to know it would be a few years before the estate would recover sufficiently to pay all the expenses. "I thank you for it."

"Your father didn't think it was generous."

"My father and I didn't see eye to eye about a great many things," Liam said sharply. "Your father gave you an independent income for *your* benefit, not for my father's and not for the estate's. You had, and still have, every right to do with it as you please. Willowsbrook should be able to support itself twice over. The fact that it *can't* quite support itself is my father's—and *his* father's—fault, not yours."

After a long pause, Elinore said, "Would you like more tea?"

What he'd like was a hefty glass of that whiskey, but he had the feeling they'd only chewed the edges of whatever she'd wanted to talk to him about. "Please," he said, holding out his cup. He waited until she refilled both their cups. "Would you mind if I sold the town house in Durham?"

"The estate and any other property is yours now, Liam. You may do with it as you please."

"Would you mind?" he persisted.

When she looked at him, he saw a bitterness in her eyes she'd never allowed to show before. "There's nothing in that place that I value."

No, there wouldn't be, not when his father's string of mistresses had spent more time there than she had. Well, that was one burden and expense he could easily shed. He'd write to his man of business and set things in motion to sell the town house and its contents.

"Won't you need the town house when you have business in the city?" Elinore asked.

Liam shook his head. "I can rent rooms easily enough for the two times a year when the barons formally meet."

He felt a pressure building inside him, and he clamped his teeth to try to keep the words back as he'd done for so many years. Perhaps it was because the conversation was already difficult that he couldn't hold it back anymore. "Why didn't you leave him? He was a bastard, and you deserved so much better. Adultery is grounds for severing the marriage vow. You had income of your own, so you were never dependent upon him. Why did you stay?"

"I had three reasons," Elinore replied quietly. "You. Brooke. And Willowsbrook."

There was something about the way she said "Willows-brook" that made him think she was talking about more than the estate.

"You're the baron now. You have authority and power, not just on the estate and tenant farms but over the villagers and the free landowners, as well. You can use that authority and power for ill or for good."

"I'm aware of that."

"How you act will set a precedent for the rest of the people here."

Liam snorted softly. "My father thankfully didn't set much of a precedent."

"If he'd ordered that something be done, that order would have been obeyed. The squires and magistrates in each village would have seen it carried out."

Liam rested one hand lightly over his mother's. "He still had to obey the decrees that the council of barons agree upon for the good of Sylvalan."

"The barons have the power to change the decrees or make new ones, regardless of what the rest of Sylvalan's people want. And a baron can impose his will over the people in the county he rules no matter what the decrees say."

She looked pale and unhappy, and he didn't know what she wanted from him. "To what use do you want me to put my new authority and power?" he asked gently.

"I want you to protect the witches at Willowsbrook—the Old Place this estate took its name from generations ago when your father's kin first came here to live and work the land."

Liam sighed, withdrew his hand. "Mother—"

"I have something to tell you," Elinore said hurriedly. "A secret I'd kept from your father because of a few things he'd said on our honeymoon. But you have to know. You have to understand."

"Understand what?"

Agitated, Elinore set her teacup on the table, then walked to the glass door. She stared at the world beyond the glass for a minute, as if she needed to draw strength from the view. Then she turned to face him.

"My great-great-grandfather was a witch's son," she said quietly. "He was the eldest son, but the Old Places always belong to the women of the family, and he wanted something to call his own. When he was a young man, he left home with his mother's blessing. He traveled for a few years, learned a bit about several trades as he worked for his food and lodging and a few coins to rub together. Then, one day, he saw a piece of land that made him want to put down roots, so his mother and grandmother helped him scrape together enough money to buy the land and build a small cottage.

"He had a gift for knowing what the land could yield and what needed time to ripen. He was canny when it came to business—and he was canny when it came to people. Like the land, he could sense what each could yield and when something or someone needed time to ripen.

"He prospered, and the people he dealt with prospered, as well.

"When he eventually married, he took a witch for a wife. They had several children, and the family continued to prosper. By then, his merchant business was turning a good profit, and he built a large, rambling country house.

"His eldest son went into the business with him, while the other sons and daughters found their callings in other kinds of work. In time, some of them fell in love, got married, and had children, and their children had children.

"And so it went. And while the family never hid their ties to the witches who lived in several of the Old Places, they also didn't flaunt those ties. As generations passed, not all of the spouses could make the same claim of having ties to an

Old Place, and the gifts that come down through the blood became watered down or disappeared altogether." Elinore paused, then shook her head. "Not disappeared. Nuala says the Mother's gifts sometimes sleep in the blood, waiting to reappear again." She smiled sadly. "The name means nothing to you, does it? Our nearest neighbor for all of these years, and you don't even know who she is."

"Of course I know," Liam said testily. "She's one of the witches."

Elinore walked back to the sofa and sat down, folding her hands in her lap. She sighed. "Yes, she's one of the witches. She's also my father's cousin, several times removed."

Having no idea what she expected him to say, Liam drank his now-cold tea to give himself a little time. Given his father's animosity toward the witches who lived in the Old Place that bordered the estate, he understood quite well why his mother had never mentioned this aspect of her family heritage. But . . .

"As you said, it was several generations ago," Liam said, thinking she was worried about his feelings toward her changing. "You've no reason to feel shame because of it."

Elinore's eyes widened. "I'm not ashamed of my heritage. If I regret anything, it's that my gift from the Mother is so weak." Then she looked slightly annoyed. "Perhaps it's because it came down through the paternal line in my branch of the family that the men's gifts from the Mother were less diluted. My brother certainly has a stronger connection to water than I do to earth."

Liam opened his mouth, then shut it again before he said anything. What was she trying to tell him? That she *regretted* not being a witch? How could she *want* to be like them?

"Mother," he began hesitantly. "I can appreciate your concern for those . . . women . . . who live in the Old Place since they're distantly related to you. But they're *distantly* related."

"To me," Elinore replied. "But not so distant to you." She took a deep breath, let it out slowly, then looked at him. "The youngest of them is your half sister, one of your father's bastards. She's four years younger than you, and she's not distant, Liam. She is family."

"No!" Unable to sit anymore, Liam restlessly prowled the room. As he passed the table, he snatched up the decanter, splashed some whiskey into a glass, and downed it. He poured another two fingers into the glass, but, this time, resisted the urge to gulp it down.

"No," he said again as he continued to prowl around the room. "She's no more family than any of the other bastards my father seeded in the women he seduced. I know you established a fund to help those women and assist the children in learning a trade so that they could have a living, but they've never been acknowledged as *family*."

"No, they never have." Elinore looked down at her hands. "I'm not proud that I couldn't find it in my heart to accept the children, but it is, I think, an understandable failing. But Keely is different. She was only fourteen when your father took her, and what he did to her scarred her mind in ways that time has never healed. And with the talk and stories that are starting to be told about witches, your sister—"

"She's *not* my sister!"

"—is more vulnerable than any of those other children."

"If she's four years my junior, that makes her twenty-three," Liam said. "She's no longer a child."

"Which doesn't change the fact that she needs your protection." Elinore stood up. "They all need your protection, Liam. There are troubles in the east. Things are happening there that threaten every woman, not just the witches. My cousin Moira—"

"Oh, yes, cousin Moira," Liam said nastily—and then realized he'd used the same tone of voice his father had always used when Moira was mentioned.

"Did you know that the girls in her village were turned away from school last fall? The baron who rules Pickworth declared that too much learning is unhealthy for females. It makes them unfit for the duties that are beneficial to a man's family. So now they are permitted to learn how to read and write and do sums to the extent that it is sufficient for them to run a household. By those standards, Brooke should be learning nothing more than how to do fine needlework and write out a menu rather than learning how to think for herself."

"You misunderstood what Moira said," Liam insisted. "Or she exaggerated something sensible, turning it into the ridiculous."

"Sensible? Do you call leaving women totally dependent on the men in their families, with no way for them to earn a living on their own, sensible? What about the Widow Kendall? Should she have become little more than a beggar when her husband died instead of running the merchant store and making a good living for herself and her children? Or maybe she should have accepted any man who offered to marry her, whether she cared for him or not, trading the use of her body for sex in exchange for food and lodging for herself and the children. It isn't sensible, Liam. All it does is turn women into unpaid domestic help and legal whores."

"*What?*"

"If a woman is controlled by the male head of her household until she marries, performing whatever duties are required to provide him with a comfortable, well-run home, and then has to spread her legs when she does marry in order to earn her food and lodging, what would *you* call it?"

He said nothing for a moment, staggered by the crudeness

of her words. "What's wrong with a man taking care of his family?" he finally asked. "What is so wrong with him making decisions for his children or younger siblings since they would be too inexperienced to always make good decisions for themselves?"

Elinore sighed. "There's nothing wrong with those things, Liam. But I'm not talking about children. I'm talking about grown women, independent women who are as capable of thinking for themselves and making choices about their lives as any man, who are now being forced back into being as dependent as a child. I don't think a strong, healthy community can exist with that kind of forced dependence, but it's my gender that is vulnerable. You, being a man, may see things differently."

Liam shook his head. "You've misunderstood something."

"No, I think I understand perfectly what is at stake. I don't think the eastern barons care about healthy communities anymore," Elinore said. "I don't think they care about anything but having domination over women, over the land, over life." She paused, then added bitterly, "But I will not stand by and let it happen here."

"It would never happen here, so it's a moot point." Liam angrily circled the room.

"Won't it? Your father was going to make the same decree, forbidding girls to receive more than three years of formal education. He was also going to follow the example of some of the eastern barons and forbid women of any age to read *anything* that wasn't approved of by the male head of the household. And he was quite pleased to inform me that the barons were considering a new decree that would prevent a woman from owning property in her own name, or running a business, or even having an independent income."

"But that would mean—"

"That your father would have had control over my income. He could have spent it as he pleased, and I wouldn't have seen another copper from it except what he chose to dole out to me."

Liam shook his head. His father had made some dark hints about changes in the wind, but this?

"Even if he wasn't just baiting you for some cruel reason," Liam said slowly, "it still has nothing to do with the witches."

"It has everything to do with them!" Elinore's hands clenched. "Don't you see? These troubles all have the same root. The witches were the first to be destroyed in the east. Once they were gone, other things began happening to the rest of the women. It's not that far a step from killing one kind of woman to enslaving the rest."

"That's nonsense, and you know it!" Liam shouted. "Why are you pushing this?"

"Because I'm afraid!" Elinore's breath hitched. It took several seconds for her to regain control. "I'm afraid for myself, but I'm more afraid for Brooke because I don't want her to live in fear that any thought she has, any comment she makes, anything she does might give a man an excuse to brutalize her. If these decrees are passed, fear and pain are the only things she'll know."

"You're jumping at shadows, Mother, and I've heard quite enough of this." Realizing he still held the glass of whiskey, he drank it.

Spinning around, Elinore rushed to the work basket next to the chair near the windows. She pushed aside the needlework, pulled something out of the bottom of the basket, strode back to the sofa, and tossed two objects on the cushions.

Liam studied the strips of leather that had brass buckles and were connected to what looked like a leather tongue.

Harness of some kind, but, for the life of him, he couldn't figure out what animal a harness like that would fit.

"It's a scold's bridle," Elinore said, her voice deliberate and cold. "A tool and a punishment to teach females never to speak unless their words are pleasing to a man's ears. You don't like what you've heard? You don't like the feelings and opinions I've expressed? That's your answer, Baron Liam. You're bigger than I am, and you're stronger. Will you force me down to the floor and shove that leather tongue into my mouth and buckle that bridle around my head? Will you use your fists to subdue me when I fight you so that when you order me to open my mouth to be bridled I'm too frightened and hurt too much to do anything but obey?"

Liam swallowed hard to keep down the whiskey that threatened to rise up in his throat. "He did that to you? He did that?" He suddenly understood the days, a few months ago, when his mother had barely spoken, had moved so carefully, had denied there was anything wrong. The whiskey glass slipped from his fingers, hit the carpet, but didn't break. "Why didn't you tell me?"

"If I'd said anything, he would have hurt Brooke."

Liam looked at the second, smaller bridle. "Did he—? Did he ever—?"

"No," Elinore said. "If he had, he wouldn't have lived long enough to choke at his mistress's table. I would have cut the bastard's heart out before then."

A long, uneasy silence hung between them.

"You have a choice to make, Liam. You can give me your word that you'll do whatever you can to protect the witches in the Old Place."

"And if I don't give you my word?" he asked hoarsely.

"Then I will pack my things, take my daughter, and go live with my kinswomen."

If she'd pulled a bow and arrow from beneath the sofa and

aimed it at his heart, she couldn't have shocked—or hurt—him more.

"You'd leave me? You'd walk away from your son to live with *them?*"

"I wouldn't be walking away from my son since I would already have lost him. I'd be walking away from the Baron of Willowsbrook and any control he might have over my life."

"Mother . . ." Liam rubbed his hands over his face. "If you left like that, everyone in the village would know inside of a week. We'd be laughingstocks."

"I don't have the luxury of considering hurt feelings," Elinore replied quietly. "Not when my daughter's life is at stake."

Anger burned through him. "Do you truly think I'm capable of hurting Brooke? She's my little sister."

"I know what my son would, and wouldn't, do. I don't know what the new baron is capable of when he doesn't get his own way."

He looked at her pale face and clenched hands. Pain lanced through him when he admitted to himself that she meant every word.

"You make your choice, Liam. Then I'll make mine," Elinore said.

"I can't give you an answer. I—I can't think. I need to think."

He strode out of the room, slamming the door behind him. He left the house and headed for the stables. A hard ride. That's what he needed. A horse that required his attention and energy as a rider. Maybe fresh air and speed would help clear his head so that he could think again. But, right now, he needed a little time not to think at all.

When Liam reached the stables, Flint, the stable master, gave him a sour look. Nothing new about that. Flint had been the old baron's man and had always resented taking orders from anyone else—including the baron's heir.

"You'll be wanting the gelding again?" Flint asked, his tone implying that unsaddling the gelding had wasted the time of one of his men.

"Yes," Liam said curtly. He turned away to wait for the horse, then turned back. "No. Have Arthur saddle Oakdancer."

Flint's expression soured even more, but he turned his head to call out, "Boy! Saddle the stallion for *Baron* Liam."

One of these days, he's going to use that tone with me and find himself looking for a new position, Liam thought as he took a few steps away from the stable. His feelings were too raw, and butting heads with Flint now would only add to the resentment most of the men felt toward the boy for being the only person besides Liam who could handle the big bay stallion.

"So you want to buy a stallion from me?" Ahern said, scowling at his guest.

Wondering if his father had been right about this being a fool's errand, Liam set the small glass of ale on the scrubbed kitchen table without tasting it. "Yes, sir."

Ahern was silent for a long moment. Then, looking at the woman who kept house for him, he said, "The lad will be staying for supper."

"Good for the lad," the woman replied tartly. "He—and the rest of you—just might find some supper to be had if you take your business out of my kitchen and back to the stables where it belongs."

Ahern flashed the woman a quick grin before draining his glass. "Come on then," he told Liam as he walked to the kitchen door. "Let's see if you'll suit one of the youngsters."

Liam offered the woman a weak smile of apology for in-

*truding on her domain—an effort that was wasted since
she'd already turned her back on him to fuss with something
near the sink. He eyed the sugar bowl on the table. Not finely
ground, as it was in many of the gentry houses these days, but
broken up into small lumps. After another quick glance to
make sure the woman wasn't watching him, and keeping his
back to the kitchen door, he snitched a couple of lumps of
sugar and stuffed them into his coat pocket as he turned to
follow Ahern back to the stables.*

"It's been said that you raise the finest horses in Sylvalan," Liam said, stretching his legs to keep pace with the
older man.

"There's truth to the saying," Ahern replied.

Well, so much for flattery, *Liam thought.* Not that he'd actually thought it would help. *The other things that were said
about Ahern being gruff and difficult to deal with were
equally true. The old man sold horses when he chose, to
whom he chose. And no amount of money could seal the bargain if Ahern decided against a man for some reason.*

They walked silently for several minutes until they
reached a fenced pasture where a dozen young stallions
grazed. Heads came up. Ears pricked. Then they all returned
to their grazing.

Ahern climbed over the fence. Liam followed.

"Stand there," Ahern said, pointing to a spot on the
ground before walking a few feet away.

"But—"

"Stand."

Liam stood. And waited.

Nothing happened.

"How can you keep them pastured together?" Liam
asked.

"I don't tolerate bad manners."

From man or horse, Liam concluded, biting his tongue to keep from saying anything else to fill the silence.

Then the wind shifted just enough for the horses to catch the scent of the two men. Suddenly they were all in motion, cantering in a large circle as if to show off their paces. Two of them veered away from the rest, headed toward the men, wheeled, and galloped to the far end of the pasture. Two more broke away from the circle, moved off a ways and began grazing. One by one, the young stallions lost interest in the men until only one, a bay, trotted toward Liam.

Slipping his hand in his pocket, Liam brought out one of the lumps of sugar, loosely clasped in his fist.

The stallion came forward more slowly now.

Hoping to hide the sugar from Ahern, Liam cupped his hand and held it out. "Hello, lad," he said quietly. "Come to make friends?"

The stallion was quite willing to make friends with a man who offered sugar. While the horse took the treat, then licked Liam's palm to get the loose grains of sugar, Liam petted him and kept talking.

"You're a fine-looking lad, aren't you?" Liam said. "A very fine lad."

The stallion nodded, then nipped at the pocket of Liam's coat.

Liam gently pushed the horse's muzzle away from the pocket. The horse gave him a shove that was less than gentle.

"You'd best give him the other lump of sugar before he knocks you down," Ahern said, walking toward them.

Feeling his face heat, Liam gave the horse the other lump of sugar.

Ahern studied Liam and the bay. Then he nodded. "You'll do for him. His name is Oakdancer. Come along now. There's work to be done before the two of you leave here."

Liam thought the old man had meant settling on a price or taking care of paperwork. Instead, he found himself in the training ring for the rest of the day while Ahern put man and horse through their paces.

By the time they left Ahern's farm two days later, he and Oakdancer were comfortable with each other, and the old man's parting words, "He trusts you as a rider," were the finest compliment he'd ever received.

His father had sneered when he brought the stallion home. . . .

"*Oakdancer? What kind of name is that for a horse?*"

. . . but Liam had been astute enough to see the envy in the old baron's eyes.

The stallion, on the other hand, had hated the old baron on sight. Had hated Flint and the rest of the stable men. For that first year, Liam had taken care of Oakdancer, since the horse wouldn't tolerate the other men—until Arthur showed up one day, a pale, starving youth who was looking for any kind of work. He had an almost magical touch when it came to horses, and Oakdancer responded to him as if they'd been friends their whole lives.

"Here he is, Baron," Arthur said, leading Oakdancer out of the stables.

"Thank you, Arthur," Liam replied. He mounted, took a moment to test the feel of the saddle. No, there was no need to tighten the girth. There never was with this horse.

Arthur stepped back, brushed a finger against an imaginary cap brim, then retreated inside the stables.

Liam kept the stallion to an active walk until they were away from the house and stables. The moment he eased the reins a little, Oakdancer lifted into an easy canter that swiftly changed to a gallop.

They flew over the land, and for a few short minutes,

Liam's world narrowed to the horse beneath him, the wind in his face, and the land that rose up and flowed away.

Then they reached Willow's Brook—and the bridge.

Oakdancer pricked his ears and dashed for the bridge.

Liam sat deep in the saddle and reined the resisting horse to a halt.

Oakdancer tossed his head. Snorted. Stamped a foot.

That bridge, Liam thought as he studied the stones that looked as if they'd come together on their own accord to span the brook. *What is on the other side of that damn bridge?*

The Old Place. A place his father had forbidden him to set foot, threatening disinheritance as well as a beating if Liam ever disobeyed. A bad place, his father had said. No place for good, decent men.

If what Elinore said was true, his father had crossed that bridge at least once. Of course, he doubted if anyone in this county thought his father had been a good, decent man.

The Old Place. The home of the witches—the women he had to come to terms with, somehow, if he was going to prevent his mother from leaving the family home with his little sister.

"Come on, boy," Liam said. "Let's find out what's on the other side of that bridge."

After crossing the bridge, they trotted down the road, such as it was, for several minutes before the house came into sight.

He wasn't sure what he expected. A tumbled-down cottage. Or a neat cottage. Maybe even a small stone house.

This was an old manor house that rivaled any gentry home in the neighborhood, with the exception of his family home. To the right was a stone arch, large enough for a wagon to pass through, that connected the main house to another building.

Dismounting, Liam led Oakdancer toward the arch. No servant came out to take charge of the horse. Peering up at the house's windows, he didn't see anyone peering back. Had they gone somewhere? Did they even have any servants? Until now, he'd never wondered about them. Not really. They'd been one of the forbidden things of childhood, but, as he grew older, it always seemed easier just not to think of them. Now he was standing in front of the witches' house. He was standing in the Old Place. And he had no idea if he should knock on the door, as he would have done with another neighbor, or ride away.

"At least I can tell Mother that I tried," he muttered, turning toward Oakdancer.

As he gathered the reins and prepared to mount, a woman yelled, "Idjit! Drop that, you mongreled excuse of a flea-infested dog!"

The reins slipped from his hands before he realized he'd responded to that angry command. His heart jumped into his throat. Would they curse him for daring to step onto their land? If that were the case, he wouldn't show them his back while they were doing it.

"Idjit!"

Liam turned and took a step forward at the same moment a small black dog, its tail happily curled over its back, ran through the arch toward him. A piece of white linen was clamped firmly in its jaws, its length flapping and dragging on the ground.

Grinning with relief that something else could qualify for a mongreled excuse of a dog, Liam dropped to one knee and held out a hand. The dog, with what Liam would have sworn was laughter in its eyes, loped toward him, tossing its head to show off its prize. When the dog got close enough to tease and invite him to play, Liam grabbed one end of the linen with one hand at the same time he grabbed the dog by the scruff with the other. Ignoring the hand that held it, the dog opened its jaws to get a better grip on its prize. Liam whipped the linen behind his back and stood up.

The dog watched him, its mouth open in a grin as it danced back and forth in front of him.

"Game's over," Liam said, glancing up to see a dark-haired woman run through the archway, then skid to a halt.

The dog raced around him, forcing him to turn to keep the linen away from it.

"Idjit!" the woman said sternly, placing her fists on her hips. "Sit!"

The dog stopped racing around Liam, stood on its hind legs, and turned in a circle.

"Sit!"

The dog lay down, then rolled over twice.

"Did someone drop him on his head when he was a puppy?" Liam asked.

"It's possible," the woman replied, her lips twitching with the effort not to grin. "He's either very dumb or very smart. We just can't tell which it is." Then she really looked at him, and humor gave way to uncertainty. "You seem familiar, but . . ."

Taking a good look at her, Liam felt his heart jump into his throat for the second time in the past few minutes. The young woman standing before him looked more like his sister than Brooke did. She had dark brown hair like his, the same woodland eyes. Her face was a feminine variation of his own. He'd hadn't realized how much he'd wanted to be able to dismiss what Elinore had said—or at least think of this woman with the same emotional distance he managed with his father's other bastards. But he couldn't dismiss what had been said, couldn't maintain a distance. With her, the word *sister* hummed through him. A like mind. A like heart. Someone who saw the same world that he did and yet saw it differently. He felt as if one of them had been gone on a long journey and had finally come home, and they just had to get reacquainted all over again.

Except he'd never seen her before, had never spoken to her, had no idea if she really was of like mind where *anything* was concerned. And he didn't want to feel anything toward her. He hadn't come here to feel anything toward any of them.

She still seemed to puzzle over who he was—until she looked over his shoulder and noticed the stallion. Then her face became hard and cold. He knew that expression, too. His father had worn it often enough.

"So," she said with icy courtesy. "The new baron has come to pay a call. Why?"

"Because I am the new Baron of Willowsbrook," he replied quietly. Remembering the linen he still held, he took a step forward and offered it to her. "I hope it's not ruined."

She reached for it slowly, as if reluctant to take anything from his hand. "It's nothing that washing it—again—won't fix."

An awkward silence hung between them.

"Why are you here?" she said.

"Because—" Frustrated, Liam raked his hand through his hair. How was he supposed to explain this?

"You've paid your brave courtesy call to the witches," she said, her voice vicious and sneering. "You can ride on now."

"No, I can't."

"Why not?"

"I don't want to lose my family!"

There were winter storms in her eyes now. "Not even the old bastard of a baron had had the balls to insult us like that on our own ground—although he certainly caused us other kinds of pain."

"I meant no insult," Liam said.

"Of course you didn't." Her hands fisted. "You imply that we'll cause your family harm, without provocation, and *you don't think that's an insult?*"

"No. Yes." He closed his eyes for a moment. There wasn't time to put his thoughts in order. If she walked away now, he knew instinctively that she would never listen to him again. "We're kin. Distant kin. On my mother's side."

"I'm aware of that."

"And we—you and I—are closer kin. Because of our father."

"*Your* father. He was never mine, thank the Mother, and for that I am grateful."

"You should be," Liam snapped. "At least you didn't grow up under his fist."

They stared at each other.

"Baron—" she began.

"Liam," he said. "My name is Liam."

She hesitated, her reluctance obvious, before she said, "I'm Breanna." She took a breath, blew it out slowly. "What—?"

"What's *he* doing here?" another voice wailed.

Liam looked over at a woman clinging to one side of the arch. Her brown hair glinted with red where the sun touched it, and was cropped short, like a boy's. She just stared at him.

"Keely," Breanna whispered, taking a step toward the woman.

Breanna's mother. Liam glanced at Breanna, not sure what he should say or do.

"He's *dead*," Keely wailed. "You *told* me he was *dead*." Then her face filled with a rage unlike anything Liam had ever seen. "Get away from her." She moved toward him. "*Get away from my girl!*"

"Keely, no!" Breanna shouted.

The land rolled beneath Liam's feet. Suddenly, clots of

earth flew straight at him. He threw up his arms to protect his head and face, felt a clot hit his upper arm hard enough to bruise. Two others hit his ribs and thigh.

"No!" Breanna shouted.

Wind tugged at his coat, lifted him off his feet, and shoved him to the ground. It roared in front of him. He heard the dog yelp, heard Oakdancer's neigh of fear.

"Keely, stop it!"

"I won't let him have my girl! He won't hurt my girl!"

"This is Liam, Keely. *Liam.*"

Squinting to protect his eyes, Liam raised his head enough to peer over his arms. An arm's length in front of him, wind and earth swirled furiously, blocking the women from his view. He rose to his knees, unsure if it was safer to stay where he was or try to run.

"You *told* me he was *dead!*"

"The old bastard *is* dead," Breanna said sharply. "His body was given to the Mother to feed the worms, and his spirit has gone to wherever spirits like his go when they pass through the Shadowed Veil."

Liam saw movement at the edges of the swirl. Then Breanna dragged Keely around it to where they could all see each other clearly.

"This is Liam," Breanna said. "*Elinore's son.*"

Keely shook her head fiercely. "Liam is a boy. A nice boy. I've seen him riding on his pony."

A bleak sadness filled Breanna's eyes for a moment. "He was a boy. He's grown up now."

"He looks like the baron," Keely whispered. Her eyes began to fill with blank rage again.

"He *is* the baron, but he's *Liam.*" Breanna grabbed Keely's shoulder and pivoted. "Look who he brought for a visit."

The blank rage slowly faded as Keely stared at the stallion. A smile lit her face. "Oakdancer!" Then she frowned, leaned toward Breanna, and whispered, "I didn't hit him with a clot of earth, did I?"

"Not likely," Breanna replied dryly. "He's a horse. He knew enough to get out of the way."

Sidling past Liam, Keely walked over to the stallion and began petting him.

"Are you all right?" Breanna asked, offering him a hand.

He slipped his hand into hers, not because he needed help getting to his feet but simply because she had actually offered it.

"A couple of bruises," he said, trying to sound dismissive as he brushed dirt off his clothes. In truth, now that it was over, fear put a tremor in his hands. The power these women could wield—and what they could do with it—was something else he'd never given much thought to. He looked at the swirling wind and earth. "How—?"

"Keely's branch of the Mother is earth. Mine is air. It was the fastest way to stop her from hurting you." Breanna raised a hand. The swirling wind gradually slowed, depositing a pile of earth in front of her. She sighed. "Edgar is going to be annoyed about having the drive torn up like this."

"Edgar?"

"The groundskeeper. We take care of the kitchen garden and our own flower beds, but he maintains the rest." She hesitated, her gaze fixed on Keely and the stallion. "What did you mean about losing your family?"

"There's been trouble in the eastern part of Sylvalan. Bad trouble. My mother is worried about what might happen if that trouble comes here."

"So what is it you want from us?"

"I don't want anything from you," Liam said. It sounded harsh, so he went on quickly. "My mother wants me to use my position as the Baron of Willowsbrook to keep you and your family protected."

"And if you don't?"

He swallowed hard. "She'll leave the family home, taking my young sister with her, and move in with her kin."

"With her—" Breanna's eyes widened. "Here? She'll move in *here?*" Using both hands, she pushed her hair away from her face. "That would certainly be grist for the gossip mill, wouldn't it?"

"I don't give a damn about that," he said sharply, but remembering to keep his voice low to avoid disturbing Keely. "They're my family. I love them. I don't want to lose them."

Understanding softened Breanna's face. "I know how that feels." She sighed. "I'll talk to Nuala. She'll be more persuasive where Elinore's concerned."

"Thank you."

Breanna hesitated, seemed to be arguing with herself. "Is that the only reason you came here?"

It seemed crude right now to admit that it was, so he said nothing.

She winced a little. "You see, I'd wondered if you'd also come to demand a stud fee."

Liam felt his jaw start to drop. "A—a *stud fee?*"

Color suddenly blazed in her cheeks. A little defiant, she lifted her chin to indicate the stallion. "Well, that one comes visiting when he pleases, doesn't he? It wasn't as if we'd planned on . . ." She huffed.

"You had a mare in season on one of those visits," Liam concluded.

"And him acting the ardent lover, and not a fence that can keep him out when he puts his mind to getting over it."

Liam tucked his hands in his pockets—and firmly tucked his tongue in his cheek. He hoped it took her a little longer to fumble through this explanation. He was enjoying seeing her flustered.

"It wasn't like there was anything we could have done about it by the time Clay came running to tell us your horse was helping himself to our mare."

Liam made little coughing noises to keep from laughing out loud. "So what did you get out of his helping himself to your mare?"

"A filly."

"Can you afford to keep her?"

Breanna's eyes slashed at him. "We aren't paupers."

"I didn't think you were." Especially after seeing the house and the well-kept grounds. "But that doesn't mean you'd want an extra horse."

She looked uncomfortable again. "There's good bloodlines on both sides, and she is a sweet little thing. I would like to keep her."

"Then let's just consider the filly a peace offering," Liam said quietly.

"Thank you."

"Well." He scuffed the toe of his boot in the dirt. "I'd better collect my horse and get back to my work." He watched the dog trot up to Breanna, dragging the linen that must have blown away while Breanna had dealt with Keely's wrath. The dog sat at her feet, looking up at her until she took the offering and gave the expected praise. "And I'd better let you get back to your own work."

Breanna studied the dog. Then she looked at him, the light in her eyes making him want to check to make sure his purse hadn't been stolen. "How old is your sister?"

"Ten," he replied cautiously.

"Wouldn't she like a dog?"

"I'm not taking him."

"He'd be a fine companion for a young girl."

"He'd be a domestic disaster."

She drew in a breath to say something else, then simply grinned. "He is that. But you could consider him a peace offering."

He grinned back at her. "Your keeping him here is a much better peace offering."

She wrinkled her nose. "Come along, then. I'll walk you over to your horse."

He fell into step with her, keenly aware of how easily their strides matched.

"Keely," Breanna said quietly. "Oakdancer has to go home now."

Keely pouted, reminding Liam of Brooke. "Arthur hasn't come to fetch him yet."

"He's not going home with Arthur," Breanna said firmly. "He's going home with Liam." She gave the stallion a pat as she slipped an arm around Keely's shoulders and moved her away from the horse.

Liam mounted. "Ladies."

"Blessings of the day to you, Liam," Breanna said.

How much had it cost her to say those words? Liam wondered as he held Oakdancer to an easy canter all the way home. How hard had it been to grow up with a mother who had never grown beyond childhood emotionally? That had been his father's doing, the scars Elinore said time hadn't healed. And yet . . .

Breanna was his sister. She was a witch. She had power that frightened him now that he'd seen a small demonstration of it. And yet she was a woman like any other.

A sister.

A witch.

He wasn't sure how he felt about that, how he felt about her. But he knew he'd find another reason, before too many days had passed, to cross that bridge again for another visit.

*　　*　　*

"You liked him."

Standing next to Nuala as they watched Keely throw a stick for Idjit to fetch, Breanna nodded reluctantly. "Yes, I liked him. I didn't expect to, didn't want to."

"He's your brother," Nuala said quietly.

Breanna shook her head. "He'll never be that."

"Never is a long time. Things can change."

"Not that much."

"We may need his help. He may need ours. The family is uneasy about the things that are happening in the eastern villages. Harsh words are being said about witches, and that has the elders worried, too. Some of our cousins will be coming for the Summer Solstice—and they may be staying for quite some time."

Breanna turned to look at her grandmother—the gray that streaked the dark hair, the lines that accented a strong face. "Are you worried?"

Nuala remained silent. Then, "Yes, I'm worried. I dream of water that turns dark from the gore spilled into it. Keely has had a couple of nightmares recently about trees that weep blood. What about you, Breanna? What have your dreams carried in them?"

"Wind that turns black, becomes filled with wings and fangs. And everything it touches dies." Remembering those dreams made her shiver.

Nuala nodded. "So, you see, I have reason to be worried. And the Small Folk have told me that the Fae have been skulking about lately."

Breanna shrugged, but her voice had a bite to it. "The Fae come and go as they please and don't care whose land they use to do it." Not that she'd actually seen any of the Fair Folk. Well, perhaps once, when she was still a girl and had snuck out of the house one restless summer night to take a walk. But those riders she'd glimpsed at a distance in the moonlight could have been anyone.

"They've never questioned the Small Folk before, never paid any attention to anything beyond themselves," Nuala said.

Breanna frowned. "What would they question the Small Folk about?"

"Us." Nuala took a deep breath, let it out slowly. "It seems the Fae have developed a surly interest in us."

"Why?"

"I don't know. The Fae don't do anything that doesn't serve themselves, so it has to have some benefit for them."

"Did the cousins say anything about the Fae taking an interest in them?"

Nuala shook her head. "When there's a wolf at the door, you don't worry overmuch about the fox raiding the henhouse."

"I don't like it."

"Neither do I. So it may be in our own best interest, as well as the interest of those who are coming to us, not to dismiss Liam as a potential ally—especially when we may have enemies gathering in Tir Alainn as well as in this world."

Chapter Three

Morag, the Gatherer of Souls, sat back on her heels and stared with dismay at the profusion of little green plants before her.

"It's easy, he says." She almost snarled as she said the words. "Just pull up anything small and green that doesn't belong in that patch of the garden, he says. Mother's tits, Neall, how am I supposed to know what doesn't belong here?"

"That doesn't belong," a voice said. A slim stick came over the waist-high kitchen garden wall and pointed to a spike of green. "That's grass trying to find a home for itself in well-turned earth."

Morag looked up. Ashk, Bretonwood's Lady of the Woods, stood on the other side of the garden wall, smiling at her.

Pushing at the strands of black hair that had escaped from the ribbon she'd used to tie it back, Morag gave Ashk a sour smile in return. "Are you certain? If I pull up the wrong thing, Ari will be upset and Neall will spend the rest of the year teasing me about it. 'We're having grass soup tonight because Morag weeded out the peas.' Or the beans. Or whatever it is that's supposed to be growing here."

"The rest of the year?" Ashk said, her voice full of laughter. "You're Clan now, darling Morag. You'd be lucky if he didn't mention it for the next *ten* years." She leaned farther over the wall and studied the little green plants. "But you may be right. Those might be the beans. Or the peas."

"In other words, you don't know either."

"I can tell you what grows in the woods, but in the kitchen garden . . ." Ashk shrugged. "But I *am* certain that *that*—" She pointed again with her stick. "—is grass and doesn't belong there."

Morag leaned forward, grasped the shoot of grass firmly between thumb and forefinger—and couldn't bring herself to pluck it from the soil, to tear its roots out of the Great Mother. Last summer, she'd been steeped in death—cruel, vicious death—while she discovered the presence of the Inquisitors and uncovered why their destruction of the witches also meant the destruction of Tir Alainn. She had gathered too many spirits and taken them up the road to the Shadowed Veil so that they could pass through to the Summerland beyond. But here, staying in this Old Place with Ari and Neall, she was almost overwhelmed by the heady feel of *life*. So much of it, all around her. She didn't want to hear Death's whisper, not even for a weed.

"Day and night," Ashk said softly. "Shadows and light. Life and death. They're all part of the turning of the days, Morag. All pieces of the world. Life can choke out life. Weeds can leave no room for other plants to grow. Some harvesting must be done."

"Are we talking about small green plants, Ashk?" Morag asked. The understanding in Ashk's woodland eyes was as compelling as it was disturbing.

"We're talking about life," Ashk replied. She looked up, her gaze focused on the woods that bordered the meadow where Ari and Neall's cottage stood. "This is the growing season. This is the time when the Lord of the Woods is called the Green Lord, the time when life is bursting into the world.

But no one forgets that when the Green Lord walks, you can see the shadow of the Hunter, which is his other name."

Morag rested her hands on her thighs. "My sister pointed out that there are no forests in Tir Alainn. I told her it was because life and death walk hand in hand there, that it was because forests have shadows and they're too alive to be perfect."

Ashk's gaze returned to Morag. "Then you do understand. Pluck the weeds while they can still be plucked. The grass has its own place to grow. Let it grow there. But keep it out of the garden where it doesn't belong."

As they watched each other, a tension grew between them. Then a happy bark made Ashk turn, and the moment was broken.

"Ah," Ashk said. "Here comes the person who can tell you what is weed and what is not."

Getting to her feet, Morag saw Ari walking toward them while Merle ran exuberant circles around her. The big animal, half shadow hound, was still young enough to be puppyish in his behavior and had been acting even more so since being reunited with Ari.

When Ari reached one of the gates that opened into the big kitchen garden, she rested a hand on Merle's head. "Go run and play in the meadow," she said. "I'll be right here with Morag and Ashk."

Merle just looked at her and whined.

"It's all right," Ari said. She leaned toward him. "Go chase a bunny."

With another happy bark, Merle turned and raced across the meadow, a black-streaked, gray shape. Only the tan forelegs gave away the fact that he wasn't pure shadow hound.

Looking at the two women, Ari smiled ruefully. "When I

closed him out of the bathing room last night, he sat at the door and howled."

"We heard him," Ashk said dryly. She laughed when Ari's eyes widened.

"You may not have really heard him," Morag grumbled, "but Neall and I certainly did." And no command or scold could move the animal away from the bathing room door. She had taken the puppy when she left Ahern's farm last summer, but Merle had never forgotten Ari, the first person who had loved him without reservation.

"Give him time," Ashk said. "He's been with you only a few days. He doesn't trust yet that a closed door doesn't mean you'll go away."

"I know," Ari said, opening the garden gate. "At least Neall has convinced him that he can't sleep in the bed with us."

Ashk smiled. "The next step will be convincing him that he can't always spend the night in your bedroom."

Ari blushed. Then she frowned at the empty basket at Morag's feet. "I came out to help you weed."

"You're supposed to be resting," Morag said as Ari sank to her knees, braced one hand on the ground in order to lean over, and neatly plucked the shoot of grass out of the soil.

"I rested," Ari said, sounding a bit defensive. She tossed the grass into the basket and busily continued to weed that patch of the garden.

Life can choke out life, Morag thought as she sank to her knees beside Ari and reached to pluck a small plant from the soil.

Ari grabbed Morag's hand. "That's a bean plant." She pointed to a sprout right beside it. "That's a weed."

"How can you tell?" Morag muttered. "They look the same."

"No, they don't. Their leaves look different."

Maybe those leaves looked different to Ari, since witches were the Daughters of the Great Mother and drew their power from Her four branches—earth, air, water, and fire—but to Morag, they were all just sprouts of green that made the ground look soft and fuzzy.

"Besides," Ari said, "I want to do the work now, before I get so fat with the babe I can't get up off the ground by myself." She sighed. "Our first harvest here, and I won't be able to do more than waddle around while others do the work."

"It was quite thoughtless of Neall to have his way with you after the Winter Solstice feast and not take into account you might be waddling by the harvest season," Ashk said dryly.

Morag looked up at Ashk. There was something sharp behind the words that were teasingly said.

Ari didn't seem to notice. She blushed fiercely, then laughed. "All right. We enjoyed each other, and neither of us was interested in counting on our fingers that night to see when a babe might come."

Wanting to turn the conversation to something else, Morag said, "You planted a lot of beans. You must like them."

Ari wrinkled her nose. "I like peas better, but Neall likes beans. I want to be sure enough plants grow so that he can eat all the beans he wants fresh and still give me enough to can so that he'll have some over the turning of the seasons."

Glancing at Ashk, Morag was surprised to see pleasure and pain in equal measure on the other woman's face.

"Are you feeling well?" Ashk asked quietly. "Neall mentioned that you've nodded off a few times almost before you've finished eating the evening meal. You shouldn't be that tired after sleeping during the day."

"I—" Ari looked around, as if checking to make sure it

was still just the three of them. "I don't really sleep during the day."

"Oh?"

"When Neall and I went to Breton last month, I traded some of the weavings I'd done over the winter for fabric to make clothes for the babe, and something for me to wear while the babe's still growing in me. And I got a fine piece of linen to make Neall a shirt for the Summer Solstice. I hid the linen among the rest of the fabric because he would have dug in his heels about me getting something for him that cost so dear." Ari hesitated, took a deep breath, then let it out slowly. "All those years when Neall lived with Baron Felston, he never had anything new, anything fine. All his clothes were Royce's cast-offs. But this is Neall's home; this is his mother's land. He's gentry here, and a Lord in his own right. So I want him to have something new and fine. And I want it to be a surprise, so I can work on it only when I'm supposed to be resting because that's the only time when Neall takes care of chores that aren't close to the cottage and I can be sure he won't walk in before I can hide the shirt."

What's going on in your head and heart, Ashk? Morag wondered as that mixture of pain and pleasure filled Ashk's face again before the woman looked away.

"Fair warning," Ashk murmured. "The young Lord approaches."

Ari started weeding vigorously.

Morag rose to her feet, feeling oddly protective but uncertain why that was so.

Neall strode toward the kitchen garden. He frowned when he reached the wall and saw Ari.

"You're supposed to be resting," he said.

Ari looked over her shoulder. "I rested. Now I'm teaching Morag how to weed the garden."

"I already told her how to do that."

"And now I'm *showing* her how to do it."

Before Neall could say anything more, Ashk said briskly, "Come, young Lord. While Morag has her lesson, it's time for yours."

Morag watched Ashk and Neall walk toward the woods. Neall looked human, but his father had been half Fae and his mother had been a witch, a Daughter of the House of Gaian. Ever since their arrival here last summer, after he and Ari had fled from Ridgeley and the Inquisitors who had come there to destroy Ari because she was a witch, Ashk had been teaching him how to nurture the power that had lain dormant within him, how to be a Lord of the Woods.

That much Morag had learned from Neall in the handful of days since they had welcomed her as friend and family and invited her to stay with them. But there were things she sensed weren't being said when she spent time with the Fae who lived in this Old Place. More often than not, when she asked a question, the answer was, "That is for Ashk to answer." And Ashk, who could be quite forthright about many things, turned away far more questions than she answered.

Who are you, Ashk? I've never seen a Lord or Lady of the Woods rule over a Clan the way you rule this one. Who are you that you can command this kind of obedience? That's the real question no one will answer. Not even you.

"The weeds are down here," Ari said.

"What do you do with the weeds after you've pulled them from the soil?" Morag asked, putting aside the questions that had no answers.

"They go in the compost piles at the end of the garden," Ari replied. "The heat of the sun, the rain, and the wind all help turn them into a rich food for the earth."

Earth, air, water, and fire. The four branches of the Great Mother. The four branches of power that were the heritage of witches.

Life and death. Shadows and light. Witches understood those things, too.

Morag sank to her knees beside Ari. "All right. Show me what to weed."

Ashk wandered the forest trails with Neall, her thoughts and feelings too scattered to remain focused on the intended lesson. Neall wasn't paying much attention either. There were times in the woods when one could drift peacefully with one's thoughts turned elsewhere. And there were times when a moment's inattention could be fatal. A snapped twig, a subtly different scent in the wind were enough warning for her, but Neall was still learning to use the gifts that had come from his father and couldn't afford to be careless.

Although, Ashk thought, *when the teacher's mind wanders, it's hard to fault the student for the same thing.*

"Since it's only your body that trails along with me, should we end the day's lesson?" Ashk asked mildly.

"What?" Neall looked puzzled; then he smiled an apology. "Sorry. My mind was elsewhere."

"When you're in the woods, young Lord, keep your mind with you."

"Yes, Lady." He hesitated. "There's nothing wrong, is there? With Ari or the babe?"

"Why would you think there was?"

"You all seemed so serious when I approached the kitchen garden, so I wondered if Ari had mentioned something to you and Morag that she wouldn't have told me."

There were plenty of things Ari had said, none of which she wanted to discuss with the young man standing nearby.

"Ashk—"

"If you must know, we were comparing the cocks of the lovers we've known." She spoke without thinking, answering him the same way she answered Padrick whenever he prodded her about something that she didn't want to talk about. Padrick always laughed and held up his hands in surrender, knowing she'd talk to him when she was ready—or wouldn't talk if whatever was on her mind wasn't hers to tell.

She wasn't prepared for the stricken look Neall gave her before he turned away.

Fool, she thought. *You not only stepped off the trail, but you also landed in a tangle of thorns.*

"So," Neall said quietly. "How do I compare?"

Ashk stared at him. "*Neall.* I was teasing."

The uncertainty in his eyes revealed things he'd kept well hidden until now.

"Ari chose you, Neall."

"There wasn't much choice," he replied. "Not after the Inquisitors showed up in Ridgeley."

"She made her choice before they came," Ashk replied sharply. "That's what you told me. Was it a lie?"

Neall shook his head. "But I can't help wonder if . . . I wonder if I disappoint her as a lover, if she feels with me as much as she felt with . . ." His voice trailed off. He wouldn't meet her eyes.

"If she feels as much with you as she felt with the Lightbringer," Ashk finished. Her emotions soared, as ferocious as they were protective. "Ari chose you, not Lucian. *You.* He's not the one who's been warming her bed all these months. It's not his child she carries. Has she ever given any indication that what you share in bed doesn't please her as much as it pleases you?"

"Of course not," Neall replied hotly. "She'd never say anything even if—"

"If what?" Ashk said, just as hotly. "If you think she doesn't enjoy your lovemaking, you should pay more attention. The two of you—" She broke off, trying to hold back feelings that had been building inside her for months. "You're more like your father than you know."

"What do you mean?" Neall asked.

Ashk laughed softly, a pained sound. "Kief used to worry over whether or not he was good enough for Nora, whether or not he pleased her as a lover. Your grandmother didn't approve of him, you know, because he wasn't a witch's son or even pure Fae. But he loved Nora, and she loved him in that quiet, deep way she had. She planted beans that first summer. Lots of beans. Because they were his favorite. He didn't understand it was a declaration of love, didn't understand that passion doesn't always burn hot and bright on the surface, not when it's deeply rooted in the heart."

"I remember them," Neall protested. "I remember their laughter, how they looked at each other. I was a child when they died, and maybe I didn't understand what those looks meant, except that I always felt warm and safe, but I would have known if they were unhappy with each other. I would have felt it."

Ashk leaned against the nearest tree. "You can't see how you and Ari look at each other. For me, it's like seeing Nora and Kief again. The way you work together, laugh together, squabble about chores. The way you both look on some mornings, it's obvious you spent a long night in bed and didn't spend much of that time sleeping." She sighed, closed her eyes. "There are times when I've come here and seen this dark-haired woman hanging out the wash. I almost call out Nora's name before she turns and I know it's Ari." She opened her eyes and fixed her gaze on Neall. "It's easy for passion to blaze for a short time when you don't have to consider all the small day-to-day things that make up the rest of a person's life. It flares hot and burns out quick, unless it's nourished. When it came down to a choice, Lucian couldn't offer enough to give her a reason to stay. Consider that the next time you doubt, young Lord of the Woods. A Daughter of the House of Gaian chose you over the Lightbringer, the Lord of the Sun."

Neall picked up a small dead branch and idly broke it into pieces. "I don't remember my grandmother. When did she die?"

"She hasn't yet." Ashk saw his eyes widen. "She lives on Ronat Isle with her Lord of the Sea, her selky man."

"But—"

"Cordell's gift is water, but it's the wildness of the sea that calls to her, not the quieter songs of rivers and streams. This Old Place is too far away from the sea for someone like her. By the time I came to live here, she had left for good, leaving Nora and the land in her own mother's care."

Neall snapped to attention. "Came to live here? This wasn't your Clan?"

No matter how she turned, she was still caught in those emotional thorns. "No. But I needed . . . a different place . . . so my grandfather brought me here where I would still have kin. That's why—" She bit her lip.

"Why what?" Neall asked quietly.

"I didn't know." The words burst out of her. "I was nineteen when Nora and Kief died. My path wasn't something I could change, so I couldn't keep you here with me."

"Ashk." Neall reached out to touch her arm in comfort.

She stepped away from him. "I thought it would be for you the way it had been for me. People who were kin who would become family. I thought they would take care of you."

"They did take care of me."

Tears stung her eyes. "No, they didn't. 'Poor relation.' I know what that means among the gentry in the human world. They had no right to say that to you. They had no right."

Neall sighed. "Ari cares about me. I think she's colored things blacker than they were."

"And I think you try to heap flowers over a pile of shit to cut down the stink. It doesn't make it any less a pile of shit."

He said nothing for a long moment. "You told me I had to leave in order to learn the ways of my father's people. And I did. And now I've come home. If I'd never gone to live with Baron Felston, I never would have known Ari. Shadows and light. Isn't that what you keep showing me during these walks through the woods? She's my light, Ashk."

"If I hadn't left my family and gone wandering, I wouldn't have ended up here in the western part of Sylvalan," Kief had said. *"I wouldn't have ended up with Nora."*

"Come on," Neall said quietly when she didn't respond. "I'll walk you back to the Clan house."

A subtle change in the woods instantly commanded her attention. The power was old and waning, but it still called to her.

"No," Ashk said. "I have other business. You go home."

He studied her a moment, then bowed and turned to leave.

"Neall." She hesitated, then decided she could tell him this much. "Ari planted beans this year. Lots of beans. Because they're your favorite."

She watched him absorb the message. Even after he left, she remained where she was, sensing his presence in the woods. When she was certain that he wouldn't come back, she turned and followed the trails that led to the oldest part of the woods.

She walked for several minutes, listening to the chirping of birds and the chattering of squirrels. Finally, she saw the stag, standing so still beside the girth of an old oak tree. If he'd been a true deer, his antlers would have been young and velvet-covered in this season instead of a full, mature rack. But he was one of the Fae in his other form.

"Kernos," she whispered. It had been many years since he'd been the Green Lord, since he'd been *the* Lord of the Woods. That didn't matter. Not to her, anyway.

She approached him slowly, bowed when she stood before him. "You honor me with your presence, Grandfather."

He didn't move. Just watched her with those dark eyes.

"There are shadows gathering in other parts of Sylvalan," she said quietly. "If they aren't stopped, they'll creep into our part of the land, too."

He turned and walked up the trail, his left hind leg dragging a little, just as it did in his human form ever since the brain seizure three years ago. He'd regained most of his strength, but his left leg still dragged a little and his speech was a bit slurred.

Obeying the silent command, Ashk followed him.

The Clan where he lived was a day's journey from here. He shouldn't be traveling so far alone. Not anymore. Not that there was anything that would dare touch him while he was in her home woods.

He had been there for her. Always. He had taught her to be a Lady of the Woods, and he'd trained her to be so much more.

He was the one who had knelt beside her the first time she'd made the transformation to her other form. He was the one who had petted her, soothed her, encouraged her while the rest of her family recoiled from what she'd become. A rare form. Dangerous. Nothing was safe from her in her other form.

She followed him until they came to a meadow deep in the heart of the woods. He bounded forward into the sunlight. She remained at the edge of the woods, in the shadows, pained by the knowledge that he was no longer fast enough to outrun a predator, no longer strong enough to stand and fight and win.

He looked back at her, waiting.

He used to bring her to this meadow to play. He'd change into the stag and let her chase him. When she was young, he ran just fast enough to let her almost catch him, just fast enough not to bruise her pride. When she got a little older, he ran faster, making her work to keep up with him.

She remembered the day when she caught up to him, ran side by side with him. She remembered the day when she realized she could outrun him—and still ran beside him.

And she remembered the day when he stopped suddenly and she ran past him. They'd stared at each other in that sunlit meadow, and she'd felt his silent, final command.

Taking a slow, deep breath, Ashk stepped into the meadow, changed into a shadow hound.

The stag bounded away.

Her gray, black-streaked coat stood out against the sunlit green, but in the shadows of the woods, or in the moonlight, she would blend in, a predator who wouldn't be seen until her fangs sank into a throat. There was nothing in the woods—not stag, not wolf, not wild boar—that could stand against her in this form.

The shadow hound raced after the stag, snarling and snapping at his heels, running just fast enough to give him the thrill of the chase but not fast enough to bruise his pride.

Chapter Four

Hearing the bell that rang in the Inquisitors' study room, Ubel headed for the door that led down to the confession chamber he and the other Inquisitors had helped Master Adolfo create in this country house that had been lent to them by a Sylvalan baron. His stride was swift yet unhurried, the only outward sign of his confidence in the security of his position, which was something the other Inquisitors envied—especially since last autumn when the Master Inquisitor returned from this magic-blighted land to the safety of his own country.

Despite his alacrity in answering the summons, he heard the bell ring again—faintly now, since he'd almost reached the stairs that led to the cellar. The Master must be feeling impatient.

Ubel smiled. Not an indulgent smile, but a smile of relief. Adolfo had been too lenient these last few months, too . . . passive. He drank too much, and he no longer exercised his rod to maintain his vigor. The battle he had fought in Sylvalan last summer had left its marks on him—both physically and mentally. But, perhaps, wringing a confession out of this particular captive had restored some of the Master's potency.

As Ubel entered the confession chamber, Adolfo turned to face him. The Master Inquisitor, the Witch's Hammer, was a large man, middle-aged and balding, with a lean scholar's face and gentle brown eyes that never revealed the man's razor-sharp mind or burning dedication to the task that had consumed most of his life.

"Ah, Ubel," Adolfo said. "My left hand."

There was something sharp, almost hateful, under the words.

Ubel ignored it. It was one thing for a man like Master Adolfo to want assistance in softening a witch to confess her crimes. It was quite another to *need* assistance. The fight with the Gatherer had left Adolfo with a useless, dead left arm. "What is your will, Master Adolfo?"

"I'm done with the bitch," Adolfo replied. "She has nothing more to offer us. Take her back to the Old Place where you captured her and release her."

Ubel looked at the young Fae woman, who was staring at him with terror-blind eyes. She was securely strapped to the worktable, so there was nothing she could do to avoid any of the softening necessary to extract a full confession.

"It's doubtful there are any Fae remaining in that Old Place to see her," Ubel said. He'd made sure of that. After he, along with a double handful of Inquisitors and guards, had killed the witches who had lived in that Old Place, his men had waited at the end of the shining road that led to Tir Alainn. When it started to close, the panic-stricken Fae who came down that road to reach the human world were easy targets. A few had escaped the arrows, but far more had fallen. The last one to stumble into the human world before the shining road closed was this young Fae female. He'd captured her and brought her back to the manor house for Master Adolfo to question.

"It doesn't matter if the Fae see her or not," Adolfo said. "Someone will find her, sooner or later. She will serve as a warning to everyone in Sylvalan that even the Fae cannot escape the Inquisitors' justice."

Ubel nodded, still studying the woman. "We'll cut the bindings around her legs after we reach the Old Place."

"There's no need. She can untie herself once you leave her."

Ubel looked at the bindings around the woman's legs. He looked at the hands Adolfo had pounded with a mallet until all the bones had broken. He smiled. "Very good, Master Adolfo."

"But take the spiked bridle when you leave," Adolfo said. "There's no point in wasting good workmanship. And," he added softly, "I have hope that I will need that particular bridle again for another Fae bitch."

Out of the corner of his eye, Ubel saw Adolfo shiver, saw the way the older man's right hand trembled as he brushed it over his head, and knew Adolfo was thinking about the Gatherer. Just as he knew she was the reason the Master Inquisitor hadn't ventured away from this house since he'd arrived in Sylvalan a few weeks ago to oversee the continued purge of the witches in this land.

"The barons' council will meet at the end of next week," Adolfo said after a moment. "Once you're rid of the bitch, I want you to take three Inquisitors and ride to Durham. Be alert. Listen well. The procedure we introduced in the spring has been successful in solidifying the eastern barons' position and their alliance with our own goal to rid the land of magic. Now they have to convince the other barons in Sylvalan to follow their lead. I want to know who is resistant. They will have to be dealt with."

And we'll walk the streets of Durham pretending to be visitors or merchants from Wolfram, trying to eavesdrop on conversations instead of being able to demand answers from any man, no matter his rank. "Yes, Master Adolfo," Ubel replied, then regretted saying anything at that moment. Adolfo wouldn't ignore the surly tone.

"You have some objection?" Adolfo asked sharply.

Ubel stiffened; then he turned to face Adolfo. "It insults our great work that we must hide who we are, that we must sneak in and out of the villages here like petty thieves."

Adolfo stared at him long enough to make Ubel uneasy. Then he said gently, "Last year, we came to this land as honest men to help the barons eliminate the magic that stood in men's way. We did our work openly, educated the villagers and peasants alike so that they would understand what vile creatures witches truly are and why other females needed to be disciplined to keep them from being ensnared by the Evil One. Because we did the work openly, good men died, Ubel, including my own nephew. When it was over, I was the only one who was still alive." His right hand lightly touched his left arm. "And even I, the strongest among us, the Master Inquisitor, the Witch's Hammer . . . even I did not escape untouched. So we must fight in other ways this time. We must be cautious, careful. We must use all our skills to soften the land and the people until they are ready to yield to everything we will teach them. And they will yield, Ubel. They will yield because there will be no turning back. Then men will rule as they were meant to. But until that time comes, I will not trust the lives of my Inquisitors to the assurances of Sylvalan barons. Not again. So, for now, you must cloak your honesty and do the work secretly."

Chastened, Ubel looked at the floor. "Yes, Master Adolfo."

Adolfo walked to the chamber door. He turned, looked back at Ubel. "Keep me informed—and take care, Ubel. The Fae's presence in this land makes our work twice as dangerous."

Ubel looked up, stood straight and tall, and said fiercely, "We will rid the world of the witches and the Fae."

"Yes," Adolfo replied, giving Ubel a small but approving smile, "we will."

Ubel waited until he could no longer hear Adolfo's footsteps before he turned his attention back to the woman strapped on the table.

Her hair, dirty and tangled now, was a plain brown, but there were lighter streaks in it that were almost as blond as his own hair. Her eyes were a greener blue than his own eyes, and her face was shaped just differently enough that she would never be considered pretty in the human world. But it was her pointed ears that revealed the animal inside her—the animal that made her less than human and, therefore, expendable. If men could not control it or rule over it, a thing had no place in the world. Which meant her kind had to be eliminated because the Fae would never be ruled by men.

And this one wasn't even significant among her own kind. When he'd ordered his men to capture her, he'd dropped his bow and stripped off his coat, throwing it over her head to confuse her if she tried to change into her other form to escape them. A little brown bird had fluttered beneath his coat.

One of the men had emptied a food sack, and they'd put her in it. He'd felt her frantic movements all through the ride back to the country house.

Just an insignificant little brown bird—with valuable information.

"Change back to your human form," Adolfo said. *"We simply want to talk to you. We want to understand the Fae. Change back so we can talk, and then we'll let you go."*

And, oh, after a bit of softening, how that little bird had sung.

The witches weren't just the key to keeping the magic alive in the Old Places, they were the key that kept the shining roads open, giving the Fae access to the human world. *That* was why, after the witches in Wolfram had been eliminated, the Fae had disappeared, as well. By destroying one, the Inquisitors could destroy *both* kinds of creatures whose presence threatened men's ability to rule.

Turning away from the Fae woman, Ubel walked over to the bell rope and pulled it so that the bell would ring in the sequence that told Assistant Inquisitors that their presence was required. He would let the Assistants bring the woman up to the wagon while he prepared for the journey to Durham.

He would be Adolfo's eyes and ears. He would be the Master's left hand. And he would make sure he was in a position to know which barons might try to thwart the Master's great plans for this land.

Chapter Five

Lyrra followed behind the packhorse Aiden led. The forest trail they'd taken after leaving the main road wasn't wide enough for them to ride side by side. Just as well.

Tears stung her eyes. One spilled over, ran down her cheek. She brushed it away, refusing to give in to grief. Aiden would be grieving, too, but both of them needed to stay alert.

The magic in this Old Place was swiftly dying. Which meant the witches who had lived here were already dead. When the Daughters of the House of Gaian fled from an Old Place to escape whoever meant them harm, the magic faded slowly. Being Fae, she could feel the difference.

Aiden had been reluctant to travel farther into the Old Place once they'd gone in far enough to feel the change. But she'd insisted that they needed to find out if any of the Fae whose Clan territory was anchored to this Old Place had managed to escape from Tir Alainn before the shining road through the Veil closed, trapping them beyond the reach of the human world . . . or even their own kind.

The wind shifted slightly, bringing the smell of decay and rotting flesh.

Aiden reined in suddenly, his attention on a cluster of dead trees they'd have to pass between in order to continue on this trail.

Lyrra studied the trees neighboring the dead ones. What were those dark clumps in the branches?

"Lyrra," Aiden said in a quiet, strained voice. "Turn the mare. Go back up the trail as fast as you can. We need to get back to the road or find a meadow, a field. Anything with sunlight."

"Aiden . . ."

Pieces of the dark clumps on the trees fell off, spread bat-like wings, and flew straight for them.

Nighthunters!

Lyrra wheeled the mare. The horse needed no urging to gallop recklessly back the way they'd come. Fae horses had silent hooves, so she couldn't hear Aiden's gelding and the packhorse behind her—but she heard the hungry, angry squeaking of the creatures the black-coated Inquisitors created by twisting the magic in an Old Place. The nighthunters were flesh eaters—and they were soul eaters.

Sunlight, sunlight, Lyrra chanted silently. They had to get out of the shadows of the woods. The nighthunters didn't like sunlight. Why hadn't she yielded to Aiden's reluctance to enter this Old Place? He'd spent close to a year on the road and would have seen far more Old Places that had been stripped of their magic than she had in the few weeks she'd been traveling with him.

He was behind her, closer to the danger that flew in pursuit. If something happened to him because she'd insisted . . .

Her mare suddenly veered left, almost throwing Lyrra out of the saddle. She hung on grimly, letting the animal choose the way and hoping the mare's instinct would get them to safety in time.

It felt like they'd been fleeing for hours when the mare slid down a bank, splashed through the shallow stream, then scrambled up the other bank.

A few heartbeats later, they galloped out of the trees into a sunlit meadow.

Thank you, Mother, Lyrra thought as she slowed the mare. *Thank you.*

Then she looked back, expecting to see Aiden. And saw nothing but the trees.

She reined the mare to a stop. Slid out of the saddle. Stared at the trees.

Behind her a horse neighed a greeting.

Spinning around, Lyrra saw the black-haired woman riding toward her.

No, Lyrra thought, sinking to the ground. *Not Morag. Not the Gatherer. Go away! He doesn't need you! It's not his time! Aiden!*

"Lyrra?" the woman said, dismounting so quickly she stumbled before catching her balance and running the rest of the way to where Lyrra sat on the ground. "Lyrra? Are you hurt?"

Lyrra looked at the woman who now knelt beside her. She pressed her hand against her mouth to hold back the weeping. If she started, she wasn't sure she would stop.

Not Morag. This was Morphia, Morag's sister. The one who was called the Sleep Sister and the Lady of Dreams.

"Are you hurt?" Morphia asked again.

Lyrra shook her head.

"Are you alone?"

"I—" *I don't know.* "Aiden . . ."

Morphia looked around. "He must have followed a different trail through the woods. That's him, isn't it?"

Lyrra twisted around, saw Aiden and the horses cantering toward her.

"Aiden!" she cried, scrambling to her feet. She ran to meet him.

He barely waited for his gelding to stop before he was out of the saddle, rushing toward her. He pulled her into his arms. Held on tight.

"Are you all right?" he asked hoarsely, kissing her cheek, her neck, anything he could reach without letting go of her.

"I'm fine. I'm fine. And you?"

"I'm fine."

She pulled back far enough to really kiss him, looked at his face, then gave him a shove that startled him enough to break his hold and make him step back a couple of paces. Anger burned through her, sweet and hot.

"You did it deliberately, didn't you?" she shouted. "You kept going along the forest trail so the nighthunters would follow you instead of me. *Didn't you?*"

"Of course I didn't," he replied sharply. He raked his hand through his black hair. "Mother's tits, Lyrra, you disappeared down that game trail so fast, there was no chance to follow you. So I followed the trail I was on until I could head in the same direction you did."

"With those nighthunters chasing you every step of the way!"

Anger flashed in his blue eyes. "They weren't behind me once you disappeared. I thought they'd gone after you!"

He was the Bard. He could be a facile liar when he wanted to be. And he was lying to her now. If he'd truly thought the nighthunters had gone after her, he would have abandoned the packhorse and followed the game trail she'd taken. But a man and two horses offered more prey than a woman and a horse—especially when he'd been behind her.

Lyrra's temper, goaded by fear and relief, soared. "You can keep your lies and your self-sacrificing—"

"Stop it!" Morphia hurried toward them. "Stop it!"

Hearing pain beneath the anger, Lyrra bit her tongue to prevent herself from telling the other woman to stay out of a private quarrel.

"What's wrong with you?" Morphia demanded. Her voice trembled. Broke. "You stand before the person who is dearest to you, knowing that person is alive and well and safe, and all you can do is quarrel?" She pressed a hand against her mouth and turned away from them.

Lyrra looked at Aiden. Together, they went to Morphia. Aiden put his arms around her while Lyrra stroked her hair.

"You've had no word from Morag?" Aiden asked quietly.

"None. Lucian and Dianna made good on their threat. She's been shunned by all the Clans. *No one* will say if she'd visited their Clan. *No one* will acknowledge seeing her. She said she had a task to do, so we parted ways a few days after we left Ahern's farm. I went back to our home Clan. I haven't seen her since. I knew she wouldn't go to any of the southern Clans, since they would be too close to Dianna and Lucian's Clan. I've looked for her in the midlands and the north. I thought she might have come back to the eastern part of Sylvalan since the trouble is here, so I—"

"It isn't safe for a woman to travel in the east, especially a woman traveling alone," Aiden said sharply.

"And well I know it," Morphia replied bitterly. "There was a place," she continued softly. "I was called there by need so great I couldn't deny it. So many human women crying out. So much pain, so much fear. I felt their dream, helped them shape it, saw it as if I was standing just beyond reach. I stayed as long as I dared to feed the magic that would let them dream together because it would fade once I was gone, but I knew I had to get away from the east and whatever it is the humans have done there." Giving Aiden a wobbly smile, she stepped back from his embrace.

"Where will you go now?" Lyrra asked. "Back to your home Clan?"

Morphia shook her head. "I'm going to find Morag. I'm going to the western Clans."

Lyrra glanced at Aiden, relieved that he looked as startled as she felt.

"But . . . Morphia . . . ," Lyrra said. "They're the *western* Clans." Clans the rest of the Fae avoided whenever possible because there was something about those Fae that made them all uncomfortable.

Determination filled Morphia's eyes. "I know they're . . . different . . . from the rest of us. Maybe different enough not to dance to the Lightbringer's tune and shun Morag for doing what she had to do. Besides, that's the only place left to search, so that's where I'll go."

"Why don't you ride with us for a while," Aiden said.

"You're heading south?"

He shook his head. "North."

"Then I thank you, but no. I'll keep riding south until I find a shining road through the Veil. I'll be able to travel faster through Tir Alainn." She turned away, started walking toward her horse, then turned back to look at them. "I will find her. I won't turn away from her simply because Lucian and Dianna want to punish her for doing what was right."

"It doesn't matter that she was right," Aiden said. "The Fae who have shunned her still sleep easy at night."

Morphia gave him a strange look. "Some of them no longer sleep easy." She raised her hand. "May your dreams be gentle ones."

Lyrra felt a little tremor go through her body. It hadn't occurred to her that the Sleep Sister could have a darker side to her nature. "And if the dreams are not gentle?"

"Then, if I were you, I would try to understand whatever they're trying to tell you."

Aiden slipped his arm around Lyrra's waist. She leaned against him as they watched Morphia mount her horse and ride away.

"Let's get away from this place," Aiden said.

Lyrra didn't argue, didn't remind him that they hadn't

tried to find out if any Fae had made it to the human world
before the shining road closed.

As she mounted her mare, she suddenly realized why
Aiden was less generous in his concern. He would have ridden this way last summer, when he'd left Ridgeley—and
Brightwood. He would have warned the Clan whose piece of
Tir Alainn was anchored to this Old Place. He would have
told them about the Black Coats. He would have told them
who the witches are and why they needed to be protected.

And still the witches here had died. Despite everything he
had said or tried to do, the witches had died. Was it any wonder that he probably felt the Clan deserved whatever had happened to them?

Trying not to take more than his share of the narrow bed,
Aiden stared at the ceiling of the tiny room. With the window open, he could hear the men in the tavern below. He
should have been down there, playing his harp, singing his
songs, listening to the news and rumors about what was happening in other villages. He didn't have the heart for it
tonight, so he'd paid for the room, the meal, and stabling for
the horses out of the rapidly diminishing coins he and Lyrra
had left. No chance of filling his purse from the Clan chests.
If the Clan chests still existed in those lost pieces of Tir
Alainn, they might as well be sitting on the moon or at the
bottom of the sea for all he could reach them.

The witches had died. More Daughters of the House of
Gaian lost. And the presence of the nighthunters meant that
the Black Coats hadn't been driven out of Sylvalan as he'd
hoped when he'd seen no further sign of them over the winter months. Or else they'd come back. If that were true, what
could he say that he hadn't already said to make the Fae listen and heed his warnings? If they wouldn't listen to him, the

Bard, was there anyone besides the Lightbringer and the Huntress whom the Fae wouldn't dare ignore?

There was one. He'd have to think about that. Think hard about it. But right now . . .

He turned his head and looked at Lyrra, who lay with her back to him. As a Fae lover, he could simply have left, offering to return when and if she was ready to welcome him back to her bed. As the Bard, he could have had a heated argument with the Muse about who was right and who was wrong back at the Old Place. As a husband, he had the bad feeling that he should apologize—except he couldn't figure out what he should be apologizing for.

"I would have stayed behind you if I could have," he said quietly. "I truly wasn't sure where you'd gone, and I was past the game trail so fast it wasn't safe to turn back."

"Stayed behind me," Lyrra muttered.

Aiden winced at the anger in her voice.

She rolled over and propped herself on one elbow to look down at him. "Stayed behind so that if those creatures caught up to us they would have swarmed over you instead of me."

"I hadn't thought of it like that," he protested. Not consciously, anyway.

"We can't afford to lose the Bard."

He focused on the ceiling again, not quite sure why her words stung so much. "There would be another to take my place."

"Not for me," she said quietly. She raised one hand, rested it on his chest just over his heart. "One day I'll have the words to tell you how it felt to reach the safety of sunlight and realize you weren't there. One day I'll tell you how it pained my heart to stand alone for those moments, not knowing if you were coming back to me. One day. But not tonight."

She kissed him in a way that made him forget every song

he ever knew. He reached for her, then hesitated. Pulled away enough to catch his breath. "Lyrra . . ."

She smiled at him; then she released the glamour magic to reveal her true face, the feral beauty of the Fae. Suddenly, she seemed wild and strange, something that frightened him a little and excited him even more.

" 'Tis a custom between husbands and wives," she said, stretching out over him. "We quarreled today, did we not?"

"We did?" He couldn't remember, not while he was staring into her woodland eyes.

"We did," she replied. "And when a husband and wife quarrel, they have to make up."

"They do?"

"They do." She nipped his chin. "So we're going to make up, and you're going to prove you came to no harm."

He wondered briefly if it was the danger they'd faced in the Old Place or the fact that he still wore the glamour that gave his face the illusion of being human that made her more aggressive and demanding. Then she kissed him and he didn't care what the reason was.

"Let's try not to break the bed," he gasped.

She kissed him again, and he didn't care about that either.

Chapter Six

L iam hesitated for a moment, then knocked on his mother's morning room door. Entering the room, he saw her at her small desk, writing in that hurried yet careful way she had.

"A moment, if you please, Liam," she said distractedly.

"Of course."

He smiled as he wandered around the room while she finished her letter. His father had always been furiously insulted if Elinore didn't stop whatever she was doing to give him her total and immediate attention. There'd been some fierce arguments about the value of her work for the village and the estate compared to properly sympathizing with her husband about the inadequate shine of his boots. He knew which his father had considered more important.

Elinore set aside her pen, then turned in her chair to smile at him.

She was more relaxed than he'd seen her in a very long time, and she smiled at him a lot lately—ever since he'd gone to the Old Place to introduce himself to the witches there.

"I met Nuala while I was out riding today."

"Yes?"

"She told me you called at the Old Place yesterday. And she gently suggested that I remain here at the estate. She said

anyone who intended to bang heads with Breanna deserved a sympathetic ear waiting for him when he got home."

He'd mumbled something to the effect that they hadn't banged heads, but he suspected Nuala, who obviously knew her granddaughter very well, had the right of it. Dealing with Breanna was similar to dealing with a goat—if you weren't careful, getting knocked off your feet would become a regular occurrence.

"What can I do for you, Liam?" Elinore asked.

It was a simple thing, really, but he suddenly felt awkward. "The council of barons is meeting at the end of the week."

"I see," Elinore said in a voice that gave him no clue about her reaction to that news. "So you'll be leaving in a couple of days?"

"Tomorrow. It'll give me time to take care of some business in Durham before the council meets." *I'm not meeting a mistress,* he wanted to shout at her when he saw the way her face seemed to close him out. *And even if I was looking to spend time with a woman, I'd be breaking no vows since I've made none.* "Is there anything I can bring back for you while I'm there?"

"No, thank you."

"Books?" Liam prodded. Elinore loved books.

She shook her head, then paused. "Well . . . Perhaps a book of stories suitable for Brooke?"

He walked over to her chair, knelt on one knee beside it, and rested his hand lightly on her arm. Her eyes widened, and he wondered if she were going to scold him for kneeling by her chair now that he was the baron. Oh, she wanted to. He could tell by the way she lightly caught her tongue between her teeth to keep herself from saying anything. He grinned at her.

"Come now," he coaxed. "It would be a shame for me to

be standing in a bookshop and only come away with one book. Just one book for yourself?"

She looked away from him. A bit of color rose in her cheeks. "There was mention a few months back that Moira would be having a new book out soon, and I do enjoy her stories—and not just because she's my cousin."

"Done." He kissed her cheek, then stood. "I'd better see to the rest of my arrangements if I'm going to leave early tomorrow morning."

He was glad she didn't ask him what arrangements. He wasn't sure how to explain the decision he'd reached.

As he left the manor, intending to go to the stables to have Oakdancer saddled, he saw a young man riding toward him and waited.

The young man raised a hand in greeting. "Good day to you, sir."

"Good day," Liam replied.

"Could you tell me where I would find Old Willowsbrook? When I inquired in the village, they directed me here, but this isn't quite the place. It's been a few years since I've been there, and I seem to have forgotten the way."

A few years ago, the man before him would have been a boy—certainly too young for courier work. Which meant he was lying about having been to the Old Place before, and that made Liam uneasy. "What business do you have there?"

"Begging your pardon, sir, but it's none of yours."

"I'm the Baron of Willowsbrook," Liam said, his former courtesy turned cold. "So it is my business."

The young man paled a little. "I've a letter for one of the ladies there."

"Which one?" Why was he pushing? It truly *wasn't* any of his business. If the man hadn't lied in the first place, he might simply have given him directions and let him go.

"Mistress Nuala."

Liam extended one hand. "I'm going that way. I'll see it gets delivered."

The young man paled a little more. "My instructions were to place it in Mistress Nuala's hand personally. 'Tisn't important or anything," he added hurriedly. "You understand how ladies can be at times about making sure letters reach the right person, although why they make such a fuss is beyond me. My sister is a right fusser about things like that. I happened on a letter a friend of hers had written to her. Hand delivered it was, too, so I thought— Well, I was younger then. But there it was, four pages, sir, filled with discussion about ribbons and the length of sleeves and the different shades of green needed to do some embroidery. Four pages! And they, my sister and her friend, always got right stiff about having their letters delivered properly."

"Probably because your sister's friend also had a younger brother," Liam said coolly. The man was lying with every breath. Oh, he was telling the truth about having a sister, Liam was certain of that, which only made the lie about the letter's unimportance more damning. Whatever he was delivering to Nuala was something he didn't want anyone else to know about—or connect him to—and it occurred to Liam that Elinore's concern about the witches needing his protection might have weight.

"Very well," Liam said. "I'll ride with you, since I'm going that way. Follow me."

"Yes, sir."

Not happy, but trying not to show it, the young man waited while Arthur saddled Oakdancer. Once Liam was mounted, they rode to the Old Place in silence.

"Breanna!"

Shading her eyes, Breanna looked up at the housekeeper, who was leaning out an upstairs window. "Glynis?"

"You've got company coming. Best look sharp."

Wondering if that was a suggestion that she should change out of the tunic and trousers she'd been working in or simply a warning, Breanna shrugged, then walked to the arch. Liam and Oakdancer were easy enough to recognize, but it took her a moment to place the other man.

When they were a few feet away, the men reined in.

"Good day to you, Mistress," Liam said.

Had he forgotten her name? Breanna wondered.

It was his quick glance at the other man and the stiff way he held himself, as if ready for a fight—and the question in his eyes, directed straight at her—that told her he wouldn't give her name to a stranger, and he'd make that stranger's life a misery if she even hinted there was cause.

In a flash of insight, she realized Liam would react the same way if a stranger approached his little sister, Brooke. This wasn't about being a baron—although she was sure he'd make use of the power the title gave him. This was about being an older brother.

Not sure how she felt about that—pleasure and confusion danced inside her in equal measures—she turned to the other man, and said, "Cousin Rory?"

The young man sagged in relief. "It's glad I am to see you, cousin Breanna."

Breanna narrowed her eyes and put her hands on her hips. "Why?"

"Well, there is that," Rory muttered. "Father sent a letter and things to Nuala, asked me to deliver them personally."

"Then you can use the kitchen door same as the rest of the family," Breanna said tartly.

Rory flashed a grin at her, brushed his fingers against the brim of his hat as a salute to Liam, then urged his horse through the arch.

"There's no point having him go through the front door,"

Breanna said, walking toward Liam while he dismounted. "He'd just head straight for the kitchen anyway, wouldn't remember to stop and wipe his feet, and then he'd have Glynis chasing him with a broom for mucking up her clean floors."

Liam just stared at her.

"You've never been chased by an annoyed woman with a broom," Breanna decided.

"No," Liam said faintly, "I've never had the pleasure."

She studied his boots. "Well, if you're wanting the experience, just walk through the front door and don't wipe your feet."

"I'm the Baron of Willowsbrook."

"From the ankles on up, you're the Baron of Willowsbrook. From the ankles on down, you're dirty boots on a clean floor. I'll give you odds which part of you Glynis will notice."

"If you don't mind, I'll stay where I am," Liam muttered. He was appalled to realize that a tiny part of him wanted to find out if a woman would really whack a baron with a broom because he tracked dirt on her floor.

"So," Breanna said, wondering where his mind had wandered off to. "Besides giving Rory an unwanted escort, what brings you here?"

"Does he really have a sister who writes long letters about ribbons and the length of sleeves?"

She studied him more carefully. He didn't look like the stallion had tossed him, but she wasn't sure *something* hadn't addled his brain. "He does have a sister, a year younger than me. I've never known her to write a letter about ribbons and sleeves, but if you make the mistake of asking, she *can* write you a page or two about which kinds of quills can be sharpened to the best point and hold that point the longest to produce the clearest hand when toting up numbers in a ledger." She shrugged.

"Mother's mercy," he said. He started petting Oak-dancer's neck.

"Liam?" Breanna said gently. He really was starting to worry her.

"Yes?"

"You're here."

"Yes."

"Why?" That came out a little sharper than she'd intended, but at least it got his attention focused again.

"Oh. I'm going to Durham tomorrow for a few days, and I . . . uh . . . I wondered if there was anything you'd like me to bring back for you."

She gave him her best wide-eyed sweet look—which probably didn't look anything like what she'd intended, since all the color slowly drained out of his face. "You mean you'd shop for ribbons and lace if I asked you to?"

That's mean, Breanna, she scolded herself. *If he faints at your feet, you've only yourself to blame.*

Liam cleared his throat. "I— If that's what you might be needing."

He'd do it. He looked miserable right now, and probably wished he'd never offered, but he'd do it.

"Why would you do that?"

"You're my sister, and—"

Breanna stiffened. "I thought we'd settled that the other day."

"We settled that you wouldn't acknowledge my father as your own. We didn't settle if you would or wouldn't acknowledge me."

As what? A brother? There were plenty of the old baron's bastards who would be happy to acknowledge Liam as a brother. Why did he want that from her and not them?

"I need to think on it, Liam," she said quietly. "I've thought of you for a lot of years as simply the baron's son, and that never made me feel like we were kin. I need to think on it."

Liam nodded.

"I thank you for the offer, but there's nothing we need from Durham. We have kin who are merchants, so it's easy enough to get something if we can't find it in the village." He looked so discouraged, she added hesitantly, "Perhaps a book?"

His smile was slow in coming, but it eased a strange tightness in her chest.

"I think I can manage a book," he said. "I won't keep you from your work any longer." He mounted Oakdancer, then looked down at her. "Good day to you, Breanna."

"Blessings of the day to you, Liam."

She stayed where she was, watching him until he'd ridden out of sight.

I'll think on it, Liam. I don't know that I'll give you the answer you seem to want, and I don't understand why you want it, but I'll think on it.

When she went back inside the house, Rory looked up from the soup and bread he was busy shoveling into his mouth. "Nuala wants to see you. In the morning room."

"Don't talk and eat at the same time," Breanna said as she walked through the kitchen. "You'll choke."

Nuala was standing by a window, just staring out at the land. On the table near her sat the letter and two large bags that must have come from Rory's saddlebags.

"Some of our kin will be visiting us this summer," Nuala said quietly.

Breanna glanced at the letter. "We'd had word of that before. They're coming for the Solstice."

"Sooner than that, I think. Trevor was as careful about what he said as he was about what he didn't say. But reading between the lines, I'd say he's worried about what may be decided at the next barons' council, and he wants the girls to be someplace else when the new decrees are announced. He also sent enough gold and silver coins to keep us all for a couple of years if it comes to that."

"If the barons make a new decree, it will apply to all of Sylvalan, not just the eastern part."

"We're still farther away from the troubles that have been touching the east." Nuala turned away from the window and looked at Breanna. "And we live at the foot of the Mother's Hills. You know as well as I do that nothing the barons decree will make any difference in the Mother's Hills."

"I know." Breanna took a deep breath, let it out in a huff. "I'd better give Glynis a hand in polishing up as many guest rooms as we can."

Nuala just nodded and turned back to the window to look at the land.

All through that day, as Breanna helped Glynis prepare the rooms, her mind circled around one thought: Liam would be at the barons' council, and if there was trouble heading toward her family, he would tell her soon enough.

Chapter Seven

"**L**ady Morag, have you seen Ashk?"

Morag studied the young man rapidly approaching her. She couldn't remember his name, but she'd seen him with the group of adolescents Ashk affectionately called "the pack."

"She's at the Clan house," Morag said.

The young man grinned. "I wanted to give her fair warning. She's about to have visitors." He touched two fingers to his temple, giving Morag a jaunty salute before jogging down the forest trail that led to the Clan house.

Morag continued along the trail away from the Clan house for another minute. Paused. Looked back.

Turning in a slow circle, she opened herself to her power as the Gatherer and listened.

Death always murmured in the woods, just as life murmured there. But she heard no whisper from Death that indicated she was needed. Besides, there was the youth's grin to consider—and the fact that Ashk had been oddly distracted while she'd been showing Morag some of the trails in the woods. Added to that was Ashk leaving her abruptly about an hour ago "to take a bath."

Whose arrival could be important enough that this Clan's Lady of the Woods would feel compelled to look her best in order to receive them?

A chill went through Morag. She could think of two Fae

whose arrival might cause some excitement among the Clan here—the Huntress and the Lightbringer. The Lady of the Moon and the Lord of the Sun, the Lord of Fire.

Would Dianna or Lucian visit a western Clan? The rest of the Fae in Sylvalan tended to avoid the Fae in the west whenever possible. There was no reason those two would visit here. Unless, somehow, they'd heard that Ari was still alive and now lived in this Old Place.

But there was that youth's grin and Ashk's desire to look her best. Considering Ashk's opinion of Lucian and Dianna, Morag didn't think Ashk would make any special efforts for either of them.

Morag shifted to her other form, spread her black raven's wings, and flew along the forest trail back to the Clan house.

Just to be safe. Just to be sure. As soon as she'd satisfied herself that these visitors were no threat to Ari and Neall, she'd return to the cottage.

As soon as you've satisfied your own curiosity, she admitted frankly. *You want to see who could fluster Ashk.*

Morag landed just out of sight of the Clan house, changed back to her human form, then walked the rest of the way. She reached the Clan house at the same time Ashk walked out one of the doors.

"How do I look?" Ashk asked, turning in a circle to show off the summer-green gown and the brown, richly embroidered overvest.

Like a gentry lady—except you have the pointed ears and feral looks of the Fae, Morag thought. "You look lovely."

Ashk's woodland eyes had a sparkle Morag hadn't seen in them before.

A horn sounded through the woods. Ashk's nostrils flared slightly, as if she were trying to catch a scent on the wind.

"They're here," Ashk said. She smiled at Morag. "Come and meet them." Not waiting for Morag's response, she walked toward a dark-haired man on a gray gelding and a young girl on a black pony as they slowly rode into view of the Clan house.

Gentry, Morag decided as she moved to a position where she could watch Ashk as well as the strangers. That's why she saw the boy riding behind the man. Seen straight on, the boy had been hidden.

"Lady Ashk," the man said with formal politeness.

"Baron Padrick," Ashk replied just as formally. "Come and be welcome."

Morag scanned the faces of the other Fae who were watching this meeting. They didn't seem concerned or wary that the local baron had come to the Clan house. No, they seemed amused by the formality of the greeting. Just like the young girl on the black pony, who was rolling her eyes—which, in turn, made the boy scowl at her.

"I brought someone to see you," Padrick said. Reaching an arm back, he helped the boy down before dismounting.

The girl, grinning now as she watched Ashk, dismounted and led her pony closer to Morag.

Ashk studied the boy before giving Padrick a quizzical look. "You've brought a visiting baron to see me?"

Morag wanted to join the young girl in rolling her eyes. What was wrong with Ashk? It was obvious the boy was the man's son. Anyone could see that by looking at them.

The boy, both pleased and embarrassed, said, *"Mother."*

Ashk stared at him coolly. "Mother? You're mistaken, sir. My son is a boy of eleven years, while you are a tall, handsome young man."

"Mother! It's me, Evan. Truly, it is." He looked up at the man beside him. "Father, tell her."

Morag stared at the man, then at Ashk. Father? Mother? Ashk had mated with the local baron?

Ashk tipped her head to one side, considering. "I'd know who you are for certain if I got a hug." She opened her arms.

When the boy glanced at the people around him and hesitated, Padrick said, "Lad, if you haven't learned yet to recognize a good offer when you hear one, then I'll be glad to take your hug as well as my own."

"You're getting a hug?" Ashk asked.

"Indeed I am," Padrick replied.

The boy took a self-conscious step toward Ashk. Then another. When Ashk smiled at him, he closed the distance between them in a rush.

Padrick looked over at the girl and winked. She gave him a sassy smile in reply.

After a few moments, Padrick said, "Step aside now, lad. It's my turn."

Evan squirmed out of his mother's embrace and stepped aside, grinning.

Padrick stepped forward—and received a bit more than a hug as a welcome.

"I'm Caitlin. Who are you?"

Morag turned her attention away from Ashk and the baron to the girl now standing beside her. She had blue eyes like the baron, but her hair was ash brown, like Ashk's. And it was Ashk's face looking up at her, younger and human, but the connection was still obvious.

"Are you visiting from another Clan?" Caitlin asked.

"Yes, I am."

"She's Neall and Ari's friend," Evan said, joining them. "She's staying with them. Father told me."

"He told me, too," Caitlin said, sounding a little fierce. "I was just being polite."

Both children looked over at their parents, who were still embracing.

"When I was little, I thought it was awful that men had to

kiss ladies that way," Evan said thoughtfully. "But now that I'm older, it doesn't seem like such a bad thing. I may even try it some time. When I'm a bit older."

"Only husbands are allowed to kiss that way," Caitlin said. "And they're only allowed to kiss their wives."

"Husbands are allowed to kiss other ladies."

"Are not."

"Are, too. Father kisses ladies who are friends. Like Ari."

"But not *that* way."

"Of course not *that* way."

" 'Cause if he did, Mother would tear Father's throat out."

"And if Mother kissed another man that way, Father would throw her in the dungeon and not let her out until she promised never to do it again."

Caitlin scowled. "We don't have a dungeon. And even if we did, Father would *never* do that to Mother."

Evan frowned at his younger sister. "Guess not. But he *would* be very angry."

"Yes, he would," Caitlin agreed.

Bloodthirsty little beasts, Morag thought.

Then they both looked at her, a bit too thoughtfully for her comfort.

"What's your gift?" Caitlin asked.

Morag hesitated. "I'm the Gatherer."

She expected them to move away from her. The children in other Clans, once they learned who she was, had tended to keep their distance. Instead, Evan's and Caitlin's eyes brightened.

"You're the only one of Death's Servants who can gather a spirit before the body dies," Evan said excitedly. "Have you ever done it?"

"There are times when it is kinder to let the spirit go on to the Summerland if the body is failing and the person is suffering," Morag said carefully.

"Have you ever gathered someone because they did a bad thing?" Caitlin asked.

Morag thought of the Inquisitors she had gathered last summer when they were still healthy and whole in order to stop them from killing the witches. That wasn't something she was going to try to explain to these children. "Mostly I gather those whose flesh has already returned to the Great Mother."

"But if someone did a *bad* thing, you *would* gather them, wouldn't you?" Caitlin persisted.

"Of course she would," Evan replied. "She's the Gatherer. So if sea thieves were attacking a merchant ship and she saw them doing it, she'd send the sea thieves to a watery grave to save the good merchants. Wouldn't you?"

"Ah . . ." What was she supposed to say to this boy who was looking at her with such approval?

"But she wouldn't gather someone just because they did something that was a *little* bad," Caitlin said. "Because that wouldn't be fair. Would it?"

"No, that wouldn't be fair," Morag said. "Did— Did your parents tell you that? That I— That the Gatherer would take you if you didn't behave?"

The children shook their heads.

"Oh, no," Caitlin said. "They would *never* say that. Besides, you have to take care of the important gathering, so you wouldn't have time to gather everyone who did something a little bit bad."

"When we were little, Mother used to say if we did something very bad, she would dunk us in the privy," Evan said.

"And we wouldn't be allowed back inside the Clan house until we washed ourselves and our clothes well enough to smell tolerable," Caitlin added.

"So one day we decided to find out how bad it would be if we *did* do something bad enough that Mother would dunk us," Evan said. "So we tied a rope to a tree near one of the privy houses and brought the other end in with us so that we could climb back out."

"It was bad," Caitlin said, wrinkling her nose. "And we never did get the shoes clean enough to be tolerable. Mother threw those back down the privy hole. And when Father came to take us back to the estate, he wouldn't let us bring the clothes back into the house even though we'd washed them."

"And he made us take another bath," Evan said.

"But we never did anything bad enough to make Mother dunk us in the privy hole," Caitlin said proudly. "And now that we're older, we don't do things like that anymore."

"I'm so glad," Morag said faintly. A bit desperate, she looked around and felt almost weak with relief when Ashk and Padrick joined them.

Ashk smiled at the children. "There's someone waiting to greet you. Just follow that path. You can leave the pony here," she told Caitlin. Then she frowned at Evan. "Why *did* you ride behind your father? Where's your pony?"

Evan gave Ashk a sweet smile. "I lent it to Ari, along with my little pony cart. It's small enough to fit on most of the forest trails, and that way Ari won't have to walk so much when she's gathering her plants this summer."

"That was very thoughtful of you," Ashk said.

Padrick coughed. "Go on now. And remember to come back. You're the guest of honor at this feast, and we can't begin without you."

The children grinned at him. Evan dashed down the path. Caitlin shoved the pony's reins into her mother's hand and ran after him.

"Morag?" Ashk said. "You look pale. Aren't you feeling well?"

"I've been talking to your children."

"Oh, dear," Ashk and Padrick said.

"I've never met children quite like them."

Ashk gave her a cool look. "They're not so different from other children."

"Not the children here in the west," Padrick said. "But, perhaps, different from the children who had grown up knowing only Tir Alainn?"

"Yes," Morag said, relieved he understood—and then wondered *why* he understood so well.

"My Lady," Padrick said, looking pointedly at Ashk.

"Morag," Ashk said, "this is Padrick, the Baron of Breton—and my husband. Padrick, this is Morag, the Gatherer."

"I'm pleased to make your acquaintance, Lady Morag," Padrick said.

Morag stared at both of them. Husband? Not just mate?

She must have looked as startled as she felt, because Padrick said, "The gentry require a legal heir to a baron's estate, so Ashk indulged me in following the human custom of marriage."

"I see," Morag said. But she didn't see. Not really. A baron and a Lady of the Woods. Gentry and Fae. Not just living separately side by side in their own little pieces of the world, but weaving those pieces together.

Do you know how different all of you are from the rest of the Fae? Morag wondered.

The feral amusement in Ashk's woodland eyes told her clearly that Ashk, at least, was quite aware that the Clan's acceptance of her union with a gentry baron would be incomprehensible to Fae beyond the west.

When she saw that same feral amusement in Padrick's eyes, understanding struck her as hard as a physical blow. She hadn't looked beyond the human face and the gentry title, hadn't considered there might be a reason to look beneath the surface. She should have considered it, especially after living with Neall and Ari for the past few days.

Padrick might be gentry and a baron, but he was also Fae.

"The children are returning," Ashk said after a moment of long silence. "Shall we join the others for the feast?"

As the late afternoon gave way to evening, and the feasting gave way to the dancing and the music and the stories, Morag couldn't shake the feeling that when she'd crossed into the territory of the western Clans, she'd crossed more of a boundary than she'd realized.

Declining to participate in another dance, she sat beside Ari, glad to have a moment when she could watch instead of being swept along in the celebration.

"Why didn't you tell me Ashk was married to the local baron?" Morag asked, feeling a little hurt that she'd been excluded from what was, after all, common knowledge among this Clan. It reminded her too sharply that she was still an outsider, might always be an outsider.

"It didn't occur to me," Ari said. Then she hesitated. "You've said very little about where you've been over this past year, but I think we've all sensed it was a hard journey, for the heart as well as the body. You've had enough things to adjust to in the few days since you've come to live here." She lightly touched Morag's arm. "They're different from the rest of the Fae, aren't they?"

Morag looked at the men and women laughing and dancing, and almost—*almost*—understood something that had been eluding her since she'd arrived at this Clan house. "Yes, they're different."

In her bedroom at the Clan house, Ashk lay on her back in bed, dreamily watching the candlelight play with the shadows on the ceiling. The night air dried the sweat, chilling her skin except where Padrick's arm lay heavy and warm across her belly and his head rested on her shoulder.

"If I were still a randy young man, my cock would already be willing to try again," Padrick said.

"Hmm," Ashk replied, too sated to think of anything else to say.

Padrick raised his head. "That's the best you can do, woman? You're supposed to say something flattering."

Ashk turned her head to look at him. "A seasoned lover is better than a randy young man."

He grunted. Dropped his head back down on her shoulder.

Ashk smiled. "So what were the three of you talking about this evening? You looked so serious."

"Who?"

Now Ashk grunted. "You know very well who. You and Evan and Neall."

"Oh. That. If you must know, we were comparing the size of our cocks."

Ashk snorted. "Oh. Well. Must have been embarrassing when Evan came out the winner of that little contest."

"You've never had any complaints when I stand at attention, wife," Padrick grumbled.

She just grinned.

"Well," he said, rolling onto his back. "You might as well know. Since you started it, you'll have to finish it."

"Started what?" Ashk said, sitting up so that she was in a better position to give her husband a narrow-eyed stare. "Finish what?"

"You should learn to be more careful about what you put in writing, darling wife."

The way Padrick was smiling at her made her nervous. "I didn't put anything in writing."

His smiled widened. "Oh, now. Who was it who was feeling maudlin a few months ago because her firstborn was away at school on his birthday?"

"I wasn't feeling maudlin!" But she had been. She'd just hoped Padrick hadn't noticed.

"And who was it who fretted over only being able to send gifts that wouldn't be remarked upon at a gentry school?"

"That's perfectly understandable," Ashk said defensively, sensing a trap but not able to see the shape of it.

"And who was it who wrote that firstborn son a letter and told him that because he wasn't home to celebrate his birthday, he could choose his gift when he came home?"

"So?" When he didn't say anything, she wondered how he'd enjoy being shoved out of bed. "What's that got—?" She began to see the shape of the trap. "What's that got to do with Neall?"

"And who is it, my darling wife, who has some of the finest horses in the county?"

"A horse?" Ashk stared at her husband. "I never said Evan could have a horse!"

"And you never said he couldn't."

"He's too young to have a horse. Besides, he has a pony."

"No, he doesn't. He lent the pony, and the little pony cart along with it, to Ari."

"But—"

"Our boy learned more in this past year than could be found in schoolbooks. He's made friends with a couple of boys from a well-to-do merchant family from eastern Sylvalan, and the three of them went over every word of that letter as if it were a contract full of fine print."

"But—"

Padrick burst out laughing. "Oh, you should have heard him, Ashk, telling Neall how he'd been thinking of Ari walking through the woods for hours at a time to gather her plants, and her with a babe heavy in her belly, and how, being another man, he could appreciate that Neall would be carrying a bit of worry about that, which is why he offered Ari the loan of the pony and the cart, even though it meant he wouldn't have a mount of his own. And then observing, just casual-like, that there's that one gelding that Glenn brought with him when he came west to join Neall and Ari that really was too small for a grown man—"

"But an acceptable mount for a lady," Ashk protested.

"—but it was a good horse, and it would be a shame to let it go to waste."

Ashk opened her mouth, then shut it with a snap of her teeth.

"Yes," Padrick said, grinning at her, "he softened Neall up like the sun softens butter."

"It isn't right to take advantage of Neall," Ashk growled.

"Considering the wink he gave me after Evan walked away, I'd say Neall's got a fair amount of horse trader in him, too."

Ashk screamed—but quietly enough not to cause a commotion that would have people banging on the door wanting answers.

"So when you and Evan go over to bargain for the little horse, don't make Neall do all the work of haggling himself down to the price he has in mind. You have to do your share in this bartering."

"I don't barter."

Padrick took her hand, his expression turning serious. "Yes, you do. All the time. Just not for small things. Not for things like this."

Ashk studied his face, studied the way the candle flame gave it light and shadows. "When do you have to leave for the barons' council?"

"I should have left already, but I wanted to bring Evan home before I went. Don't be worrying now," he added, brushing her hair behind her shoulders. "I'll go up to Tir Alainn and use the bridges between the Clan territories until I get to the southern end of the Mother's Hills. That will save me a day's travel, if not more."

"You'll need to ride a Fae horse if you're planning to use the shining roads."

"I can cloud a stable lad's mind well enough for him to see nothing more than a fine but ordinary horse," Padrick said.

"I know," Ashk replied, smiling.

"And I can use the glamour to hide this gentry face behind the mask of looking Fae so that my presence in Tir Alainn won't upset the Clans beyond the west."

What would Morag have said if I'd told her that I loved a man who, because of the mingling of bloodlines over generations, was not only a gentry baron, but Fae, as well? Ashk wondered. If she'd shown contempt for our marriage, which is how I suspect other Fae beyond the western Clans would respond, it would have killed the friendship slowly growing between us. So whose feelings was I protecting by saying nothing until she was thrust into meeting Padrick and the children today? Morag's? Or my own?

"I have to go, Ashk," Padrick said softly. "It pains my heart to leave you, but I have to go to this council."

She pulled herself from her own thoughts and realized he was genuinely troubled. "I know that. We each have the duties that go with who we are." She studied him carefully. "What troubles you, Padrick?"

When he didn't say anything, she waited. She'd learned over the years that when he had something on his mind, he collected his thoughts and then strung them together like beads before presenting them to her.

"Many things," he finally said. "I didn't like what I heard at the barons' council last autumn. Didn't like what I was hearing at the club where I'd dine so that I could listen to more than the other barons braying their opinions at each other. There were things happening back east last summer that bode ill for all of us, and it was as much what wasn't said as what was that troubles me—especially when I could put those things together with what Neall told me about the Black Coats."

Ashk shivered. Neall had been more willing to talk to Padrick than to her, but she'd learned enough from Padrick to share his uneasiness. And it occurred to her that if she truly wanted to know more, the person to ask was Morag.

Well, she *would* ask Morag. But not tonight.

"I'm also troubled by the merchant boys," Padrick continued.

"You don't approve of them as friends for Evan?" She wasn't sure she approved of them since she was fairly certain Evan wouldn't have thought of trying to corner her into buying him a horse at his age if there hadn't been two coin-counting little brains helping him look at a mother's loving words as a chip on the bartering table.

"They're fine lads. Intelligent and lively, yet courteous and respectful. No, it's not the boys themselves, but . . . There are good schools in the east—better schools than you can find in the west if the eastern barons can be believed. A wealthy merchant family is minor gentry. They wouldn't have any trouble getting the boys into a school in the east. So why would an eastern merchant family send their boys so far from home?"

"Because they don't care enough about the boys' feelings to let them stay close to home?" Ashk said.

Padrick shook his head. "They care. The boys mentioned that their uncle, who captains one of their ships, brought his ship in to the nearest port and took a coach the rest of the way to bring them gifts from the family and spend the Winter Solstice with them since there wasn't enough time for them to go home. When I went down to fetch Evan, their uncle was also there, and we talked for a bit. He mentioned that he'd like to find a nice harbor town here in the west, a place where he could establish a port of call for the family business. He said it all easily enough, but when he learned I was a baron, he was also quick to mention how it would benefit the towns here to have goods brought in by sea."

Ashk stared at her husband. "He was offering a—what do you call it? A bribe?"

"In that he implied any goods I might be interested in could be gotten for a leaner price than I could get them elsewhere, yes, it was a bribe."

Ashk sputtered. "What makes him think you'd accept such a thing—or that a man whose estate sits a day's ride from the coast would have any influence?"

"But I do have influence, don't I?" Padrick said quietly. "At least, at one harbor where there's only a paper baron for whom I've been casting an absentee vote in the council for the past several years."

"You really think he'd be interested in a . . . a safe harbor surrounded by a village that has very few human residents?" Ashk said doubtfully.

"There's power in him, Ashk. Not Fae, but there's something in him that I recognized. And I think he sensed the magic in me, which is why he risked talking to me in the first place. I don't think he's looking for a safe harbor for his ship or that he gives a damn about expanding the trading territory to fill his family's coffers. I think he's really looking for a safe harbor for his family, something that's established before they may need it. I think that's why those boys are going to school here in the west. Safe harbor." Padrick paused. "He also mentioned that his wife and young daughter were going to be visiting kin this summer, a place that borders the Mother's Hills."

A shiver went through Ashk. Not fear, exactly. More like the feeling of stepping into deep, cool shadows after spending time out in the sun when its heat lay heavy on the skin.

Watching her, Padrick nodded. "Oh, he never said the words. He was careful about that, always watching me to see if I understood and accepted or if he had said too much. But he mentioned that their kin's property was fine land, and held a fine woods. An old woods."

"An Old Place," Ashk said softly. "You think his family has roots in the House of Gaian?"

"I'm not sure if they wanted to impress me or Evan, but before he could stop them, his nephews were boasting about how their uncle had never lost a ship at sea, had never limped into port after a bad storm. They said when a storm blew up, their uncle would stand at the bow of his ship, would tie himself to the railing if need be, and call to the sea—and no matter how fierce the storm, no matter how high the waves, the sea would let his ship pass safely through."

"Mother's mercy."

"So, yes, I think it's safe to assume his family has roots in the House of Gaian. And that puts them all at risk."

"You'll find a safe harbor for him and his," Ashk said, not really asking a question since she realized he'd almost set his mind to doing just that.

"I wanted to talk with you first."

"You'll find a safe harbor for him and his," she repeated.

Padrick sighed as if he'd just been relieved of a great weight. "They have a shipping office in Durham. I have the name of the cousin who runs it. I'll leave a message to be passed on."

And I'll talk to Morag, Ashk thought.

"While I'm gone, I'd like the children to stay with you."

"Of course. I can play lady of the manor for a week or two."

"No. I'd like them to stay here. With you."

Ashk sorted through the feelings she heard behind the words—and didn't like them. "I know your people aren't that comfortable with dealing with me, but—"

"They're more comfortable than you seem to think," Padrick said sharply. "Mother's tits, Ashk. The farm folk don't leave trinkets or other little offerings in order to placate the Fae as they might do in other places. They do it in the hopes that whoever they're leaving it for might show up while they're still there, might talk with them a bit. Do you realize how many of them showed up at Neall and Ari's door when they arrived here last summer, offering a bit of baking or a dish of food? How many of the men gave up a day of working their own land to help Neall? How many of the women came to clean the cottage because Ari was still too fragile to do the heavy work by herself? Those things weren't done out of fear of the witch and the young Lord of the Woods. They were done because the people wanted to know Ari and Neall."

Ashk looked down at their joined hands. "I didn't realize. Not completely. The truth is, I'm still not comfortable being around most humans. Many of their ways still seem strange to me."

Padrick put his other hand over hers. "It hasn't been so many years that both sides have tried to know each other more openly. Before that, we were always aware of each other but, for the most part, always apart."

"I'll stay at the manor house. It will be good practice for me to deal with the people when you're not there to take care of things."

"No," Padrick said firmly. He paused. "My people are servants or farmers. In the village, they're merchants and tailors and seamstresses and bakers. They're good people, but . . . they're not the Fae. They don't grow up with a bow in their hands. While I'm gone, it will ease my heart to know the children are safe here—with you."

"If I make that promise to ease your heart, what will you promise to ease mine?" Ashk asked. "Where you're going, you'll find no safety in the woods."

"I'll take care, wife. That I promise. And I'll be home as soon as I can."

When he leaned forward to kiss her, she turned her face away, then put one hand on his shoulder to let him know she wasn't refusing his touch but there was something more to say.

"My grandfather is in the woods."

"I thought that's who you had sent the children to see before the feast," Padrick said. "I'm sorry he didn't choose to join us. Was he feeling poorly after the journey?"

She felt herself stepping away from the light, going deeper into the shadows of the woods, could almost hear blood dripping from her knife onto the leaves beneath her feet. Not today. Not tomorrow. But soon. Soon.

"The old Lord is in the woods," she repeated, putting a sharper emphasis on the words. "He hasn't come to the Clan house. He hasn't changed to his human form at all since he arrived."

"I see."

But he didn't see. Not really. His Fae heritage had lain dormant inside him—and might have remained dormant if they hadn't become lovers, if it hadn't been awakened by the continued presence of her strength and particular gift. He understood her Clan better than she understood his humans, but he didn't understand this.

Padrick took a deep breath, let it out slowly. "I'll talk to Forrester when I stop at the manor house to pick up my saddlebags. He and his gamekeepers will keep an eye out for your grandfather."

"It's not that—but I'm grateful to you for thinking of it."

Ashk closed her eyes. Pieces of the past few days were swirling around in her mind, trying to form a pattern. She just couldn't see it yet. "First Morag arrives. Why here? Why now? Did she truly choose the road at random that led her to this Clan, or was her gift guiding her here, so subtly she still doesn't realize she was summoned? Then my grandfather, the old Lord of the Woods, arrives. There's something he knows, something he senses. But he keeps to his stag form, stays in the woods because it's the clearest way he has to show me whatever it is that brought him here. And you're approached by a sea merchant whose family has ties to the House of Gaian. They're all connected. Somehow." She shook her head. *The pattern won't come if you try to force it. Think of something else.* Her eyes snapped open. "Curse the barons' council twice over! You won't be back home in time for the Summer Moon."

Padrick studied her carefully, as if trying to decipher her change in mood. "And will you go out walking that night, darling Ashk?"

"Oh, I'll go out walking that night, but I won't be wearing a form any other man would want to cuddle."

He grinned. "I love the feel of your fur beneath my hands. All thick and soft."

She narrowed her eyes. "No. It's too hot, and I'm shedding something fierce."

"Ah, well, then. I'll give you a good brushing when I get home."

"And if you let anything but your eyes roam that night, I'll pluck you, my fine hawk."

He took her hand, pressed it against his cock. "The bird's already plucked, but quite willing to be petted."

Laughing, Ashk pulled him down on top of her.

Chapter Eight

"I am sorry, but with the baron away and the mistress not at home, I do not have the authority to offer you shelter."

Faced with the butler's genuine concern, Aiden tried to hide some of the weariness that had plagued him for the past two days. He worked to give the man a smile. "I understand. With the troubles in the villages east of here, it is wise to be . . . cautious . . . of strangers." Touching fingertips to temple in a salute, he turned away from the door and started walking back to where Lyrra waited with the horses.

"Minstrel."

I am the Bard, the Lord of Song, Aiden thought bitterly as he turned back toward the butler. Such a civilized gift of magic, being the Bard—and so useless in the face of what he and Lyrra had recently seen.

The butler took a few steps away from the house, glanced around to see if anyone else was about, then said with quiet intensity, "You are a man with an open mind?"

"About most things," Aiden replied. But not where the Inquisitors were concerned. Never where they were concerned. Especially not after— No, he couldn't think about that. He had to keep his mind focused on the immediate task of finding food and shelter for Lyrra and the horses.

"I do not believe the baron would object if you used the lanes on the estate instead of going back to the main road since that would lengthen your journey," the butler said, giving Lyrra a worried look. "Go on past the stables and follow the brook until you reach a stone bridge. Cross the bridge and follow the lane. The ladies who live on that land sometimes offer shelter to travelers."

Aiden almost asked why he needed an open mind toward anyone willing to offer shelter—and then he understood what the butler was carefully not saying. His heart lifted one moment, then began pounding anxiously the next.

Please. Great Mother, please don't let us be too late this time.

When he mounted his horse, Lyrra made the effort to raise her head and look at him. She was pale from exhaustion, and the dark smudges under her eyes seemed deeper than they'd been even an hour ago.

"Just a bit farther," he murmured as he gently urged his horse forward. "Just a bit farther."

She didn't ask where they were going or how much "a bit farther" really was. She just slumped in her saddle and let her mare follow the packhorse Aiden led.

He didn't dare let her see how much she worried him. She'd withdrawn from him. Withdrawn from everything. All her energy, all her focus was on staying in the saddle and going forward. Her sleep, like his, had been restless the past two nights, torn by dreams of blood and pain. He wondered if she, too, heard that young voice pleading to be allowed to die. He couldn't ask because he didn't want to remind her of anything that might not be preying on her mind.

As if either of us is going to forget. He wondered if there would be a story or a poem from her that would be a cry of rage and sorrow. And he wondered what wild, grieving song would rise from him one day.

When he reached the stone bridge, he hesitated.

"An Old Place?"

Hearing hope and horror in equal measure in Lyrra's question, he looked back at her and said carefully, "The butler at the manor house said the ladies here sometimes offer shelter to travelers."

There was something so terrible about the way she stared at him that he turned away from her.

The witches at the last Old Place they'd come to had also offered shelter to travelers. That's what the Small Folk had told him bitterly. If someone asked for shelter, it was given. So there hadn't been anything strange about four men coming to that house at dusk one day. Four men who looked like dusty, weary travelers.

The Small Folk hadn't become uneasy until the second day because it had rained the first day after the strangers arrived, and, noticing one man go to the barn to tend the animals, they had reckoned everyone else had chosen to stay inside out of the wet.

But the second day, the men left late in the afternoon—and rode out in a hurry.

That's when some of the Small Folk went to the house and found the warding spells that usually protected the house were gone. So they went inside—and they found the witches.

Two hours later, Aiden and Lyrra rode up to that house.

The youngest witch was still alive, had been left in a room with the bodies of her mother, grandmother, and elder sister. The men, whom Aiden strongly suspected were Inquisitors, hadn't been worried about leaving her. There was nothing anyone could have done to mend her poor tortured body.

Please, let it end. Please, let me die. Please.

If he'd known where to find Morag, he would have begged her to come to that house and take the girl's spirit from that suffering body. Without the Gatherer, he and Lyrra and the Small Folk did what they could to make her more comfortable, which was pitifully little.

Please, let me die. Please.

Lyrra stayed with the girl while he and the Small Folk dug the graves for the other three women. He didn't ask the small men if any of the Fae had bothered to make themselves known to the witches. At one point, while he was resting his back and hands, he wondered if he should ride up the shining road to Tir Alainn and warn the Fae that the road would be closing soon. Then he looked at the half-dug grave and went back to work. The Fae could take care of themselves. When had they ever done anything else?

The girl died at dusk on the second day after they'd arrived at that Old Place. While Lyrra washed the body, he and the small men went out to dig another grave.

They'd barely broken ground when one of the small men noticed the swarm of nighthunters flying toward them and gave a cry of warning.

Shouting at Lyrra to close the windows, Aiden dropped his shovel and ran to the barn. The house was still sturdy enough, but the barn had been neglected, and he couldn't leave the horses in a structure that would make them easy prey.

It didn't occur to him until he led the horses out of the barn that he didn't have a chance of reaching the house before the nighthunters attacked.

A stone shot from a sling knocked one of the nighthunters down. The small men shouted at him to make good use of his legs as they shot clods of dirt and small stones at the creatures.

He ran to the house, got himself and the horses inside. The small men continued to hold off the nighthunters long enough to reach the house, too. They huddled together that night, listening to the nighthunters' bodies hitting the shutters as the creatures tried to find a way into the house. Then they listened to the screams of agony from the three ghosts when the creatures finally abandoned the living and sought another kind of sustenance by devouring the spirits of the dead.

The next morning, knowing what would happen once the sun went down, none of them could bring themselves to bury the girl. So they dug up earth and covered her with it where she lay on the bed. They put a bowl of water on the bedside table, set the stub of a candle next to it, and, for a few tense minutes, opened the bedroom window to let in fresh air.

Earth, air, water, fire. The four branches of the Great Mother.

He didn't know if there were special words that should have been said, so he played his harp for a few minutes. Lyrra sang a poem about witches that she had written last winter and that he'd recently set to music.

Then they closed up the house, saddled the horses, said good-bye to the Small Folk, and rode away.

Now here they were with only a bridge separating them from another Old Place.

Aiden took a deep breath, let it out slowly. Brushed his heels against his gelding's sides to urge the animal forward.

A small stone hit his boot.

"Deceiver," a voice hissed.

Aiden looked down. Even knowing what to look for, it still took him a moment to locate the water sprite standing on a flat stone near the bank of the brook. She stared at him with such loathing, he couldn't suppress the shiver that went through him.

"Deceiver," she hissed again.

"We mean no harm," he said quietly.

"Then show the Daughters your true face. Let them see who stands before them before they bid you welcome." She waited a moment. When he didn't respond, she gave him a knife-edged smile.

Aiden urged his horse forward, not sure what he expected,

but not feeling easy until Lyrra was across the bridge. When he looked back, the sprite had climbed the bank high enough to peer over the edge. Her eyes were still filled with loathing, and her smile was still knife sharp. He wondered if she had a particular reason for disliking the Fae, or if it was simply because the Fae had always dismissed the Small Folk as insignificant, lesser beings who were expected to obey the Fair Folk's commands.

He almost turned back, almost tried to tell her about the Inquisitors and why it was necessary to keep watch. But if his own kind wouldn't listen to him, there was no reason to think she would trust anything he might say. So he continued down the lane, with the packhorse and Lyrra trailing behind him.

Strength flowed from the land, filled him with every breath he took. It made him dizzy, as if he'd drunk too much strong wine, and so thirsty for more he wanted to gulp it down. Fighting to stay alert, he looked up and saw the Mother's Hills.

The Fae avoided the Mother's Hills. Perhaps it was simply because there were no shining roads there that anchored Tir Alainn to the human world, and there were no Old Places. Perhaps there *was* something . . . strange . . . about those hills. Or perhaps the Fae said the hills were strange because they sensed that they weren't welcome there.

When they came in sight of a manor house, Aiden reined in, waited for Lyrra to come up beside him. She studied the well-kept house, then looked at him.

"Perhaps I misunderstood what the butler said," Aiden said carefully. The homes they'd seen in the other Old Places had ranged from large cottages like the one Ari had lived in to places that were little better than one-room hovels. Neither of them had seen a manor house like this in an Old Place. The signs of gentry prosperity were unnerving. They'd seen no sign before now that witches lived this well.

"The magic is still strong here," Lyrra said, but there was a trace of doubt in her voice.

"And the water sprite referred to the ladies as Daughters." Aiden sighed. "Come on, then. We won't find out anything standing here."

As they rode toward the house, a dark-haired woman raced through the arch that Aiden guessed led to the stable yard. She slid to a stop when she saw them.

"Did you see a black dog and a string of sausages?" she demanded.

"No, Mistress," Aiden replied. "I regret we have not."

The woman put her hands on her hips and yelled, "Idjit! Come back here, you feeble-minded excuse for a dog!"

Since they were here to beg food and shelter, Aiden didn't think it prudent to point out that a dog who could steal sausages probably wasn't feeble-minded.

No dog appeared. Not even a bush rustled to indicate where the thief might be hiding.

The woman let out an exasperated sigh, then turned to study Aiden and Lyrra. There was a friendly wariness in her eyes that made Aiden uncertain if they would get much help here but also made him feel relieved that she wouldn't assume all travelers were good people.

"Blessings of the day to you," she said.

"Blessings of the day, Mistress," Aiden replied. "I'm Aiden. This is my wife, Lyrra."

She studied them, then studied the carefully wrapped instruments tied on the packhorse. "Minstrels?"

"Minstrel and storyteller," Lyrra said.

"The Bard and the Muse," Aiden said.

"Aiden!" Lyrra looked shocked.

Aiden smiled at the witch. Let her draw her own conclusions about a couple of entertainers who had enough gall to use titles that belonged to the Fae and yet couldn't coax an audience to part with a few coppers. Not that they'd tried to earn any coins in the past couple of days, despite having an empty purse.

"I'm Breanna," the witch said.

"That's a lovely name."

She ignored the flattery while her sharp eyes continued to study them. "You look like you've had hard traveling the past few days."

Aiden's smile faded. He heard the catch in Lyrra's breathing and wondered what he could say in explanation if she suddenly burst into tears.

"Yes," he said. "It's been hard traveling."

Breanna said nothing for a long moment. Then, "Come this way. Clay will see to your horses."

She led them through the archway and called for Clay.

After they handed over the horses, they followed Breanna to the house. Aiden slipped an arm around Lyrra's waist, as much to offer comfort as to provide support.

Breanna stopped at the threshold, drew a gold chain from beneath her shirt, and held up the pendant. "Do you know what this is?"

Yes, he knew what it was. "It's a pentagram." The witches' symbol for their connection with the Mother, the symbol for earth, air, fire, water, and spirit.

"Do you understand who we are?"

"You're the Mother's Daughters."

The way her eyes widened and then narrowed told him he'd made a mistake of some kind, but his mind and body recognized this as a safe place to rest, and it was getting harder to think clearly, getting harder to move.

"Come in and be welcome," Breanna said, stepping across the threshold.

Aiden felt tears sting his eyes as he helped Lyrra enter the house. He blinked quickly to banish them. How could he explain why a simple phrase could effect him so much? How could he tell these women that he'd feared he'd never hear that phrase again, that he'd always arrive too late? How could he say nothing when he knew what might happen the next time a stranger rode across that stone bridge?

"Breanna?" An older woman with gray-streaked dark hair entered the kitchen, followed by a middle-aged woman wearing a fashionable gentry riding outfit. "We have guests?"

"Entertainers," Breanna said. "They need a place to stay tonight." Turning toward Aiden, she added, "This is Nuala, my grandmother. And this is Elinore . . . a neighbor."

"And mother of the Baron of Willowsbrook," the middle-aged woman added.

She wants us to know these women have connections, Aiden thought. Said to the wrong person, that could put her family in as much danger as the witches. "Ladies."

"They need some food," Breanna said.

"They might also appreciate a bath," Nuala said. Then she smiled, her expression sympathetic and slightly amused, as if she understood exactly how hard a choice she'd just presented to them.

"Bath, is it?" another voice said as shoes clomped to the inner kitchen door. "I'll say they need a bath. Mother's tits! You can smell them two rooms away!"

"Glynis!" Nuala said sharply.

The woman stepped into the kitchen far enough to see Aiden and Lyrra. Her face reddened.

"I—" Lyrra stammered. "If we could have a bit of water . . ." Her breath caught on a sob. Crying, she turned toward Aiden, who wrapped his arms around her as he glared at Glynis.

"Oh," Glynis said. "I never meant—"

Nuala cut her off. "You've said quite enough for the moment." She and Elinore went to Lyrra, gently drew her out of

Aiden's arms, and led her away. "Come along, now. Come. You're worn to the bone. We'll prepare a nice bath and a bite to eat. You'll feel easier in no time. You'll see."

"Aiden!" Lyrra half turned back.

"He'll be fine," Nuala said, continuing to lead Lyrra out of the kitchen. "Breanna will look after him."

Not knowing what else to do, Aiden stepped back across the threshold, taking himself out of the house. Beside the door was a simple wooden bench, much like the one that had been at Ari's cottage. Was that common to a witch's house, or simply a practical way to give whoever worked in the kitchen a place to rest outdoors for a moment?

He sat on the bench, resting his back against stones that were still cool despite the growing heat of the day.

A few moments later, Breanna sat down on the other end of the bench.

"You don't have to keep me company," Aiden said wearily. "I smell."

"Yes, you do," Breanna replied calmly. "But that's something soap and water can fix easily enough."

"Breanna," Glynis said, hovering in the kitchen doorway.

Aiden kept his eyes fixed on the neat yard, so different from the other witches' homes he'd seen in Old Places. He didn't want to look directly at this woman, didn't want to have to say anything to her. As tired as he was, he didn't think anything he said right now would be courteous.

"Thank you, Glynis," Breanna said, taking a pewter mug and a plate from the woman.

"I'll— I'll just go prepare the water for the gentleman's bath."

"That would be good." Breanna waited until Glynis left before she held out the plate and mug to Aiden. "Here. Have a bit to eat while you're waiting."

"Thank you." He took a sip of ale, fought the urge to drain

the mug. They'd found enough fresh streams on the journey to keep supplied with water, but the ale created a different kind of thirst, and it wasn't one he could afford to indulge when it was already so hard to keep his wits sharp. After taking another sip of ale, he put a thick slice of cheese on a piece of fresh bread, folded it one-handed, then bit into it.

"If the ale isn't to your liking, I could get you something else," Breanna said as he finished the first piece of bread and cheese.

He smiled as he put more cheese and bread together. "It's better ale than I've tasted in a good many days. But if I drink it as heartily as I'd like, I'll likely be asleep before the last swallow."

She didn't smile back. Just studied him. "Tell me something, Bard."

He stiffened, then gave her a rueful look. After all, he was the one who had told her he was the Bard.

"Are you wandering without two coins to rub together because you don't entertain well enough to earn a purse when you play, or has it really been a hard road?"

He set the bread and cheese back on the plate, his appetite gone. "We're very good entertainers. We just haven't had the heart to play in the past few days."

"Then I'm sorry that your heart holds your hands and voice captive."

It always does, Aiden thought. *But it usually speaks its truth through the songs.* "Mistress Breanna, there are things I should tell you about what is happening in the eastern villages, things your family especially needs to be on guard against."

"Then you'll tell us," Breanna replied. "But they'll keep for a little while." She turned her head toward the kitchen. "First you'll have your bath and a bit of a rest. After the evening meal will be soon enough for us to listen to what you need to say."

Would a few hours make so much difference? They could. If the Black Coats came riding up to this house, they could.

Please, let me die. Please.

A shudder went through him. He reached out, not quite touching Breanna. "As grateful as I am for your hospitality, I beg you, Mistress Breanna, be careful who you welcome into your house. Be wary of strangers, especially men—especially if there's more than one of them. Keep your warding spells strong. Please. Evil is riding the roads these days, wearing the faces of men."

He watched her face pale a little. Then he wondered if he'd been too abrupt. She seemed to go away from him, her thoughts focused elsewhere.

A moment later, she focused on him again. "Come along," she said briskly. "I'll find you some clothes to wear so that yours can get washed."

He followed obediently through the house until she showed him into a guest room that had a corner screened off as a bathing area.

"Your lady is in the adjoining room," Breanna said. "I suggest you knock. I also suggest you wear something more than a towel before you enter."

He pushed his dirty hair away from his face. Mother's tits, he was looking forward to being able to soak himself clean. "I understand. I wouldn't want to distress the ladies."

Breanna just looked at him, wide-eyed. Then she grinned. "Oh, you wouldn't be distressing them. I'm sure Gran and Elinore would enjoy the opportunity to admire a handsome man, but being the object of their attention while wearing something that could become unknotted at any moment might be distressing to *you.*"

He could picture it. And he could almost hear the tune that

would go with the song about a man caught in just such a position. Have to have plenty of instrumental bridges for the laughter to die down before the next verse, and—

He was suddenly aware that Breanna was watching him.

"Makes a fine picture, doesn't it?" she said.

He winced at the purely female amusement in Breanna's voice. He could barely hear the tune and didn't have one line of the lyrics yet, but he knew *exactly* what tone of voice Lyrra would use when she sang her part of that song-to-be.

Laughing, Breanna left the room, closing the door gently behind her.

He quickly stripped out of his clothes, leaving them where they fell, and hurried behind the screen. More than just a hip bath. A good-size tub filled with water.

He'd just settled into the tub, sighing with pleasure, when a brisk knock was immediately followed by the bedroom door opening.

"Aiden?"

"Breanna?" He looked around for some way to cover himself, even though he couldn't see her through the screen—which meant, he sincerely hoped, that she couldn't see him.

"I found some clothes for you. Can't do anything about the boots, but the rest will do for the evening."

"Ah . . . thank you." *Go away!*

"I'll take your clothes. Anything in the pockets that can't get introduced to soap and water?"

"Ah . . ."

"For a silver-tongued minstrel, you're a bit stingy with words, aren't you?"

"I'm—" He knew he should meet that teasing with something sharp and witty, but his brain and his tongue failed him. After a moment's silence, he heard her chuckling as she gathered up his clothes and left him alone again.

He finished his bath and put on the clothes Breanna had left for him, then knocked on the adjoining room's door. He found Lyrra there, alone, slowly combing out her hair. She wore a soft white shift that left her arms bare and fell just past her knees. The way she looked aroused him, and he wondered if she'd be interested in using the bed for something other than rest.

Then she stood up to greet him and swayed to keep her balance.

He crossed the room, put his arms around her, and led her to the bed.

"You need to rest now," he said quietly.

"Don't leave," she murmured.

"I won't leave." He settled them both on the bed, her head resting on his shoulder.

"Do we have to go tonight?" she asked. "Nuala said we were welcome to stay."

Her voice, so carefully stripped of emotion, made a more eloquent plea than anything she could have said. She was exhausted, physically and emotionally. They both were. This was a good place, a strong place, a safe place. They needed all those things right now.

"We can stay tonight," he said, brushing his lips against her forehead.

She relaxed against him and fell asleep.

A good place, a strong place, a safe place. He'd do whatever he could to help the witches who lived here keep it that way.

It was his last thought before sleep claimed him.

Breanna hesitated a moment, then opened Aiden's and Lyrra's saddlebags and removed all the clothing. They didn't have a clean garment between them. What was the point of washing the clothes they'd been wearing and leaving the rest? Who knew when they'd have another chance to wash everything?

With the clothing removed, there wasn't much left in the saddlebags, which is why she noticed the sheets of paper tucked in special pouches in each of their saddlebags. Her fingers itched to pull out a few sheets to see what stories or songs might be written on them. Perhaps they had some new songs, something she hadn't heard every other minstrel who came through the village sing. It wasn't quite courteous to ask guests to sing for their supper, but, maybe, if they weren't too tired, Aiden and Lyrra would be willing to oblige with just a song or two. And maybe they wouldn't be too upset about someone looking through their papers to see if there *was* a new song or two.

She firmly closed the saddlebags to avoid temptation, and said, "That's all the clothing."

Glynis just nodded and dropped the clothes in the wash tubs. She stood motionless, her arms deep in the soapy water. "I didn't mean to make the lady cry," she muttered. "I thought it was Clay and Edgar coming in for a bite."

"Whether you meant to be hurtful or not, the words cut just as deep," Breanna replied. "And even if it had been Clay and Edgar, it wasn't a kind thing to say."

"Don't know why I do things like that." Glynis sniffed, then got on with the work of washing the clothes.

You do it because you've also traveled a hard road, Breanna thought, walking across the small yard to the stables to check on the horses. *You're like a dog that's been hit so many times it snaps at any hand held out to it, even when it wants to be petted.*

Glynis had come to them three years ago, hungry and bruised in body and soul, looking for any kind of work that would provide her with food and a place to sleep. So they hired her as cook and housekeeper—and didn't ask about a past they could sense held far more memories of pain than pleasure. Her way of dealing with other people, even people she liked and cared for, was to make cutting remarks. She usually felt regret as soon as the words were out, but that didn't stop her from voicing the next opinion.

Understanding that didn't mean it could be overlooked, not when it hurt other people. But that was something Nuala would deal with.

And she guessed that if the Bard hadn't been so obviously exhausted, there would have been more than one woman reduced to tears in the kitchen.

Breanna glanced at the house. Their guests were in rooms at the front of the house where the noises of everyday activity would be less likely to disturb their rest.

The Bard. He'd stiffened when she'd called him that. He must have forgotten he'd said it. Why would he react that way, as if she'd found out something about him he hadn't wanted known?

She could think of one reason—and she didn't like where that thought led.

"Clay?" she called.

"Breanna." He stepped out of an empty stall and nodded to her. "I put all the gear and the packs in the stall here."

"That's good. I don't think their instruments will come to harm there."

"Wanted to talk to you about their horses."

Oh, dear. "They're sound, aren't they?"

Clay laughed, but there was no humor in it. "Oh, they're fine horses. *Fine* horses. With silent hooves."

She puzzled over that for a minute before she realized what he was saying. Where would two entertainers get horses like *that* unless . . .

"Oblige me, if you will. Go down to the brook. See if

there are any water sprites near the bridge who might have seen our guests. Perhaps they could tell us something."

"Thought that's what you'd say." Clay went over to another stall and opened the door for the gelding that was already bridled.

"Oh. Mention that he'd said they were the Bard and the Muse."

Nodding to indicate he'd heard her, he was mounted and gone before Breanna could get her thoughts to settle.

She was still standing in the same spot when he returned.

"Found one," he said. "She seemed to be waiting for someone to come from the house before she went off to tend to her own business."

Breanna found it hard to swallow. "What did she say?"

" 'He gave her true words if not his true face.' " Clay looked at her grimly. "What are you going to do about them?"

"I'll talk to Gran. It . . . it may be best not to mention this to anyone else. At least, not right now."

"You be careful, Breanna."

"I will."

When she found Nuala and Elinore, she babbled something, she wasn't even sure what. But it was enough for Elinore to leave the room on the pretense of needing to use the water closet.

Not sure how much time she'd have, Breanna blurted out her conversation with Aiden and then the message from the water sprite. Nuala just listened in silence.

"What do we do?" Breanna asked.

"Nothing," Nuala said. She raised a hand to stifle Breanna's protest. "We do nothing. We offered them hospitality, and hospitality is what we will give. We'll make no mention that we know—or at least suspect—who they are."

"They didn't come honestly."

"The Fae seldom do," Nuala replied dryly. "But it's evident to anyone who looks that those two have had a hard time lately—and anything they can tell us about what is happening in the eastern villages is more than we know now. So we will say nothing. Perhaps the reason they hide what they are is not so deceitful as it seems."

"Perhaps," Breanna agreed reluctantly. Then she smiled, but there was no humor in it. "The Bard did warn us to be wary of strangers." *And wary we will be.*

Lyrra woke first, not sure what had pulled her from sleep.

Somewhere outside, a dog barked again. A happy sound. Just conversation, nothing more.

She smiled. The sausage thief sounded quite pleased with himself about something.

Carefully moving away from Aiden, she got out of bed. He grunted, rolled on to his side, and continued sleeping. The fact that the dog didn't wake him told her much. At any other place where they'd stayed recently, even an inn, a barking dog would have awakened him instantly. There was something here he trusted enough to take the kind of deep rest he needed.

Tears stung her eyes as she gathered up the simple gown that had been left for her and slipped into the adjoining room to dress. The house was much finer, but the *feel* of the place reminded her of Ari's cottage.

She hoped that Ari and Neall had found a good place, a safe place.

Pushing away thoughts of Ari that would lead to other, more painful, thoughts of the things she and Aiden had seen, Lyrra found her way downstairs. She hesitated at the kitchen door, reluctant to face the sharp-tongued woman again. The kitchen was empty, so she hurried out the door and headed for the flower beds where Breanna was working.

Breanna saw her coming and rose.

When Lyrra got close enough to see the cool look in the witch's eyes, she hesitated. "I just came out to admire the flowers. I don't mean to interrupt your work."

"I was finished here," Breanna replied. "Why don't we sit on the bench under the tree. I could use the shade now."

What had happened, Lyrra wondered, to put that coolness in Breanna's voice and eyes?

"You slept well?" Breanna asked.

Lyrra made the effort to smile. "Better than I have in quite some time."

"Where will you be going when you leave here?"

"Oh—" *To Tir Alainn, now that we've finally found an Old Place that has a shining road open.* "I'm not sure."

"If you take the trail that leads into the woods," Breanna said, pointing in the general direction, "and keep heading for the Mother's Hills, you'll find the road you're looking for."

A chill went through Lyrra, but she wasn't sure if it was caused by Breanna mentioning a road or mentioning the Mother's Hills. "What road is that?"

"The shining road." There was anger mixed with the coolness in Breanna's voice now. "Isn't that where you're headed?"

Lyrra looked away. The prudent thing would be to feign ignorance, but she was suddenly tired of half-truths that were no better than lies. "You spoke to the water sprite."

"It's an odd thing, that. We *live* here. The Small Folk *live* here. We talk to each other and help each other. Unlike the Fair Folk, who come by whenever they want something but don't even have the courtesy to acknowledge the presence of those who live here. So you can tell your kin that I'm a good shot with a bow, and if they keep bullying and badgering the Small Folk, I'm going to start shooting them for trespassing."

Lyrra gripped the bench so hard her hands ached. "Do you

want us to leave?" she asked, not sure how she'd explain to Aiden why they were no longer welcome.

"Don't be foolish," Breanna snapped. "The way the two of you looked when you rode in, it was obvious you wouldn't have stayed in the saddle for another mile."

"Then what do you want?"

"The courtesy of honesty."

With sharp relief, Lyrra released the glamour that hid her true face behind a human mask. She turned to look at Breanna. "Is this honest enough?"

Breanna studied her for a moment. "You're lovely. Why do you hide what you are?"

"Why?" Lyrra replied softly. "Habit. Perhaps arrogance is the reason we show our true faces only when *we* choose to show them. Or perhaps we're like the hares that exchange their brown coats for white when the seasons change. We hide the most obvious means of recognizing what we are so that we don't stand out." She paused. "I'm sorry the Clan here has been discourteous. That wasn't our intention when we tried to get the Fae to pay more attention to the witches."

Breanna stared at her. "Why would you want to? Why would *we* want that attention?"

"The shining roads are anchored to the Old Places. And it is the presence of the Mother's Daughters, the witches, in the Old Places that keeps those roads anchored to the human world, that keeps Tir Alainn existing."

"So this sudden interest in us is just to make sure we don't bolt and leave you gasping like a fish thrown up on the bank."

Lyrra winced. "That's part of it. But the other part was to protect you, to keep you safe."

"From what?"

"From the Black Coats, the Inquisitors. That's why Aiden and I are traveling. To gather news, gossip, any information we can find to keep the Clans informed—and to warn the witches."

"So you've been to other Old Places? You've given your warnings elsewhere?"

Lyrra shuddered. "We've been to other Old Places. We didn't reach them in time to give any warnings. The witches were already gone—or dead." She closed her eyes, felt the warmth of Breanna's hand on her arm.

"I think what you have to tell us will be hard enough to say once," Breanna said quietly. "Let it go for now. After the evening meal, you and Aiden can tell us what needs to be told."

Lyrra nodded, grateful for the reprieve.

The dog barked.

Breanna made a sound that might have been a growl.

Opening her eyes, Lyrra saw the black dog racing toward them, having left the company of a short-haired woman and a young girl, who waved at them before disappearing into the house.

The dog stopped a few feet in front of the bench and barked as if determined to let the whole county know there were strangers at his house.

"Oh, shut up, Idjit," Breanna muttered.

The dog barked and danced in front of them, paying no attention to the command.

"*Sit*, Idjit," Breanna said firmly.

The dog stopped barking, ran a couple of steps, then leaped as if someone were holding a hoop for him to jump through. He turned and leaped again.

Breanna sighed. Then she looked at Lyrra and smiled.

Lyrra was always suspicious of merchants who smiled like that.

"Wouldn't you like to have a dog on your travels?" Breanna said brightly. "He'd be a good companion, and he could warn you when strangers approached."

"Like he warned you?"

Breanna waved that aside. "And he can do tricks."

"He's . . . interesting." Was that noncommittal enough?

"I'll give you twelve coppers to take him."

"He's not that interesting."

Breanna huffed. Lyrra looked toward the house.

"I've already been warned not to offer him to young girls," Breanna said sourly.

Lyrra laughed. It felt good to laugh, felt good to talk with another woman, felt good not to hide what she was.

She was still chuckling when she noticed Aiden walking toward them. The dog watched him, too, and didn't let out a single yip.

"Some guard dog," Lyrra muttered.

"You'll never be surprised by a squirrel," Breanna replied with a straight-faced sincerity that made Lyrra laugh again.

That's how Aiden found them, laughing over something neither was willing to explain. Lyrra saw his surprise when he got close enough to see that she'd released the glamour. After a moment's hesitation, he released the glamour, as well, then bowed to Breanna.

She studied both of them, then asked, rather wistfully, "Are you really the Bard and the Muse?"

"Yes, we are," Aiden replied.

"I don't suppose . . ." Breanna shook her head.

Lyrra frowned. "You get little entertainment here?" It was hard not to remember Ari, and how she wasn't welcome in the nearby village and was excluded from any amusements that might have been available.

"Oh, there are entertainers who come by, and we'll go into Willowsbrook from time to time when a minstrel stops for a day or two. But they don't know any *new* songs."

Aiden grinned as he looked at Lyrra. "We have a new song or two."

The wretch. He was going to trot out that mouse song.

"And we'd be pleased to do a song or two for all of you," Lyrra said. She gave Aiden a clench-toothed smile.

"That's wonderful," Breanna said. "I'll see if Elinore and Brooke want to stay for the evening meal so that they can hear you, too." She hesitated, looked at both of them.

"Perhaps your other guests would find so much honesty disconcerting?" Lyrra asked, guessing that Breanna was wondering if the gentry would feel easy dining with the Fae.

"Perhaps," Breanna said a bit ruefully.

Lyrra glanced at Aiden. They resumed the glamour that gave them human masks.

Breanna gave Aiden a speculative look as the three of them walked back to the house. "How would you like—?"

"No," Lyrra said firmly, "he would not."

"I wouldn't?" Aiden asked, sounding confused.

"No, you wouldn't."

"You didn't even give me a chance to offer the twelve coppers," Breanna protested.

"He wouldn't take them."

"I wouldn't?" Aiden said.

"No," Lyrra replied, "you wouldn't." She looked at Breanna. "And if you don't mention it again, we'll play an extra song."

Breanna grinned. "That's the best offer I've had."

"It's the *only* offer you've had."

"That, too."

Two women in charity with each other and one confused man walked into the house to wash up for the evening meal.

Aiden tuned his harp. It had been a good decision to talk after the evening meal and save the songs for last. He could give the ladies here something sweet to sleep on after he and Lyrra had told them about the things that were happening in eastern villages—and in the Old Places. And it had been wise of Nuala and Breanna to cut up a couple of apples and send Keely and Brooke out to the stables to give the horses a treat. He wasn't sure what had happened to Keely that had kept her a child in a woman's body, but neither she nor Brooke were emotionally old enough to hear the things he'd had to say.

And he wasn't sure what was causing the undercurrents between Elinore, Nuala, and Breanna. They weren't newly acquainted; there was too much familiarity for that. But something new had been added recently that had changed things between them. The baron, perhaps? Elinore had mentioned that she was the mother of the Baron of Willowsbrook, so the man was probably in his twenties. Had his attentions suddenly turned toward Breanna? Her face was strong rather than pretty, but it was the kind of face that any but the shallowest man would find attractive.

Wasn't his business, but he found himself wanting to find a way to tell Breanna not to settle for less than she deserved. So he ended up singing "Love's Jewels" as the first song, wondering if she would understand the message.

Then, giving Lyrra a wicked grin, he sang the mouse song. His lady was in fine form, singing her part with just enough pique he could tell she was itching to smack him with the tambourine.

During that song, he learned what it felt like to have an audience die on him, despite his best efforts. Clay and Edgar, who had been invited to listen to the singing, sat with their arms across their chests and their heads down. Keely and Brooke grinned a little, but neither of them could appreciate all the lyrics. Nuala, Elinore, and Breanna just stared at him.

The two older women sat with a hand lightly circling their throats. Breanna had her fingers pressed against her mouth.

He got to the end of the song, wondering if he'd just convinced them all that he really *couldn't* earn enough coppers to pay his way, when the laughter started. Coughing chuckles from Clay and Edgar as they glanced at the ladies. Then a sputtering from the ladies that ended with all three women holding their sides because they'd laughed so hard and the men guffawing and slapping their thighs.

"Oh, my," Elinore said when she finally caught her breath. "Oh, my." She dabbed her streaming eyes with a handkerchief, then grinned at Lyrra. "I'm sure there must be compensations for him singing that song in public."

That produced another round of laughter when Lyrra's cheeks flamed with color.

Aiden was feeling a bit warm, too, especially seeing the way Breanna grinned at him.

"I'm sure the next time they travel this way, there will be a poem to complement that song," Breanna said sweetly. "'Ode to a Bath,' perhaps?"

Aiden choked.

Lyrra looked at him, then looked at Breanna. "Oh? Perhaps we should talk."

"Perhaps we should," Breanna agreed.

Perhaps he should just find a hole and hide in it.

Clearing his throat, he played a quiet tune that had no words since he wasn't sure how well he could sing at the moment anyway. By the time Lyrra told a story and the two of them had sung another song, the daylight was waning and it was time for Elinore and Brooke to go home.

"I'll saddle the horses and see you home," Clay said.

"Oh, there's no need for you to do that," Elinore said. "There's enough light. We'll be fine."

Aiden saw the grimness in Clay's expression and knew the man wouldn't forget what he'd said.

"I'll see you home," Clay said again before he left to saddle the horses.

That reminder sobered all of them, but not enough to spoil the evening. After Elinore and Brooke left, they all lingered in the parlor, talking about small things and politely hiding yawns. No one mentioned that they were waiting for Clay to return before closing the house and seeking their beds.

When he and Lyrra finally bid good night to the others and went up to their room, he loved her well before they both drifted off to sleep.

Chapter Nine

Liam stared with dismay at the empty spaces on the bookshelves. Nolan's Book Salon was smaller than the other establishments in Durham that sold books, but Nolan was a man who clearly loved books, and there was almost nothing that couldn't be found in his store.

Something's happened here, he thought, feeling a chill run down his spine as he walked over to the shelves. He scanned titles for a few minutes, looking for Moira's new book. He didn't find her new book. He didn't find *any* of her books.

He started scanning names instead of titles. All men. Where were the women authors? Was Nolan in the process of rearranging shelves? Why would he move the female novelists and leave the males here?

"Ah, Master Liam. Have you returned to add to your own library?"

Liam turned at the sound of Nolan's voice. The man hastily closed the door that led to the small office and storeroom, then stepped up to one side of the counter.

Liam studied Nolan for a moment before walking over to stand on the other side of the counter. The man's smile was forced, brittle. His eyes were grief-weary.

He's been drinking, Liam thought.

"Perhaps I've come at a bad time," Liam said.

Nolan waved a hand. "Not at all. What can I do for you, Master— I beg your pardon. It's *Baron* Liam now, isn't it?"

There was fear in Nolan's eyes now as well as grief.

"I came to see if you had a copy of Moira Wythbrook's new book." Liam tried a smile. "My mother requested that I ask for it particularly."

Nolan pulled himself up to his full height, which barely brought his head equal to Liam's chin. Patrons of Nolan's Book Salon good-naturedly teased the small man, saying the reason there were so many step stools for customers to sit on while they perused books was that Nolan wouldn't be able to reach his beloved books without them.

"I am an upstanding citizen of our beautiful land," Nolan said with chilled dignity. "As such, I obey the dictates of the baron in whose county I live."

"What does that have to do with Moira Wythbrook's books?" Liam asked.

"The barons have decreed that it is harmful to carry the work of female scribblers."

"Female *what?*"

"Females are of weak intellect, and it is harmful to indulge them by publishing or selling their work, which is inferior to the books written by men. It produces immodest feelings in ladies that make it difficult for them to fill their place in society. Therefore, their books are no longer sold, and no further books by female scribblers will be published."

Liam took a step back from the counter. Maybe Nolan was drunker than he seemed. Why else would the man be spouting such horse muck?

"What happened to the books that were already published?" he asked. "You still have copies of those."

Nolan shook his head. A sheen of tears filled his eyes. "They were collected by the magistrate's guards . . . and burned."

Burned.

As Master Liam, he could have staggered over to one of

the step stools and collapsed to give himself time to absorb what Nolan had said. *Baron* Liam could not permit himself that kind of luxury.

"Just here in Durham?" he asked, his voice barely above a whisper.

Nolan shook his head. "The barons who rule the eastern counties have all made the same decree. If it is accepted at the next council of barons, that decree will hold true for all of Sylvalan."

Not in the county I rule. Liam stepped up to the counter, put his hands on it, then leaned forward. "Forget I've become a baron," he said with quiet urgency. "I've been buying books from you for years—for my mother and younger sister as well as for myself. You must have known the magistrate's guards were coming. I've seen that warren you call a storeroom. If you wanted to hide some books in there, *no one* would be able to find them. You wouldn't have let them burn all the copies. You wouldn't."

"Do you want me to lose everything?" Nolan cried, but he, too, kept his voice down.

"You would have kept at least one copy of each of those books so that the work wouldn't be completely lost when the fools who made that decree came to their senses."

"I have nothing. I swear to you—"

"Give the copies to me. I'll make sure they get back to my estate safely. I'll hide them until this . . . situation . . . is settled."

Liam reined in impatience while Nolan studied him for too long.

"I have nothing," Nolan finally said. "I— I already packed the copies and sent them away."

"Where—?"

The bell above the shop door tinkled.

Liam looked over his shoulder at the blond-haired, blue-eyed man who stepped into the shop. A cold uneasiness settled over him as the man met his eyes for a moment before turning to scan the shelves.

He's looking to make sure nothing is here that shouldn't be. Liam glanced at Nolan, noticed how pale the man had become. How would someone else, someone suspicious, view this close conversation?

Pushing back from the counter, Liam said, "Since that book isn't in stock, perhaps you could suggest another? Reading before I retire is a habit of long-standing."

"Of course," Nolan said, bustling over to one of the shelves.

Liam followed, aware that the blue-eyed stranger had turned to watch them.

"This one is excellent," Nolan said, pulling a book off the shelf.

His back to the stranger, Liam made a face. He recognized the author, had tried to get through one of the man's books once before. Prosy old bore. Well, it wouldn't keep him up late. He'd be asleep ten minutes after he opened the book.

"And this one," Nolan said, going over to the far-too-empty shelves and selecting another book. "This one has been recently published. A book of instructional essays. Very popular. I'm told that it's one of the few books most heads of families consider suitable material for the females in their families and have consented to permit the ladies to read."

Consented to permit the ladies to read? Liam could imagine what Elinore—or even Brooke—would say if he tried to dictate what they could or couldn't read.

Which made him wonder what happened to women in the eastern part of Sylvalan who *did* express such opinions.

Feeling numb, Liam paid for the books and waited while Nolan carefully wrapped them in brown paper and string.

As he turned to leave the store, he noticed the stranger was still watching him.

There was no reason for the animosity he felt toward a man he didn't know and hadn't even seen before. But the feeling was there, and he wasn't going to dismiss it.

He spent the rest of the day wandering, feeling oddly off balance. The streets of Durham were familiar, and he recognized the buildings. But it felt as if he kept turning down familiar streets and finding himself in a strange place. The women in the shopping district were all dressed in plain gowns with high necks and long sleeves. Drab clothing—grays, browns, dark greens and blues. Not the kind of garment worn to catch a man's eye. They wouldn't look at him, wouldn't even acknowledge his "good day" when he passed them.

He stopped at a shop where he'd often picked up a new shawl for his mother. The woman who owned the shop stood behind her counter. When he asked about shawls, she laid out a selection on the counter, offering none of the assistance she used to give him in order to make the right choice. Every move said plainly she no longer cared if anyone bought anything at her shop, which made him wonder how she expected to remain in business.

His last stop in the afternoon was an art gallery. By then, his mind was prepared for what he'd find. His heart wasn't.

The empty places on the walls seemed like a terrible accusation. All the paintings by female artists were gone. When he asked the owner, he was told that women were capable of creating pleasing little sketches for the amusement of their families, but they weren't capable of creating *art*. Never mind that the women whose work no longer hung on the walls had been hailed, just a few months ago, as some of the finest artists of their generation.

Feeling unsettled and a little sick, Liam passed a group of

men his age standing before a painting, loudly proclaiming its brilliance. He stopped for a moment to look at the painting, then shook his head and left the gallery. If his stable hands had slung soiled straw at a white sheet and then framed the result, it wouldn't have looked much different from the "brilliant" painting.

When he returned to the family town house, he ate the evening meal because his body needed food, and because he couldn't afford any physical weakness when he sat at his place in the barons' council tomorrow.

Maybe there was an explanation for all of this. Maybe.

And maybe there was another explanation for the straight bruises on the shop owner's cheeks. Faint bruises. Faint enough that, at first, he'd thought it was a trick of the light. But when he closed his eyes, he could see the straps of the scold's bridle that Elinore had flung between them when she'd given him the ultimatum of accepting the witches as her kin or losing his family. Straight straps that could bruise tender skin if they were cinched too tight.

Alone in his room, too uneasy to even try to sleep, he unwrapped the books he'd bought. He set the prosy old bore aside, then opened the other book. Perhaps having some knowledge of what was now considered suitable reading material for females would prepare him for whatever he was going to face in the barons' council in the morning.

Chapter Ten

Aiden's hand hovered over the case that held his small harp. He shook his head, let his hand fall to his side. Under normal circumstances, he would have met with any bards who lived in the Clan or were there visiting. He would have listened to any new songs they had created and shared his own. But these weren't normal circumstances, and he wasn't in the mood to bring his harp to play idly in one of the common rooms.

Crossing to the window, he looked out at the garden that made up part of this courtyard. Beautiful. Perfect. No tangles of weeds, no blighted flowers. Nothing out of place. That was Tir Alainn. The rain was always soft, gently soaking into the ground. No storms here to turn roads into mud. No lack of food, so the belly never tightened with hunger. Beautiful rooms, beautiful clothes, sprawling Clan houses that could rival the finest estates in the human world. And all of it required so little labor from the people who lived here.

A sanctuary. A place to rest from the toil of the human world. But the Fae weren't the ones who toiled in the human world. What had they *ever* done to earn the right to be here?

Sighing, Aiden left the room that had been granted him and Lyrra for their stay, although he doubted either of them wanted to stay very long. A cold welcome didn't encourage a person to linger in a place.

No matter. There was work to do here. Witches were still

dying. Pieces of Tir Alainn, and the Clans who lived there, were still being lost. But here . . . If the Clan ignored the warnings *here*, it would be Breanna and Nuala and Keely who would die.

He entered one of the common rooms in the Clan house. Lyrra stood at the other end of the room, her lips set in a tight, grim line as she listened to several older women.

No doubt haranguing her for turning her back on the Lady of the Moon and leaving Dianna to shoulder the burden of keeping the shining road open so that her Clan's territory in Tir Alainn remained in existence.

If they knew we weren't just lovers but had made a vow of loyalty in the human fashion, they'd probably exile us on the spot, Aiden thought sourly. He started to scan the room—and was surprised to see a familiar face this far north. Smiling, he walked over to the brown-haired man whose attention was fixed on the group of women with Lyrra.

"Falco! Well met," Aiden said.

"Aiden."

There was just enough tension, just enough hesitation in Falco's voice to stop Aiden from taking another step forward.

"What brings you here?" Falco asked, his brown eyes now scanning the room.

Aiden studied the Lord of the Hawks. There was too much anxiety in Falco's eyes. "We're here to rest—and catch up on any news that has been passed along through the Clans."

"Aiden . . . maybe this isn't a good time for you—"

"So," a male voice said loudly from another part of the room. "The Bard has decided to grace us with his presence. Where's your harp, Aiden? Aren't you going to subject us to another mewling song about witches?"

Recognizing the voice, and seeing the way Falco's face

paled, Aiden turned slowly to face the man who now stood in the center of the room.

"Lucian," Aiden said politely. "Well met."

Lucian, the Lord of the Sun, the Lord of Fire, said coldly, "We aren't 'well met,' Bard. *You* saw to that. No, we are not 'well met.' I doubt we ever will be."

"I regret the loss of your esteem, but I don't regret the reason for it. I can't. Not after the things I've seen. And, yes, Lucian," Aiden said, his voice rising, "I *will* sing my mewling songs about witches, and I *will* say the words that need to be said, and I *will* keep saying those words until the Fae start listening, start heeding, start *doing* instead of standing back and watching witches die and then wailing because there's a cost to not listening, not heeding, not doing. *How many of them have to be tortured to death before you'll listen?*"

"We are doing what is necessary to make sure the witches don't leave the Old Places," Lucian said.

"What?" Aiden demanded. "Hemming them in? Taking away whatever means they might have to flee before the Black Coats kill them? If the Fae are doing what is necessary, where were they when the Inquisitors destroyed the witches in the villages south of here? Where were they, Lucian? Where were they when the Mother's Daughters were dying in agony?"

"The witches are *not* the Mother's Daughters," Lucian said, his voice rising to meet Aiden's. "They are *witches*. They've somehow bound their small earth magic to the Old Places, making their presence there necessary for the Fae to have what is rightfully ours."

Aiden stared at the man who had been a friend as well as kin through their fathers. "Rightfully ours?" he asked, his voice becoming quieter as pain lanced through him. "Rightfully ours. What have we ever done to deserve Tir Alainn? The witches created the Fair Land. It's been their power that has kept it in existence. What have we ever done to earn the right to be here?"

"We don't have to do anything," Lucian said fiercely. "We. Are. The. Fae."

"Has 'Fae' become another word for parasite?" Aiden asked bitterly, his temper pushing aside all prudence as his mind's eye put before him images of hovels, of broken-down cottages, of broken bodies. "We feed off the labor of others, giving nothing in return."

"If there are any parasites, it's the witches, who have sunk their claws into the Old Places so that we *have* to keep watch over them in order to protect what is ours."

"They're the Mother's Daughters," Aiden cried passionately. "*They're the House of Gaian.* When are you going to accept that?"

"*Never!*" Lucian shouted. "And I insist that you stop spreading those lies. The House of Gaian disappeared a long time ago."

Aiden shook his head. "*They* are the House of Gaian. They are the Pillars of the World, the ones who created Tir Alainn. Mother's mercy, Lucian, we have written proof of—"

"We have nothing!"

"We have the journals written by a family of witches, which are the record of their history and the Old Place in their keeping."

"We have the scrawlings of women who wanted to be more than what they were," Lucian said. "Where is your proof that there's any truth to what was written? A passing bard could have told a tale about the House of Gaian generations ago, and the woman who heard it took it for herself, claiming to be something she was not, something she *never could be.* One family, trying to assuage their own inadequacies by pretending to be something they're weren't. Have you come across any other mention of it, Bard? Have you?"

I've lost them, Aiden thought, knowing none of the Fae in this room had missed his moment of hesitation. "No," he said quietly. "I have not found any other record that the witches are the House of Gaian."

"Then, by my command, there will be no more talk of this. Not here. Not in the other Clans. Is that understood?"

The Lord of the Sun. The Lord of Fire. The male leader of the Fae.

Lucian, you've condemned us all. "I understand, Lightbringer," Aiden said softly.

He couldn't look at Lyrra. Maybe it would be better if she severed her ties with him, went back to her home Clan, or *any* Clan instead of traveling roads that were getting more and more dangerous.

The Lightbringer had commanded, and he would obey— up to a point. He would be exiled for what he intended to do—assuming that he *could* do it—but he couldn't see any other road left open to him.

Bowing formally to Lucian, he left the common room and retreated to the room he shared with Lyrra, knowing she would follow him there in a little while. The things he needed to tell her were best said in private.

Lyrra watched Aiden leave the room, her heart aching for him.

One of the older women next to her *harrumphed* in satisfaction. "It's about time the Lightbringer put the Bard in his place and put a stop to these . . . *tales.*" Her eyes slid to look at Lyrra. "And you would do well to take another lover, a man who will bring no shame to you or your Clan."

Lyrra gave the woman her coldest stare. "If my Clan

thinks my being with the Bard shames them, then I have nothing to say to them, nor they to me."

She walked away before she could say anything else that would cause trouble. She knew, without doubt, that her words would find their way to her Clan within a handful of days—and she knew, without doubt, that if she went back to her Clan while she was still with Aiden, they *wouldn't* have anything to say to her.

She moved from one end of the long room to the other, paying no attention to what was around her until a hand firmly grasped her elbow. She tried to pull away. When she couldn't, she turned toward the person who held her.

"This is an open-air room," Falco said. "Another few steps and you'll go right over the balcony. Since you can't sprout wings, it would be a hard fall." He smiled shyly, hesitantly. "Blessings of the day to you, Lyrra."

A witch's greeting. The same greeting he'd offered every morning when she'd lived at the cottage that had belonged to Ari's family, as if to remind himself of the young witch he'd been acquainted with briefly. Or to take to himself one small custom that belonged to the Mother's Daughters.

"Blessings of the day to you, Falco," Lyrra replied softly. Dear Falco. A year ago, he'd been an impetuous young man, too quick to speak without thinking, so sure that the Fae, who called themselves the Mother's Children, were superior to anything else that lived in the world. Then he went down to the Old Place with Dianna, Aiden, and her to celebrate the Summer Solstice with Ari, and, that night, saw the power a witch could command. The past year had been a hard one for everyone in the Clan whose piece of Tir Alainn was anchored to the Old Place near Ridgeley, but Falco had surprised her. He'd accepted the need for so many of the Fae to remain in the human world in order to keep the shining road open with more grace than she'd thought he had in him. And he'd been a friend to her during all the months she'd stayed at the Old Place to be the anchor the others needed to keep the magic alive.

"What brings you so far north?" she asked.

"I'm . . . visiting." He released her arm and walked the few remaining steps to the balcony.

Lyrra followed him, trying to sort out all the nuances in his voice. "Did you come with . . ." Lucian's name stuck in her throat. She wondered if it always would after today.

"No," Falco said, staring at nothing. "It was unfortunate timing that he arrived here the day after I did. He . . . wasn't pleased."

"You're entitled to some time away from the home Clan to . . . visit," Lyrra said, still trying to decipher the underlying meaning to his words. For a Fae male, "visiting" meant enjoying the bed of one, or more, ladies in the Clan where he was guesting. If Falco had become restless for that kind of "visit," there were other Clans closer to his home Clan where he could have found a lover for a few days.

"You're not going back," Lyrra said, suddenly understanding. "That's why you've come this far north. You're not going back to your home Clan."

"No," Falco said, his voice holding a deep-rooted unhappiness. "It's not like it was when you were there, Lyrra. Dianna left you there to do what *she* had promised to do, but you never took it out on the rest of us. You never—" He bit off the rest of the words.

Lyrra rested a hand on his arm. "Darling, I know Dianna can be difficult, but—"

"Difficult?" There was more than unhappiness in his eyes. There was anger, too. "She resents all of us. Her kin. Her Clan. Nothing we do is good enough. Ever. She'll jump her pale mare over the wall enclosing the kitchen garden and trample the young plants past saving, then complain about the sparsity of the food set before her. We give her more than her share of the food grown in the human world because it *does* taste better than what we grow in Tir Alainn, and she takes even more than that. She has two rooms of her own while the rest of us sleep wherever we can, and it's not enough. If she walks into a room, she gets the chair. If she walks into the kitchen, she expects to be served food, no matter the hour. And she reminds us, constantly, that her sacrifice is the reason the rest of us can still ride up the shining road and enjoy Tir Alainn."

"Hush, Falco, hush," Lyrra said, glancing over her shoulder to see too many of the Fae starting to pay attention to them. "Don't call attention to yourself." *Think before you speak,* she pleaded silently, knowing it was useless. He may have matured in many ways, but he was still Falco.

Surprisingly, he paused, then continued speaking quietly. "She resents me most of all."

Lyrra frowned. "But . . . why? You did everything you could to help the others get settled in the human world. And I'm sure it would have been harder on all of us if you hadn't hunted to provide some meat for the table."

"That's just it, don't you see? I hunted, at Dianna's command, to provide Ari with some meat after Dianna gave her that puppy. And I hunted for you."

"Not just for me," Lyrra protested.

"So I'm not doing anything . . . special . . . to show my appreciation for Dianna's sacrifice. And she resents that the other Fae in the Clan ask me what Ari was like. They want to know anything I can remember about her and about the night we were at the cottage to celebrate the Summer Solstice. I'm not a bard," he added quickly, "and I'm not trying to tell a tale. Truly I'm not. But . . ."

"But everyone is so unhappy because Dianna is acting like a selfish fool that they've begun to wonder about the witches, about Ari, about how things might have been if they'd tried to know her before it was too late," Lyrra finished for him. *And that's exactly the kind of wondering that could change the Fae's attitude about truly helping the witches. If Lucian and Dianna are determined to have the rest of the Fae continue to believe that the witches are supposed to be some kind of servants to us, they'd be especially displeased about a shift in attitude in their home Clan.*

Falco nodded. "And Lucian is furious because Dianna gave him a cold welcome when he came back to Brightwood to see her. *He* can go anywhere he pleases. *He* isn't chained to the human world. So Dianna resents her twin for all the things he can still do, and Lucian is bitter about her reaction to him as well as losing Ari."

A twinge of guilt pushed at Lyrra. She couldn't give Lucian any hint that she knew what really happened to Ari. She *couldn't.* But if his heart ached for the loss of someone dear to him . . . "Did he truly care so much for Ari?"

"Don't waste your sympathy on Lucian," Falco said harshly. "I've heard the Lightbringer rarely sleeps alone, and rarely spends more than two nights in the same bed. The only reason he still thinks about Ari at all is because he didn't have her until *he* was ready to walk away—and because she'd chosen to wed a human instead of being his mistress until he tired of her. Well, she would have wed the man if the Inquisitors hadn't gotten to her first," he added in a sad voice.

Lyrra sighed. An hour spent talking to her own kind made her feel as weary as spending a day traveling over a hard road in the human world.

"They both resent you and Aiden," Falco said. "You know that, don't you?"

"Because I chose to go with Aiden instead of remaining at the Old Place so that Dianna wouldn't be inconvenienced. Yes, I know."

"Because of that, yes. But more because you supported Morag when she refused to bring Ari back from the Summerland instead of siding with them. That's really why both of them will deny anything you say about the witches."

"Morag is the Gatherer," Lyrra said angrily. "She did what she had to do."

"I know. But they exiled her because of it, Lyrra, and if you're not careful, they'll do the same to Aiden and you."

Would it make any difference? Lyrra wondered. *We're hardly welcome as it is.*

"What can I do?" Falco asked.

Lyrra shook her head. "You've done all that you could, Falco."

Now he shook his head. "I believe you and Aiden. I believe the witches deserve whatever help the Fae can give them. What can I do?"

"The Fae are already keeping watch over the Old Place this Clan's territory is anchored to," Lyrra said carefully.

Falco snorted. "They go down the shining road, find one of the Small Folk, and demand to know what the witches are doing. That's hardly keeping watch. They never actually go close enough to *see* anything."

Something in his voice. Something beneath the annoyance. Wistfulness?

Suddenly, Lyrra understood exactly what Falco was asking—and why. He wanted a way to justify getting close enough to become acquainted with the witches who lived at Willowsbrook.

"Well," she said cautiously, "the witches who live at that Old Place aren't very pleased with the Fae upsetting the Small Folk." *And Breanna threatened to shoot any Fae she found trespassing on her family's land.* Having met Breanna, she didn't think it was so idle a threat as it might have been coming from someone else.

"You've met them?" Falco asked eagerly.

Lyrra winced. Mother's tits. Today she was as bad as Falco usually was about speaking without thinking. But she had to say something now, and she simply couldn't lie to him. "Yes, they gave us shelter last night."

"You *stayed* with them? What was it like? Did you tell them you were Fae? Would they really be upset about having another visitor if the Small Folk weren't bothered?"

How was she supposed to answer when she could see anticipation instead of unhappiness in his eyes?

"I think if approached cautiously, and respectfully, it might be possible to become acquainted with them."

He smiled at her. "I'll be careful, Lyrra. I promise."

She pictured a careful Falco—or as careful as Falco ever was—meeting Breanna. If the Lord of the Hawks expected every witch to be like Ari . . . Poor Falco. She couldn't turn down what he was offering since she and Aiden had gotten so little help from the Fae, but at least she could send him down to the human world with one important piece of advice.

Placing a hand on one side of his face, she said, "Falco, if you *do* decide to make the acquaintance of the witches in this Old Place, don't let Breanna talk you into taking the dog."

Well, Lyrra thought a few minutes later as she left the common room and made her way back to the room she and Aiden shared, *at least I've made one man I care about happier. Let's see what I can do for the one who is dearest to me.*

When she slipped into the room, she saw Aiden on the bed, one arm flung over his face to hide his eyes. He gave no indication he knew she was there until she lay on her side next to him.

"Perhaps . . . ," Aiden said. He swallowed hard. "Perhaps

it would be better if you went back to your home Clan for a while."

She wanted to ask him if he'd tired of her already, but the sharp tease would only bruise them both. So she said, quietly but firmly, "We're in this together, husband."

He moved his arm so that it rested behind his head. His blue eyes didn't hold the passionate anger they would have at another time. Instead, she saw determination and . . . fear?

"What are we going to do?" she asked.

"We've been forbidden to do anything useful in Tir Alainn, and nothing we've done in the human world has made any difference."

"You're backing down because Lu— the Lightbringer demands it? You're giving up?" She couldn't believe that of him. *Wouldn't* believe that. But when he turned his head and stared up at the ceiling instead of continuing to look at her, she felt a ball of sickness grow inside her.

"The Lightbringer has managed to silence the Bard," Aiden said. "There's no point in wasting time or words here, so I'm not going to waste either of them."

"Then what are we going to do?"

He took a deep breath. Let it out slowly. "How did the Lord of the Sun and the Lady of the Moon become the leaders of the Fae? He doesn't command the sun; she doesn't command the moon. How did they become the ones to whom the rest of us yield?"

Lyrra frowned, wondering where he was going with this. "The Lord of the Sun is also the Lord of Fire, which is a powerful thing to command."

"An elemental thing, you could say."

"And the Lady of the Moon commands the Wild Hunt."

"Which must have had more of a purpose at one time than simply riding over the countryside with a pack of shadow hounds."

She sighed in frustration, still unable to follow his thinking.

"Fire is a branch of the Great Mother. If it burns long enough and hot enough, it can sweep away anything on land, which is good reason to yield to the one who wields that power. And no living creature can stand against the Wild Hunt if it's the chosen prey."

"Which brings us where?" Lyrra asked, frustration making her voice sharp.

"Which brings us to finding the only one among the Fae who commands enough power to defy the Lightbringer and the Huntress and walk away from the encounter intact."

Lyrra stared at him for several seconds. An odd chill went through her, a shiver of fear that she had no rational reason to feel. "You want to find the Lord of the Woods? *The* Lord of the Woods?"

"The Hunter," Aiden said quietly. "Yes."

"But . . . Aiden . . . no one has seen the Hunter in *years*. No one's even *heard* anything about him in years."

"I know."

"Then why do you think he would help us protect the witches, even if we *can* find him?"

Aiden said nothing for a long moment. Then, "The day came when the old Lord of the Woods felt his power waning and knew the time had come for another to ascend to the full power of the gift and become the Green Lord and the Hunter. And so it was, at the full moon nearest Harvest's Eve, that he went to a clearing in an old woods and waited for the young Lords to test their strength against him to see who would ascend and become the new Lord of the Woods."

"And the young Lords came," Lyrra said, taking up the story both of them knew so well, "but none of them were strong enough. None of them could match the waning strength of the one who commanded all of them."

"Then another Lord stepped into the clearing, a stranger the others had never seen before. The stranger walked to the center of the clearing and faced the old Lord of the Woods, and all those who had gathered there felt the power rising— a fierce, joyful power that burned like a hot sun compared to a waning moon—and they knew this stranger was the new Lord of the Woods. The old Lord changed into the mighty stag that was his other form, and waited for the young Hunter to shape an arrow of magic, fit it to the bow, and send it into his heart, stripping him of his magic as was the custom."

"And the stranger did shape an arrow of magic and fit it to the bow. Then the new Lord of the Woods shot the arrow into the ground in front of the old Lord's feet, and said, 'I will take the burden of your duties with a glad heart, but I will not take from you the power that made you what you are. For you have walked in the shadows and the light for all these long years, and your strength, your experience, your wisdom are still needed in the world. Go in peace. Merry meet, and merry part, and merry meet again.' "

"The stag lowered his head, then turned and walked away from the clearing. When he was gone, the other Lords of the Woods came, one by one, to kneel before the Hunter and offer their loyalty, swearing to obey the commands of the new Lord of the Woods. And so it was, that night near Harvest's Eve, and he who came into power that night still rules the shadows and light of the woods and all things in it."

Lyrra said nothing, feeling the echo of Aiden's last words whispering through her.

"He changed things, Lyrra," Aiden said. "Before that night, every time a Lord or Lady ascended to rule over all the others who had that same gift, the one whose power had waned was stripped of all of it, if not killed outright, in order to ensure that there would be no rivalry between the old and the new. By letting the old Lord walk away, the Hunter changed the waning and waxing of power from a battle between rivals to a ritual where the duties of power were passed on to the one best able to take up the task. When I ascended to become the Bard, I didn't strip the old Bard of his gift of song. You didn't strip the old Muse when your time came to command that power. And we would have, because it was the custom, if it hadn't been for the story of how the Hunter came into his power."

"Some still strip the power from the old to prevent any rivalry," Lyrra said.

"And some always will. But many no longer do. If the Hunter could show compassion *that* night, he might be willing to hear what we have to say about the witches and why they need the Fae's help."

Hopeful. Doubtful. Lyrra wasn't sure which was the strongest feeling pulsing through her. "Where would we even begin to look?"

"Where no one has thought to look."

She puzzled over that for a moment. Then her eyes widened. She sat up on the bed and stared down at him, wondering if he was feverish. "The west? You want to go to the *western* Clans?"

"Think about it, Lyrra." Aiden sat up to face her. "He hasn't been seen in years. But we know he's still the Lord of the Woods because if he *wasn't*, another would have ascended to become the Hunter. No one knew who he was that night. No one knew what Clan he came from, and I don't think he *ever* said where he came from, even during the time when he *did* travel to the other Clans so that the other Lords and Ladies of the Woods would have no doubt about who ruled them. Then he disappeared again. Where else could he be?"

"Perhaps . . . in the human world, living there the same way Ahern did?"

"Even if that's so, it still has to be in the west. All of us who ruled a gift knew where the Lord of the Horse was, even if few approached him. But no one knows how to locate the Hunter, and maybe that's because we avoid the western Clans. If we approached one of those Clans and asked for him, I wonder how long it would really take to find him."

What was it about the Fae from the western Clans that made the rest of them so uneasy?

"There's another reason why the Hunter might be willing to help us," Aiden said softly. "'Merry meet, and merry part, and merry meet again.'"

Lyrra frowned. "I've always wondered about that. It's such an odd saying, and it's only in that story because the Hunter said it."

"I wonder if Breanna or Nuala would find it an odd saying."

Could the Hunter have taken those words to himself the same way she and Falco had taken Ari's ritual greeting to themselves?

"If that is a witch's saying . . . ," Lyrra said carefully.

"Then the Hunter might already be acquainted with a witch or two."

Lyrra didn't bother to remind him that plenty of Fae males had been acquainted with witches—for as long as it took to bed them and breed them—but they hadn't actually understood anything about the women they were mating with.

"When do we leave?" Lyrra asked.

"Tomorrow. Early. Even using the bridges between the Clan territories, it will still take a couple of days to reach the north end of the Mother's Hills and then head west."

"And what will we do today?"

"We'll rest." Aiden brushed a finger gently down her cheek. "Lyrra, this won't be easy, even going through Tir Alainn as much as we can. Are you sure you—"

"Do you think the Fae in the western Clans have any stories we haven't heard before?" Lyrra asked, deliberately cutting him off. "Maybe a song or two that even *you* haven't heard?"

"It's possible," he said cautiously.

"And if I stay behind, you would promise to listen to any new stories as carefully as you listen to the songs and tell them to me when you got back."

"Yes, of course I would." He smiled at her, looking regretful and relieved.

"Ha!" She rolled off the bed so that she could stand with her hands on her hips. "You'd listen to them well enough to snip them here and nip them there so that they'd fit into a melody that suddenly came into your head, and the only thing *I'd* get is *your* version of the story instead of the story itself."

"But—"

"Why don't I go instead, and you stay here? I'll listen to the songs and bring them back to you."

His mouth slowly opened, but no sound came out. "Lyrra . . . You know I love you, and you have a lovely voice, but, darling, you never catch all of a song when you only hear it once. Most of the lyrics, yes, but never the tune."

"Well, I can turn the song into a story so that I remember all of the words."

He looked scandalized.

"You don't approve?" she asked sweetly.

He rolled off the other side of the bed to stand and face her. "No, I don't approve! A story and a song are *not* the same thing!"

"In that case, Bard, it would seem we have to go together. You to hear the songs, and I to hear the stories. And we'll find some way to convince the Hunter to help us. Together."

His breath came out in a huff that turned into a laugh.

"Very well, Muse. Together." He came around the bed and held out his hand. "Shall we stroll through the gardens for a little while? I think my wife could use a little courting."

Smiling, she slipped her hand into his. "I think my husband could use a little of the same." A thought occurred to her, and she voiced it before she could change her mind. "What made you think of the west?"

He studied her for a moment in a way that made her sure her guess was correct.

"Morphia," he said. "She was going to the western Clans to find Morag since there was nowhere else to look. It made me wonder if the Hunter might not be there, too."

"Do you think Morphia has found Morag?"

"When we reach the western Clans, perhaps we'll find out." Aiden kissed her gently. "Let it go now. There are miles between us and any answers. For today, just let it go."

Lyrra leaned toward him. "When we come back from our stroll through the gardens, will you play for me?"

"On the harp?"

"If you insist."

He grinned, hesitated, then opened the door. "After our stroll, I'll play you any tune you care to name."

"I don't catch all of a tune with only one hearing. You said so yourself."

He burst out laughing, and was still laughing when he pulled her through the open door. "Come along, then. I want a bit of romancing before you have your way with me."

And that, Lyrra decided when they reached the gardens, was one of the reasons she'd fallen in love with him. The Bard would never leave the romance out of passion—which suited the Muse perfectly.

Chapter Eleven

Liam shifted in his chair as another eastern baron droned on about how about his county's prosperity had increased since he'd destroyed the vile creatures in the Old Places who had caused his people so much harm and how important it was for *all* the barons to take strong action to protect the people in Sylvalan's towns and villages from the Evil One's lures.

None of them actually came right out and said they'd hired men called Inquisitors to murder women who had a gift of magic and owned vast tracts of land that the barons couldn't touch. None of them actually said it was the women in their communities who were suddenly too weak-willed and weak-minded to avoid this evil that most of the barons beyond the eastern part of Sylvalan had never heard of except in these chambers. But that's what was being said under what was actually spoken.

Liam shifted again. Ignored the sour look from the old baron sitting in the chair on his right. The man reeked of cologne, adding another stink to the body odor and brandy that had been generously imbibed during the midday break. If this was all the barons' council did, why make the effort of the journey?

Because you and the people who matter to you have to live with whatever decrees are made here. Why else would the western barons travel so far twice a year?

Gritting his teeth, he sat up straight and forced himself to pay attention. Not that he hadn't been hearing the same thing all day yesterday as well as this morning. Kill the witches, acquire the Old Places for your own profit, strip all the other women in your county of the right to be anything but a man's property, and the *men* in your county will prosper. And since they were all men here, they had everything to gain and nothing to lose.

Nothing except their honor, their sense of what was right and wrong, and the trust of the women who were a part of their lives.

The baron finished his speech and returned to his seat in the council chamber. A smattering of applause came from the part of the chamber where the eastern barons sat. There was nothing but stony silence from the rest of the room.

Liam raised his hand, as he'd done over and over again yesterday afternoon and this morning, indicating he wanted a chance to speak.

The Baron of Durham, who presided over the council meetings, looked straight at him before calling on Baron Hirstun to speak.

Another eastern baron. More verbal puke about the dangers of the Evil One and the need to exterminate *all* the witches in Sylvalan so that the people who look to the barons to keep them safe will not fall prey to the cruel magic these terrible females spawn.

"I am pleased to report that all paintings and books that have been deemed unsuitable have been properly destroyed so that they no longer create unhealthy thoughts in those whose minds are too delicate to shoulder the burdens of keeping our counties—and our country—prosperous," Hirstun said. "I am also pleased to report that the procedure the esteemed physicians in our communities have learned recently to curb female hysteria has been entirely successful."

Procedure? Liam wondered, noticing how many of the eastern barons were nodding their heads in agreement. What procedure? If the eastern barons were going to try to push through a decree that *all* the barons would be expected to follow, they could damn well be more specific about what they were ordering done—and why. They'd spent the past day and a half filling the room with words and saying nothing. When a vote was finally called, how was anyone supposed to know what he was agreeing to?

Straining to hold his temper, he tugged at his collar, felt a trickle of sweat roll down his neck. Mother's tits! Why did they have to make the chamber room so warm?

When Baron Hirstun finished and returned to his seat, Liam wasn't the only one to raise his hand to speak. He noticed several of the barons from the north and midlands now wanted a chance to take the floor—and not all of them were younger men.

The Baron of Durham didn't give any of them so much as the courtesy of looking their way before calling on another eastern baron.

Heat flooded through Liam, the kind of heat that usually presaged a spectacular loss of temper. Unable to remain seated, he leaped to his feet, pushed past the two other barons who were on his left, and found himself standing in the aisle with his fists clenched, almost panting with the effort to draw in enough air.

"We have heard from the eastern barons," Liam said loudly. "We have heard the same things over and over again—words with plenty of fat and no meat. It's time to let others speak."

"You are newly come to your title, and this is your first time in the council," the Baron of Durham said coldly. "It is customary for the senior members of the council to speak first. And it is a measure of wisdom that those who are so junior they haven't even learned how to properly address the council should just listen and heed the words of those who have far more experience in ruling the land and the people who live there."

"Then let the senior members from the north or south or midlands speak," Liam insisted.

"You, sir, are out of order," the Baron of Durham shouted. "You will be seated!"

"No, sir, *I will not.*" Liam strode down the aisle. When he reached the front of the room, he turned to face the other barons. Grim faces. Furious faces. He was burning up. With anger. With fever. He couldn't tell. Didn't care.

"It's true that I've newly come to the title," Liam said, struggling to hold his temper. Ranting would only kill any sympathy he might find in the barons beyond the east. "And it's true that this is my first time attending the barons' council. But becoming a baron doesn't mean I relinquished my sense of what is decent, of what is *right.* I didn't relinquish my education or my understanding of the world I live in and the people who live in it with me. I've listened to what has been said here in the past two days. I don't have any answers, but I do have one question that I think *needs* to be answered." He held out one hand in appeal. "What has happened to us? What has happened to our pride in our country and our pride in our people? We're being told that women are too weak-minded to entertain ideas. We're being told that the only creative things they are suited for are the embroideries to decorate their homes. No. Not even *their* homes. Their fathers' homes. Their husbands' homes. We're being told that their writings are emotional scribbles that cause unhealthy feelings in others. We're being told that girls should not be permitted to attend school for more than three years—just long enough to learn their sums and to read and write so that they don't have to impose on the males in their families to keep the household accounts or write the invitations for a dinner party. We're being told that women don't have the intellect to run a business. We're being told that the only purpose women have is to provide a comfortable home for their fathers and brothers or their husbands once they marry. This is what we've been told in these chambers over and over again."

Liam paused, took a deep breath, then continued before the Baron of Durham could start demanding that he take his seat. "My question to all of you is this: *When did we change?* Women are weak-minded? How many of our schools are well run by women who have studied and trained to teach the children? Women are weak? Tell that to the farmers' wives who tend their houses and children and still go out to help their men with the planting and harvesting. A year ago, we had women novelists and poets and playwrights. We had musicians. We had painters whom we hailed as brilliant, remarkable talents. A year ago, we had women successfully running their own shops. Can you actually sit there and tell me that those women lost all of that talent, lost all of those skills *in the past year?* That women have changed so much they can no longer do what they've been doing for generations?"

He shook his head. The anger was draining out of him, sorrow taking its place. "*They* haven't changed. But I'm afraid to think what we'll become if we agree to the eastern barons' solution for prosperity. If women are no more than a body in bed to use and breed, are men really any different from the rutting bull that covers the cows? Will we really feel more like men if we see fear instead of affection in the eyes of our mothers and sisters and wives? Will we really go home in a few days, look at the women in our villages and in our family, and suddenly see weak creatures incapable of making a decision without first getting our approval? I don't think so.

So I ask you again: When did we change? *Why* did we change? And if we continue to do these things that will tear our people and our families apart, will we truly be able to look in the mirror and not see something monstrous and evil looking back at us?"

He looked at the barons. Grim faces. Thoughtful faces. Uneasy faces.

"I never heard of the Evil One until I took my seat in these chambers yesterday morning," he said quietly, "but I'd like you to think about one last thing. If there really is such a creature, where did it come from? What if these ideas about women and the things that are being done in the villages in the eastern part of Sylvalan are the work of this . . . *thing*? What if it's like a plague that buries itself in a man's mind and makes something terrible seem right? If that is the case . . ." Liam swallowed hard. "If that is the case, then the ones who died were the victims of this madness, and the ones who did the killing, or ordered the killing to be done . . . *they* are the Evil One's servants. *They* are the ones we should be on guard against."

The heat inside him was gone, leaving him feeling sick and shaky.

Silence.

Finally, the Baron of Durham said, "This meeting is adjourned until tomorrow morning when the votes will be taken on the decrees that have been proposed."

His legs shaking, Liam walked up the aisle toward the chamber's door. Alone. No one else rose from their chairs; no one spoke. But his eyes briefly met those of an acquaintance, a baron about his age who had wed at Midsummer last year. Donovan gave him a barely perceptible nod. Encouraged, he glanced at the far end of the room where the western barons sat. None of them were looking his way—except Padrick, the

Baron of Breton, who held his eyes for a moment before looking away.

As he reached the chamber door, Liam noticed the blond-haired, blue-eyed man staring at him with brutal intensity. It was the same man he'd seen in the bookseller's shop.

You'd have no trouble using a scold's bridle on a woman and claiming you were doing it for her welfare, Liam thought. *You'd enjoy using your fists on her even more.*

He opened the chamber door and quickly walked through the corridors until he reached the doors that would take him out of the building.

Perhaps he *was* becoming ill. He had no reason to think those things about a man he didn't know. But there was something about the man that made him uneasy, something that didn't *feel* right.

He saw a hackney cab draw up a couple of buildings away to let out a fare. He ran to catch it before the driver turned the horse back into the flow of carts and carriages. As he opened the door and climbed inside, he thought he heard someone call his name. But he didn't turn to look, and he didn't hear the hail again. Just as well. He didn't want to talk to anyone, didn't want to think. He just wanted to get back to his town house and rest until this shaky feeling went away.

Ubel stared at the closed door long after the Baron of Willowsbrook had left the room. Finally, he turned to study the remaining barons, his blue eyes assessing the damage that had been done by Baron Liam's passionate speech.

The eastern barons were protesting to everyone around them that just because they'd only recently been able to put a name to the source of trouble that plagued Sylvalan didn't mean it hadn't *always* been there.

Fools. They were spilling oil on a small fire, encouraging it to turn into an inferno. If any of them had thought to say the obvious—that it was *Liam* who was under the influence of the Evil One—and had expressed concern for his family and the people he ruled, they may not have sufficiently persuaded any of the other barons to their side, but they wouldn't seem to be the very thing Liam had accused them of being: men who were so greedy that they'd sanctioned killings for their own financial gain.

Of course, he could understand their fear. If they couldn't sway enough barons to vote with them tomorrow to pass the decrees that would assure that the restrictions they'd placed on the women in their control would be carried out throughout Sylvalan, they would be standing alone. That would be bad enough. But if the other barons became incensed enough because of that bastard's speech to demand that all rights and property that had been taken from women be restored . . .

A few short months ago, the eastern barons might have grudgingly given in to avoid the censure that could have proved troublesome to their purses. But since those barons had ordered the new procedure done on the females in the counties they ruled . . .

They couldn't admit they were wrong. Not after *that*. And if the other barons didn't vote for the decrees, there was a strong chance that the people in those counties would turn on the barons. It had happened in a few villages in Wolfram after the procedure was ordered—and in Wolfram, the people *knew* the Inquisitors stood behind the barons' orders. It had required cleansing two villages of the Evil One's presence—cleansings that had left a handful of children as the only survivors by the time the Inquisitors were done—before the people had surrendered to the next step in assuring that men would remain the strong rulers of their families, their land, and their country.

But there weren't enough Inquisitors here in Sylvalan to

carry out such a cleansing to teach the people how pernicious the Evil One could be.

Ubel pushed those thoughts aside and concentrated on the barons. He was Master Adolfo's eyes and ears in these chambers, and he needed to be alert.

Some of the northern barons—the ones who had already stripped the best timber from their lands—were listening to the eastern barons. And some of the southern barons, who had gone as far as eliminating the witches in their counties, seemed interested enough that they could be persuaded to take the next steps. But the midlands was rich farmland, and most of the barons who ruled there received a comfortable income from their estates and tenant farms. They had no incentive to change and become true men who didn't have to pander to the females in their families. And the western barons . . .

He didn't know what to think of them. Silent men. Uncomfortable men. If there was one of them who needed to be swayed to the eastern barons' argument, it was Padrick, the Baron of Breton. The man listened to everything and said nothing, but Ubel had seen the way the other western barons subtly deferred to Padrick, almost as if they were a little afraid of him. So there had to be something more to the man than what could be seen on the surface. Which meant it was likely that whichever way Padrick voted, the rest of the western barons would follow.

Which meant the vote would go against the decrees the eastern barons had proposed, and the odds were good that, before the summer ended, the barons themselves would be burned at the stake by the enraged villagers they now controlled.

But Liam had done something even worse than put the eastern barons at risk, as far as Ubel was concerned. He'd questioned the Inquisitors' motives. He'd accused them of being the Evil One's servants. How could the Inquisitors do their great work if they had to fear for their lives every time they rode into a village? What Liam had done was remind the barons of that song that was still being sung in taverns—the song that referred to the Inquisitors as Black Coats and users of twisted magic. It seemed every minstrel knew every word and every note of that song, even when the man couldn't recall where or when he'd heard it. It was as if it had ridden on the air to lodge in men's brains. Now a *baron* was taking up the tune in a slightly different way, but the end result was the same—all the effort that had gone into helping the eastern barons say things in just the right way to get the vote they needed was likely for nothing.

It was fortunate that Master Adolfo had decided to use the yacht one of the Wolfram barons had put at his disposal. He had arrived in Durham yesterday afternoon, and although Adolfo refused to leave the yacht, Ubel was pleased to have the Witch's Hammer so close at hand. There wouldn't be any delay in conveying information or receiving orders.

There was one thing, however, for which Ubel needed no orders. The Sylvalan barons needed to be shown before they reconvened tomorrow morning that defying the eastern barons was the same as defying the Master Inquisitor. Once they understood how costly that defiance could be, they would also understand the need to vote as they should to ensure that Sylvalan did not remain infested with witches and other kinds of female power. Yes, they needed to be taught that there was a penalty for defying the Master Inquisitor.

And Liam, the Baron of Willowsbrook, would be that lesson.

Your father understood the necessity for making changes that will keep Sylvalan strong.

Liam stepped out of the club where he'd had dinner,

turned up his collar against the drizzle that had begun falling, then looked around for a hackney cab that he could take back to the town house.

Baron Hirstun's bitter statement had done nothing but convince Liam that opposing whatever the eastern barons were trying to do was right. As soon as Hirstun uttered those words, Liam had recalled with painful clarity the scold's bridles his father had acquired for his mother and sister. Yes, his father would have enjoyed having a way to silence any opinion but his own—and he would have enjoyed even more being able to take control of Elinore's inheritance to spend as he pleased. There was no doubt in Liam's mind that his father would have voted for the changes the eastern barons were proposing. It must have been an ugly surprise to those men to discover that the son was a different kind of man from the father.

Liam sighed. Not a hackney cab in sight.

The sigh turned into a grimace as his belly clenched and a queer shiver went through him. Had the beef he'd eaten for dinner been a bit off? The sauce that had been poured over the beef hadn't been to his liking, and after the first two bites he'd scraped off as much of it as he could. Not that he'd had much appetite anyway. It had taken hours for the sick, shaky feeling to go away this time. He wouldn't have gone out at all if he hadn't felt the need to listen to whatever comments might be dropped by the other barons in a last effort to convince their colleagues to support their side of the vote— whichever side it might be.

There was nothing more he could do tonight, and nothing he wanted more than to return to the town house to relax for a little while before getting a good night's sleep. Tomorrow would be a difficult day, no matter how the vote turned out.

No point standing around getting wet, Liam thought as he started walking back to his town house.

There was a noticeable lack of traffic on the streets at an hour that, a year ago, would have been considered the prime of the evening. From what he'd gathered from the men who had been in Durham for a few weeks, there was also a noticeable lack of social activities. The women who were usually the premier hostesses who planned the balls and parties and musical evenings when the barons and other gentry gathered in Durham had made no effort this year. Even the ones who *had* planned such evenings at their husbands' command had done so with so little enthusiasm that the affairs felt more like a gathering of mourners than a party.

Liam spotted a hackney cab heading in the opposite direction, but it was past him before he could raise his hand to hail it.

He grimaced as his belly clenched again and kept walking. Sweat suddenly broke out on his forehead. His legs and arms felt oddly heavy, as if he were trying to walk through deep water.

He passed a narrow alley between two shops that were closed for the night. A few moments later, he heard two pairs of footsteps behind him.

He tried to walk faster but couldn't seem to get his legs to respond.

The footsteps got closer. His heart beat harder.

A little farther behind him, he heard the *clip clop* of a horse's hooves and the rattle of wheels on the cobblestone street.

Maybe he should turn and face whoever was now following him. Maybe he should dash into the street and hope whoever was driving the vehicle saw him in time to stop the horse. Maybe—

"Boy!" a voice full of annoyance shouted.

Liam turned, staggered back a step as a wave of dizziness washed through him.

Two large, rough-looking men stared at him for a moment before taking another step toward him.

"Boy!" the voice shouted again.

A hackney cab pulled up. The door swung open. Padrick, the Baron of Breton, got out of the cab and strode toward Liam, his expression harsh enough to make the two rough-looking men hesitate.

"Mother's tits!" Padrick exploded, brushing past the men. He clamped a hand around Liam's arm in a grip hard enough to bruise. "When I told your father I'd keep an eye on you while you were in town, I had no idea he'd saddled me with a snot-nosed drunken wastrel! Well, your evening on the town has come to an end, laddy-boy, and I'll not listen to a word otherwise."

Stunned, Liam started to raise one hand toward his nose to see if he needed to use his handkerchief, but Padrick hauled him toward the cab with a force that almost pulled him off his feet.

"Get in," Padrick snarled, shoving Liam through the cab's open door.

Liam sprawled, his upper body on the seat, his legs on the floor. Padrick stepped on him as he entered the cab and slammed the door shut.

The cabby set his horse to a fast trot, quickly leaving behind the two men who had followed Liam.

With an effort that made his arms shake, Liam maneuvered himself into a sitting position. "I'm not drunk," he said.

"No, you're not drunk," Padrick said with quiet anger. "You're a fool. A courageous, passionate young fool. Where are you staying?"

"The family town house." He was sweating heavily, and being rattled around in a fast-moving vehicle was making his gorge rise.

Padrick huffed. "If they were waiting for you at your club,

they'll be waiting at your town house." He leaned his head out the window and shouted, "Cabby! Pull up at the end of the next block."

Liam watched as Padrick pulled out a folded piece of paper and the stub of a pencil from his jacket pocket.

"Here," Padrick said, pushing them into Liam's hands as soon as the cab stopped moving. He left the cab, returning a few moments later with one of the cab's lanterns. "How did you get to Durham? Horseback or carriage?"

"Horseback," Liam gasped. Why was it so hard to breathe? "But a groom drove an open cart to carry my trunk."

"Fine, then. Write a note to your butler. Tell him he's got thirty minutes from the time he receives this note to have your valet pack your trunk and have the groom get your horse and the cart ready to travel."

"Travel?" He wasn't traveling any farther than it took to get to the town house.

"Tonight's the Summer Moon, and the sky is clear. They'll be plenty of light to travel by."

"I'm not—"

"You're getting out of Durham. Tonight. Before whoever decided you were an enemy gets a chance to finish the job."

"I don't know what you're talking about."

Padrick grabbed Liam's arm. "The only reason those two men didn't drag you into an alley and beat you to death was because their minds were clouded long enough that they weren't sure you were who they thought you were. But once it wears off and they realize they've been tricked, they'll come after you again. Now write the note, Liam."

Yes. Write the note.

He laid the paper on the seat, gripped the pencil, and struggled to make his hand shape the words. By the time he folded the paper and wrote the town house's address on the outside of it, he was shaking badly.

Padrick took the paper and the lantern, went out to speak to the cabby. When he returned, the cab took off at the same brisk trot.

"Where are you taking me?" Liam asked faintly.

"To my room at the hotel," Padrick replied. "It's closer. And we should be safe there for long enough. I need to pack and settle my account, and you need— Well, I think I have something that will help you."

Liam didn't argue, didn't answer. Mother's tits. The club he belonged to was supposed to be one of the best in the city. How could they serve beef that had gone bad? Was that why they'd poured that sauce over it? Because they'd known it had gone bad? Irresponsible of them. And he would tell whoever was in charge exactly that.

He must have faded out for a bit, because the next thing he knew Padrick was hauling him out of the cab and into a modest hotel.

Only two flights up to Padrick's room, thank the Mother, and every step a misery.

Padrick unlocked the door, pulled Liam through the small sitting room and into the bedroom. He pushed Liam to the floor near the window, then retrieved the chamber pot. He was back a few moments later with a small bottle in his hand.

"Drink this," Padrick ordered, holding out the bottle to Liam.

Liam shook his head. He couldn't drink anything.

Making a vicious sound, Padrick grabbed Liam's hair, yanked his head back, and poured the contents of the bottle down his throat.

Liam choked, then gasped for breath when Padrick released him. "You bastard. I've already got food poisoning."

"What you've got, laddy-boy, is poisoned food," Padrick said harshly. "A meal prepared especially for you."

Liam stared at Padrick. "Poisoned? Why?"

"Because you stood in that council chamber and said everything the eastern barons and the Inquisitors who seem to be controlling those barons didn't want anyone to say. You made the other barons wonder if these new ideas were coming from their own people or from someone outside of Sylvalan who might have his own reasons for wanting to have our society ripped apart. You made them wonder *exactly* what was happening in those eastern villages. And you pointed a finger at the men whose appearance in Sylvalan started all these changes. I don't think the poison was meant to kill you, which is a small blessing, just make you weak enough that you wouldn't be able to fight or escape the men they sent after you."

"Lucky you came along, then."

"I was looking for you," Padrick snapped. "I didn't want to hear tomorrow morning that you'd been found in an alley somewhere with your head smashed in."

Before Liam could say anything, his belly clenched again. He got his head over the chamber pot before he became violently ill.

"What did—?" Liam gasped. "What—?" Another wave of sickness threw his stomach past his teeth.

"A purge," Padrick said. "Whether it's a mild poison or something strong enough to kill you, you have to get it out of you as quickly as possible." He pushed the window open, leaned out far enough to take deep breaths of fresh air.

Liam wondered why a baron would feel the need to carry a purge, but he didn't feel well enough to ask.

"Are you through?" Padrick asked.

Liam nodded weakly. "It's not just my dinner, it's my stomach as well that's filling the chamber pot."

Padrick put a cover over the chamber pot, then helped Liam to the bed. "You rest a bit while I pack my things."

"There's no reason for you to leave. And we both have to stay for the vote. We have to."

Padrick rested one hand on Liam's shoulder and leaned over until they were eye to eye. "Get it through your stubborn head, Liam. One way or another, they're going to make sure you don't walk back into that chamber tomorrow morning. And not just for the vote. If you die, who becomes the next baron?"

"A cousin of my father's. I think."

Padrick nodded. "And if he's a man who can be swayed—or bought—to the eastern barons way of thinking, what will happen to your family?"

Liam thought of Elinore and Brooke . . . and shuddered.

"You'll best serve your family and your people by staying alive. And that means getting out of Durham." Padrick went to the wardrobe, took out the saddlebags, and packed swiftly. When he was done, he turned to Liam. "I have to go out for a few minutes. Will you be all right?"

Liam nodded. He felt hollow—and fragile enough to shatter. He knew Padrick was right, and yet . . . "You don't have to go. You could stay for the vote."

Padrick paused at the bedroom door. "Laddy-boy, if these Black Coats are as smart as I think they are, they'll figure out quickly enough who helped you tonight. I don't fancy getting a knife in the back because of it, and you're in no shape to ride alone. Besides, getting myself killed would seriously annoy my wife, since I promised her I'd be careful while I was here. You rest for a bit. I'll be back shortly."

"Come on, laddy-boy," Padrick said, hauling Liam to his feet. "Time to try your legs."

Liam stared fuzzily at Padrick. "I thought you were going out for a few minutes."

Padrick studied Liam carefully. "I've *been* out. And so, it seems, were your brains." He paused. "Can you walk on your own? Don't answer that. I shouldn't have bothered to ask." Settling his saddlebags over one shoulder, he draped one of Liam's arms across his shoulders.

"If someone sees us . . . ," Liam said weakly.

"You've had too much wine, which you inconveniently sicked up when you got to my room," Padrick said quietly as he led Liam through the sitting room and into the hotel's hallway. "I told a couple of the western barons who are also staying at this hotel that you'd received distressing news from home, but you're too ill to travel by yourself so I agreed to go with you. They're seeing to getting my horse saddled and hunting down a hackney cab for you."

"Can you trust them?" Liam asked, gripping the banister as tightly as he could to steady himself as they made their way down the stairs. "What if they . . ." He suddenly realized he was trusting his life to a man he knew only by sight, and Padrick was trusting men he didn't know at all.

"They won't raise their hands to do me harm," Padrick said softly, grimly. "They know full well if they did, they could never go home again, they could never go anywhere near the western part of Sylvalan and be safe." He paused, then added, "The barons aren't the only ones who rule in the west, Liam, and they aren't the most powerful."

The words buzzed in Liam's mind, but he couldn't get them to make sense. The smell of sickness clung to him, making him wish he'd thought to rinse his mouth to cleanse it.

A hackney cab stood waiting. A saddled horse waited behind it. He didn't see the other western barons. Either they didn't want to be seen helping Padrick, or they'd been told *not* to be seen helping for their own safety.

He would have stopped to get a better look at Padrick's

horse, which was the finest animal he'd ever seen, but Padrick hustled him into the cab and closed the door.

Liam heard Padrick give the driver the address of his town house. The cabby clucked to his horse, and they set off at a brisk pace.

Liam closed his eyes, trying to gather his strength. The *clip clop* of the cab horse's hooves soothed him, almost lulling him to sleep.

He opened his eyes. Only one set of hooves. Had Padrick stopped to talk to the other barons after the cab had set off? Had he been delayed by something simple like a loose cinch? Or had he been detained by another pair of rough-looking men?

Twisting around, Liam stuck his head out the cab window to look behind him.

Padrick, riding a few lengths behind the cab, made a sharp movement with his hand.

Liam drew back into the carriage, his heart pounding strangely.

Padrick's horse made no sound as it trotted on the city street. No sound at all.

Not sure what to think, he tried not to think at all until he reached the town house. Trembling from the effort, he got out of the cab by himself—then realized the cabby had driven him directly to the mews behind the town house. He staggered over to the cart that already had his trunk in the back and leaned against it to take some weight off his shaking legs.

"Baron Liam!" Kayne, the upper footman who had been acting as his valet, touched Liam's arm briefly, his worried expression making his plain face look harsh.

One groom ran to the kitchen door to inform the butler that the baron had arrived. Hogan, the groom he'd brought with him from Willowsbrook, stood nearby, looking surly.

His father's man, Liam thought sickly. His father's servants. Except for Kayne, who'd been hired the day after he'd arrived in Durham to replace the upper footman who had gone out to run an errand and never came back. The rest of the servants, Kayne had told him the next evening, were speculating that the man had run off with a parlor maid that he'd been courting, a young, pretty woman who worked for a family a few doors down.

Padrick rode up beside the hackney, handed the driver a few coins, then moved his horse to one side to allow the cabby to turn his horse and cab.

"Is everything ready?" Padrick asked as soon as the cab was gone.

Liam almost said yes. Then he looked at the saddled gelding and said, "Bring him over here."

Hogan led the gelding closer to the lanterns.

"The saddlebags are empty," Liam said sharply.

Kayne stammered, "There was no need to use them, Baron Liam. Everything fit in the trunk."

Knowing his anger was unjust but unable to stop it from rising, Liam pushed away from the cart, stumbled over to the gelding, fumbled with unsteady fingers to untie the saddlebags, and finally pulled them off the horse. Heat crept through him, filled him.

Not now, he thought as he walked back to the trunk. *Merciful Mother, don't let my temper give me the shakes now.*

"Not your fault, Kayne," he said, opening the trunk. "You couldn't know there are things I always carry with me." Like the miniatures of his mother and sister. He rummaged through the trunk until he found the velvet pouches that protected the miniatures. He stuffed those into one saddlebag, along with a change of linen. The small case that held his toiletries went into the other saddlebag, as well as the purse that held the coins he'd brought with him.

Hogan took the saddlebags from him. Tied them securely to the gelding's saddle.

By then the butler had reached the mews.

"Baron Liam," he said. "Did the gentleman find you at your club?"

A chill went through Liam, smothering the heat. "What gentleman? What did he look like?"

"He had fair hair and blue eyes," the butler replied. "He said he had an urgent message for you. When I said you were not at home, he asked for your direction."

"So you told him where to find me," Liam said softly.

The butler stiffened. "It did not seem out of place to do so. He was, as I said, a gentleman."

Liam glanced at Padrick, who said nothing. Didn't have to say anything.

"Yes, he found me," Liam said. "He had . . . troubling . . . news, which requires my immediate return to Willowsbrook." No reason not to confirm the story Padrick had already told the western barons.

"Let your groom take the cart and head out of Durham by the north road," Padrick said. "We have another stop to make, so we'll catch up with him as soon as we can."

Another stop? Liam didn't ask, certain he wouldn't get an answer. He just looked at Hogan and said, "You have your orders."

"Let me accompany you, Baron Liam," Kayne said quickly. "It's obvious the news from your estate has distressed you to the point of being ill. You should have someone along to look after you."

Liam managed a smile. "My thanks for the offer, but there's no need. I'll be fine." He mounted the gelding, waited for the wave of dizziness to pass, then looked at the butler. "If anyone asks for me, tell them that I've been called away."

He looked at Padrick, who simply turned his horse and

rode out of the mews and into the alley. After a moment's hesitation, when he clearly heard the sound of a horse's hooves, Liam followed.

The sickness from the poison must have affected his hearing, Liam decided. It wasn't possible for a horse not to make a sound on cobblestone streets. He'd been so busy trying to stay upright in the cab, he'd become delusional. That's all it—

As soon as they turned out of the alley and onto another street, Liam heard only one set of hooves on the cobblestones. His own horse's.

Padrick urged his horse into an easy trot, a pace that covered distance without looking like the riders were in a hurry. A typical pace for young men in the city—when they weren't riding like fools.

Liam gritted his teeth, concentrated on staying in the saddle. "This isn't the way to the north road."

"We're taking the west road out of the city," Padrick said. "We'll circle around. The horses are fresh, so we should be able to catch up with your groom on the north road soon enough."

"And if someone's waiting for me on the north road?" Liam demanded.

"Then your man will have a better chance by himself," Padrick replied sharply. "It's you they're after, not the people who work for you."

You don't know that, Liam thought bleakly. He continued to follow Padrick toward the west road because he was still too weak and sick to do otherwise. But when they left the city and he saw the road ahead of them lit by the full moon, he reined in, too uneasy to continue.

"What's the matter?" Padrick asked, turning his horse so he and Liam faced each other. "Are you feeling too sick to ride? Here." He extended a hand. "Give me the reins. I'll lead your horse. You just hang on to the saddle. When we catch up to the cart, you can ride with your groom."

Which is what I should have done in the first place. "I have a question that needs an answer before we go any farther."

Padrick made an impatient sound. "What answer do you need that can't wait?"

"Who are you?"

Padrick gave Liam a strange look. "Has that poison addled your brains? I'm Padrick, the Baron of Breton."

Fear. Temper. Sickness. It was an uncomfortable mix sliding around inside him. "Let me rephrase the question," Liam said. "*What* are you? You ride a horse that makes no sound on a city street. You indicate the other western barons wouldn't dare harm you, which means you have far more power over them than anyone in the council realizes."

"Not I," Padrick said quietly.

"And you conveniently appear to help me, claiming I've been poisoned and those men had been sent to kill me. You seem to know too much and say too little. So I ask again: What are you?"

Padrick said nothing for so long, Liam wondered if he should try to make a run for it back into the city. Then, "I am the Baron of Breton. I am gentry." Padrick paused before adding, "And I am Fae."

Liam swayed in the saddle, not sure if it was shock or sickness that suddenly made him so weak. He was on a moonlit road, alone, with one of the *Fae?*

"So now you have to decide, Baron Liam," Padrick said. "Are you going to risk riding with one of the Fae on the night of the Summer Moon, or are you going to take your chances and ride north alone, or back to the city, and hope you don't meet anyone who wants to finish killing you? I'll ride north with you to help you get home. Or I'll keep riding west."

It wasn't a hard choice when there really was no choice. "If I'm going to be riding with one of the Fae tonight, shouldn't it be a fair maiden who gives me a come-hither look?" Liam asked. Relief swept through him when he saw a glint of humor in Padrick's eyes.

"You're stuck with a man, and I save my come-hither looks for my wife."

Liam grinned. The sickness was still there, and the worry about his family and what might happen in the council tomorrow, but he felt a little boyish excitement, too. "Let's ride."

Turning his horse, Padrick held the animal to an active walk.

Liam chafed at the slower pace, then realized it was a chance to ask a few questions. After all, he'd never met any of the Fae before.

"You're riding a Fae horse. That's why I couldn't hear it on the streets."

Padrick nodded. "A Fae horse has silent hooves, unless it wants to be heard."

Liam admired the gelding. "I've never seen a finer horse. Well, maybe I've seen as fine."

"Oh?" Padrick said, giving Liam a long look.

"When I bought my stallion, Oakdancer. There were some 'special' horses that weren't for sale, and I saw them only at a distance. Oakdancer's light on his feet, but not like your gelding."

"Where did you acquire your stallion?"

"From a man named Ahern."

Padrick nodded. "He must have seen something in you to sell you one of the half-breds."

"Half-breds?"

"An animal bred from a Fae horse and a human horse. He

raised the finest horses in Sylvalan. But that was to be expected, since he was the Lord of the Horse."

"The—" Liam's jaw dropped. "Ahern? *The* Lord of the Horse?" He thought back to the days he'd spent at Ahern's farm when he'd gone to buy the stallion—and the odd way Ahern had gone about choosing the right horse for the rider . . . and the right rider for the horse.

"So you've already met the Fae, laddy-boy, even if you weren't aware of it," Padrick said.

Who could have guessed that gruff old man was Fae, let alone the Lord of the Horse? "I heard he died."

"Yes," Padrick said softly, grimly. "He died helping a young witch escape from the Inquisitors. Come along. We have a fair amount of road to put behind us tonight." He urged his horse into a canter.

Touched a wound, Liam thought as he brought his horse alongside Padrick's. Maybe it wasn't just his own people and the witches who had reason to look hard at the Inquisitors. And maybe that was a good thing. "Do you think the Fae will help us?" he asked, raising his voice to be heard.

"I can't say what the Fae in the rest of Sylvalan will do," Padrick replied. "But I can tell you this—if the Inquisitors come to the west, they'll die."

Liam judged they'd been riding for an hour, taking farm lanes and going cross-country at times before they reached the north road. A few minutes after that, he saw the cart up ahead, overturned in the middle of the road. He saw the downed horse and the blood turning the road black in the moonlight—and he saw the man's body.

He kicked his horse into a gallop to cover the remaining distance. It slid to a stop when it scented the blood, throwing him heavily against its neck. He slid out of the saddle, but managed to keep a firm grip on the reins. Not that it would do any good. The horse wouldn't stand. Not with the scent of blood so strong in the air.

"Give me the reins," Padrick said. "I'll see to the horse."

Liam handed the reins to Padrick, then stumbled toward the man in the road. Falling to his knees, he turned the man over gently, saw the cross bolts, heard the wheezing rattle of breath.

It wasn't his groom. It was Kayne, the upper footman.

Kayne opened his eyes, stared at Liam. "They killed me," he said, gasping with the effort to speak.

"Hold on," Liam said. "We'll find some help for you." Hollow words since he knew they couldn't reach anywhere fast enough to save the man.

"They killed me," Kayne said again, sounding baffled. "I was riding out to warn them that they needed to watch for two riders, but they killed me before I—" He struggled to breathe.

Liam sat back on his heels. "You were going to betray me? Why?"

"They— They said I had the gift. That I didn't have to remain a servant. They said if I did a good job of keeping a watch on you for them, they would train me to be an Inquisitor. I'd be a powerful man then, even more powerful than a—a baron. But . . . they . . . killed me."

Kayne stared up at Liam with dead eyes, his expression still baffled.

Padrick cursed softly. "He must have sent word to them somehow the moment he was told to pack your things." He dropped to one knee, placed his hand on Liam's shoulder. "Liam, we have to get away from here. Now. This attack couldn't have happened that long ago or he wouldn't have still been alive. There's no way of knowing if the men working for the Inquisitors are ahead of us or behind us, but they can't be that far away. And either way, we've got to put some distance between us and this road."

"Hogan was a Willowsbrook man," Liam said. "He wouldn't have let someone else drive the cart and leave him behind to make his own way back home. Which means he's wounded or dead, back on the road somewhere."

"We can't look for him," Padrick said firmly. "And we can't stay here."

"I wonder if the footman Kayne replaced actually ran off with the parlor maid. Or was that the first death?" He shook his head, struggled to his feet with Padrick's help. "Where do we go?"

"Where's your estate?"

"Northwest. Near the Mother's Hills."

"Then that's where we go. Without the cart, we don't have to stay on the roads. That'll make it harder for anyone to find us."

Padrick led Liam to the horses and held the reins while Liam mounted.

"I'll do," Liam said, answering Padrick's unspoken question.

Nodding, Padrick mounted his horse and turned toward the west. "Then let's ride."

In the early dawn, Ubel boarded the yacht and quietly entered the cabin.

"Well?" Adolfo asked softly, his doe-brown eyes giving no hint of what he was thinking.

Ubel bowed his head. "We failed, Master. That bastard eluded us. He shouldn't have been able to, but he did."

"It was a sound plan," Adolfo said quietly, calmly. "Even if you didn't receive my consent before starting it."

Ubel accepted the gentle-sounding reprimand, knowing that, even crippled, Adolfo could inflict a harsh punishment.

But it angered him. He wasn't an apprentice Inquisitor. More often than not, especially in these last few months, he'd made his own decisions about what needed to be done, had given orders to other Inquisitors. He'd never been reprimanded for it—until now. That, too, was one more thing he was going to lay at Baron Liam's doorstep, one more thing the baron would pay for.

"It was a sound plan," Adolfo said again. "Why didn't it work?"

"He had help," Ubel replied, resentment swelling inside him. "First with avoiding the guards who had waited for him at his club, then in getting out of the city."

"Who?"

At least he could offer that much. "Padrick, the Baron of Breton."

Adolfo poured a glass of wine, drank slowly. "So. There will be two barons missing from council later today. Probably not enough to change the outcome, not after that young bastard's speech yesterday, but it means we can't afford to have any other barons becoming indisposed right before the vote. That would cause too much talk, too much speculation of the wrong kind." Setting the glass on the table, he reached down, pulled up a bag, and dropped it on the table.

Ubel heard the *clink* of shifting coins.

"There's nothing we can do about the coming vote, but that doesn't mean we can't take care of other problems," Adolfo said. "Send four men to Willowsbrook."

Ubel smiled.

Adolfo shook his head. "We'll prepare the ground this time. Ripen the people until they're ready to listen. No one is to go near the baron's family. Three of the men will draw as much magic as they can from the land and turn it back on the baron's estate and the village. The other will find a reason to spend time in the village tavern and use his Inquisitor's gift to plant a few thoughts in the minds of the people around him. By the time he leaves, I want the tavern owner to be certain that the cause of the village's sudden ills is because the young baron is too weak—or too bewitched—to act against those who are the Evil One's servants, and the Evil One has found a place to take root. Let him fight against his own people's fears and troubles. That will keep him occupied for the time being."

"And the other baron? What about him?"

Adolfo reached for his glass, took a sip. "He must be punished for interfering with us. You'll see to it personally, Ubel. Take five men to assist you. I want no mistakes this time." He sipped again. "It doesn't matter if the four men reach Willowsbrook before the young baron, but it's important that you reach Breton before Baron Padrick. If he's still helping the whelp, he'll be delayed a couple more days, so you shouldn't have any trouble arriving ahead of him if you ride hard. I want it done and all of you gone before he returns home."

"And what is it you'd like done, Master?"

"Give his people a gift that flies in the dark. Then find out what is most dear to him—and destroy it."

Chapter Twelve

With Aiden beside her, Lyrra rode toward the mist at the edge of the world. Rolling hills, sparkling streams— they vanished into that wall of white that defined the borders of each Clan's territory. Islands of land that had been created out of dreams and will, according to the entries the Crones in Ari's family had written in their journals. Islands that were anchored to the human world by threads of magic the Fae called the shining roads—and anchored to each other by shining threads of magic they called bridges.

She'd never wondered how the bridges could shorten the distance between one Clan's territory and another, how it was possible to cover the same distance in a few minutes that would require a half-day's ride in the human world. It was part of the magic of her world that she'd simply accepted, like the rest of Tir Alainn.

She looked at the mist and the two shining arches that indicated the two bridges that connected this Clan to others.

Aiden reined in, studied the two arches, then looked at her. "We can still change our minds."

Lyrra pressed her lips together. They'd talked about this last night. Both bridges led to Clans that were northeast of here. One bridge connected with the Clan that was a good day's ride from this place; the other connected to the Clan that would be a two-day journey in the human world.

She didn't like the longer bridges. Never had liked them.

It took a few minutes to ride the shining road to the human world. It took thrice that long to cross even the shortest bridge, when all you had beneath you was a wide, shining path that created a tunnel through the mist. It took thrice again that long to cross one of the longer bridges. It felt so much longer when you were riding through that tunnel in the mist, watching for that archway on the other side. She didn't want to take that long bridge, but even using those shining threads as much as possible, it was still a long journey to the west, and the days were bleeding by so fast. The Summer Moon had come and gone last night, and every day it took them to find the Hunter was another day when more witches—and more Clans—might be lost.

"We need to swing around the Mother's Hills as quickly as possible in order to head southwest. We're of one mind in that." She waited for Aiden's nod of agreement. "Lucian took the bridge to the neighboring Clan early this morning. If we ride in after him, it will just be the same scene as yesterday. Since we're both heading north to go around the hills, we'll continue having the same scene. The long bridge will cut two days off the journey—and put us ahead of Lucian. Last night that seemed like the best choice. It still does."

"All right, then," Aiden said, still studying the shining arches. "Let's not waste the time by sitting here." He gave his horse the signal to move on, the packhorse obediently following behind him.

When he reached the arch to the long bridge, his horse snorted, danced a little.

"Easy boy," Aiden soothed. "Easy. It's just another bridge. You've seen hundreds by now." Coaxing but firm, he urged the horse forward, rode into that tunnel through the mist.

Lyrra followed. Her hands tightened on the reins when her mare tensed and planted its feet as soon as it was on the bridge, refusing to go forward.

"Follow Aiden," Lyrra said quietly. "Follow the others. You don't want to be left behind, do you?"

After another moment's hesitation, the mare trotted forward, expressing its unhappiness about being on the bridge with a gait so rough Lyrra clenched her teeth to keep from biting her tongue.

They hadn't gone that far when they caught up to Aiden and the packhorse. In fact—she looked back over her shoulder—she could still see the archway that led to the Clan territory they'd just left.

The animals shifted uneasily, as if they didn't like what was under their feet. Aiden stared at the tunnel ahead of them, frowning.

He handed the packhorse's lead to Lyrra. "Stay here. I want to ride up ahead just a bit."

"I'll go with you," Lyrra said quickly.

Aiden gave her a look that silenced further protests. "Stay here."

She watched him trot away from her, then became occupied with getting her mare to stand. When she looked up again, tendrils of mist drifted across the shining bridge.

Her mouth went dry, making it impossible to swallow. Her heart began beating fast and hard.

Then . . .

"Lyrra! Go back, Lyrra! *Go back!*"

Aiden's voice sounded oddly muted, but she heard fear in it—and something close to panic.

She turned her mare, aimed the animal for the archway, and dug her heels into the mare's sides.

The mare leaped forward into a headlong gallop, the packhorse matching the pace.

Lyrra glanced back, almost lost her balance.

Stay ahead of him. Stay ahead of him. He'll hesitate if you start flagging.

She screamed. In terror. In defiance. She wasn't sure. But the sound of her voice, so raw and primal, produced another burst of speed from the mare and the packhorse.

Aiden was behind her, his horse galloping flat out. And behind him . . .

A silent avalanche of mist filling the tunnel, rushing toward them. The shining bridge disappearing under it. And Aiden barely a length ahead of it.

She felt the difference in the mare's pace, felt how the animal was suddenly working for each stride, as if they'd hit a patch of boggy ground.

She emptied her mind of everything but the archway, so close now but still just out of reach.

Closer. Closer.

The mare and packhorse shot through the archway into the perfect morning light that bathed Tir Alainn.

Lyrra reined in hard a few lengths away from the bridge, then twisted around in her saddle.

The tunnel started collapsing near the archway, but she could make out the dark shape of a horse and rider.

Almost there. Almost there. Aiden Aiden Aiden.

She saw the horse gather itself to leap for the firm safe ground ahead. She heard Aiden's cry, as raw and primal as hers had been. She saw the shine that had been the bridge vanish just as the horse leaped.

The horse's forelegs landed solidly on the ground of Tir Alainn. But the hind legs . . .

One back hoof touched the edge of the world. Slipped as the edge crumbled.

Nothing under those back hooves now. Nothing but mist.

Aiden kicked out of the stirrups, dove for the land in front of him. He hit the edge at his waist, dug his fingers into the ground to find something, *anything*, to hold on to as the edge crumbled and he slid back into the mist.

The horse flailed for another moment before it fell into the mist, screaming in terror.

Lyrra tumbled out of the saddle in her haste to dismount and reach Aiden. She dropped the mare's reins and the pack-horse's rope and ran toward him.

More of the ground beneath Aiden suddenly crumbled. He kept fighting to find a hold in Tir Alainn while the weight of his own body pulled him down, until only his head, shoulders, and arms were visible.

"Lyrra . . . don't," he gasped when she dropped to her knees in front of him and reached out to grab one of his wrists. "You can't . . . hold me."

"I can. *I will.*"

"You . . ." He looked beyond her.

She twisted around.

Two riders cantering toward them. Two Fae males.

"Help us!" she shouted, waving her arms to get their attention. "*Help!*"

The riders stopped. Stared at Aiden for a moment. Turned around and cantered back the way they'd come.

Lyrra stared at them. They'd seen her and Aiden. They'd *seen.*

"I love you," Aiden gasped. "Remember that."

"I'm *not* going to lose you." Lyrra surged to her feet. Ran to the horses. Grabbing the reins and the lead rope, she pulled the horses as close as she dared. She made a hasty knot in the end of the lead rope, hoping it would be enough. There wasn't time to make a loop.

She saw Aiden slip a little more.

Getting as close as she could, fearing that any moment more of the edge would crumble, she held out the lead rope, dangling it next to his left hand.

"Grab the rope, Aiden. Grab the rope." When he hesitated,

she screamed at him, "If you go over the edge, I'll leap with you!"

He grabbed the rope with his left hand.

"Hold on," Lyrra panted. "Hold on." She forced herself to move quietly toward the nervous horses, her own nerves shrieking to *move move move*.

She grabbed the mare's reins. Tied them to the rope. Closed her hands over the knot. "Back up now. Back!"

Aiden's face was contorted with pain, fear, and the effort to hold the rope as the horses slowly pulled him out of the mist.

His left hand started to slip. Letting go of his tenuous hold of the ground, he grabbed the rope with his right hand. The move turned him on his side.

More of the edge crumbled beneath him.

"Back!" Lyrra cried, pulling with the horses. "Back! *Back!*"

His chest now rested on solid ground. His hips. His knees.

Lyrra pulled with the horses. Pulled and pulled until Aiden's feet were an arm's length from the edge.

He let go of the rope. Rolled onto his belly and crawled a bit farther before he collapsed.

It took her a moment to open her hands and let go of the reins and the rope. Once she did, she ran to him, tears streaming down her face.

"Aiden. Aiden." She touched his shoulder.

With a moan that was almost a sob, he rolled over.

A hawk screamed.

Looking up, Lyrra saw it dive toward them, then back-wing until it landed on the ground and changed shape.

Falco ran over to them, dropped to his knees beside Aiden.

"What happened?" he said. "Are you hurt, Lyrra? Aiden, can you speak? How bad is it?"

"The— The bridge collapsed," Lyrra said.

Falco frowned, looked over at the place where the archway had been. "Why were you attempting to use the long bridge when you knew it was unstable?"

Fear changed to anger in a heartbeat. "How could we know it was unstable?" Lyrra snapped.

"We were told," Falco said, staring at her in confusion. "Something started weakening the bridge about a fortnight ago, and the Clan has been warning guests not to use it to travel to the other Clan territories. The Clan matriarchs mentioned it when I arrived."

"They didn't tell us," Lyrra said. "They didn't mention it when we arrived yesterday. They didn't mention it this morning when they came into the common room where Aiden and I were having something to eat."

"They didn't—" Falco paled. "Why would they do that?"

"Because they're Fae," Aiden said softly, bitterly. He raised one arm to cover his closed eyes—but not before Lyrra saw the single tear escape. "If the Bard disappeared in the mist while using a bridge they'd warned him not to take, who would be inconvenienced? Another with the gift would ascend to become the Lord of Song, and perhaps the next one wouldn't be so insistent about playing the same wearisome tune about protecting the witches."

"But they *didn't* tell you," Falco said. "Lyrra just said they didn't."

"If we were both lost in the mist, they could claim they'd told us—and there would be no one who could call them liars," Lyrra whispered.

"But . . ." Falco sat back on his heels. "But that seems like such a . . . *human* . . . thing to do."

"Is it? If that's the case, perhaps we've become more human than we want to believe."

Falco winced. Lyrra didn't blame him. The Fae had held

the conceit of being superior to every other living thing for so long, it wasn't easy to consider that the worst flaws in their nature might be something they had in common with humans.

Aiden tried to sit up. When he started to fall back, groaning, Lyrra and Falco supported his shoulders to help him.

"We have to keep going," Aiden said.

Red streaks on the side of his torn shirt caught Lyrra's attention. Blood. "You *are* hurt!"

"I'm all right. I can travel. We need to travel."

"First you need to have the Clan healer take a look at your hands," Falco said, helping Aiden stand up.

His hands? Lyrra gasped when she looked at Aiden's scratched, abraded hands. "Mother's mercy, Aiden."

Aiden looked at Falco. His blue eyes were so filled with bitter despair Lyrra wanted to cry out from the pain of just seeing it.

"Do you really think I'd trust this Clan's healer with my hands?" Aiden asked. "I could end up crippled from a few scratches." He turned, stumbled on the first step. Catching his balance, he started walking toward the Clan house in the distance.

Lyrra stared at him, not sure what to do with him or for him. His frustration with the rest of the Fae had been turning bitter for a while now, but she didn't know what would happen to either of them if he continued down that road. She wouldn't leave him. She knew that much. Not just because, as a woman, she loved the man, but also because, as the Muse, she believed in what he was trying to do as the Bard.

"Can you get the horses?" Falco asked quietly. When she nodded, he ran to catch up to Aiden.

As Lyrra untied her mare's reins from the packhorse's lead rope, she saw the two men stop. Their voices were too low to hear the words, but it was obvious they were arguing about something. Gathering the reins and lead rope, she hurried to catch up to them.

"Don't be a fool, Aiden," Falco said heatedly. "Do you think they'll care if you harm yourself to spite them?"

Harm himself? Lyrra's heart leaped in her chest.

"I'll ask no favors," Aiden snarled. "Not from them."

"Then don't. But you can get back to the Clan house faster and use what you need to clean those wounds if you ride the mare instead of walking."

Aiden winced as his hands began to ball into fists. His shoulders sagged. Then he smiled ruefully. "If I can lose an argument to the Lord of the Hawks, I suppose I'm really not fit enough for a long walk."

"There's nothing wrong with that sharp tongue of yours," Falco muttered before adding, "Then be sensible and get on the horse."

Lyrra mounted the mare, wincing when she heard Aiden's grunt of pain as he mounted behind her. After accepting the packhorse's lead rope from Falco, she urged the mare into an easy canter.

A moment later, a shadow passed over them. She glanced up, saw the hawk flying just ahead of them. Falco, keeping watch.

When they reached the grounds of the Clan house, Aiden pointed to a fountain. "Over there."

She slowed the mare to a walk, guiding the animals to the fountain.

Aiden dismounted. He pulled off his shirt and dropped it in the fountain. He sat on the fountain's edge, pulled the shirt out of the water, and used it to wash the bloody scrapes on his side.

Falco landed near the fountain, gave Lyrra a worried look.

Dismounting, Lyrra approached Aiden. He ignored her and continued to use the shirt to wash his right side. Then he dunked his hands in the fountain, gritting his teeth as he scrubbed as much dirt as he could out of the cuts and scrapes.

Lyrra turned back to the mare, trying not to let her exasperation show. Stubborn, foolish . . . *man*. Did he really think a quick wash in a fountain was going to be sufficient?

Fine, Lyrra thought irritably as she opened one of her saddlebags and took out a linen shift. *That's just fine. If he wants to pretend we're in the middle of nowhere in the human world instead of at a Clan house and we need to make do with whatever we've got, that's just fine.* She drew the small knife out of its sheath in her boot and cut the linen shift into bandages.

Aiden stood up, shivering and definitely unsteady on his feet. He dropped the ruined shirt beside the fountain.

"Are you done?" Lyrra asked tartly. She bit her tongue. *Now you're sounding like one of those wives who starts all the trouble in certain stories.*

Aiden just nodded.

She saw nothing but weariness in his face, as if all the emotional fire in him had been quenched. She wrapped his hands, then made a pad to cover the worst of the scrapes on his side, securing it with more strips of linen that she tied around him. When she was done, she studied her makeshift bandages and suppressed a sigh. They would serve until she could find something better.

"You need a shirt," she said, turning toward the horses. Then she froze for a moment. Almost all his clothing was in his saddlebags. Gone now. Well, there was still the fine garb he wore for special occasions. That was on the packhorse. At least he still had that much—and his instruments. Those would have been a crueler loss than the clothing. Clothes could be replaced, and the only other thing in the saddlebags . . .

It hit her like a blow. She absorbed the emotional punch, then pushed it aside.

She reached for the bag that held his fine garb.

"No," Aiden said. "I won't wear that. Not here."

Knowing her emotions were too raw and anything she said would be regretted later, she just glared at him. "You need a shirt."

"No, I don't."

There was a hint of pleading in his voice that almost broke her heart.

"Let's ride, Lyrra." Aiden closed his eyes for a moment. "Let's just ride."

Where? But she didn't ask. She mounted the mare and waited for him to mount behind her.

Falco handed her the packhorse's lead rope. "You're going to try the other bridge?" he asked worriedly.

"No," Aiden said. "We're taking the shining road back to Sylvalan."

She couldn't see how that was going to help them, but she didn't argue. She smiled at Falco, hoping to convey some of her gratitude for his friendship and help. "Blessings of the day to you, Falco," she said softly.

"And to you, Lyrra. Aiden." Falco stepped back.

Suddenly aware of the Fae who were watching from the terraces on this side of the Clan house, Lyrra sat up straight in the saddle. "Be careful, Falco," she whispered.

She guided the horses around the fountain, keeping them to a walk until they were past the grounds of the Clan house and she saw the stones that marked the shining road. She urged the horses to a canter, tried to prepare herself for any reluctance they might have after being terrified on the bridge. But both horses pricked their ears and increased their speed, as if the safety and reassurance they wanted was at the other end of the road.

Maybe it is, Lyrra thought.

She heard Aiden's soft moan as they reached the shining road. She felt him shudder and press his head against her shoulder.

With her mouth pressed in a grim line, she kept the horses in the center of the shining road.

Not much longer, Aiden, love, she thought. And once they returned to the human world? Then what? She couldn't answer that. Didn't want to think about it. Right now, she needed to find some help for Aiden.

When they reached the end of the shining road, Lyrra tried to rein in the mare, but the animal fought the bit, swerving toward a wide game trail. Not in the mood to argue with a horse, Lyrra let the mare canter along the trail and wondered if the animal had any sense of where it was going.

Apparently it did. A few minutes later, they reached the green lawn and gardens behind the manor house. Lyrra caught a glimpse of Keely and Breanna working in the garden before the mare swerved again, heading straight for the stable block.

Seeing them, Clay left the horse he was grooming and walked toward them quickly.

"Easy now," Clay called. "Go easy now."

The mare and packhorse slowed to a walk, blowing and sweating.

Clay held his hands out, palms up.

The horses walked right to him, lipped his empty palms.

"Looks like you've had a bit of trouble," Clay said.

"Yes," Lyrra replied. She felt Aiden shudder, felt that shudder travel from his body into hers.

"Lyrra. Aiden." Breanna approached from the side, sounding a little breathless as she slowed to a walk to avoid startling the horses. "What's—? Oh, Mother's mercy. Come on now. Come on. We'll get him into the house."

Clay took the lead rope from Lyrra. "I'll take care of the packhorse. Breanna, you lead the mare to the house; then let her go to come back to the stables."

Breanna gripped the reins just under the bit and led the reluctant mare to the house. Nuala and Keely waited at the kitchen door.

Breathing heavily, Aiden dismounted. Nuala and Keely helped him into the house.

Lyrra dismounted, then grabbed the saddle, her legs suddenly feeling as if she had no bone in them. "Clay has a way with horses."

"A gift from his father, which was the only thing his father ever gave him," Breanna replied with enough of an edge that Lyrra flinched. "Mother's tits. That wasn't a thrust at *you*." She released the mare and wrapped an arm around Lyrra's waist when the horse trotted back to the stables. "Where's Aiden's horse?"

Tears filled Lyrra's eyes, spilled over. "Gone."

"Here, now." Breanna led Lyrra to the bench beside the kitchen door. "Sit down and rest. There now. There you go."

Shaking, Lyrra sank down on the bench.

"Are you hurt?" Breanna asked, resting a hand on Lyrra's shoulder.

Lyrra shook her head. Her body wasn't hurt, but her heart . . . She was certain her heart was sorely bruised.

"I'll be right back. Just rest."

Lyrra leaned back against the stone wall and closed her eyes. She heard quiet sounds, murmuring voices in the kitchen. But not Aiden's. Why couldn't she hear Aiden?

She stirred, almost too weary to make the effort. Wouldn't have tried at all if she didn't need to find out about Aiden.

She turned toward the kitchen door just as Breanna

stepped out carrying two tankards and a plate of bread and cheese.

"Can you walk as far as the tree?" Breanna asked.

"Aiden?"

"Gran is taking care of things. She has the touch for it." She smiled. "And she figures he'll stay more docile if he doesn't feel that he has to act manly for your benefit."

Lyrra followed Breanna to the bench under the tree.

"Fresh cider?" Lyrra said after taking a sip from one of the tankards.

Breanna made a face. "Let's just say there was an . . . incident . . . with Idjit and some of the stored apples. So there's plenty of fresh cider and apple tarts."

Lyrra started to smile, picturing Breanna dealing with the small black dog, but as she glanced back at the house, the smile faltered.

"What happened, Lyrra?" Breanna asked softly. "Were you attacked?"

"No." *Not in the way you mean.*

"Where's Aiden's horse?"

The tears came again. "Gone."

"Stolen?"

Lyrra shook her head. "It fell off the edge of the world."

"Mother's mercy." Breanna paused. "And everything Aiden was carrying with him was lost with it?"

"His clothes and personal things, yes."

"What about . . ." Breanna bit her lip. "I wasn't trying to pry, and I truly didn't look, but I noticed the papers when I emptied your saddlebags the other day to have the clothes washed. Those were his songs, weren't they?"

"Yes."

Breanna looked so sad, Lyrra wasn't sure she could stand it.

"His songs are gone?" Breanna asked.

"He still has them. In his h-hands and his heart." Lyrra gulped, trying to stop the sobs that were swelling in her throat.

Breanna took the tankard and set it at the end of the bench with her own and the plate. She slid over, gathered Lyrra in her arms. "Cry it out. Gran says sometimes tears are the only way to wash out the heart's wounds."

Lyrra let grief and the terror she'd felt in Tir Alainn flow through the tears. With her head resting on Breanna's shoulder, she told the witch about the bridge collapsing and her gut-deep fear when Aiden hung there at the edge of the world.

"He seems like a good man," Breanna said slowly. "Why would the rest of the Fae do nothing to help him?"

Lyrra hesitated; then she said carefully, "He believes, as I do, that the witches are the House of Gaian."

Breanna shrugged. "Why should that matter to the rest of them? We *are* the House of Gaian."

Lyrra raised her head. Sat up slowly. "You remember that?"

Breanna tipped her head, obviously puzzled. "We live at the foot of the Mother's Hills. How could we forget?"

"Some . . . Well, we've actually met only one other witch to speak to, and *she* didn't know." Only the Crones in Ari's family did, after reading the journals of those who had come before them.

Breanna looked in the direction of the hills. "If they've forgotten who they are, what else did they forget?"

"I don't know. But Ari . . . Ari was someone I would have liked to have as a friend. I wish there had been time to know her better."

"Where is she?"

"She's . . . She disappeared after the Black Coats came."

Breanna sighed. "Well, I'll mention it to Gran. This may

be something the elders should know about—if they don't already. But that's for Gran to decide." She handed the tankard to Lyrra, folded a piece of bread around a slice of cheese. "Here. Have a bite to eat, and drink the cider. Are you tired?"

Weary to the marrow of her bones. "I'll do. Why?"

Breanna studied her. "Come spend an hour with me in the garden. I think you need what earth can give."

Aiden woke to the cheerful sound of water singing over stone. That made no sense. He was laying in a bed in one of the guest rooms in Nuala's house—the same room he'd been given before. There wasn't a brook close to the house, so how could he hear one?

Turning his head toward the sound, he opened his eyes and stared at the bowl on the table beside the bed. With a few grunts and groans, he managed to sit up and slide his legs over the side of the bed so he could get a better look.

Arranged stones filled the center of the bowl. Water rose up between them, spilling down over the stones' edges.

A brook in a bowl, Aiden thought, smiling. But how was it done?

Curiosity got him out of bed when nothing else would have at that moment.

He found clothing on a chair. The belt and the boots were his, but the shirt and trousers had belonged to someone else. Still, he put them on, grateful for the loan—and tried not to curse too loudly when his bandaged hands and side made the task of getting dressed a fumbling challenge.

A comb and brush had been left on the dressing table beneath a small mirror. He picked up the brush, looked in the mirror—and froze.

His true face, his Fae face, stared back at him.

He and Lyrra had forgotten to use the glamour when they'd returned to the human world.

Breanna had seen his true face, so she'd probably told the others he and Lyrra were Fae. That's why they hadn't seemed surprised. Or maybe they were too intent on helping him to really notice the shape of his ears and the feral quality of his face.

Unsure if that made him feel relieved or uneasy, he brushed his hair and left the room.

He wandered back to the kitchen, since it was the only part of the house he was familiar with. Glynis escorted him to a parlor, where Nuala sat near an open window, doing some needlework.

She rose when he crossed the room, placed one hand lightly on the side of his face, and studied him for a long moment.

"You look better," Nuala said.

I look Fae. But he wasn't comfortable pointing that out to her, so he asked a question. "The . . . fountain . . . in the bedroom. How did you do that?"

Her woodland eyes twinkled with amusement before a soft smile curved her lips. "Water is my strongest branch of the Mother, and I have a connection with earth and fire, as well. So it's not so difficult to ask water and stone to dance together to soothe a weary heart."

He'd been dazed when she and Keely had led him into the kitchen and sat him down at one end of a worktable. But he remembered how Nuala had quietly murmured while she ran her fingers over his hands and Keely poured water over them. He remembered seeing bits of dirt and stone rise up out of his flesh to be washed into the bowl on the table.

"You called the earth out of my hands," he said.

"It didn't belong there." Her fingers trailed down his cheek before she lowered her hand. "It's almost time for the evening meal. Why don't you sit and rest a bit?"

Aiden took a step back, shook his head regretfully. "As

much as we enjoy your hospitality, Nuala, we have a long
journey and can't delay."

She gave him a stern look that made him want to scuff his
toes against the carpet. "Do you have a grandmother?"

"Yes." *Although I doubt she'd be willing to acknowledge
me now.*

Nuala nodded, as if he'd given her the answer she expected. "I am old enough to be your grandmother, and since
yours isn't here, I will stand for her this evening. You, young
man, will stay here tonight to rest and gather your strength
for the journey ahead. As soon as Breanna and Lyrra join us,
we will discuss your plans to see what can be done to ease
the journey."

"But—"

She pointed to a small sofa that faced the windows. "Sit."

He sat. And he wondered how different the Fae might
have been if the grandmothers in the Clans had perfected that
tone of voice.

Nuala returned to her chair and picked up her needlework.

After a few minutes, he relaxed. Under different circumstances, he could see himself sitting in this room for an hour,
idly playing his harp, perhaps even picking out a new tune
while she quietly worked on her embroidery. There was so
much peace and strength in this room, in this house.

"Why are there no men here?" he asked, a question more
for himself than directed to her.

Nuala didn't even glance up. "No men? Then Edgar and
Clay are . . . ?"

Aiden shrugged, winced a little when the movement
pulled the scabs forming on his right side. "I meant . . . companions." Lovers, actually, but he wasn't going to say that.

"My husband died when Keely was still a child. Because
of what happened to her, she will never think of a man in that
way. And Breanna hasn't yet found the man who touches her

heart. As for other kinds of companions . . ." Nuala's lips twitched. "That, grandson, is none of your business."

Aiden grinned.

The door opened, and Breanna and Lyrra walked into the room.

"Aiden!" Lyrra cried, rushing over to him as he struggled to get to his feet. She wrapped her arms around his neck and kissed him with an intensity that made him blush, since he knew Breanna and Nuala were watching with great interest. "How do you feel?"

He wrapped his arms lightly around her. "Better." She, on the other hand, looked exhausted and yet peaceful. "What have you been doing?"

"I worked in the garden." She turned her head and gave Breanna a dark look. "And I turned the compost piles."

Breanna just smiled and took the other chair near the windows. "I just let you learn one of Gran's lessons: Given time, even muck will change into something that nourishes."

"Did I phrase it that way?" Nuala asked mildly.

"No, you phrased it much more nicely, but the lesson remains the same."

Smiling, Nuala put her needlework aside. "Sit down, you two. There are things to discuss."

Aiden eased himself back down on the sofa. Lyrra sat beside him, one hand on his arm as she rested lightly against his left shoulder.

"Now, Aiden. You've lost your horse."

Grief stabbed through him. No one knew what happened to those who got lost in the mist. He couldn't say if the horse was dead, injured, or wandering around alive until lack of food and water killed it. It was easier to believe it had died swiftly, cleanly.

"Yes," he said.

"We don't have a horse we can offer you, but I could inquire tomorrow if the baron would be willing to lend you a horse."

Aiden shook his head. "I thank you for the offer, but to travel as we do, I would need a Fae horse. I doubt any would be found in the baron's stable."

Nuala nodded. "I thought that would be the case. So. What are your plans?"

He felt Lyrra tense beside him. She wasn't going to like the decision he'd made at some point while he'd slept. "We need to reach the western part of Sylvalan as soon as we can. So we're going to go through the Mother's Hills."

"*Aiden!*" Lyrra pulled away from him. "We *can't* go through the Mother's Hills."

"Why not?" Breanna asked.

"Because . . . because the Fae don't go into those hills. We just don't."

"Why?"

"Because we're afraid of them," Aiden said quietly. "I can't tell you why. It's never spoken, but it's understood that we do not go there. But I don't see that we have a choice."

"We have a choice," Lyrra said heatedly.

"What choice?" Aiden snapped. "To add more days and delays to the journey?"

"We don't even know it will be worth it!"

"We won't know anything if we don't try!"

"I think I know why the Fae don't like the Mother's Hills," Nuala said quietly.

A chill went through Aiden, banking his temper.

"It's an Old Place," Nuala continued. "*The* Old Place. From the northern tip to the southern end, the Mother's Hills are the home of the House of Gaian. The power there . . ." She shook her head. "I don't think the Fae would want to have to acknowledge the power that lives in the Daughters and Sons of the House of Gaian. So they've stayed away until they've forgotten why. If what Lyrra told Breanna is true, that whole families of witches have forgotten who they really are, then it would be easy for those witches to come to believe they are less than what they are. And far easier to believe that a people who appear only occasionally in the human world are more powerful."

"We do have gifts of our own," Lyrra muttered.

"I didn't say you didn't. I only offer a reason why the Fae may have avoided the Mother's Hills."

A long, thoughtful silence.

Then Aiden said, "Can we cross through the hills?"

"As long as you offer no harm, you'll come to no harm." Nuala reached into her work basket, pulled out two wooden disks strung on thin cords of leather. She handed them to Aiden and Lyrra. "Here. Wear those where they can be seen."

Aiden studied the disk. On one side was a rough image of a willow tree in front of some wavy lines that probably were meant to be water. The carving had been stained somehow to stand out against the lighter wood.

"We have kin in the Mother's Hills," Nuala said. "That is our family symbol. Show it to anyone you meet there. They will know you guested with us ... and that you were welcome."

"Thank you," Aiden said, slipping the leather cord over his head.

"We can also give you a purse to pay for food and lodging on the journey."

"Nuala," Aiden protested. "We can't—"

"Grandson."

He knew there was only one thing to say in response to that tone of voice. "Thank you, Grandmother."

Nuala smiled.

A brief knock on the door before Keely opened it and

stuck her head in the room. "Glynis says she's ready to serve the meal."

"Thank you, Keely." Nuala rose. "I think that's all we need to discuss." She walked out of the room.

As soon as Nuala left, Breanna chuckled. "Ah, Aiden, you looked good sitting there like a hooked trout, just thrashing around and getting nowhere."

His pride stung, he said with as much sarcasm as he could muster, "Thank you, Breanna."

"Oh, it's I who should be thanking you." Breanna grinned. "It was a treat to see someone else on the receiving end of that tone of voice. Even more of a treat to discover that even the Bard can't argue against it."

Aiden gave her what he hoped was a scalding look. Her grin just got sassier. Sighing, he gave up. His sharp tongue and his way of shaping words might intimidate the Fae most of the time, but he had a feeling that Breanna, with a lifetime of practice behind her, would have come out better in this "discussion" with Nuala than he had.

With Lyrra's arm tucked through his, he slowly followed Breanna out of the room.

"Grandmother?" Lyrra whispered, looking at him a bit wide-eyed.

"An honorary one."

"Do you think you're going to acquire any more grandmothers on this journey?"

"I sincerely hope not." One was more than he could handle.

Chapter Thirteen

Ashk rode beside Evan on the wide forest trail that led back to the Clan house. He was doing well on this practice ride with the new horse—easy hands and good seat—and the horse had a sweet way of moving. A good partnership for the time being, but she'd noticed how the small gelding's attention tended to stray whenever it heard Caitlin's voice. The horse accepted her son as its rider, but it was far more attached to her daughter. Ah, well. The animal wouldn't pine for Evan when he outgrew it.

I did what you'd asked, Padrick, Ashk thought dryly. *I did my part of the bargaining—or tried to, anyway—and Neall managed not to kill himself choking back the laughter as we wrangled down to the price he wanted. Of course, offering twelve coppers and six rabbits might not have been where I should have started my end of the bargaining.*

She tried not to sigh out loud. Despite the time she'd spent with humans because of being Padrick's wife, she still couldn't understand why they enjoyed this haggling for goods. But watching Neall fight to keep a straight face gave her more understanding for why the merchants in the village were so hesitant to name an amount whenever she became interested enough in something to inquire about its price. She'd probably shocked them by paying the asking price—and probably terrified them into worrying that the baron would be along shortly to demand an explanation for what he would consider out and out thievery. Which probably explained why there were always a few coins tucked into whatever she'd purchased. She'd simply thought it was a custom among merchants to return a bit and had given the coins to the children to spend.

And Padrick, she suddenly realized, had simply smiled all these years when he saw her remove the coins from a package and had never said a word.

As they came in sight of the Clan house, Ashk saw the horse and rider. She recognized both. She still reined in, raising a hand to signal Evan to stop, as well.

"It's Gordon, Mother," Evan said. "I wonder what he's doing here."

Nothing good. Ashk studied the groom who worked in her husband's stable. She'd made a point of riding over to the manor every couple of days since Padrick had left for the barons' council, so whatever had brought the groom to the Clan house was out of the ordinary—something the servants didn't feel could wait for her next visit.

"Stay here." She looked at her son, saw him flinch, and knew he was seeing something in her face that reflected the side of her that even the other Fae approached cautiously. "If I tell you to ride, you turn that horse around and head for the heart of the woods. Do you understand me?"

"But, Mother—"

"Do you understand?"

His eyes widened. "Yes, Lady."

She caught a glimpse of something coming along on the trail behind them. Her hand slid down to the large hunting knife strapped to the outside of her right boot. Then she caught the flutter of black between the trees and relaxed. Morag, coming back from her own ride with Caitlin.

Brushing her heels against her horse's side, she rode toward the Clan house and the man waiting for her.

Had he been too fearful to enter a Clan house of the Fae? Or had the invitation never been given?

A compromise, she decided, noticing how a couple of the Fae men holding crossbows hung back—and how the other men who were closer to their guest were still standing where they wouldn't interfere with a clean shot if one were needed. But they'd given the groom a mug of ale and had brought a bucket of water for the horse.

Gordon smiled when he saw her, obviously relieved by her presence. How ironic since, with the exception of Morag, she was the one he should fear the most.

"Lady Ashk," Gordon said, settling for a brush of his fingers against his cap when he realized he couldn't bow without spilling the ale.

"Is there a problem at the manor?" Ashk asked.

"Not a problem exactly, but Finlay asked could you come to the manor. Some boxes for the baron, but the man that brought them said he won't leave them until he talks to the baron. Then he said he'd speak to the baron's lady since he was just remembering that the barons were having a big meeting in the east. So that'd be you, Lady Ashk. Will you come?"

"Just one man?" Morag said sharply as she rode up beside Ashk.

Ashk watched the groom's eyes widen. Dressed in one of her black outfits, there was no mistaking who Morag was.

"T-three, Mistress. Lady." He looked at Ashk, a silent plea in his eyes to help him say the right thing to the Gatherer.

"Three men," Morag said quietly. There was nothing gentle in that quietness.

"T-the captain of the ship and two of his men," Gordon stammered.

Padrick had said nothing about expecting a shipment. So who was this captain, and why had he come to Breton?

Ashk looked at Morag. "Will you come with me?"

Morag studied Gordon a moment longer. "I'll come."

Ashk glanced at the men standing near the groom. A moment later, two ravens and a hawk took flight, heading for the manor—and for Ari and Neall's cottage, since it was between the Clan house and Padrick's estate. Two would remain close to the cottage to keep watch; the other would continue on to the manor to give warning if it was necessary.

Well, Ashk thought as she and Morag rode away from the Clan house at an easy canter, *Gordon will have a tale to tell the other grooms when he gets back. It's not often a human sees any of the Fae change to their other forms.*

They rode in silence, not quite fast enough to satisfy the need to cut off any trouble before it could take shape, but prudent enough that they could keep the pace without risking the horses' legs on a raised tree root or their own necks on any low-hanging branches. Not that there were either on this trail, which was frequently traveled and well maintained. Especially now that Ari drove the pony cart along this trail to visit the Clan house.

Leaving the woods, they let the horses stretch into a gallop, flying over the open land. No sign of Neall or Glenn out in the fields, for which Ashk was grateful. There wasn't time to stop, and nothing she could tell either of them even if she did.

Then they passed through another short stretch of woods that formed the boundary separating Neall's land from the land worked by Padrick's tenant farmers.

Not so far in terms of distance between the Clan house and Padrick's estate, but the distance between human and Fae had felt vast—until she fell in love with a man who was both gentry and Fae, a man who had shown her it was possible to take the best from each and create something better than either could be alone.

They eased back to a canter when they were close enough to the manor to be noticed. Ashk used the glamour to create a human mask. The people who worked for Padrick knew what she was, but there was no reason to let these unexpected visitors know more than was needed.

Morag, however, made no attempt to hide what she was, and Ashk didn't ask her to. Why waste the breath? Besides, it would give her time to study these men and decide what to do about them. Who would be paying attention to *her* when Morag was standing in front of them?

They rode into the stable yard and dismounted. Ashk murmured, "Walk," to her horse and heard Morag murmur the same. Two grooms came out, touched two fingers to their foreheads in a salute, then stood back. They knew better than to try to take the reins of a Fae horse. When the horses were cooled down, the grooms would offer water and wait for further orders.

She paused, noting the small wagon, the two horses in the paddock for visitors that Padrick had built next to the stable—and the two men leaning against the paddock rails where the shade tree outside the paddock offered relief from the sun.

Turning away, Ashk strode to the manor with Morag easily matching her stride. How must they look to a stranger? One dressed in the brown-and-green trousers and tunic that were favored by the Fae of her Clan and the other dressed in slim black trousers and a split overdress that floated around her.

The front door opened before she reached it. Finlay, Padrick's butler, said, "Lady Ashk, this gentleman asked to speak with you." Nothing in his voice implied that she'd been anywhere except for a long ride from which she was just returning.

The man, who had been sitting on a bench next to six

boxes, rose quickly to his feet. Whatever greeting he'd intended to give died when Morag walked through the door. His eyes widened. His breath seemed to catch in his chest. The healthy color in his face drained away.

"Blessings of the day to you," he said—then winced a little when he realized *what* he'd said.

"Blessings of the day," Ashk replied, studying his face more intently. Not the greeting he'd intended, but the one that came more naturally to him. He had woodland eyes, that brown-flecked green like her own. And she suspected that, like her, there had been a witch somewhere in his lineage. Perhaps fairly close, considering that it was a witch's greeting that flowed from his lips when he was too startled to think.

"I beg you'll forgive the intrusion, Lady, but—"

"I might," Ashk interrupted, "if I knew who you are."

His face flushed. With effort, he focused his attention on her. "I'm Mihail, the captain of a merchant vessel. I'm here to deliver these boxes to Baron Padrick."

"Why? The baron didn't mention he was expecting anything."

Mihail looked uncomfortable. "He's not. That's why I wanted to talk to him."

Ashk smiled. "Since he isn't here, you'll have to talk to me."

He shifted uneasily, as if recognizing there was a threat in those words but not knowing why it was so.

"What's in the boxes?" Ashk asked.

"Books," he replied promptly.

Books? That could be good. Padrick always brought back a book or two when he had to go to Durham for the barons' council. He had a fine library, the best in the county and probably beyond. He'd even brought some books for her, which she'd puzzled over, both fascinated and appalled by the actions and behavior of the people until he'd explained that these were stories that had been written down and were to be taken in the same way as the stories and story-songs that were told or sung by the Fae. Once she understood that, she was still fascinated and appalled—and grateful that the humans who lived near the Old Place had never done *anything* like the people in the stories—but she'd also come to appreciate that the books were a fine entertainment on a winter's night. Sometimes she'd end up howling with laughter when Fae were mentioned in a story, because it was obvious the person who wrote it had never set foot in an Old Place let alone met any of the Fair Folk.

"Why did you bring them here?" Morag asked.

Ashk jolted, suddenly aware that she'd dropped her guard when Mihail mentioned books. *Fool. Stop acting like a gentry woman who doesn't know how swiftly a predator can strike.*

"There's a bookseller in Durham," Mihail said. "He and I have had an arrangement for the past few years. I take some of his books and sell them to shopkeepers in the ports where I transport goods that come into Durham. Neither of us makes much profit, but it's a tidy little business, since it's easier to take the books along the coast than sending them overland." He shifted his feet, cleared his throat. "When I was there recently, he had the regular order waiting—but he also asked me to take these books and find a safe place for them. The barons had declared that these books were no longer suitable reading and were to be destroyed, and the magistrate's guards would be along any day to take all the copies he and the other booksellers had. He wanted to save what he could. Otherwise, when the barons finally came to their senses, these books, these stories, would be lost.

"I brought a cart late that night and drove it to the alleyway door. I took the books and promised I would find a safe place for them."

"Why are these books no longer suitable for reading?" Ashk asked.

His eyes filled with restrained anger. "Because they were written by women, Lady Ashk. And the eastern barons have decided that women aren't capable of writing anything that is worthy of being published or read."

Ashk felt Morag stiffen—and she wondered what Padrick would say about this when he returned home.

"Why bring them to Padrick?" Ashk said. "He, too, is a baron."

Mihail hesitated. "I met Baron Padrick when I went to fetch my nephews home from school, and he struck me as a decent man. One who would understand."

"The merchant boys," Ashk said, feeling another jolt run through her. "You're their uncle." *The uncle who stands at the bow of his ship in a storm and asks the sea for safe passage. The uncle with woodland eyes. The man who talked to Padrick about finding a safe harbor in the west for his family's ships—and his family.*

"Yes, Lady."

"Where are the boys?" She knew her tone was too sharp, but she couldn't help it.

There was something wrong with Mihail's smile. The affection was real, but the smile itself was a lie. "They're still with me. They're on the ship."

You meant to take them home, but you kept them with you. Why?

"And where is your ship?"

Now he looked worried. "We put in at a harbor about a day's ride from here. I'm not sure of the name of the village. The people there . . ." He shrugged. "If you're willing to take the books, my men and I will be on our way. We're only a few days past the Summer Moon, so there's still plenty of moonlight. We should be able to travel well enough and get back to the ship by dawn."

"He stays here tonight," Morag said abruptly.

Mihail glanced at Morag, but he addressed Ashk. "I'm grateful for the offer, but I need to get back to my ship."

Morag turned to Ashk. "He stays here tonight." Then she was out the door before Ashk could say anything.

"Lady Ashk," Mihail said.

Ashk had turned toward the door when Morag left. As she turned back to face her reluctant guest, she dropped the glamour that hid her true face.

He stared at her. "I thought you were—"

"Padrick's wife. I am. I'm also Fae."

He held out a hand, a silent plea. "I have to return to my ship."

Ashk shook her head. "If she says you stay, then you stay."

"Why?"

"Because she's the Gatherer, and she wouldn't insist that you stay for no reason."

He paled again, and there was fear in his eyes now. It was one thing to wonder if the woman standing before you was the Gatherer; it was another thing to *know* it. "My ship . . ."

"Will be safe enough."

"The villagers weren't pleased to have a strange ship come into their harbor."

No, they wouldn't be. "Your ship and your people will be safe enough."

"How can you be sure?" Mihail demanded, his concern overriding his fear.

"Because you have woodland eyes," Ashk replied quietly. "Those eyes mark you as witches' kin. So the harbor folk will wait and see what comes when you return."

Mihail nodded reluctantly. "Then I thank you for your hospitality." He hesitated. "Why does she want me to stay here?"

"I don't know," Ashk said. *But I intend to find out.*

"Why do you want him to stay?"

Morag turned from the flower bed she'd been staring at to find Ashk standing a few feet away from her. She hadn't heard the other woman approach, but Ashk always moved silently. "He seems like a decent man."

Ashk nodded. "He seems to be."

"When he mentioned going back to his ship, I saw a flicker of a shadow on his face, and when I went out to look at the men who came with him, I saw the same flicker. But Death isn't whispering here. Death isn't waiting for him but still might find him."

Ashk studied Morag. "An accident on the road?"

"I don't know." She smiled, but there was no humor in it. "I can see only what I can see, Ashk. Only hear the messages Death sends."

Ashk walked over to a bench and sat down. After a moment, Morag joined her. They said nothing for a while. Odd how a silence between them never seemed too long or too short. It was simply a resting place.

Finally, Morag said, "I'll go with him tomorrow. Perhaps Death is waiting for him along the road and there's nothing that can be done. But if he dies, I'll always wonder if my being there would have made a difference."

"We'll both go with him," Ashk said. "I think it best that I talk to the folk in that village—just in case the merchant captain finds himself needing a safe harbor."

Chapter Fourteen

The Mother's Hills were the most beautiful piece of Sylvalan Aiden had ever seen—and he wished with all his heart that he didn't have to take one more step forward, that trying to find the Hunter was a foolish idea, that they could turn around and go back to Willowsbrook.

He was sure he could have convinced Lyrra to turn back and take the long northern roads around the hills. He might even have convinced himself if it wasn't for the very last thing Breanna had said to them before they left the Old Place and entered the Mother's Hills.

Merry meet, and merry part, and merry meet again.

The same words that had been in the story of how the current Hunter had ascended to his power. The *only* story the Fae told that had those words. Merry meet, and merry part, and merry meet again. Those words made it far more likely that the Hunter had known witches, or, at the very least, had heard of the wiccanfae and might be willing to help him and Lyrra convince the rest of the Fae to do *something* before it was too late to do anything.

But the power in the hills staggered him. It felt as if every leaf, every blade of grass, every pebble under his boots breathed in that power then breathed it out again.

Perhaps they did. Nuala had said this was *the* Old Place, the home of the House of Gaian.

A year ago, the Fae had thought the House of Gaian had

been lost long ago. And it had been—to us. We didn't know
who the wiccanfae were or why their disappearance from an
Old Place caused a shining road to close and a piece of Tir
Alainn to vanish in the mist. A year ago, when we searched
to find information about the Pillars of the World, we didn't
know any of those things. If we'd ever set foot in these hills,
we would have understood all of them.

He brushed his fingers over the wooden disk Nuala had
given to him. There was no magic in it, no protective spell he
was aware of. It wasn't any different from a family crest, the
kind the human gentry seemed to take such stock in. But
touching it made him feel easier. A family of witches had be-
friended two of the Fae. Surely that would mean something
to those who lived here—if they actually met any of them.

Nuala had also warned them not to use the glamour while
they were in the Mother's Hills because the people here
would be able to sense the magic in them and would not feel
kindly toward the deception of a human mask.

He felt naked without that mask. It was safer to look like
the people around you. Especially when you were in a place
where your kind weren't usually welcomed.

He looked up at Lyrra, who was riding her mare and leading the packhorse. "Do you want to rest for a while?"

Lyrra shook her head. They were in another stretch of
woodland, and her focus was on the trees and bushes on her
side of the road.

There was plenty of open land in the hills—meadows and
pastureland where they'd seen animals in the distance, grazing. But when they came to another piece of the road where
the trees formed a canopy overhead and they stepped from
the light of a summer day into the shadows of the woods . . .

Eyes watched them from those shadows. He saw no one,
and he suspected if any of the Small Folk lived here, their

magic was too pale for him to sense over the power in the land. But he felt those eyes watching the two of them.

Up ahead the road returned to open land and the bright dazzle of summer light.

Aiden quickened his pace, his reluctance to go forward warring with the desire to get into the open again. But he'd gone only a few steps when the mare pricked her ears and whinnied a soft greeting.

He froze, his eyes scanning the woods to find what had caught the mare's attention, and he knew Lyrra was doing the same.

"Are you lost?" an amused voice asked.

Aiden didn't see the man until he stepped away from the tree he'd been leaning against. Dressed in brown and summer green, he'd blended into the woods.

"You were expected a while ago, so we began to wonder if you'd gotten lost." The man glanced at Lyrra, but the smile that followed that glance was directed at Aiden. "Then again, there are some pretty spots between here and Willowsbrook that are fine places to linger on a summer's day."

Aiden's fingers brushed the wooden disk. "You were expecting us?"

"Cousin Breanna sent a message this morning. A man, a woman, and two horses coming our way from Willowsbrook."

Since Lyrra had turned mute, Aiden had no choice but to be their spokesman. Besides, his curiosity was now a dreadful itch. "How could she send a message after we left and have it reach you before we did?" Could there have been a faster way? No, Breanna had escorted them to this road herself and said it was the clearest way and the easiest to follow.

The man smiled. "A whisper on the wind. A scent in the air. Not as precise as words on paper, but easy enough to read if you know how." He whistled softly. A horse trotted out of the trees, its hooves making no sound on the road.

A Fae horse? Aiden wondered. *What was a Fae horse doing here?*

"There's only a couple of miles to go before we reach the village," the man said as he mounted his horse. "If you ride behind your lady, we'll cover the distance faster, and you'll have some time to rest before the evening meal." That male smile flickered again.

When Aiden mounted behind Lyrra, she turned her head and whispered, "He thinks we're late because we stopped to make love instead of traveling."

Resting his mouth near her ear, he whispered back, "It's a reasonable assumption." And at a different time and in a different place, they might have done just that.

"How can we be late when we didn't know we were expected?"

"Lyrra." Aiden squeezed her waist lightly, well aware that the man who was now their escort might not be close enough to hear the words but was intelligent enough to guess at the conversation.

Their escort guided his horse over to them and gently tugged the packhorse's lead out of Lyrra's hand. "Why don't I lead the packhorse," he said, his eyes twinkling. "It looks like you two have your hands full as it is."

"I— I— I—" Since that was the only sound Lyrra seemed capable of making, she subsided into silent fuming, her cheeks brilliantly colored by embarrassment or temper.

Aiden just closed his eyes, considered what the Muse could do when she finally regained her ability with words, and decided he didn't want to think about it.

Their escort set his horse into an easy trot with the packhorse trotting with him, leaving Lyrra and Aiden no choice but to follow.

After a few minutes, when their escort looked back to see
what was keeping them, Aiden murmured to Lyrra, "I think
it would be wise to be a bit more friendly." Her only response
was to urge the mare forward until they were riding beside
the man.

There was one simple, common way of bringing a
stranger one step closer to possibly being a friend. "I'm
Aiden. And this is Lyrra, my wife."

"Skelly," the man replied.

Aiden waited for Lyrra to say something. Anything.

"I'm . . . in a mood," she finally said through gritted teeth.

Skelly laughed. "That's a bit like saying the sun is warm,
the rain is wet, and the wind can blow sweet or fierce. Men
are no strangers to women's moods. Even the Great Mother
has them." He glanced at her, considering.

Air whistled out from between her teeth.

"Men have moods, too," Aiden said quickly.

"Oh, that they do, and, according to women, what we lack
in variety we make up for in quantity."

Lyrra grunted. It might have been a choked-back laugh.
Aiden wasn't sure.

"A few years ago," Skelly said, "another fellow and I
were both taken with the same fair lady, and she seemed to
enjoy our company without giving a hint as to which one she
preferred. Wicked thing to do to a young man's heart—although my sweet granny would have said it wasn't our hearts
that found the young lady so compelling. Well, we did what
young men do. We strutted and bragged. We swaggered and
boasted. Annoyed the patience out of everyone around us.
After this had been going on awhile, my sweet granny took
us both over to a pasture where the rams were doing a bit of
deciding among themselves about who might be courting the
fair ewes. And she told us if we were going to act like rams
in most ways, we could settle things by butting heads the

same way the rams did, and leave the rest of the village out of it. 'Twas a sobering moment, I can tell you, when the other fellow and I looked at each other and decided the fair lady really wasn't worth a cracked head. And she wasn't worth it. While we'd been busy strutting and bragging, what did she do but go and fall in love with a quiet merchant's son who lived in another village. So the other fellow and I went to the tavern one night and drowned our mutual sorrow with a few too many tankards of ale. And I can tell you, those rams never had a headache like the ones we had the next morning."

"And what about the fair lady?" Aiden asked.

"Oh, she married her quiet merchant's son, and they've been happy ever since."

Lyrra's eyes narrowed as she turned her head to study Skelly's face. "You made that up. All of it. From the fair lady to the rams, right down to your sweet granny."

"Ah, no," Skelly protested. "I've got a sweet granny. Indeed I do. And if I'd ever been so foolish, she would have done just what I'd said."

"But you made it up," Lyrra insisted.

Skelly smiled at her. "I've been known to tell a tale or two on a winter's night. Or a summer one, if you're counting. There are some among every kind of people who hold the tales close to their hearts. And whether the Muse whispers so that I have to listen close or shouts in my ear, I still listen. And I tell the tales that come to me."

Lyrra looked as stunned as Aiden felt. Did Skelly know who they were? Did he know who *Lyrra* was? Had Breanna managed somehow to convey *that* in her message on the wind?

"So it's glad I am that cousin Breanna set you on this path. Your packhorse carries instruments, and since the Muse hasn't been whispering much lately, I'm hoping you have a few new stories and songs you'd be willing to share."

Lyrra looked down at her mare's neck. "The Muse has been whispering—and shouting for all the good it's done—but perhaps those stories aren't meant for you. Perhaps you don't need them, and that's why you don't hear them."

"Perhaps. But how can anyone know if a story is needed until it's heard?" Skelly shrugged. Looked a little uncomfortable. "I'm thinking . . . I apologize for teasing you. The stories about the Fae always make them seem so . . ."

"So much like rams?" Aiden finished dryly.

"Well," Skelly hedged. "Just more outspoken, you could say, about . . . earthier matters."

What kind of stories did witches tell about the Fae? Aiden wondered. *And how many tankards of ale would we have to tip before I could coax a couple out of him?*

"Perhaps we could trade a story for a story," Lyrra said, echoing Aiden's thought.

Skelly grinned. "There's some that will have to wait until the children are put to bed before they're told."

"I know a few of those."

"I'll hold you to that, storyteller," Skelly said. "But we're here, and it's news the family will be wanting."

"We've news to give," Aiden said, realizing how much his mood had lightened in the past few minutes now that it was once more shadowed by what was happening in the east beyond the Mother's Hills. And he hoped that, when the letters Nuala and Breanna had written to their kin and sent along with him were opened and read, there would be no one in the small village they rode into who would be grieving for lost kin.

They'd been given the guest room in a house that belonged to one of Nuala's cousins. After they'd done what everyone seemed to assume the Fae did almost every waking minute, Lyrra sighed contentedly, stretched her arms over her head—and started giggling.

"What?" Aiden said, turning his head to look at her.

"This picture of two men in a pasture, pawing the ground with their feet before running toward each other to crack their heads together just popped into my head."

"Are they naked men?" Aiden asked, rolling over to prop himself up on one elbow.

She looked thoughtful. "They should be, shouldn't they? But I can't quite seem to get them there."

"I won't say I'm disappointed."

"You would never do anything so foolish, would you?"

"I think it's safe to say I'll never try to crack another man's head with my own." But he wondered if she'd think all the nights he'd worked on a tune, hoping the song would impress her, amounted to the same thing. "Besides," he added, resting a hand on her belly, "you're taken. And I'm taken. So the only heads we have to butt are each other's."

"I think some of the ladies were disappointed to see a ring on my left hand."

"I think some of the men were equally disappointed."

She smiled at him. "We'll give them some good tunes tonight."

"The best we have."

She closed her eyes and drifted into sleep.

Aiden settled down and tried to sleep, but the songs danced through his mind.

They'd give their hosts the best songs they had—but not all of them would be joyful.

"It's an imposition, and I know it," Skelly said. "But the lad got so excited when he'd heard it was the Bard himself who was staying in the village overnight, it would have broken his heart to refuse him."

Smiling, Aiden waved off the explanation. "I've listened to plenty of apprentice minstrels. I can listen to another."

"Well, that's just it, isn't it?" Skelly said, looking uncomfortable. "He's not an apprentice minstrel. Just a boy who loves to play music."

The words pained him, but Aiden kept his smile in place. "That's how we all begin."

Maybe it *had* been a bit of head butting, as Lyrra so curtly put it when she found out, to tell Skelly that the Fae guesting in his village were the Bard and the Muse. It had certainly delighted him to see Skelly's mouth fall open—and to watch the man's eyes almost pop out of his head when he thought back to the conversation on the road and realized he'd been talking about the Muse *to* the Muse. Maybe it had been a need to let the witches know that the Fae had something to offer and didn't come down the shining roads just for their own amusement.

Whatever the reason, by the time he'd finished the tankard of ale Skelly had poured for him at the evening meal, the news had run through the village, and the small gathering that would have been held in the tavern had turned into a large gathering in the village square. Benches and blankets were being carted out of people's homes and set up to face the bench cushioned with folded blankets that he and Lyrra would use.

The wiccanfae might not think much of the Fae in general—and he wondered how different their welcome would have been if he and Lyrra hadn't been wearing the tokens Nuala had given them—but it became clear that they were hungry for the gifts the Bard and the Muse could offer.

And that cut at him. He didn't hoard his gift, didn't keep it for just the Fae. He'd come across many a human musician who just needed the spark kindled a bit for it to catch fire and truly shine. But, until a year ago, he, like the rest of the Fae, had used the shining roads in the Old Places without thinking about the people who lived in those places—when he noticed them at all.

"If the crowd that's gathering doesn't make him nervous, let him play," Aiden said.

"His nerves are dancing, and I'll be surprised if he manages to get out more than a word here and there, but I'm grateful to you for giving him the chance."

Don't be grateful for what we should have done for the people who are the Pillars of the World. Just another thing we chose to forget along the way.

With a smile, Aiden turned away to help Lyrra set out the instruments. He settled on the bench and tuned the harp. By the time he was done, his half-healed fingers were so sore, he knew he wouldn't be able to play.

The next time we come by this way, I'll play for them.

He pondered that certainty for a moment and knew it was true. They *would* come back this way to share their songs and stories.

By the time everyone had assembled, it looked like every person within shouting distance was in the village square, crowded up as close as they could get in order to hear.

In order to keep the bargain Skelly had made, some of the musicians made their way to the front of the crowd, stood a little to one side of Aiden and Lyrra, and began to play.

The first tune was a familiar one. Aiden had heard variations of it in the Clan houses as well as in human taverns. The singer was nervous, and her voice tended to fade more often than not. But the applause from the crowd gave her and her companions more confidence, and her voice was steady for the next song.

The third song was one he'd never heard before, and he

found himself leaning forward to catch the words and the tune, almost grinding his teeth when the singer kept faltering. It wasn't until Lyrra slid over and gave him a hard jab with her elbow that he realized it was his own intense stare that was unnerving the singer. He lowered his eyes and, with effort, kept himself from leaping up and demanding that she sing it again. There was time. He'd corner her later.

After the musicians, Skelly stood up and told a story about his sweet granny, who was, apparently, the stern woman sitting on the other side of the square with her hands folded and her hair scraped back into a bun that must have made her scalp ache. It made Aiden's scalp ache just looking at her. And the expression on her face was fierce enough to frighten any rational man.

Obviously, Skelly wasn't a rational man, because he continued his story, gesturing now and then toward his sweet granny. When he finally got to the punch line, the first person to burst out laughing was his granny. The laughter transformed her face, and her eyes sparkled with mischief. As she pulled the pins out of her hair, she said, "Ah, Skelly. That story gets worse every time you tell it."

Aiden heard Lyrra's soft grunt, and he knew she, too, had taken the bait without realizing there was a hook in it. Seeing the grins on the villagers' faces and how the old woman now *looked* like a sweet granny, he understood that the scraped-back hair and the fierce expression were props for Skelly's story. Something he was sure everyone else in the village had known.

Then the boy came up with his small harp. After bowing to Aiden and Lyrra, he sat on the small bench Skelly brought over for him, settled himself, and began to play a song he wrote himself.

The boy had potential. Aiden felt his Bard's gift swell with the desire to kindle that spark until it burned brightly.

The song, on other hand . . .

When the boy finished, he lowered his head. The applause from the crowd was more a response to his courage than an indication of pleasure.

Then the boy raised his head, looked Aiden in the eyes, and said, "It's not a good song."

"No, it isn't," Aiden replied gently. "But it *is* a good first effort. With time and practice, you'll write better songs." He reached for his harp.

"Aiden," Lyrra whispered fiercely. "You can't play the harp yet. Your fingers aren't healed."

"They're healed well enough for this song." He set his fingers on the strings, suppressed a wince, plucked the first chord, and sang.

He watched the boy's eyes widen in disbelief and disappointment—and something close to hope. He watched the adult faces in the crowd settle into a painfully polite expression. And he knew by the look on Lyrra's face that she would, at that moment, gladly deny knowing him.

It was, if one wanted to be kind, a bad song. And he sang all five verses and their refrains.

When he was done, he handed the harp to Lyrra, flexed his painfully sore hands, and smiled at the boy. "That was the first song I ever wrote. I was about your age. But with time and practice, I've gotten a bit better." He took a breath and began to sing "The Green Hills of Home." It was a song about a traveler, alone and lonely, yearning for a place far away. It was a song about a man, alone and lonely, yearning for the lover who wasn't there. He'd written it over the winter, when he'd been traveling and Lyrra had been at Brightwood.

Her voice joined his, harmonizing. She didn't even try to play the harp, so there was nothing but their voices, filled with the same remembered yearning.

When the last note faded, he watched people brush away tears—and felt the sting of tears in his own eyes.

Lyrra began plucking a simple tune on the harp, something that had no words. Aiden chose one of the whistles and joined her, letting the song flow through him. They used it as a transition song, when the audience needed time to settle again. Then he sang the song about the Black Coats—and watched the adult faces turn grim. Lyrra followed it with the poem about witches that he'd set to music. After that, they did a few romantic songs, gradually moving toward songs that were lighter and humorous. By the time they got to "The Mouse Song," people were grinning and stifling chuckles—but a lot of them seemed to be watching something over Aiden's shoulder.

That's when he felt the presence of something moving softly behind him, coming closer and closer. He could almost feel the heat from a body, warm breath against his cheek. His nerves jumped, but he didn't turn around. If there were some danger, surely the people watching would give him warning.

Lyrra glanced around. Her eyes widened. She choked back a laugh and kept on singing. But she couldn't manage the annoyed tone she usually did with that song.

When they finished, Aiden slowly turned his head toward the warm breath just above his left shoulder. He stared at the black muzzle, the nostrils breathing in his scent. He looked up into a brown eye. He noticed the pricked ears. Slowly raising one hand, he rested it lightly on the muzzle, and whispered, "A dark horse. It's a dark horse."

"A herd of them came up from the south last summer," Skelly's granny said. "A few stayed in the southern end of the Mother's Hills. The rest kept moving north. Some of them wintered here. When spring came, they continued heading north. All but this one."

Aiden twisted on the bench to get a better look at the animal. The dark horses had disappeared after Ahern, the Lord of the Horse, died last summer. Fae horses were more intelligent than human horses, and the dark horses—Ahern's "special" horses—were the most intelligent of all. None of the Fae had been able to find out what happened to them. Had Ahern given some last command that had sent them into the Mother's Hills instead of going up one of the shining roads to Tir Alainn? Or had it been instinct that had driven them here?

"Who does he belong to?" Aiden asked.

"No one," Skelly replied. "I've had a saddle on him a time or two, and he's well trained. But he's made it clear he wasn't for any of us. We've had the impression he's been waiting for something."

"Sing another song, Bard," Skelly's granny said. "Sing another song."

Lyrra quietly plucked the introduction to "Love's Jewels." Aiden sang, unable to turn away from the horse focused so intently on him. Seeing a dark horse, remembering Ahern, it made the events of last summer flood back, and by the time he'd reached the last line of the song, his throat was tight.

"I'm sorry," Aiden said to the horse. "I can't sing any more tonight."

The horse snorted softly, a disappointed sound.

"There will be time enough to sing him another tune," Skelly said, smiling.

Puzzled, Aiden turned toward the man.

"Looks to me like he's chosen his rider," Skelly said. "And you have a horse."

Chapter Fifteen

It was late afternoon when Morag, Ashk, the merchant captain, and his two men crested the low hill and looked down on the tidy village spilling out from the bottom of the hills toward the harbor and the deep blue of the sea. A little ways out, a string of islands formed a breakwall that protected the harbor from the sea's moods.

To Morag's untrained eye, the harbor looked like the sort of place sailors would be keen to tuck their ships into when they weren't out earning their living on the water. So why weren't there more than two large ships moored to the docks? Why did all the boats but those two look like small fishing boats?

And what was it about this tidy village that bothered her?

She glanced at Mihail, saw the way he flinched while trying to pretend he didn't notice that glance. He'd been tense and taciturn all through the journey back to this village. The tension had increased as they got closer—and the shadows continued to flicker across his face.

She suppressed a sigh. She'd hoped those shadows would go away once they'd left Padrick's estate, hoped that whatever trouble might draw Death to this man had been left behind. But the shadows had remained, no more constant than they'd been when she'd first seen them, but there nonetheless.

She hoped the kindness that had guided him to take the

books from the bookseller in the first place and then make the journey to Padrick's house wouldn't be repaid with pain.

Ashk had ordered the footmen to put the boxes of books in the library. After her reluctant guests had gone to bed, she and Morag had gone back to the library and opened the boxes.

Women's names stamped on the books' covers below the titles. All women. And only one copy of each work. But as the two of them opened the boxes, wiping away stray tears now and then, they'd realized the bookseller had tried to gather up as many as he could to save them from being confiscated by the magistrate's guards and burned.

Only one precious copy of each work. There might be others, tucked away in gentry libraries throughout Sylvalan. If, somehow, the spread of the Black Coats' poisoned words could be stopped, perhaps other copies would escape the fire. But if they were lost, the stories those women had shaped out of words and heart would exist only in that room where she and Ashk had sat, both of them wondering if those writers would find some comfort in knowing their stories were still in the world.

As they descended toward the village, Morag noticed the other things. Scattered houses surrounded by pastureland where cows, horses, and sheep grazed. Other houses with large plots of plowed land full of the bright green of young plants.

Did the humans in this village divide their skills and the goods this way? Did some raise the cattle for the milk, meat, and leather while others raised sheep for wool and meat, and still others did the spinning and weaving to supply the cloth for the clothes they'd all wear?

Whatever curiosity she had about the humans who lived here vanished when she looked to her right and saw the stream that tumbled down the hills to feed a tiny lake. The mouth of the lake dropped in a series of small waterfalls before the stream reclaimed the water and finished making its way down to the sea. But it was the odd gathering of stones on one side of the waterfall that captured Morag's attention as well as the attention of Mihail and his men. She reined in to take a longer look at the same time Mihail halted the wagon.

Ashk, who had been riding a little ahead of them, looked back and grinned, then rode back to join them. "Those are fish stairs."

Morag gave Ashk a stare of her own.

Ashk's grin widened. "Fish stairs," she repeated. "While the salmon are fine leapers, especially when they have the incentive to return to their home stream to spawn, only the strongest were managing to get back up the falls and return to the stream. At some point, someone argued that, while it was a fine thing for the best leapers to get back to the spawning grounds to breed, if they found some way for the second-best leapers to make it back to the spawning grounds, there would be more fish to catch and eat and sell. And a salmon doesn't have to be the best leaper in the world to taste good. So they built the stairs—and the fish have shown abundant gratitude ever since."

"It's a marvelous idea," Mihail said. "It's a wonder I've never seen the likes of it before."

"All it takes to build one is muscle and desire—or a connection with earth and water," Ashk said.

Morag watched Mihail's face change from open curiosity to shuttered tension. What had there been in Ashk's last comment that he heard as a threat?

They rode silently down into the village, and as they passed the oddly clustered houses and shops, Morag noticed the number of villagers who came to their doors to study the strangers—and then follow them down to the harbor. Mihail and his men noticed, but Ashk, who usually paid attention to everything, ignored the growing crowd.

By the time they reached the harbor, Mihail was so tense, it was almost unbearable to be near him. There was already a crowd of hard-eyed men near the long pier where one of the larger ships was moored.

Morag shifted in her saddle. Those men glanced at her, then averted their eyes. She suspected that meant they recognized who she was. Good. Perhaps they would think twice about causing any trouble while the Gatherer rode in their midst.

A man stepped forward and placed one hand on the cart horse's reins. "I can take him for you now," he told Mihail.

After murmuring his thanks, Mihail climbed down from the cart, his eyes on his ship—and on the two boys standing at the bow waving to him. He lifted his hand to return the greeting, but Morag saw worry in his eyes.

Mihail turned to Ashk, who had dismounted and was now studying him calmly. "Lady Ashk," he said, giving her a small bow as any merchant would when addressing a baron's wife. "I thank you for your hospitality, but now it is time for us to continue on our journey."

The only warning was a sudden gust of wind a moment before one of the men shouted, "Captain!"

Morag looked toward the sea. Felt her breath catch.

The wave rose out of the water. Rose and rose until it was twice the height of the merchant ship's tallest mast—and headed straight for Mihail's ship.

"NO!" he cried. He tried to turn, to run to his ship, but men roughly grabbed him and his two men, preventing them from going anywhere.

Morag started to turn toward them, not sure of what she intended, when Ashk gripped her arm.

Feeling ill from her own restrained fury, Morag watched

the wave, heard the frightened cries of the two boys and the other men on the ship.

And she saw the young woman suddenly appear on deck. She looked toward the docks, looked directly at Mihail, then lifted her hands as she turned to face the wave.

It kept coming toward the ship, but slower now. Slower.

The woman faced it, her hair blowing in the wind, her hands raised.

The wave stopped, a deadly curve of water foaming white at its crest.

Morag wondered if she was the only one who heard Mihail whisper, "Jenny." She couldn't tell how long the woman and the wave faced each other before the wave slowly, quietly sank back into the sea, leaving nothing more than ripples to gently rock the boats.

The woman lowered her arms. Sank to the deck as the crew and the two boys rushed to her side.

Ashk snarled, "A *witch* is part of your cargo? You neglected to mention *that*."

Now Morag gripped Ashk's arm, unsure what the other woman intended. She *knew* Ashk had no objections to witches, so something else must have sparked that temper.

"She isn't cargo," Mihail snapped with more heat than prudence.

"But she *is* a powerful witch," another voice said.

Everyone turned to the dark-cloaked woman as she pushed the hood off so that her white hair gleamed in the sun.

"Cordell," Ashk murmured, shaking off Morag's restraining hand.

"What difference does it make that she's a witch?" Mihail said, his voice full of anger and desperation. "She does no harm with her gifts, no matter what the Black Coats say."

Cordell started to reply, but her attention was caught by something happening on the ship.

Morag watched the woman, Jenny, shake off the hands helping her, then march to the other side of the ship, where she disappeared over the side. A few moments later, she strode along the pier and shoved her way through the crowd until she was standing a step ahead of Mihail, facing Cordell, who had a little smile playing on her lips.

"How dare you break the creed we live by?" Jenny shouted.

"Jennyfer," Mihail said softly, warningly.

"And what creed is that?" Cordell asked politely.

"Do no harm," Jenny snapped.

"We cannot always live by that creed," Cordell said. "Not if we would protect what we love."

"That may be so, but we did nothing to deserve *that*." Jenny flung out one arm, her hand pointing to the harbor. A fountain of water burst out of the harbor, then spilled back down, creating more ripples to rock the boats. She didn't notice what she'd done any more than she noticed the villagers' sudden wariness as they watched her. "We came here to deliver goods to an inland baron. While my brother made the delivery, the rest of us stayed on the ship so that we wouldn't soil your precious village. Well, the delivery is made, and you have no right to hold us here."

"Brother?" Ashk said quietly, studying him carefully.

Mihail jerked free of the men holding him. He took a step forward so that he stood side by side with Jenny. His hand brushed hers. Held on.

"Yes, I'm her brother. And proud to be so."

Cordell looked toward the ship. "And the boys? Are they yours?" She shook her head. "No, you're too young for them to be yours."

"They're my—our—older brother's sons," Mihail said reluctantly.

Cordell pursed her lips as she watched Jennyfer. "You connect with the sea."

"I love the sea," Jenny said.

Cordell nodded. "I felt the song of your power in the tides, but when you didn't leave the ship and make yourself known to the villagers . . . I apologize for any fright I gave you and the others on the ship. If you hadn't stopped the wave before it reached the ship, I would have. It was meant to draw you out, to find out how you would react."

"Now you know," Jenny said, anger still simmering in her voice.

"Now I know." Cordell gestured toward the cart. "The cart isn't elegant, but it will do. Come with me. Let the boys come, too. No harm will come to them." Her lips curved in an amused smile. "As I will it."

"We should get back to the ship," Mihail said.

"You have to wait for the tide in any case, so you may as well take a look at our 'precious village.' "

Judging by the carefully blank looks on Mihail's and Jenny's faces, Morag wasn't certain they would have to wait for the tide, but she couldn't see how they'd be able to reach their ship or get out of the harbor safely unless she was willing to gather the souls of half the village to give them a fighting chance. And she would never be able to justify taking so many lives—especially, she realized, when the shadows were no longer flickering on Mihail's face.

"Ashk," she said softly.

Ashk shook her head. "It's out of our hands now."

They waited for Mihail's men to return to the ship and escort the boys to their uncle. When the boys were introduced to Ashk, they bowed with great dignity, then spoiled the effect by grinning at her and asking if Evan had gotten the horse he'd wanted.

"Yes, he did," Ashk replied with sour amusement before mounting her horse.

Morag mounted her dark horse while Cordell was carefully helped into the driver's seat beside the village man who took the reins. Mihail, Jenny, and the boys climbed into the back. The crowd moved aside to let the cart pass.

Thinking this would be a tense and futile tour, Morag got her next lesson about dealing with children in the human world.

"Uncle Mihail," one of the boys said excitedly. "We saw little selkies."

"We did!" said the other. "They were swimming around the ship."

"We wanted to go down to the pier so we could talk to them better, but Jenny wouldn't let us." He gave his aunt a dark look. "We wouldn't have hurt anything."

"We pointed out the ship's name, *Sweet Selkie,* that was written on the stern and told them how we got to name your ship."

"And they got to swim in the harbor. *We* didn't get to swim in the harbor." Wounded, mutinous looks at both aunt and uncle.

Morag noticed how hard Ashk was pressing her lips together in an effort to keep a straight face. She noticed the way Jenny and Mihail just rolled their eyes, as if they'd heard this complaint at every port. And she noticed the slight shaking in the driver's shoulders, and wondered how long the man would be able to suppress his laughter.

"And *they* don't have to go to school and have lessons," one of the boys said.

"Oh, but they do," Cordell said, turning in the seat. Her eyes danced with laughter, but she kept her expression admirably serious. "For how else can a young selkie grow up to be a good selkie?"

The boys' mouths fell open. "They do?"

"Of course. If they don't learn their numbers, how can they report to the fishermen to tell them how big a school of fish is? If they don't know compass bearings, how can they tell where the fish are? And don't they need to learn what kinds of fish are good to eat and which should be avoided? And what is safe and what can harm them? And while it's the bards who create the songs, if the little ones don't learn to sing them, how will they remember who they are and where they came from? No, there's much a little selkie has to learn."

That managed to silence the boys for a noticeable few seconds. Then, "But they still get to swim in the harbor when the lessons are done."

Cordell nodded. "There is truth in what you say, but not all of us can be selkies."

Before the boys could reply, Cordell began pointing out things in the village. The women in this family baked the finest bread. The men in that family tanned leather. This family did spinning and weaving. That family had skilled seamstresses and tailors. Someone else made candles. Another was the blacksmith.

Clusters of neat cottages that continued to tug at Morag. The village just didn't look quite . . . *right* . . . somehow, and yet she was certain if it was in a different place, she would know why it also looked familiar.

Then she realized Ashk was watching her as well as watching Mihail and his family's reaction to the village.

At the edge of the village, on a little rise of its own, they stopped at a sprawling stone building. Cordell climbed out of the cart and waved at them to join her as she walked to the wrought-iron gates.

Following behind the rest of them, Morag walked through the wide passageway to a lovely but neglected courtyard.

The house surrounded it except for the passageway leading to the street and an archway in one back corner. Doors on each side, opening into the courtyard.

Cordell led them through the archway. Another courtyard. More doors. And a couple of arched gates leading out to the stables and the back gardens.

A comfortable place, Morag thought. Which made her wonder why no one lived there.

Cordell didn't take them into the house itself. When they'd seen the courtyards and had a glimpse of the grounds, she led them back to the cart.

"What do you think of it?" Cordell asked, looking at Jenny as they rode back to the harbor.

"It's lovely," Jenny replied. "A grand and sprawling home with room and more for a lively family." She hesitated. "But no one lives there."

"No," Cordell said quietly. "No one lives there anymore. It needs loving hands—and laughter and songs filling its courtyards again." She paused. "Would it suit you and yours?"

Jenny stared at her.

"Baron Padrick wrote to me and mine about a merchant captain who was looking for a safe harbor for his family's ships . . . and his family." Cordell looked pointedly at Mihail, then at Ashk, who nodded. "Even in this part of Sylvalan, we've heard bits of things about these Black Coats. Enough to understand why you'd have cause to worry, and why you'd want another place to go if you need to run. Well, I'm a Crone now, and while I don't expect to be journeying with the Gatherer for some years yet"—she shot an amused and knowing look at Morag—"I'd feel easier if there was another of the Mother's Daughters here who felt a kinship with the sea."

"Aren't there any other witches around here?" Jenny asked cautiously.

"There are. But not every witch whose branch is water feels comfortable with the moods of the sea. There are those who are more attuned to the rivers and streams, to the ponds and the lakes. Not that they *can't* command water wherever it is, but we all follow our hearts to the right places. My own daughter, like my mother, may the Great Mother hold them both gently, had the gift of earth, and she was happy in the Old Place where she lived. But the brooks and streams . . . I had little to offer them, nor did they have what I needed. For me, it was the sea. I think it's much the same with you."

Jenny nodded.

"So. If you want it, you have a place to live and a safe harbor for your ships." Cordell hesitated, actually seemed uncomfortable for a moment. "The only question is, will you be comfortable with your neighbors?"

Morag felt the tension rise again. But not from Jenny or Mihail. It was the driver who tensed.

"I am not the only witch in my family," Jenny said slowly. "I think the question is whether or not our new neighbors could accept a family like ours."

"No," Cordell said in an odd voice. "That's not the question."

The crowd was still at the harbor, waiting. When they heard the cart, they turned to face it.

A jolt went through Morag, and she understood why the village looked different. Some of the villagers still looked human. But more—many more now that they'd dropped the glamour—had the pointed ears and feral quality of the Fae that gave even a plain face a kind of beauty.

"They're Fae," Mihail whispered.

Morag looked at Ashk, who returned the look calmly.

She knew all along. Of course she knew. Just as she knew

*that if the people here had perceived Mihail and his ship as
a threat, he and his people would have never left the harbor
alive.*

"Yes," Cordell said quietly. "They are Fae. The Old Place
is Ronat Isle, the largest island, and many make their home
there—as I do. But there have been humans and Fae who
have made this harbor their home for generations. Over time,
they built a village together. And they made families together
until it's impossible to say, 'This family is Fae, and this one
is human.' We don't bother with such things here. This is our
home, and we are its people. The question is, is a Daughter
of the House of Gaian willing to walk among them as friend
and neighbor?"

Jenny stared at the villagers. They stared back at her. She
glanced at Mihail, but he lowered his eyes and kept his expression carefully neutral. Even the boys knew enough to
keep silent.

It was Jenny's decision. Morag knew that as well as Mihail and the villagers did. They wanted *her* and her affinity to
the sea, but they would welcome any family she brought with
her.

Jenny took a deep breath, let it out slowly. Her smile was
a little self-conscious as she said, "If some of my new neighbors would be willing to lend a hand to clean up a couple of
rooms, the boys and I can settle in while Mihail and *Sweet
Selkie* go back to fetch some of the others." She bit her lip,
and her face paled a little.

Mihail reached out, rested a hand on her arm. "I'll bring
them to safe harbor, Jenny. Those who haven't already left to
visit kin, I'll bring them to safe harbor."

"Done then," Cordell said, climbing out of the cart. "If
you brought anything with you, let's get it unloaded so your
brother can be on his way." She smiled mischievously at Mihail. "And since my other branch of the Mother is air, I can

promise you fair winds and calm seas for the start of your journey."

While Mihail and several men headed for the ship and several women began the brisk business of deciding with Jenny what she and the boys would need, Ashk eased her horse out of the crowd. Morag followed.

"The shadows," Ashk said abruptly. "Do you still see them on his face?"

"No." *She's tired,* Morag thought. *This was harder for her than she allowed anyone to see.* "You weren't sure they'd be accepted."

"I wasn't sure," Ashk agreed. "Or that he could accept what he found here. And while I suspected there had been at least one witch in his family somewhere along the line, I hadn't suspected he had *quite* that strong a tie to the House of Gaian. But I thought, when it came to the villagers here deciding about him, his eyes would be in his favor, and I was right about that."

"His eyes?"

"He has woodland eyes, Morag. So do those boys. So does Jenny. A witch's eyes. Anyone who has those eyes has a bit of the House of Gaian running through their veins."

Like you, Morag thought, looking at Ashk.

"Come along," Ashk said, brushing her heels against her horse's sides. "There's a tavern nearby. The family lives above it, but they keep a couple of rooms set aside for guests—and they serve a decent meal. We can stay there tonight and get a fresh start in the morning. Besides, once Jenny and the boys are settled, Cordell will want to speak with me."

"Cordell." Morag stiffened when she finally made the connection. "She's Neall's grandmother."

"Yes. She'll want news of him and Ari."

"I thought she didn't care."

"I thought so, too, for a long time. But hearing her talk to Jenny . . . I wonder if she hadn't been right all along. Nora had loved Bretonwood, and Cordell needed the sea. She could have taken her daughter to the Old Place here, but it wouldn't have been the same. Not for Nora. Bretonwood was where her heart lived."

Morag hesitated, then said, "I wonder if Ari regrets leaving Brightwood."

Ashk shook her head. "She came to a place that needed her, welcomed her."

"Like Jenny."

"Like Jenny."

When they reached the tavern, the young man who came out to lead the horses to the stables around back barely glanced at either of them—but he beamed and cooed to the horses.

"Well," Ashk said as she slung her saddlebags over one shoulder and strode to the tavern door. "That puts me in my place."

Morag just laughed softly.

They kept the conversation light that evening, even spent a little time listening to the village minstrel who often played in the tavern. And if they were wondering what was happening at the barons' council or whether Mihail would get back in time to get the rest of his family safely out of the east, neither voiced the thoughts, giving each other the gift of silence.

Chapter Sixteen

Ubel stepped away from the other five Inquisitors and the young forester they'd captured. Not much more than a boy, really. All it had taken was a little of the Inquisitor's Gift of persuasion to coax the lad deep into the woods on Baron Padrick's estate. He would have liked to take their captive farther away, but he'd been impatient to wring information out of the boy.

Just as well. The boy had broken so quickly under the first level of softening, he'd spilled out disjointed answers to every question they'd asked.

The result was frustrating, and he was still trying to sort through the boy's words to fit them into something that made sense.

The baron had not yet returned home from the barons' council. That was good. The baron's wife was also not at home, nor were the baron's two children. The boy had been clear about that much.

But every time Ubel had asked about the baron's wife, the boy had babbled about a Lady Ashk, one of the Fae who lived at the Clan house in the Old Place nearby.

The Fae didn't have Clan houses in the Old Places. Everyone knew that. They lived in Tir Alainn and came down the shining roads for brief visits to the human world—at least, until those visits were stopped by destroying the magic in the Old Place.

When he'd pressed further about this female living in the Old Place, the boy had babbled about a witch living there. *That* made sense, and the news had excited him. Master Adolfo had told him that he and his men couldn't afford to linger at any of the Old Places they might pass on their way to Breton, so they'd been forced to allow the Evil One's servants to continue soiling the world. But a witch who lived so close to Breton . . . That was different. They could take care of *her* at the same time they dealt with the baron's wife and children.

The baron's wife. Was it possible Padrick had actually *married* one of the Fae and *that's* why the boy babbled about Clan houses? While the thought of using one of those creatures for physical pleasure was titillating in a disgusting sort of way, acknowledging her as a *person* and, worse, raising the offspring that had come from such matings as if they were decent humans was obscene.

Perhaps she *did* have a cottage in the Old Place where she stayed when she was tired of pretending to be human. Perhaps that was what the boy had meant by a Clan house. Perhaps there *were* other Fae who lived there with her. Whenever the baron was away, she probably acted the bitch in heat for any Fae male who wanted her. She couldn't do *that* in the baron's own house. Even a man lacking in decency—as Padrick surely did, since no decent man would have helped that bastard Liam escape his rightful punishment—wouldn't tolerate being cuckolded in front of the people he ruled.

Ubel studied the trees around him. Too many. Too close. Too alive. If there *were* some Fae living in the Old Place, then every bird, every deer, every rustling sound in the woods might be the enemy in animal form. Which meant they had to strike swiftly and thoroughly.

Tomorrow. The boy had said the baron's wife was expected back tomorrow. But there was still one thing they could do today.

The magic in the nearby Old Place was so strong, it seeped beyond the borders, spilling out into Padrick's land. There was more than enough here for him and the other Inquisitors to draw on, and what they would create would plague Fae and human alike.

"Ubel?" one of the Inquisitors asked. "What should we do with this one?"

Ubel looked back at the boy on the ground, bound hand and foot, a scold's bridle keeping him silent. "We can't let him go, so I see no reason why you shouldn't test all the instruments on him to be sure they're in good working order. After that, we'll dispose of him."

Master Adolfo had trained them all too well for them to act like children who had just been given a treat. But their eyes glittered with anticipation as they opened their saddlebags to carefully set out the rest of the instruments they'd brought with them.

As their leader, Ubel felt he couldn't join them, so he walked far enough away so that his presence wouldn't inhibit them. That's what Master Adolfo would have done.

By tomorrow at this time, the task would be completed, and Baron Padrick would come home to the lesson of what happened to men who tried to thwart the will of Adolfo, the Master Inquisitor, the Witch's Hammer.

Chapter Seventeen

Ashk slanted a glance at Morag. Who would have thought a couple swallows of ale too many could wash away all that reserve? "Headache still bothering you?" she asked kindly.

Morag shook her head. "I was thinking of Jenny. I hope she'll be comfortable in the village."

"She and the boys will settle in just fine," Ashk said. "And she'll have plenty of help getting the house ready for the rest of her family."

"I noticed the help," Morag replied. "So did her brother when the young man from the dairy farm showed up this morning with milk and butter, and one of the sons from the baker's family showed up with fresh bread and sweet buns, and a son from the butcher's family showed up with—"

Ashk burst out laughing. "They seemed like fine young men who won't be looking to be more than friendly and help-ful—at least until their sisters or female cousins have a chance to find out if there's a special man Jenny's waiting to have join her."

"I'm not sure her brother felt so reassured by all the help-fulness."

"She's a witch, and she can command the sea. No one in that village is going to overstep any boundaries Jenny chooses to set." Ashk hesitated. "What about Mihail?"

"I saw no shadows on his face this morning, nor any on

the faces of his crew. That doesn't mean Death isn't waiting for him somewhere along the journey, only that it wasn't close."

Ashk nodded. "Then we'll hope for an easy journey and a quick return to safe harbor. But I could see the worry in his eyes."

"Not for himself," Morag said quietly. "For Jenny. It isn't easy to leave a sister when all you can do is trust that she'll remain safe and well—especially when you know it's quite possible that she'll be neither."

Ashk didn't reply. Wasn't certain what she could say. The ale last night had loosened Morag's tongue enough that she'd talked about her sister, Morphia. It hadn't taken much effort for Ashk to hear what wasn't being said: Morag's gift had shown long before she'd actually become the Gatherer, and her Clan, without doing it intentionally, had made her keenly aware that she was an outsider, someone whose gift made the rest of them uncomfortable. Everyone except Morphia.

An outsider among her own. Ashk understood how that felt. She'd been one in her own Clan, which is why her grandfather had brought her to Bretonwood. His home Clan, before he'd left to live with his mate's Clan as was the Fae custom when a man and woman made a pledge to each other that was meant to last more than a season.

An outsider among her own, she'd found family in Neall's parents, Nora and Kief, and, later, with Padrick and the children they'd made together. She hoped Morag would find the same with Ari and Neall . . . and with her. She hadn't realized how much she and Morag had in common. Perhaps getting a little drunk and sentimental together was a fine step toward becoming good friends.

Words have shadows, too, Ashk thought. *They can hide as much as they reveal. Perhaps the first step in becoming good friends is mine to take, to tell her what I think she already senses but doesn't yet understand.* She saw the curve in the road. They had almost reached the place where this road joined the road that led to Bretonwood. Perhaps this was a good time to say the words that would bring some things into the light.

"Morag—"

Ashk suddenly reined in at the same moment Morag did, both of them listening, searching.

"Something's wrong," Ashk said softly. "There's something here that doesn't belong."

"Death is whispering," Morag said just as softly. "But I'm not being summoned in any particular direction."

Ashk hesitated for a moment, torn between loyalties. If Padrick were home, he would take care of his people and she would take care of hers. She could ride to the manor house, but if there *was* trouble, what could she do there? Wasn't that the very reason Padrick had insisted the children stay with her in the Clan house?

"Let's go home," she said grimly.

The two Fae horses surged forward and galloped down the road, stride for stride. A short time later, they reached the Clan house. Seeing the way the Fae dropped whatever they were working on and hurried toward her and Morag, she knew her abrupt return had been the only disturbance. But there was *something* out there that didn't belong.

She dismounted, told her horse to walk and cool down. Heard Morag tell the dark horse the same thing.

"Has there been any trouble here?" she asked.

The Fae who had gathered around her shook their heads.

"Well," one of the men said, "that groom from the manor house rode by this morning. Seems that one of Forrester's apprentices went missing yesterday. Forrester thought the boy might have met up with a couple of our lads and abandoned his duties in order to go fishing or have a bit of fun. When the boy hadn't returned at dusk, Forrester started to go out to look for him, but he said there was something about the feel of the woods that made him uneasy about sending men out when the light was going. The groom showed up here soon after first light to see if the boy had taken shelter with us or with Ari and Neall."

"Was the boy found?" Ashk asked, feeling worry flutter in her stomach.

The man shook his head.

"Could he—?" *You're thinking like a worried mother. That won't help anyone.* "Could he have run away?"

The man gave her a curious look. "To go where? From what the groom said, the boy came from one of the tenant farms and saw his family often enough that he wouldn't be pining for home. He liked his work, and Forrester is a fair man with those who work under him. So is the baron."

Which meant there was some other reason for the boy not returning last night. An injury, perhaps. Something that had made it impossible for him to get back to the manor house on his own.

Ashk looked at Morag. The Gatherer's grim expression didn't change.

A crow flew toward them, landed nearby, and changed into a Fae youth. "There's a pony cart heading this way."

"Everyone go back to what you were doing," Ashk said. She saw Morag walk over to the large outdoor table where members of the Clan often ate or worked. She joined Morag, settling beside her on the bench. "Anything?"

Morag shook her head. "Death is waiting."

Ashk almost asked if that was a good thing; then she realized it was wishful thinking. Whatever Morag heard or felt through her gift had become stronger. Death was now a certainty, but they still didn't know where or who it would touch.

The pony cart came in sight. Stopped where the road flowed into the sun-dappled space the Clan used as an outdoor living area—what Padrick, with a smile in his eyes, said was the Fae's equivalent to the manor house's front lawn.

Ashk didn't recognize the young man driving the cart, but she knew the farmer who got down and headed toward her with a cloth-wrapped bundle in his hands. Barry was one of Padrick's tenant farmers. He and his wife had two grown sons, and an adolescent daughter who still lived at home. The sons, who lived in their own cottages with their wives and young families, worked the land with their father and took their share of the profits.

As Barry approached the table where she and Morag sat, Ashk noticed two of her Clan's men set aside their work and wander over. Nothing unusual about that—unless you noticed one of them held a walking stick stout enough to double as a club and the other had an arrow loosely nocked in his bow.

"A good day to you, ladies," Barry said.

"A good day to you," Ashk replied. Barry had married later in his life, after his father had died and he'd taken over the tenant farm. So he was a fair number of years older than she and had the lined, grizzled look of a man who'd spent his life outdoors. But he hadn't looked *old*. Not old in the stooped, shrunken way he looked now. Before she could ask him if something was wrong, he jerked his head toward the pony cart.

"My cousin's boy," he said. "Works as some kind of clerk in one of the larger towns. Needed a bit of country air, so he came here for a visit." He shifted a little, effectively cutting off Ashk's view of the young man—and his view of her—and just as effectively putting his young kinsman directly in Morag's line of sight.

"Since he's visiting, my wife did some extra baking.

Made a couple loaves of her special sweet bread." Barry looked directly at Morag; then he set the cloth bundle on the table and unwrapped it to reveal a loaf of the bread. "Lady Ashk is partial to my wife's sweet bread. We'd heard she's been away and was expected back today, so my wife told me to bring this on over to welcome her home. When she gets home, you be sure to give it to her." He reached out, tore off a small corner of the bread. Popped it into his mouth, chewed a couple of times, then swallowed. And stared at Morag. "Lady Ashk sure is partial to my wife's sweet bread."

Morag didn't move, didn't answer. Simply stared back at him.

Ashk frowned at Barry. Why was he talking as if she wasn't there, as if she hadn't returned to the Clan house yet? Had he suffered some kind of brain seizure that had left him confused?

Barry brushed a finger against the brim of his cap. "Good day to you."

He hurried back to the cart before Ashk had a chance to thank him for the bread. When he climbed onto the seat and looked at her, she reached out, intending to pinch off a corner of the bread and eat it so that he would know she appreciated the gift.

Morag slapped her hand so hard she jerked back, feeling like a child who'd been caught trying to snitch something from the kitchen.

"You know better than that," Morag said loudly, angrily. She stood up and tossed the cloth back over the bread, covering it. "Lady Ashk is always willing to share, but it's custom that she gets the first slice. No one is going to touch this until she gets home."

Ashk stared at Morag. Was the woman still drunk? Had she been in the sun too long today on the journey back from the harbor? Was she having some kind of brain seizure, too, that she couldn't remember who she'd just spent the day with?

A little stunned, Ashk looked at the men in the pony cart—and saw the way Barry's kinsman, wide-eyed and pale, looked at Morag before slapping the reins across the pony's back and returning to Barry's farm with more speed than prudence.

As soon as the cart was out of sight, Ashk stood up, pushing the bench hard enough to knock it over. "What's wrong with you?" The queer fury in Morag's dark eyes made her uneasy.

"There are shadows on his face," Morag snapped. "They weren't there when he arrived. They weren't there until he ate the bread."

A chill brushed over Ashk. She looked at the covered loaf of bread.

"He knows who I am," Morag continued. "He knows *what* I am. That's why he ate it. So I would see what only I would see. And warn you."

The chill was still there, but it had turned into calm ice. Ashk recognized the feeling. Accepted it. Understood she was about to walk in the darker shadows of the woods. "He'll die?"

Morag didn't answer the question. "And that other man? I doubt he's any kin. He, too, recognized what I was—and he has reason to fear me. I think he's one of the Black Coats."

Ashk didn't ask why Morag thought that—especially when Morag half turned, and whispered, "Ari."

"Go," Ashk said. "You take care of Ari and Neall. I'll take care of Barry's 'kinsman.' "

Morag changed into her raven form and flew away, heading toward Ari and Neall's cottage. Her dark horse galloped after her.

Once more, the Fae had dropped their work and hurried

toward her. She wondered if they saw the same queer fury in her eyes that she'd seen in Morag's. She picked up the bread, shoved it into a woman's hands. "Lock that up for the moment. Don't allow anyone to eat it, not so much as a crumb." She pointed at two other women. "Gather the children and get them into the Clan house. None of them go out until I give consent. Get the elders inside, too." She pointed to others, giving orders. "Take some men. One group goes to Ari's cottage to help Morag; the other goes to the manor house. Warn them there may be Black Coats among us. Two of you go on to the village. Tell the magistrate so he can call out his guards. Some of the youths can go out to the tenant farms and give the warning."

"Will you sound the horn?" one of the men asked.

If she did, it would be heard far beyond the boundaries of the Clan house. But would the Inquisitors know what it meant? "Bring it."

A youth ran to the Clan house while some of the men and women changed into their other shapes and ran or flew to Barry's or headed out for the other farms to give the warning about the Inquisitors' presence. Others quickly saddled horses, gathered up bows and crossbows.

Ashk mounted her horse, took her bow and the quiver full of arrows from one of her huntsmen. The youth returned from the Clan house, held up the horn.

In anyone else's hands, it was just a hunting horn. In the hands of a Lord or Lady of the Woods, its notes could command anything and everything that belonged to the woods.

Ashk took a deep breath to steady herself. *Grandfather, stay away. Don't answer the horn.* A futile wish, but she made it anyway as she drew upon the gift that was hers and put the horn to her lips.

Flocks of birds exploded from the trees, taking wild flight, obeying commands as old as the woods. Some circled the Clan house. Others headed for Barry's farm.

As she blew the horn again, summoning, commanding, she felt the pulse of life responding to it. The woods had come alive. And the woods were angry.

She attached the horn to a ring on her saddle, pressed her heels into her horse's sides, and galloped toward Barry's farm. She didn't know if there was any way to save the man, but she wouldn't let the Black Coats have his family.

When they reached the farm, she saw two horses circling fearfully in the small paddock next to the barn. She heard the pony's terrified neighs. And she saw the saddled Fae horse dancing and rearing just outside the barn, holding three wolves at bay.

Her huntsmen circled the cottage on their silent horses. She reined in her horse a few feet away from the partially opened front door. A man's foot, shod in an old work boot, lay across the threshold. Barry hadn't even been able to get all the way inside the cottage before whatever was in the bread—or something else—brought him down.

Ashk dismounted, nocked an arrow in her bow. As she approached the door, she heard a woman's tearful voice saying, "Stop. Please stop."

She kicked the door, ready to leap into the room. It opened halfway before hitting something that stopped it. She stepped on Barry's legs to get through the opening, twisting around toward the voice as soon as she got past the door. She pulled the bowstring back.

Her arms shook with the effort. Her eyes refused to stay open and focused.

She bit her lip until it bled, using the pain to force herself to remain clear-sighted.

The woman, who was on her knees, twisted around to look at Ashk. "Please. Can you make them stop?"

The bow weighed as much as a tree. Her legs wanted to buckle. Mother's tits! What was *wrong* with her?

"Please?" the woman said.

Ashk fought to study the woman, despite the fatigue that was blurring her vision. She looked at the black hair, the dark eyes, the face that was softer and fuller than the one she knew but enough alike. "You're Morphia."

"Yes." The word came out in a relieved rush of air.

Her arms straining, Ashk raised the bow high enough so that if her fingers slipped on the bowstring she wouldn't shoot Morag's sister. As soon as the arrow was once again loosely nocked in the bow, she felt the fatigue lift. And she noticed all the bodies in the room. There were foxes and ferrets, wolves and hawks, crows and ravens, owls and falcons. A young stag lay across the legs of one of Barry's sons. There were rabbits and, Mother's tits, even a pile of field mice. The room was full of bodies tumbled over bodies. Some were Fae in their other form, but most were animals her hunting horn had summoned and directed toward this place.

"Mother's mercy!" One of her huntsmen thrust his upper body through an open window, his crossbow ready to fire.

Morphia whipped her head around to face him.

"No!" Ashk shouted, not sure to whom she was giving the command. She pointed to her huntsman. "Out. Tell the others to stay out. And have someone call off the wolves."

The huntsman disappeared.

Ashk and Morphia stared at each other.

"What did you do to them?" Ashk asked quietly.

"They kept trying to attack me, so I put them to sleep."

"You put them to sleep." Morag had told her Morphia was the Lady of Dreams, the Sleep Sister. Looking at all the bodies, Ashk didn't know if she should laugh or weep. She'd never thought of sleep as a weapon, but dropping someone into an instant, deep sleep was an effective way of stopping an attacker.

She looked down, saw Barry's legs, and shouted for one of her huntsmen. "Fetch one of our healers. Tell her she's needed here *now*."

"Jana is here. Came riding in behind us."

"Then tell her—" Ashk looked around. There was no place to work in this room, no place for another person to stand. By luck or instinct she'd managed to plant her feet on either side of a fox without crushing any furred or feathered bodies beneath her boots. But she couldn't turn around to get back out the door. "Pull Barry out the door. Carefully. Take him to the barn and do what you can for him."

As her men pulled Barry out the door, she saw the crow, sparrow, young ferret, and tiny whoo-it owl sleeping on his back. And as she turned back to look at Morphia, she noticed the Sleep Sister was cradling a falcon in her hands, her fingers nervously stroking his breast feathers.

Ashk was fairly certain that Sheridan, who was Bretonwood's Lord of the Hawks, would have been delighted to have Morphia stroke his chest—especially if he'd been in his human form and had been awake to enjoy it.

"Can you wake them a few at a time, or do you have to wake them all at once?"

"I can wake them a few at a time," Morphia said quickly.

Ashk licked lips that had suddenly gone dry. "Can you wake Barry? The old man?"

Morphia closed her eyes. When she opened them, tears filled them, spilled over. "If I wake him, he'll suffer."

"Then there's nothing we can do for him?"

"I don't know. I sense the suffering beneath the sleep, but that's all I can tell you. Morag would know, if she were here."

And Morag didn't answer when I asked. Which may have

been an answer after all. "Wake him. Just for a minute or two. I'd like him to know his warning was understood."

Morphia nodded.

"Can you wake the ones who are between me and the door? But not the Black Coat," she added, seeing another male body almost hidden under feathers and fur.

Morphia nodded again.

The fox between Ashk's feet stirred, opened its eyes, snarled at Morphia.

"No," Ashk said firmly, giving the animal a nudge with her boot. "Go home now. Go back to the fields and the woods."

The fox turned and nimbly leaped for the open door.

Birds woke, fluffed their feathers, and flew off.

As soon as Ashk could move without hurting anyone, she dashed out the door and ran to the barn. She heard the harsh breathing, stumbled toward a stall. She fell on her knees beside Barry and took one of his hands in both of hers.

"L-lady Ashk," he said. "The Gatherer . . ."

"She understood the warning. We didn't eat the bread."

"Good. Good. Didn't want to bring it. But they said they'd . . . they'd . . ."

"It's all right," Ashk said. "Your family is safe, and they'll be looked after. And those men will never bring harm to anyone again. This I promise you."

Barry's only answer was a gasp of pain.

Ashk laid his hand on his chest and walked out of the barn. Then she ran to the cottage, shouting, "Morphia!"

Animals streamed out of the doorway, so she pushed open a window's shutters, ducked to avoid the crow that flew through the opening, and climbed into the cottage's main room.

"He sleeps," Morphia said softly.

Ashk sniffed. Brushed tears off her cheeks. When had she started crying?

Then she looked at the two Inquisitors, and her tears dried up.

Morphia looked at the women. The mother was tied to a chair. The daughter was on the floor, her skirts pushed up to her thighs.

"I was looking for the Clan house," Morphia said. "I saw the cottage, and I heard someone scream."

"So you rode in, not knowing what you were up against."

Morphia's dark eyes stared through her, and Ashk thought she understood why Morphia and Morag, the Sleep Sister and the Gatherer, had remained close.

"I knew what I could do," Morphia said. "And I knew that I would do it—even if it meant they never woke."

Ashk looked pointedly at the women. "Will you wake them, Sleep Sister? Or is there a reason why they should never wake?"

"I thought it best if there was someone they knew here when they woke." She gently set the falcon on the floor, then stiffly got to her feet.

"Let's get the rest of the animals out of the house," Ashk said. There were three wolves and the falcon left. One was a real wolf. The other two were Fae. Of the three of them, only the real wolf wasn't annoyed by the unexpected nap. He just shook himself and trotted away. The other two glared balefully at Morphia until Ashk grabbed them by their scruffs and hauled them out the door.

Morphia studied the sleeping falcon. "He's a Fae Lord, isn't he?"

"He's our Clan's Lord of the Hawks."

"He's not going to be happy."

Ashk slanted a glance at Morphia. "I won't tell him you fondled his feathers if you don't."

Morphia blushed. Ashk liked her because of it.

"Just wake him up and let him preen his ruffled feathers," Ashk said.

Stepping away from the door to give him a clear exit, Morphia obeyed.

The Fae Lord stared at Morphia for a long moment before flying out the door.

Well, well, Ashk thought. *Maybe he wasn't as unaware of being fondled as I'd thought.* But she decided not to share that with Morphia just yet.

They woke Barry's son. He had a bump on his head but was otherwise unharmed. Looking at the knife beside the Inquisitor's body, Ashk suspected he would have come to great harm if it hadn't been for Morphia's arrival.

Barry's wife had bruises. So did the daughter. But there was no blood on the girl's thighs.

Another reason to be grateful to Morphia.

While a couple of her huntsmen led Barry's family to the barn, others saddled the Inquisitors' horses and tied the still-sleeping men over the saddles.

"Come," Ashk said, leading Morphia out of the cottage. "We'll take you up to the Clan house where you can eat and rest. I'll send someone to tell Morag you're here, but I think she'll stay at the cottage tonight."

Morphia stopped walking. "Morag is here? She's staying with your Clan?"

"No, she's not actually staying with us."

A skim of ice came over Morphia's eyes. "Because she's shunned by the Clans. If you don't want her, you don't want me. Just tell me where to find her."

So much anger and bitterness in those words. Because of that, Ashk swallowed the urge to snap to her Clan's defense. "Morag is welcome to stay with us, but when Neall and Ari asked her to live with them, that was her choice."

The ice in Morphia's eyes thawed. "Ari? Neall? She's all right? They're all right?"

"They're fine, and she's round with their first babe."

Morphia looked at the ground. "I'm sorry. I thought—"

"Don't be sorry. You had no reason to think otherwise. But"—Ashk gave Morphia an odd smile—"as the rest of the Fae have so often remarked, we're different here in the west."

One of the huntsmen stayed with Jana, the healer—and to keep watch over Barry's family. Another rode off to tell the other son what had happened. The rest of them rode back to the Clan house.

Ashk reined in beside a narrow forest trail. "How close do you have to be to wake them?" she asked, tipping her head toward the Inquisitors.

"Not that close," Morphia replied.

Ashk nodded. "My men will take you up to the Clan house. When you get there, wake these two."

"What are you going to do?"

Ashk looked Morphia in the eyes and said softly, "Don't ask questions."

When Morphia rode off, Ashk held up a hand to hold back the last escort. "You know where we'll be?"

"I know."

"Then meet us there. And bring the bread."

She turned her horse to the narrow forest trail, the men leading the Inquisitors' horses riding behind her. She was aware of the old stag following them and had a moment's regret that he would see her this way. There was nothing clean or honorable in what she was about to do—but she was going to do it. Not even her grandfather's opinion, or her Clan's— or Padrick's, if it came to that—would stop her.

Death called her.

Morag flew as fast as she could, already knowing she was too late to stop whatever she would find at the cottage. Death had come.

As she flew over the trees and reached the open land around the cottage, she saw Ari on her knees in her kitchen garden, her arms around a blood-spattered Merle. She saw the savaged body of a man, his fire-blackened hand still clutching a knife. She didn't think Ari could see the ghost shaking a clenched fist and silently shouting at her, but the fact that the shadow hound kept snarling convinced her that Merle knew something was still there.

She saw Neall running toward the kitchen garden, shouting Ari's name. His left sleeve was soaked with blood, and he held it tight to his body as he ran.

Glenn stood near the stables, holding a pitchfork, the dark mare and her new foal behind him. Nearby, Shadow, the dark horse she had given to Neall, kept bugling angrily as his hooves came down again and again on the man he'd already killed.

She called to the horse, a caw that was more a command than comfort. He broke off the attack, but continued trotting around the body in a wide circle, ready to attack again. He wouldn't fear the ghost beside the body. He'd been her companion for too long and had seen too many ghosts to fear one.

She felt a bittersweet pang at his response to her command, but that was the way with the dark horses. He remembered her, but his loyalty belonged to Neall now, and only Neall's assurance that they were safe would calm him.

She circled back to the kitchen garden. Neall had scrambled over the garden wall and was on his knees, holding Ari with his good arm. Merle stood in front of them, still snarling and focused on the ghost.

She landed on the garden wall, changed to her human form, and lightly jumped down into the garden. She winced at the sight of the trampled plants—and wondered if Ari would be able to eat the food that would grow in the blood-soaked earth.

Morag shook her head. Flesh was just flesh. Meat that returned to the Great Mother. And she would take care of removing the rest.

She knelt beside Neall. Rested a hand on Ari's shoulder.

"Do no harm," Ari said, sobbing quietly. "It is not our way to do harm. But I was frightened, and angry—and I let fire act as anger's voice."

"He would have hurt Merle," Neall said firmly. "He was going to kill you and the babe. You had to protect yourself."

"I told you once before that your creed serves you well most of the time," Morag said. "But it would be foolish not to use your power to protect what you love when someone intends harm. You can't deny these men came for any reason except to hurt you and Neall."

Neall mouthed the question, "Black Coats?"

Morag nodded, watched his expression turn hard.

"Neall! Is Ari hurt?"

Morag looked over her shoulder as Glenn ran up to the garden wall. A hawk landed on the wall behind Neall and Ari. A young stag bounded toward the garden, followed by several Fae on horseback. Within moments, the kitchen garden was surrounded by armed men.

Merle snarled a warning.

No one tried to go over the garden wall.

"Lady Morag?" one of the older huntsmen said.

"They both need a healer," Morag said.

Ari brushed tears from her face, smearing her cheeks with dirt. "I'm not hurt."

"Neall is."

Ari pushed away from Neall. She paled when she saw the blood on his shirt.

"It's shallow," Neall said quickly, "and it's already stopped bleeding."

"He needs a healer," Morag said firmly.

The young stag bounded away, racing up the forest trail that led to the Clan house.

"Come," Morag said, getting to her feet. "You should both go into the cottage and rest."

"I need—"

"Young Lord," the huntsman said. "I think you need to stop arguing with Lady Morag."

Morag saw a muscle jump in Neall's jaw as he clenched his teeth. Mother's tits! Couldn't he realize Ari would be calmer with him nearby?

He didn't argue, just used his good arm to help Ari get to her feet.

Glenn cleared his throat. "Neall, if you could give Shadow a whistle, it would ease things."

Neall let out a piercing whistle. The dark horse broke off circling the Inquisitor's body and trotted toward the cottage. So did the dark mare and her foal. By the time Neall and Morag led Ari to the cottage's kitchen door, the horses were waiting for them. Morag gave them a minute to reassure the animals, then hustled them into the cottage, ordering Merle to stay outside until he'd had a bath. Ari didn't need to see bloody pawprints on her floors.

Neall was right. The knife slice on his upper arm was long but shallow enough that even a novice healer could deal with it. Morag let Ari tend it, fetching the things that were needed. There really wasn't anything to do for Ari, but she worried about what the strain of the attack might do to the young witch and the babe she carried.

She made tea, using the mixture Ari had made from herbs she'd gathered and had labeled SOOTHING.

While the water heated, she tried not to pace continually

between the table where Ari and Neall were sitting and the kitchen door where Merle whined because he wasn't allowed inside. In another minute, he'd start howling to let everyone know he wasn't happy about being so far away from Ari. Which wasn't going to soothe any of them.

She made the tea, set the mugs in front of Ari and Neall—and went back to the kitchen door. How long did it take for the healer to arrive?

This time she saw the young stag—and the horse and rider following it. She opened the bottom half of the kitchen door. Merle streaked past her, but she felt too stunned to grab him. She stepped outside as the black-haired woman flung herself out of the saddle and ran toward the cottage.

"Morphia," Morag whispered.

"Morag!" Morphia shouted.

So good to hold this woman who was a sister of the heart as well as the flesh. "Merry meet, Morphia."

Morphia leaned back, her eyes full of tears, her smile brilliant with joy. "You're well?"

"I'm well. But I could use your help."

Morphia's smile faded. "What do you need?"

Morag leaned close and whispered, "The kind of restful sleep you can give." She took Morphia's hand and led her into the cottage, saying, "Come in and be welcome."

Neall jumped to his feet, his whole body tense.

Morag smiled. "Neall. Ari. Do you remember my sister, Morphia?"

Ari said, "Blessings of the day to you." Neall remained wary—until his eyes dropped to the lacings on Morphia's bodice.

"Why do you have a feather in your lacings?" Neall asked.

Morphia glanced down—and blushed an interesting shade

of crimson. She plucked the feather out of the lacings, and muttered, "I hope it wasn't one he needed."

Neall's lips twitched. "He?"

Morphia nervously smoothed the feather, then stuck it back in the lacings. "It's a long story."

"Which my sister will be glad to share—"

"No, I won't."

"—after the two of you have gotten a little rest," Morag said.

Morphia muttered. But she went over to the table and got a good grip on Ari's arm to persuade her to get up.

Morag walked up to Neall and smiled. She could tell by his expression that he remembered quite well the last time he'd tried—unsuccessfully—to deal with the two sisters. So it wasn't so hard as it might have been to coax Neall and Ari to lie down for a little while. Especially since Neall, at least, realized he was going to sleep and his choices were the bed or the floor.

A light brush of Morphia's fingers once they were settled on the bed was all it took for the two of them to fall sound asleep.

Morag grabbed Merle by the scruff and dragged the whining shadow hound outside. "No," she said firmly. "You are *not* climbing up on that bed with them until you've had a bath."

The whines increased.

"Hush!" Not that his whines were going to wake Ari or Neall, but there was no reason for the rest of them to have to listen to Merle's opinions and complaints. She closed the bottom of the kitchen door and watched Merle lope over to Glenn, probably hoping the man might have a different opinion.

Glenn looked at Morag. Morag looked at Glenn.

"Come along, laddy-boy," Glenn said. "We'll get you cleaned up."

Merle hung his head, but he followed Glenn back to the stables.

Morag turned back to the cottage. Morphia stood inside, watching her.

"What brought you to Bretonwood?" Morag asked.

"I came looking for you," Morphia replied. "I'd rather be with my sister than with the rest of the Fae."

Had it come to that? "Morphia . . ."

Morphia shook her head. "Ashk says the Fae in the west are different."

"Yes," Morag said softly, "they are."

"I'm guesting at the Clan house, but when word came that a healer was needed here . . . The healer was already occupied, so I came instead."

"You were what they needed." Morag hesitated. "Can you stay with them for a little while? There's something I need to do."

"I can stay."

Morag walked to the kitchen garden, where her dark horse waited. She stopped when the older huntsman approached her.

"We'll take care of the bodies," he said.

"I don't want them on her land. I don't want them near her. Not even as corpses."

He hesitated. "There is a place, deep in the woods, some distance from the Clan house. There are several places in the woods where we give our dead back to the Mother, but this place . . . There is good and bad in every people, Lady Morag. Wishing it wasn't so doesn't change that it is. So there is a place in the woods where we sometimes bury one of our own. Nothing will grow there but thorns and thistles. It's a cold place, even in bright sunlight."

"That will do." A place where even daylight was shadowed. Yes, that would do for the Black Coats.

Shadows.

"Something else," Morag said, resting her hand on the huntsman's arm. "Warn Ashk. Warn the Clan to be wary of the shadows in the woods. If the Inquisitors were here long enough, they could have drawn on the power in the Old Place and twisted it to create nighthunters."

"Nighthunters?"

"Creatures the Mother never would have created. They devour flesh and spirit."

The huntsman gave her a long look. "I'll tell Ashk. If these creatures are here, we'll rid our land of them."

Morag nodded. Having seen nighthunters, she didn't think it would be that easy to destroy them, but she wasn't skilled with a bow, so perhaps he had good reason to be confident of the Fae's ability to cleanse the creatures from Bretonwood.

She mounted her dark horse, gathered the Inquisitors' ghosts, and rode away. She felt uneasy about traveling along the deeper trails in the woods, but was unwilling to take the road up to the Shadowed Veil until she was away from the land that belonged to Neall and Ari.

When she left the Inquisitors at the Shadowed Veil, she said, "May you find the Fiery Pit you Black Coats seem so fond of," then galloped back down the road. She let the dark horse set the pace when they were once more following the forest trails, but didn't breathe easy until they cantered into daylight.

Death called her.

She turned away from the cottage and followed the summons to the old farmer's barn. She didn't go inside, didn't intrude on the grief she felt there. She simply gathered him gently and went back up the road to the Shadowed Veil. The

Inquisitors were gone, and she was glad. The old man didn't need to see them.

He raised a hand in farewell before he stepped through the Shadowed Veil to follow the path to the Summerland.

"Merry meet, and merry part, and merry meet again," Morag whispered.

She was exhausted by the time she returned to the cottage. Even her dark horse was stumbling with fatigue. Glenn took her horse. Morphia heated enough water so that she could take a sponge bath. She wasn't as clean as she wanted, but it was the best she could do.

While she ate a bowl of soup, Morphia told her that Neall and Ari had woken up long enough to eat; then, after being reassured that the animals had been cared for and there was nothing that needed to be done, they'd returned to bed.

Glenn insisted on sleeping in the stables. The Fae Lords insisted that she bolt the doors. She didn't argue with them. She didn't argue when Morphia led her upstairs to her room and settled in beside her. She listened while Morphia told her what happened at the farm, but, somehow, fell asleep before her sister got around to explaining the feather that had gotten stuck in the lacings.

Chapter Eighteen

Impatient and uneasy, Ubel followed country lanes and crossed open land until he reached a place where he would appear to be riding up from the south toward Breton. None of his men had returned to the meeting place, and he needed to find out why. He'd been firm about the need to move swiftly and slip away again. They were too far away from home, too far away from the united strength the Inquisitors could wield.

It should have been simple. Kill the witch living in the Old Place. Use the farmer and his family to kill Ashk if she was at the "Clan house." If she returned to the manor house with the baron's children, he and the Inquisitor with him were waiting close by to eliminate all of them.

But the four men he'd sent to the Old Place and the farmer's cottage hadn't returned, and when he'd heard that strange horn—the sound of it had made him shiver—he'd ordered the other Inquisitor to go to the village and listen for whatever news could be gleaned while buying supplies.

He'd waited as long as he could for the man to return, but the shadows in the woods behind the manor house had become too dark, too deep, and it was no longer safe to stay there. Besides, after that horn had sounded, people started stirring all around the manor like hornets whose nest had been disturbed.

He'd been careful. He'd thought through his plans. His

men simply had recognized the difficulty of meeting him near the manor house and had already ridden south to the crossroads posting house, which was their destination after they finished their work in Breton. He'd meet up with the Inquisitor he'd sent to the village, and the two of them would ride south and meet up with the others. Then he'd decide if they should continue traveling overland or take the road to the coast and go back to Durham by sea.

As he approached a small farm, Ubel saw a man and boy walking beside a pasture's stone fence. The man looked at Ubel riding toward him, then gave the boy a push on the shoulder. The boy ran to the cottage.

Ubel reined in. The man stopped walking and shifted the ax he carried so that he held it with both hands.

"Good day to you," Ubel said. "Can you tell me how much farther it is to the road that leads to the seaport town?" It pleased him to think of asking for another town so that no one would think Breton was his destination.

"You passed it a few miles back," the man said gruffly.

Giving the man a puzzled smile, Ubel shook his head. "I was told there's one just north of here."

"Next seaport town is two, maybe three days' ride from here."

"Ah." Ubel paused as if considering that information. "Breton is just ahead, isn't it? Perhaps I should find lodging there for the night."

Ubel noticed a hawk fly toward the farmer's cottage. Circle it. Another hawk glided high in the air—toward the road. Toward him.

Sweat trickled down his back. Surely they were just ordinary hawks. Even if there *were* a few Fae in the Old Place, they'd have no reason to be flying over *this* farm. Unless the boy who had been sent back to the cottage had been told to give some kind of signal that would draw the Fae here?

"They won't be welcoming strangers in Breton tonight," the man said. "Nor anywhere else around here. If you're a decent man, you'd best ride south to the posting house. It's not so far that you won't make it there while there's still daylight."

Ubel looked around as if confused. He tried not to shiver as the hawk's shadow fell across the road. "I took this to be a main road. Surely the people around here see travelers all the time."

"And most of the time we're friendly enough," the man replied, shifting his grip on the ax. "But there's been trouble here."

"Trouble?"

Grim fury filled the man's face. "Some of those whoreson bastard Black Coats came to Breton. Killed a farmer and hurt his family. Killed one of Forrester's apprentices. That's got the baron's people and the villagers stirred up."

Whoreson bastard? How dare this doltish, ignorant *peasant* say such a thing about an Inquisitor?

The man glanced up at the hawk soaring above them. "Word is they also tried to kill Lady Ashk and the witch who lives in Bretonwood. That's got the Fae riled. I wouldn't want to be a stranger riding into Breton tonight."

"Fae? You mean a few of them actually live around here?" Ubel tried to sound interested. Sweat soaked the armpits of his coat.

"A few?" The man stared at him. "The whole Bretonwood Clan lives in the Old Place. That's a sizable more than a few."

The forester boy had told the truth about there being a Clan house in the Old Place. How could he have known the boy had told the truth? He'd never heard of the Fae *living* in the human world.

"But . . . Even if someone, a stranger, *did* kill those peo-

ple, how do you know it was a—what did you call them?—
a Black Coat?"

"The Gatherer said they were. Guess she would know."

The reins slipped from Ubel's suddenly numb fingers.
The Gatherer was *here?* "What happened to the man?"

"I'm thinking you'd have to ask the Fae what happened to
those men. Or the village magistrate."

He wasn't going to ride into that village and ask the magistrate anything. And he *certainly* wasn't going to get near
the Fae—especially when there was a whole Clan out there
and the Gatherer was among them.

Ubel gathered the reins. "I think you're right, good sir. I
think it would be best if I went to the posting house to find
lodgings tonight. And I . . . I don't think I'll continue my
northern journey after all."

"That's probably for the best," the man agreed. "By this
time tomorrow, no stranger will be able to step a man's
length anywhere in the west without the barons and the Fae
knowing about it—and he won't be able to do so much as un-
button his trousers to take a piss without having to explain
himself."

"Thank you for your time," Ubel said weakly. He turned
his horse and set the pace at an easy trot. It wouldn't do to
run, to appear afraid. It wouldn't do to have anyone think he
had a reason to hurry.

He could keep riding. He and his men had hired horses
and exchanged them at various posting stations on the journey here. He could do the same on the journey back, riding
hard since he didn't care if the animal was sound when he
was through with it.

But one man, alone on the roads . . .

If the farmer was right and news could travel that fast here
in the west . . . If any of his men lived and were persuaded to
talk about the man who was their leader for this task . . .

He needed to blend in with other strangers. A seaport was a better choice for that. And a coach. Surely there were coaches at that posting house that took passengers to the coastal road and the seaports.

Yes. Better to be one among many than a lone rider easily followed.

It wouldn't please Master Adolfo that he'd lost the men he'd brought with him. It would please the Master even less that he'd failed his task in almost every way. But the winged gifts he and his men had left in the shadows of the woods were starting to stir.

Let the baron and the Fae and all the rest of them deal with *that*.

Ubel scanned the main room of the posting station, certain that his expression conveyed nothing more than anxious concern, yet uneasy about the amount of silent attention every person entering the room was receiving. If he didn't find—

There. That old woman sitting at a table by herself would suit his plans.

He swiftly crossed the room, shifting his expression to one of relief. Stepping up to the table, he rested one hand on the back of the chair opposite the one the old woman sat in. Seeing the proprietor approaching the table, he changed his expression from relief to confusion, and put all the strength of his Inquisitor's Gift of persuasion behind his words as he said, "Didn't you order a bowl of stew for me?"

"And why would I order a bowl of stew for you?" the old woman said sharply. "I don't know—" She looked up, and as her eyes met his, his gift of persuasion ensnared her.

The proprietor was now standing near the table close enough to hear everything that was said.

Ubel filled his voice with a touch of sadness and worry.

"It's me, Grandmother. It's Ian. Your grandson. We arranged to meet here so that I could escort you on the rest of your journey to visit relatives. I asked you to order a bowl of stew for me while I took care of the horse I'd hired. Don't you remember?"

"I—" The old woman studied his face, working hard to remember. "Ian? I don't . . . remember. You're . . . traveling with me?"

Ubel smiled, looking weary but relieved. "Yes, Grandmother."

The proprietor looked at both of them in turn, then said to Ubel, "The coaches will be leaving shortly, but there's time for a bowl of stew and tankard of ale."

"Half a tankard, if you please," Ubel said. He pulled out the chair and sat down, setting his saddlebags beside the chair.

The old woman was strong-willed and independent. So much so that every time he gave a little attention to his meal, she shook off enough of the persuasion that all he could do was reinforce the thought that he was her grandson and was traveling with her instead of planting additional thoughts about the journey.

In the end, her own strength worked to his advantage. By the time he led her to the counter where the tickets were sold, she sounded confused and querulous, which made it easier to exchange the ticket she'd already purchased for a coach headed farther inland for two tickets to the seaport.

As he settled her into the coach, he realized he'd get little rest until they were actually on the ship. Once they were at sea, heading for Wellingsford, what she said would make little difference. But it angered him to have a female trying to assert her own opinions instead of being quiet and obedient, so he decided he would spend the time at sea using his gift of persuasion as a hammer against her mind until she was no longer certain of anything.

He settled back on his part of the seat, pleased that he'd found a way to amuse himself on the journey.

Chapter Nineteen

Struggling to push away memories of the previous night, Ashk stared at the sunlit meadow. It was one of her favorite places, the place where her grandfather had taught her, trained her, played with her. She wanted to walk in the sunlight, feel the heat of it seep through her skin all the way to her cold bones. She wanted to follow the trail that led to the small pool where she had met Padrick on a Summer Moon night years ago. She wanted to soak in that water until she felt clean again—and she wondered if she ever *would* feel clean again. If she went there, would the blood and the pain seep into the stones around the pool? Would it settle on the bottom like some kind of emotional slime?

Have you nothing to say about what I've done here, Gatherer?

I've seen worse things done, and they were done by an Inquisitor's hand.

Last night, she had used their own tools against them—not with any skill, since she could only guess at the purpose of many of those pieces of metal, but she had used them while the Fae males who had brought the Black Coats to that thorny, barren place—and the Fae who had joined them—watched in silence and listened to the Black Coats spew out answers to every question she asked, listened to them beg and plead for the next caress of pain to stop.

She wondered how many witches had begged and pleaded

for the suffering to end—and how many times the Black
Coats had answered those pleas with more pain.

In the end, she'd used her knife because it was the weapon
that felt comfortable in her hand, and she dressed the Black
Coats as she would have dressed a deer—but without the respect she felt for a deer whose flesh would feed her people
and without the mercy of a swift, clean death before her knife
sliced through those human bellies. Their blood splashed her.
Their screams filled her ears until there was no other sound.
She heard the screams even after she stood over silent
corpses.

When she looked at her men, they looked back at her fearfully, even the ones who were predators in their other forms.

Not even a wolf was safe against a shadow hound, and
now they'd seen that side of her while she was still in her
human form.

Then, as the sky began to lighten with the dawn, Morag
road into that thorny, barren place.

*Have you nothing to say about what I've done here, Gath-
erer?*

*I've seen worse things done, and they were done by an In-
quisitor's hand.*

Morag gathered all the ghosts in that place and took them
up the road that led to the Shadowed Veil and the Summerland beyond.

Death's Mistress didn't fear shadow hounds.

Ashk blinked her eyes several times. It was just looking at
the sunlight that made them wet. Just the sunlight.

It would be some time before she could walk in the light
again. The Black Coats had created the foul, soul-eating
creatures called nighthunters, and those things were growing
somewhere in the woods. No, she couldn't walk in the light
while her people were in danger.

She turned her back on the meadow and looked at the men

standing in the shadows of the woods, the men who had followed her here, waiting for their orders.

"Send word through the minstrels and the storytellers," Ashk said. "They'll make sure everyone hears the warnings. Send it swiftly. It must reach the witches and the barons as well as the Clans."

"What should the minstrels and storytellers say?" one of the huntsmen asked.

"They should give warning about the nighthunters. One of the Black Coats, the one who led the other five, got away. He could create more of those soul-eating creatures in other places while he flees the west. People need to be careful."

"Is there anything else?" the huntsman asked.

"No stranger is welcome in the west, and if any come, no one is to talk to them about witches or the House of Gaian. *No one.* If any strangers want answers, they can come to me." It hurt, knowing what her next words might cost. "And if any strangers who come into the west are reluctant to explain to the Fae why they have come among us . . . kill them."

Chapter Twenty

Glynis set her wet, soapy fists on her hips. "If I've said it once, I've said it a hundred times, and I'll say it again. It isn't right. Lady Elinore would never stoop so low as to do a servant's work, and you're just as fine a lady as she is—and kin besides."

I don't think Elinore would refuse to help with chores if her help was needed, but her servants would probably faint from the embarrassment, Breanna thought as she slipped the handle of the basket that held the wooden clothes-pegs over one arm. She and Glynis had been arguing this point on and off ever since the woman came to work for them. "I think my dignity can survive hanging up the wash. Besides, I do it every week, and I'm not about to stop doing it just because Elinore will see me." She lifted the large basket full of wet sheets and pillowcases and left before Glynis could continue the argument.

As she walked toward the three wash lines strung between sturdy posts, she saw Clay look at the wash house, then look at her. He grinned.

Breanna stopped to give him a narrow-eyed stare. "I suppose you're going to tell me a gentry lady would rather run naked down the main street of Willowsbrook than be seen hanging out her own wash."

"Truth to tell, she probably would," Clay replied. "And it would be more entertaining for the rest of us. But I've no objection to a healthy body doing healthy work, so if you ever have an urge to shovel out horse manure, I won't be telling you it's not a fit occupation for a gentry lady."

She bit back a chuckle, shook her head, and continued her walk to the clotheslines. Setting down her baskets, she plucked a couple of clothes-pegs out of the small basket and started filling the lines with clean linens.

A light breeze from the west played with the pegged clothes as she filled one line and went on to the next. A few years ago, she and Keely had made a large flower bed of roses and lavender behind the clotheslines so that the wind would carry the scent over the clean clothes. A simple thing, but it pleased her every time she hung out the wash, and every time she slipped a tunic over her head and caught a hint of those mixed scents.

The message on the western wind a few days ago had been filled with warmth and humor. Aiden and Lyrra had reached the village in the Mother's Hills where her kin lived. She wondered if Aiden had sung any new songs—and she wondered if Skelly had told Lyrra any stories about his sweet granny. At another time, she would have been tempted to escort them the whole way herself, but the things Aiden and Lyrra had said about the Black Coats had made her uneasy about leaving her mother and grandmother.

And she wondered, as she'd wondered since the morning they left, why Aiden and Lyrra had reacted to her parting words the way they did.

Merry meet, and merry part, and merry meet again. A common saying among family and friends—at least among those who were of the House of Gaian. But they'd looked at her as if she'd given them a key piece to a difficult puzzle.

Breanna shrugged, pegged a pillowcase to the third line. Perhaps one day they'd ride back this way and she could ask them why a simple saying had seemed so important.

She was halfway down the line when she heard a flutter of wings and caught the movement of something large and brown out of the corner of her eye. Turning her head slowly, she studied the hawk that was perched on one of the posts.

"Blessings of the day to you, brother hawk."

She'd never seen a hawk quite that big before. No jesses, which meant it was a wild hawk. What could interest a wild hawk enough that it would perch on a post so close to where people lived and worked, not to mention the linens gently flapping in the breeze? Granted, sitting on that post would give a sharp-eyed bird a good view of the back lawn, gardens, and stables, but . . .

"Are you here because you spotted a few rats you thought might be tasty? If you *have* spotted any, you're welcome to them." She'd have to ask Clay if he'd seen any sign of rats. She didn't mind field mice—unless they got into the house—but rats weren't to her liking.

Since the hawk seemed content to perch on the post, she went back to pegging the sheet to the line. When her basket was empty and the line was full, she turned and saw the pillowcase nearest the post dangling by one peg—and the other peg firmly under one of the hawk's taloned feet.

The hawk seemed to be studying the brown, hard object it had captured.

"Ah, come on now," Breanna said, walking toward it slowly. "Come on. That's of no use to you. You can't eat it. You wouldn't even bother chewing on it. Come on now. Give it up."

How had it gotten the clothes-peg to begin with? Breanna wondered as she continued walking toward the hawk. Pulled it off the line with its beak? Whatever for?

"Here now," Breanna said, raising one hand toward the hawk. "Give it back and I'll—" She'd what? Offer him a bit of cold beef? He might like it, even if it was cooked, but she wasn't sure feeding him would be a good idea.

She reached for the peg.

The hawk raised his wings, making him look much, much bigger than he already did. He bent so that his beak hovered above the clothes-peg—and he watched her.

Mother's tits! This was worse than dealing with Idjit. And, she had to admit, she felt a lot more wary of the hawk's talons and beak than she did of Idjit's teeth. Maybe because she saw a lot more intelligence in the hawk's eyes than she'd ever seen in the dog's.

"Give it back," Breanna said quietly, firmly.

The hawk grabbed the clothes-peg with its beak and flew off, the downsweep of its wings almost hitting her in the face, making her duck.

"You . . . *thief.*" Incensed, Breanna chased the bird until grass gave way to the woods and the hawk disappeared among the trees.

"Thief!" Breanna shouted, shaking her fist. "You're nothing but a featherheaded thief! If you steal from us again, I'll pluck you and we'll have hawk surprise one night for the evening meal. *Thief!*"

"Breanna!" Nuala panted, having run from the house. "Whatever is the matter?"

Breanna whirled to face her grandmother. "That hawk just stole one of our clothes-pegs! We pay good coin for those pegs, and he stole one!"

"We pay a copper for a dozen of those pegs, and the only reason we pay that much is we can afford to and it gives old Jess a purpose to the whittling he likes to do. And now that he's living with his granddaughter, having a few coppers of his own lets him keep his pride and buy a treat now and then for his great-grandchildren."

"How much we paid for it isn't the point," Breanna said. "The point is it belonged to us *and he stole it.*"

"What would a hawk want with a clothes-peg?"

"Exactly!" Breanna threw up her hands in exasperation.

"Exactly," Nuala agreed. "So I ask you again, my darling Breanna, what would a *hawk* want with a clothes-peg?"

Breanna opened her mouth, closed it slowly. "What would a Fae Lord want with a clothes-peg?"

"That," Nuala said dryly, "is a different question, and, like the other, it has no obvious answer."

"It's bad enough that the Fae have been skulking in the woods, pestering the Small Folk about us, but this one just flies in here as bold as you please to watch everything we do—and steals from us."

"Breanna—"

Breanna whirled around to face the woods, took a deep breath, and roared, *"Thief!"*

"Breanna," Nuala said sternly. "Come inside now. You've had enough sun this morning. It's overheated your brain."

"It— What?"

Nuala just gave her the look that had subdued Aiden into obedience.

When Nuala walked back to the house, Breanna went with her—and saw three reasons why she should have been a little less vocal. Clay had run halfway to meet her, a pitchfork in his hands, before seeing that this was, somehow, a discussion between grandmother and granddaughter that he should stay out of. Edgar was standing near the wall of the kitchen garden, a hoe in his hands. And Glynis had come running with the big paddle she used to stir the laundry in the washtubs.

Giving Clay an embarrassed smile, Breanna hung her head and followed Nuala to the house, much as she had done when she was eight and couldn't manage to stay out of trouble for more than two days in a row.

But as she reached the threshold of the kitchen door, she looked over her shoulder at the woods, and mouthed, "Thief."

"Breanna," Nuala called through the partially open parlor door. "Would you come outside with me for a minute?"

Sighing, Breanna set aside the book she'd been trying to read. She enjoyed reading when she wanted to read, but it had always seemed a shame to spoil the pleasure of a story by remembering she'd used it to fill the hours when she'd had to stay in her room after some kind of rumpus. Of course, Nuala hadn't sent her to her room this time, since she *was* an adult, but suggesting that she stay in the parlor and find something quiet to do amounted to the same thing.

"What is it?" Breanna asked. Maybe she'd have to polish the silver. She hated polishing the silver. It was one of those tasks for which she was more than happy to side with Glynis about what was and wasn't a proper task for a gentry lady.

Not that she thought her opinion was going to matter this afternoon.

Nuala led her out the kitchen door to where Clay stood with an odd smile curving his lips. He held up a dead rabbit.

"You caught a rabbit?" Breanna asked.

Clay shook his head. "The hawk caught a rabbit. He flew over to the wood block, waited until I spotted him there, then flew off, leaving the rabbit behind."

Breanna frowned at the rabbit. "Why would he do that?"

"Maybe he didn't want to be called a thief anymore," Clay said.

Breanna felt her cheeks heat. Of course Nuala had told Clay—and probably Edgar and Glynis—what she'd been shouting about. She'd be surprised if there was anyone in the whole county who hadn't heard her.

Which didn't make it any easier when Nuala leaned toward her, and said softly, "I'd say a rabbit is adequate payment for a clothes-peg. Wouldn't you?"

The next morning, the hawk brought another rabbit. This time, he guarded it until Clay fetched Breanna. As soon as the hawk saw her, he left the rabbit and flew off.

Ignoring Clay's grin, Breanna took the rabbit to Glynis, who was quite pleased to have more fresh meat without having to make the trip to the butcher's shop in Willowsbrook.

Two rabbits for a clothes-peg didn't seem quite fair. Considering the way she'd yelled at him, he probably thought he'd taken something that had far more value than a whittled piece of wood. While she weeded the flower beds, she chewed on a kernel of worry that the bird was giving his kills to her and was going without food because of it. Which was foolish, of course. He was a Fae Lord. He'd just go back up to Tir Alainn and stuff himself with food. And perhaps amuse the other Fae by recounting how he'd caught a rabbit for the witches in the Old Place?

That thought didn't sit any better than worrying about him, so she tried to keep her mind on the weeds instead of on the Fae. Unfortunately, the Fae provided more interesting thoughts than weeds did—or any of the other chores she did during that day to keep her hands busy.

The following morning, Breanna was in the kitchen garden, hoeing her share of the rows, when the hawk flew over to perch on the garden wall, empty-handed—or empty-footed in his case.

Leaning on the hoe, Breanna studied the bird. "Blessings of the day to you, brother hawk," she said pleasantly.

The hawk just watched her.

"I thank you for the rabbits. They were very tasty, and the meat was much appreciated."

The hawk lifted his folded wings. The movement was so much like a shrug, if a man had done it, she would have translated the gesture as, "It was nothing."

"Since there aren't many of us here," Breanna continued, "there's still plenty of meat left, so we don't need another rabbit. You should do some hunting for yourself now." Of course, that wasn't true. Oh, there was a bowl of rabbit stew left, and a couple of pieces of the rabbit pies Glynis had made for yesterday's evening meal, but six adults, especially when two of them were hungry, hardworking men, didn't tend to leave much on the table after a meal.

Since the hawk didn't make any movements she could interpret as a response, she went back to hoeing the rows. He simply watched her, and she felt an odd pleasure in having his company. When he finally flew away, she was a bit sorry to see him go.

When she finished the first row, Breanna stretched to ease the muscles in her back.

The kitchen garden covered close to an acre of land. Most years, they planted half that land, leaving the other half to lie fallow. Clay dumped some of the horse manure in that fallow part, just as Glynis dumped the vegetable waste there. The combination could smell especially ripe on hot summer days, but it fed the land, keeping it rich and productive.

This year, Keely had decided they needed to plant the whole garden, had insisted the food would be needed although she couldn't tell them why she felt that way. But she'd been so insistent they'd given in and planted. There was still a small place for the compost piles, but the rest of the garden had been filled with seeds or seedlings. Traditionally, the kitchen garden was tended by the witch whose gift was earth because she was the one who could draw the best from the land. But the garden was too big for Keely to tend by herself this year, so Breanna and Nuala were doing their share of the work.

Breanna started on the next row.

What were they supposed to do with all the food? How were they supposed to can the surplus when they reached harvest time? Keely had insisted that Clay and Edgar plant extra acres of oats and winter feed for the animals, so they already had extra work. Not to mention that all the fruit trees and berry bushes and plants were showing signs of producing twice as much as last year. That, too, had something to do with the restless way Keely had walked the land this spring. Mentally and emotionally, she had retreated to remaining a child after the old baron had raped her all those years ago, but there was nothing diminished about her gifts as a witch—and after Rory's visit, and the letter telling Nuala that their cousins would be coming for a visit, and Aiden's tales about the Black Coats, Breanna knew Nuala had studied Keely's call to the land with a different eye.

Still, a handful of people spending a few weeks of the summer with them wasn't going to empty the pantry.

Nothing she could do about it except tend the land. At least she'd reassured the hawk that his debt for the clothespeg had been paid in full.

He brought her a salmon.

It wasn't a large salmon, and, judging by how dirty it was, it had seen a fair piece of the forest floor between the stream where it had been caught and the wood block where it lay.

Breanna, Nuala, Keely, Glynis, Edgar, and Clay formed a half circle around the wood block and studied the fish.

"How do you think he caught it?" Breanna finally asked. "Hawks can't swim. Can they?"

"There are fishing hawks who live around big rivers or along the coast near the sea," Nuala said.

"But he's not one of them," Breanna said. "So how'd he catch a salmon?"

"Maybe he changed to his human form to catch it," Keely said.

"Then why not stay in human form at least until he was close to the edge of the woods instead of trying to hold on to it while he flew here?" Breanna said.

"That would have been easy," Nuala said.

"He didn't hold on to it very well," Keely said, wrinkling her nose. "It's very dirty."

"His feet weren't meant to hold a fish," Nuala said thoughtfully. "Perhaps the effort is part of the gift. Perhaps this is his way of saying he'd like to be your friend."

"Or more than your friend," Clay muttered darkly.

"If *that* was his purpose, he'd have come in his human form with a pocketful of trinkets," Breanna snapped. At least, that's what the Fae in the stories did.

"If he'd brought you a necklace or a fine bracelet, would you have been impressed?" Nuala asked quietly.

"Of course not!"

"So he brought something you would value."

Breanna opened her mouth to argue, then discovered she wasn't sure she *could* disagree with Nuala's interpretation. She'd told him she didn't need another rabbit, so he'd brought her something else. Something he'd obviously worked hard to bring.

"There's no point standing here watching it rot," Glynis said. She stepped forward, hooked her fingers under one of the salmon's gills, and picked it up. "I'll just clean it off and see what we've got. Should make a nice meal for all of us."

After she walked away, Keely headed for the kitchen garden, and Clay and Edgar went back to their work.

"Why would a Fae Lord want to be friends with a witch?" Breanna asked.

"Aiden and Lyrra wanted to be friends."

"That's different. *They're* different from the rest of the Fae. Why does *this* one want to be friends?"

Nuala smiled as she ran a soothing hand over Breanna's hair. "That's something you would have to ask him."

Late that afternoon, she saw a hawk soaring overhead, but she couldn't tell if it was the Fae Lord or just one of the hawks that lived in the Old Place.

Glynis had washed off the salmon, pronounced it fresh enough to eat, and had made them all a delicious meal.

Too bad Breanna couldn't tell the hawk that—especially after one of the Small Folk showed up at the edge of the woods and asked her if she'd enjoyed the fish. There'd been laughter in the small man's voice. Apparently, several of the Small Folk had watched that little journey through the woods and had found it highly entertaining. And his parting words, "That one's not like the others," gave her another kernel of thought to chew on.

When Idjit started barking, she went to see why the foolish dog was dashing back and forth in front of the archway. She saw the carriages, wagons, and riders slowly coming up the road. One of the riders raised his hand in greeting.

"Clay!" Breanna shouted, looking back over her shoulder. "Rory and the others have come for their visit."

After she saw him lift a hand in acknowledgment, she ran out to meet her kin—and wondered why there were so many people with them.

The travelers reined in to wait for her. Rory and the rider beside him dismounted and walked to meet her.

It took Breanna a moment to recognize Fiona, with her

hair bundled up under a hat and wearing what looked like an old set of Rory's clothes.

"Merry me—" The grim expression on Rory's face and the exhaustion and anguish in Fiona's eyes killed the greeting.

"Breanna," Fiona said hoarsely. She stumbled into Breanna's arms and held on tight.

"Can the baron who rules this county be trusted?" Rory asked.

Still holding Fiona, Breanna stared at him, puzzled. "If you'd asked a few months ago, I would have said no. But Liam is a good man. You met him."

"I met him," Rory said. "But things can change."

Breanna felt Fiona shiver—and felt an answering shiver run through her own body. "What's happened?"

"The barons have gone mad," Fiona whispered. "They—"

"The baron who rules our county declared that anyone with woodland eyes was to be brought in and questioned to determine whether or not the person was a witch, one of the Evil One's servants," Rory said. "From what we heard, it's not the baron or the magistrate who's doing the questioning—and so far no one who was brought in has been seen again."

"The Inquisitors?" Breanna asked.

"We ran," Fiona said, stepping back far enough to look at Breanna. "The elders decided that we had to run. After the new decrees were posted in the village last autumn, most of us stayed away. Rory and the other men went when we needed supplies. But when the baron ordered that a . . . procedure . . . be done on all females, the elders decided we had to get away. Now."

"Procedure?"

Fiona shook her head. "They won't say what it is. Won't explain."

"They did the women in the village first," Rory said. "When I went into the village for the last time, those women looked at me with dead eyes."

Fiona's eyes filled with tears. "My mother . . . my grandmother. They stayed. All the elders in the family stayed. They said it had to look like the younger members of the family had just gone for a summer visit. They said it couldn't look like we were fleeing or we might be stopped before we could get away."

"For months now, Craig has been buying cargo for our ships that would keep in the warehouse and not spoil. Bolts of cloth from some of the far-off lands whose ships make the journey to Durham to trade. Tea. Sugar. And he's been drawing more from the family's accounts than he needed to pay for the goods and sending the gold and silver upriver. We've brought your share of it. There's no way of telling if we'll be able to get more."

"They burned Tremaine's ship," Fiona whispered. "That was the last message we got—along with Craig's plea that we get out of the eastern counties." She choked on a sob. "They burned his ship, and the men who jumped into the river to keep from burning with it never got to shore."

Breanna's knees started to buckle. "Jennyfer?" While she would never admit it to the others, Jenny had always been her favorite cousin. They had little in common except being witches, since air was her strongest branch of the Mother and Jenny's passion was the sea, but they'd always worked well together and enjoyed each other's company.

"She went with Mihail when he set sail to talk to some baron he knew in the west about finding a safe harbor for the ships and the family. Tremaine's boys went with him, too. He was supposed to sail back to Seahaven and wait for the other ships—and for those who are traveling overland to meet him there. If the other ships can't get past the barons and Inquisitors who are watching the Una River and reach the sea, his may be the only ship we have left."

"Craig?"

Rory hesitated. "He was going to stay in Durham as long as he could to keep the warehouse and the business open. He's supposed to be one of those meeting Mihail at Seahaven. We don't know if he got out of Durham in time."

"I know you weren't expecting so many," Fiona said. "We'd only intended to have the Daughters among us slip away, but we couldn't leave people behind."

Breanna looked at the carriages, wagons, and riders. Not just family watching her out of frightened eyes. It looked like some of the younger servants and farming families had come, too. But almost every one of them had woodland eyes.

"There's still some time before the Summer Solstice," Fiona said. "Those of us whose branch is earth could plant—".

Breanna shook her head. "It's already planted. Keely knew." No need to wonder now what they were going to do with the harvest. They would need everything the Mother could give.

"We can't go back, Breanna," Rory said quietly. "Not until we're told it's safe to go back."

That message would never come—and the ones who had stayed behind knew it.

"Nuala is the elder now," Fiona whispered.

Dull pain surrounded Breanna's heart. She hadn't visited her eastern kin often, but that didn't change the feeling of loss.

"Come on," Breanna said. "We may have to share beds for a while, but we'll get it sorted out."

As she led them through the archway, she realized Liam now held the lives of her eastern kin in his hands.

And it suddenly occurred to her that he should have been back from the barons' council by now.

Chapter Twenty-one

"There's the manor," Liam said with weariness and relief. "That's home."

Padrick simply nodded.

How many days had they been running, hiding? Liam wondered. Padrick had said something about the waning quarter moon, but had that been yesterday? The day before? He didn't know. Didn't want to ask.

He wouldn't have gotten home without Padrick's help. Fear had kept him in the saddle for hours the night they'd fled from Durham, but even fear couldn't battle against the effects of the poison that had still been inside him. He remembered the first posting station where Padrick had said they'd rest for a few hours. He vaguely remembered burning up and freezing at the same time. He didn't know how long they stayed at that posting station before Padrick had forced him to get out of bed, had helped him dress.

A back stairway. Stumbling as quietly as possible to the stables. Padrick saddling the horses and helping him mount. Riding away before there was even a hint of dawn in the sky.

A night spent in a bed of straw in some farmer's barn. Another posting station. Or perhaps it was a room above a tavern. Fevered dreams that left him weak and confused. Chills no amount of blankets could ease. Days and nights that bled into each other. Places that became jumbled into one place and no place. Riding into an Old Place where he saw things that *had* to have come from the fever dreams—except, when they'd ridden away, and ridden fast, tears had streamed down Padrick's face.

This morning he'd finally awakened weak but clear-headed—and close to home.

Now they were here, riding toward the house that had been in his family for generations. Tonight he'd sleep in a familiar room in a familiar bed, would eat food that had been prepared and served by people he could trust. He'd been unaware of so much over these past few days. Padrick had been unaware of nothing, and it showed in the grim exhaustion that seemed to reveal more of the Fae Lord beneath the gentry face.

As they reached the house, the front door opened and Sloane, his butler, rushed out to meet them.

"Baron Liam!" Sloane said. "It's good you're home. There's—" He stopped. Looked. "Have you been ill, Baron?"

"Yes," Liam said. There was no reason to tell anyone more than that right now.

"Has something happened here?" Padrick asked sharply.

Sloane gave Padrick an uneasy look.

"What is it?" Liam said.

"It's Lady Elinore," Sloane said. "Two people came by yesterday, a man and his wife. They had a letter for Lady Elinore. She told me to take them to the kitchen for something to eat. Then, suddenly, she was packing a trunk for herself and Miss Brooke and giving orders to have the pony cart ready instantly. As soon as the trunk was in the cart, she took Miss Brooke and the young couple and drove away without leaving any instructions."

Liam stared at his butler. "She left? My mother left and took Brooke with her?" Sickness twisted his belly. Hadn't she trusted him to at least *try* to do what was right?

"I can only guess that there was something in the letter that upset her greatly," Sloane said.

"Did she leave no word for me about where she was going?"

"No, Baron. But—" Sloane gave Padrick another uneasy look.

Fear sharpened Liam's temper. He felt the heat of it under his skin. "Whatever you have to say to me can be said in front of Baron Padrick," he snapped.

"The stallion has been fretful the last few days," Sloane said cautiously. "Refused to enter his stall one evening, and even Arthur couldn't control him."

No matter how valuable Oakdancer was, right now he didn't give a damn about the horse. He wanted to know about his mother and sister.

"The day Lady Elinore left, Arthur took Oakdancer for a run to see if he could calm the animal. He came back without the stallion, saying the horse was easier staying where he was—and he said he saw Lady Elinore and Miss Brooke there as well."

There was only one place the stallion would feel easier— the Old Place. He suddenly appreciated Sloane's efforts to tell him where Elinore and Brooke had gone without actually saying where they had gone.

"Don't allow any strangers in the house," Liam said. "No matter who they say they are or why they say they're here, don't let them in. Send a message to Squire Thurston to be wary of strangers, especially men. Tell him to pass that message along to the magistrate. I want to be informed of anyone coming to the village."

"Yes, Baron. I'll send the message right away."

"Come on," Liam said to Padrick. He dug his heels into his horse's sides, urging the tired animal to canter. It didn't occur to him until they were riding down the lane that led to the bridge that he should have offered to let Padrick stay at the manor.

When they reached the bridge, Padrick thrust out an arm that would have knocked Liam out of the saddle if he hadn't reined in sharply.

Padrick urged his horse forward, ahead of Liam's, and stopped just before his horse's hooves touched the bridge. He studied the stones and tall grass on the opposite bank.

"Blessings of the day to you, lady sprite," Padrick said.

Liam clenched his fists, impatient to find his family. Then he saw the small woman rise up out of the water and wondered if the fever dreams had returned.

"Blessings of the day," the sprite replied warily. "Fae Lord."

Padrick nodded. "My friend's family is visiting the Daughters in the Old Place."

"We know his face. He has crossed the bridge many times lately."

A water sprite. He was actually *seeing* one of the Small Folk. And they'd *watched* him every time he'd crossed the bridge to visit with Breanna and her family? "Has anyone else crossed the bridge recently?" he asked.

"Many," the sprite replied. "But none who do not belong here."

"You've seen no one else?" Padrick asked.

The sprite looked thoughtful. "Four men. They came to the edge of the Old Place farther upstream but did not cross into it. But they drew on the power here, and those who were nearby said that when they released the power again there was a . . . wrongness . . . to it. Then they left. We don't know where. We don't go beyond the boundaries of the Old Place." She tipped her head. "Were they Black Coats?"

"What do you know about the Black Coats?" Padrick demanded.

"The Bard warned the Daughters about them, and the Daughters asked us to watch, to give warning if they crossed into the Old Place. But the Black Coats did not enter, so we did no harm."

"The Bard?" Padrick said. "*The* Bard?"

"He and the Muse crossed the bridge many days ago. But they did not leave by the bridge. You will have to ask the Daughters where they went."

"Thank you," Padrick said. His horse crossed the bridge.

Liam followed, feeling a little stunned. As soon as he could, he urged his horse forward until he rode beside Padrick.

"That . . . that was one of the Small Folk," he said.

"Do you think the witches here will talk to me?" Padrick asked. "I'd like to know what the Bard might have told them about the Inquisitors."

"The Bard. You actually think the Fae Lord of Song was *here?*"

"The water sprite said he was."

A few days ago, the Fae had been nothing more than stories. Now he'd spent several days traveling with a man who looked human but was actually a Fae Lord, had seen one of the Small Folk, and had been told that *the* Bard had visited here. Maybe it was all the fever dreams he'd had that made this seem . . . normal . . . in an extraordinary kind of way.

"This is an Old Place," Liam said.

Padrick grinned, which only made him look more exhausted. "Laddy-boy, I knew this was an Old Place before I crossed the bridge. For one thing, I could *feel* the difference in the land. For another, the Small Folk don't live anywhere else."

"Why did she call the witches 'daughters'?"

"Witches are the Mother's Daughters. I guess you could say they are the Great Mother's hands, heart, and eyes."

Before Liam could ask anything else, a hawk screamed. He looked up, saw the bird diving toward them. Out of the corner of his eye, he saw Padrick's face change so that he looked like a Fae Lord.

With another scream that sounded a bit surprised, the hawk broke off its attack, circled them twice to get a good look at Padrick's face, then flew toward Breanna's house.

"What was that about?" Liam said, soothing his startled horse.

"That was a Fae Lord who, apparently, didn't like seeing two men riding toward the ladies' home."

"A Fae Lord. I didn't know there were any Fae around here." And he wondered what Breanna's reaction had been when she'd found out. He was certain she would have an opinion about Fae showing up on her doorstep. She had an opinion about everything.

"Didn't you?" Padrick said, something odd in the tone of his voice. His face changed so that he looked human again.

The next obstacle was a wall of armed men standing in front of the archway that led to the outbuildings behind Breanna's home.

Feeling the strain of a full day's ride, and impatient to see his mother, Liam was less than tactful. "Who are you?" he said sharply. "What's your business here?"

Not the best way to approach armed men, especially when two of them had bows drawn and aimed at him and Padrick and two others had crossbows.

"Who are *you?*" one of them demanded.

"That's Baron Liam," another man said, stepping up behind the armed men.

"You're Rory," Liam said, recognizing Breanna's cousin. "Tell these men to let us pass."

"You know him?" one the men asked Rory.

"He's the baron," Rory said. "Don't recognize the other one."

"If he's the *baron*, why should we let him pass?"

A window shot open with enough force that Liam started hoping the startled men had a good hold on the arrows pointed at him. Breanna leaned out the window.

"Rory, you featherhead, let them in," Breanna said testily. She ducked back inside the room.

The men lowered their weapons and stepped aside.

Liam's heart pounded, but he noticed Padrick looked like he was fighting not to grin as they rode through the arch.

"What?" Liam said.

"My wife would like her."

Mother's mercy.

Clay took their horses, giving them both a considering look after seeing Padrick's Fae horse.

For a place that usually seemed to have too few people, now Liam thought there were too many. Children who had been playing catch with a cloth ball a moment before they rode in now stared at them, too watchful. Idjit, naturally, was still focused on the ball and hadn't yet noticed the addition of two men and horses. Mother's tits! The hawk was a better watchdog than the dog!

Elinore burst out of the kitchen doorway and ran toward him, Breanna following more slowly.

Liam's arms went around his mother, holding her as tightly as she held him.

"Liam," Elinore said, her voice breaking. "I'm glad you're home. So glad."

"Mother, what's happened? Why—?" No, he wouldn't ask why Elinore was at the Old Place, not with Breanna looking so strained, as if she'd been fighting against grief.

"Was anything said at the barons' council? Was there any news?"

Liam brushed stray hairs away from his mother's face. "Why did you leave our home?" he asked quietly.

"I got a letter from Moira, and I was too frightened to stay at the estate while you were gone."

"From—" No. His father had trained him to have that reaction whenever Elinore mentioned her cousin Moira. It didn't have to be—*wouldn't be*—his reaction.

"Liam, have you heard anything about her village?"

"No, I . . ." Liam looked at Padrick, who shook his head.

"Let him read the letter, Elinore," Breanna said. "It might make sense to him then."

"Yes, of course. It's in my room. I'll get it." Stepping away from Liam, Elinore ran back into the house.

Liam took a step toward Breanna. "Who are all these people?"

"Kin," Breanna replied, brushing her dark hair away from her face. "They ran from the eastern barons and the Black Coats. The elders in the family stayed behind to cover their tracks, to hide that so many were gone. And now that we know what might have happened to them . . ."

Liam caught her arms as she swayed.

She glanced at Padrick and stiffened.

"This is Padrick, the Baron of Breton. He helped me get home." Liam forced a smile, hoping to ease her tension. "He's not a featherhead."

"At least not in this form," Padrick muttered—which made Liam wonder about the hawk he'd seen at times when they'd had to rest for an hour.

Breanna narrowed her eyes. "You're Fae? You're a Fae Lord *and* a gentry baron?"

Padrick gave her a small bow. "At your service, Mistress . . ."

"Breanna." Her eyes narrowed even more. "You don't have a sudden urge to go out and catch a rabbit, do you?"

Padrick glanced up. Following his gaze, Liam saw the
hawk soaring overhead, watching everything below it.

"No, Mistress Breanna, I have no urge to hunt rabbits at
the moment. Although, to be fair, he could hardly bring you
a deer."

"He doesn't do too well with salmon, either," Breanna
muttered. "But he tries."

Padrick chuckled. Liam wished he understood what was
so amusing.

Then Breanna rested a hand against his face. "You've
been ill," she said.

"I . . ." Liam took a deep breath, let it out slowly. "I was
poisoned."

She paled so much, Liam wondered if she was going to
faint.

"Poisoned? Why?"

"He spoke out in the council meeting against the eastern
barons and the Inquisitors," Padrick said.

"I would have died if it wasn't for Padrick's help," Liam
said.

"Mother's mercy," Breanna whispered.

"Perhaps you should sit down, Mistress Breanna,"
Padrick said gently.

She shook her head. "No. But the two of you should. Why
don't you sit under the tree there? I'll bring you some ale."

"You don't need to—," Liam said, but Breanna was already turning away and walking toward the house. He took a
step to stop her, but Padrick's hand on his arm held him back.

"She needs to do something useful," Padrick said. "And
you really do need to sit down."

They walked to the bench under the tree.

"Breanna is my sister," Liam said, settling on the bench.
"My half sister. My father . . ."

"You don't have to explain."

Breanna returned with tankards of ale. She handed one to each of them, then held out the letter to Liam. "Elinore is resting. She's frightened, Liam. We all are."

"Breanna . . ."

"Read the letter. Perhaps then you'll be able to tell her something that will ease her mind."

Breanna walked away.

Padrick took a sip of his ale, then stood up. "This is a private matter. I'll—"

"No," Liam said. He set his tankard on the bench. "I'd appreciate your opinion. And, obviously, this letter has been read by others, so whatever Moira wrote to my mother wasn't private in that way."

When Padrick settled on the bench beside him, Liam opened the letter.

Dearest Elinore,

I know my last letter must have hurt you when I told you so brusquely not to write to me again because I didn't want to hear from you anymore. I did want to hear from you, more than you can know, but I was afraid your letters might draw too much attention from the baron who rules my village and that you might suffer for it. I decided to tell you not to write because I was afraid, for both our sakes, of what you might say or the questions you might ask, and I couldn't write to you. But this letter will be my last, so I'll tell you all the things I haven't been able to say.

I have guests tonight, a young couple, recently wed, who are fleeing the eastern village where they had lived, hoping to get far enough west to escape the madness that has come over the barons here and has turned our lives, women's lives, into a barren nightmare. I have hidden them, given them food and a place to rest for a few hours. I gave them your direction, and I'll give them this letter in the hope that it reaches you.

I wouldn't send them to you if your husband still lived, but I think Liam has too much of you in him to be a man like his father. I hope with all my heart that is true.

We are less than prisoners now, Elinore. Less than slaves. Less than the animals men use. We are domestic labor who clean men's houses, cook their food, wash their clothes. And we are the whores they use when they want sex. That is what the baron's decrees have turned us into. We cannot work to earn a living for ourselves. We cannot express a thought or opinion or feeling that disagrees in the slightest way with what the men who are in charge of us think or say or feel. If we do, we are punished—sometimes publicly, sometimes privately. I've endured both. They are equally brutal. Even when the punishment doesn't do much harm to the body, it rapes the soul. Of course, the men call it discipline, the necessary force required to make us modest women who will not become the Evil One's servants.

We are forbidden to write stories and poems and plays. We are forbidden to write music, to paint, even to sketch. We can read only books men have given us permission to read, can play only the music it has been deemed acceptable for us to play.

We cannot write anything, not even a shopping list, without a man's approval, and that approval is indicated by his initials at the bottom of the page. That's why I haven't written to you. There is nothing I could say that I would want a man to see, and, because I've been known to be opinionated, I doubt I could write anything blandly enough to meet with approval. Trying to send a letter without that approval . . . One woman tried to write to family in another village farther west of here, asking if any of her male relatives would be willing to fetch her since we are no longer permitted to travel beyond the confines of our own village without the escort of a male relative. The letter was confiscated. On the orders of the baron and the magistrate, two of the woman's fingers were cut off so that she could no longer hold a pen.

We cannot talk to each other without a man present. If we do, we are brought before the magistrate and questioned ruthlessly about what was said—and telling the truth, that the conversation was nothing more than one woman seeking housekeeping advice from another, isn't believed. The women are "softened" by "small disciplines" until one of them breaks, confessing to having said whatever the magistrate or the baron—or the Inquisitor, if one is in the village at that time—has told her she said. Then, because those "confessions" usually admit to being a servant of the Evil One or having had contact with a witch, one or both women are killed.

And any man, especially if he isn't one of the gentry, who protests having a wife, a mother, a sister questioned or, may the Mother help him, tries to stop the killing after a woman has been condemned, is also condemned because, of course, no decent man would protest so he must already be ensnared by the Evil One. So even good men who are sickened by what has happened here have become harsh out of fear for their families.

But all these things are not the worst they've done to us. The baron decreed that too many incidents of "female hysteria" have disrupted the village and disturbed the community, meaning the men. A "procedure," brought over from Wolfram, I believe, was declared necessary for people's well-being, meaning the men. Neither the baron nor the magistrate nor the physicians who performed it explained what this "procedure" was, but men were assured they would not lose the use of their females for more than a few days, and that once it was done, we would be far less likely to be ensnared by the Evil One.

They cut us, Elinore. They took away that small nub of flesh so that there's no longer even the possibility of

*pleasure when we're with a man. They took that away
from all of us—not just the women in their prime, but
the elders and the girls. Maureen . . . A year ago, my
daughter began looking at the young men in the village
with interest. As the chains of the baron's decrees have
tightened around us, she looked at those same young
men in fear. Now she looks at them with soul-deep
dread. She will never know the juicy excitement of
being with a man. All she will know is passive submis-
sion. That's all any of us know anymore. It breaks my
heart when I hear her crying at night.*

*We're still alive, but we're no longer living, except
in our dreams.*

*How many of us, desperate and despairing, made a
heartfelt plea for some solace, some escape? Perhaps
many of us. Perhaps all of us.*

*One night I dreamt I was in the Old Place—not as
it is now, with so many of the trees cut down and the
meadows ripped by plows, but as it was a year ago
when the witches who had lived there still walked the
land. Maureen and I stood in a meadow, and soon
other women and girls joined us. There, for the first
time in so long, we could hold each other to give comfort. We could laugh, cry, rage, grieve without being silenced.*

*All the women from the village gathered in the
meadow of dream. That first night, I noticed a woman
standing at the edge of the meadow, almost hidden in
the shadows of the trees. I think, somehow, we had
summoned the Sleep Sister, the Lady of Dreams, and it
was her gift that made it possible for us to be together
in spirit while our bodies slept.*

*The first couple of nights, we were too relieved about
being together to think much about the woman standing
at the edge of the meadow. Then some of us began to
wonder how physically close she had to be to be able to
create this dream meadow for us, and we began to fear
what would happen to her if she were found.*

The third night, I approached her. She is truly lovely, Elinore, with her black hair flowing down her back and those dark eyes that see so much. I thanked her for the dream meadow—and I told her it wasn't safe for her to stay near this village unless she was staying in Tir Alainn most of the time, and even then it wasn't safe. Tears filled her eyes, and she told me that destroying the witches and the Old Place had also destroyed that piece of Tir Alainn. She told me she had to leave, it was too dangerous to stay, and when she left, the dream meadow would begin to fade. Some of us would be able to find it in our dreams for a few more nights, but she didn't think we would be able to find it in a way that we would be to-gether.

So I went back to the other women. We talked and talked and talked. The next night, we gathered again, but the edges of the meadow were soft, like a watercolor, instead of sharp like a painting done in oils. We made a choice that night, and we made a plan. Not all the women agreed because, they argued, we had a place to be together for a few hours. But the night after that, when only half of us were able to come together in the dream, we knew there weren't many nights left before we would be alone again, isolated again.

We cannot fight against the baron and his magistrate or the guards at their command, and we cannot fight against the Inquisitors. Even if we did, we wouldn't be able to take back our village and our lives. The other eastern barons would come in and crush us if we tried. There is only one way we can see to escape, and, at the same time, send out a warning to the rest of the women and men in Sylvalan. That is the choice we have made.

On the night of the Summer Moon, a night when the women of Sylvalan have traditionally celebrated their sexuality, we will gather at the Old Place for the last time.

The sky will begin to lighten soon. I must wake my

guests and send them on their way before too many men
are stirring.

I don't expect you to understand the choice I've
made. I hope the day never comes when you have rea-
son to understand. But I also hope that, after a time,
you'll be able to think of me again with kindness.

Blessings of the day to you, Elinore.

Your loving cousin,
Moira

Liam's hand fell limply into his lap. The fingers holding the
letter tightened on the paper as he stared at the ground just
ahead of him.

"They've gone mad," he said softly. "That's the only explanation. The barons in the east truly have gone mad. How
could they expect us to do this? To give the orders for *this*?"

"They courted ambition and other barons' purses," Padrick
said. "During all their talk in the council chamber, they were
very careful not to explain what the 'procedure' was. And I'm
not sure it's madness that has consumed them."

"What else could explain this?"

"The Fae aren't present here in the east, are they?" Padrick
asked, as if seeking confirmation.

Puzzled by the change of subject, Liam shook his head.
"You hear things once in a while about them coming down the
shining roads when they want to amuse themselves in the
human world. I've certainly heard stories about people who
have sworn they've seen one of the Fae. More often than not,
it's a young woman with a swollen belly claiming that she was
seduced by a Fae Lord, but sometimes it's someone who
needed help and was answered by one of the Fair Folk."

"In the west, the Fae's presence balances the power the
barons have in the counties they rule. No human touches an
Old Place, or the witches who live there, without answering to

the Clans. If the Fae are nothing more than visitors here in the east, there are only the witches in control of large tracts of land that the baron and the gentry can't touch. Prime timber, prime pastureland, prime hunting. If a man is greedy enough, wants that land enough, perhaps even fears that those women have power that could rival his own if they chose to use it, would he refuse the assistance of men who can promise to get rid of the witches in a way that no one will dare protest? If the Inquisitors have the means to force women to confess to things they've never done, then the baron conveniently eliminates the obstacles between himself and what he covets. Would such a man actually refuse to have a family of witches killed—especially when he doesn't have to get blood on *his* hands? I think not."

Padrick looked up at the leaves over his head and sighed. "But the blood *is* on his hands because he brought the Black Coats to his county. I imagine the eastern barons who agreed to that bargain discovered soon after that they were . . . ensnared . . . and don't dare refuse to carry out any other suggestions the Inquisitors now make about controlling females."

"I can't believe the barons who voted on the decrees would agree to have this carried out throughout Sylvalan. I *won't* believe it."

Padrick gave Liam a long, thoughtful look. "I wonder how many barons in Wolfram and Arktos said the same thing at one time. And I wonder how many of those barons who refused to follow the Inquisitors' dictates met with accidents. If you had died and the Inquisitors came to Willowsbrook to eliminate the witches and the female power they represent, would your successor have stood against them? Would he have risked his newly acquired wealth?"

"I—I don't even know who my successor would be," Liam said. "Probably some cousin on my father's side."

"You don't know," Padrick said quietly. "I think they do. I think the Inquisitors control the eastern barons now, and whoever controls the Inquisitors ... If you ever see *him*, you will see the face of evil."

A child laughed. Was quickly shushed by the others.

Such a normal sound, Liam thought. A child laughing.

Would his father have ordered this "procedure" done to Elinore? To Brooke?

Oh, yes. And the bastard would have smiled while giving the order. And he would have rejoiced if they'd taken Nuala and Keely and Breanna and ...

No. That had been a nightmare, a fever dream while they'd ridden through that Old Place. Just a nightmare. *Had* to be just a nightmare.

But Padrick had cried when they'd ridden away, too late to do anything, too fearful of who might be coming after them to stay a moment longer.

"What can I say to my mother?" Liam asked. "What can I possibly say to her about this?"

"I don't know. But I think, if they are willing, we need to talk to the Daughters."

"Not Keely. She's ... damaged. Nuala and Breanna ... yes, I think they'll talk to us." Folding the letter carefully, Liam tucked it in a pocket. He stood up—and felt old, used up. "Let's get it done."

As Padrick rose to stand beside him, a boy raced toward them, skidding to a stop a few feet away.

"Rory and Clay say there's a rider coming. Clay says it's Squire Thirsty and wants to know if the men should let him come in."

"His name is Thurston," Liam said, "and, yes, you should let him come in."

The boy raced back to the arch where the armed men waited. Liam and Padrick stayed where they were. Since the children had moved toward the stables, the bench under the tree was a good place for private conversations.

Squire Thurston rode through the archway, dismounted, and threw his horse's reins to the boy standing closest, then trotted toward the tree where Liam and Padrick waited. He was a middle-aged man who doted on his wife and was a good father to his four children. His land was well tended, his tenant farmers and servants well cared for. A cheerful man who was content with what he had, his opinion about almost everything was respected by villagers and farmers alike, which had always incensed Liam's father.

The man trotting toward them didn't look cheerful or content. There was fear, almost panic, in his face.

"Baron Liam," Thurston said, panting. "Thank the Mother you're back! Is it true, sir? What did the barons say? What are they going to *do?*"

"Do about what?" Liam asked.

Thurston gaped at him. "About what happened in Pickworth!"

Pickworth. Moira's village. "What happened?" Liam said sharply.

"I—I thought that's why you were delayed," Thurston stammered. "I thought the riders had reached Durham before the council ended and that's why . . ."

"Mother's tits, man," Padrick snapped. "Just tell us what happened."

"Baron Padrick and I left Durham on the night of the Summer Moon, after I . . . became ill," Liam said.

Thurston stared at them for a moment, as if he couldn't quite understand what they'd said. Then he whispered, "That's when it happened. On the night of the Summer Moon. The women . . ."

Liam's stomach churned as he remembered Moira's words. *On the night of the Summer Moon, a night when the women of*

*Sylvalan have traditionally celebrated their sexuality, we will
gather at the Old Place for the last time.* "What about the
women?"

Thurston's eyes shone with tears. "They killed themselves.
They killed their daughters, even the babes. They— They're
all dead, Liam. All dead. From the oldest granny to the
youngest babe. Many of them snuck out of their homes and
went to the Old Place. But even the ones who were still safely
at home . . . They're all dead. All of them."

Liam stumbled back a step, sank down on the bench as his
legs gave out.

Padrick muttered, "Mother's mercy," and wiped his hands
over his face. "How did you hear of this?"

"A rider came by yesterday," Thurston said. "Said the
barons' council had sent out messengers to warn other villages
that the men should be on their guard and keep a more vigilant
watch on the females in their communities. The rider said . . ."
He looked around, suddenly nervous. "The rider said the eastern barons were claiming this was the work of the Evil One . . .
and that witches were the Evil One's tools. That *they* caused
the madness that made the women do such a terrible thing."

Padrick swore softly, viciously.

"Liam," Thurston said. He took a moment to steady himself. "Baron Liam. I—I have a wife and two daughters. I'm
afraid for them. For all the women in Willowsbrook. What if
this madness comes here?"

"It won't," Liam said numbly. "As long as I rule this
county, the things that were done that made those women welcome death will never happen here."

"But what about the Evil One?" Thurston looked around,
lowered his voice. "And the witches?"

Liam bristled at the suspicion in Thurston's voice, but
Padrick asked calmly, "Do you know the ladies who live here?
Have you ever talked to them?"

Thurston stiffened. "Course I know them. I know all my neighbors. Fine ladies. When our youngest was born and my dear wife was feeling poorly, wasn't it Mistress Nuala who came by with a simple that she said had the strength of the earth, and didn't my wife start getting stronger within a day? And weren't they the ones, that year when we had a hard winter, who told me my tenants could take a deer or two from the Old Place and share the meat among them, and didn't that make the difference in keeping them all healthy and fed? Every year I send a few of my men over for a day during planting and harvest to give Clay and Edgar a hand with the fields, and I'll send them again this year if extra hands are needed. They're fine ladies, and good neighbors, and I won't stand by and let anyone say differently."

"They're witches," Padrick said quietly.

"I know they're witches," Thurston said testily. "Doesn't mean they aren't fine people and good neighbors."

"And yet, when you rode in here, you were suspicious of them, almost afraid to be here."

"I—" Thurston frowned. "Maybe it was the messenger's talk of the Evil One that disturbed my mind. Or maybe it was Dudley's talk about men needing to do their duty and keep their women modest so that they won't draw the Evil One to them."

A chill went through Liam. "Did you get my warning? Have any strangers come to Willowsbrook over the last few days?"

"Two men rode in a few days ago. Tucked into a big meal at the tavern, and also bought a couple of the meat pies to take with them. Dudley remarked on it when I stopped in. Said he'd told them the beef in the pies would likely spoil at this time of year if they weren't eaten soon, but the men didn't pay him any heed. They bought a jug of ale from him, too." Thurston paused. "It was after that he started talking about this Evil One."

"Four men, four strangers, would have drawn more attention than two," Padrick said thoughtfully. "They could have been buying the food for the two who stayed away from the village."

"Why would they care if anyone noticed four travelers or two?" Thurston asked.

"Because they were Inquisitors," Liam answered softly. Those men had been so close to Elinore and Brooke . . . and Breanna. If there hadn't been so many of Breanna's kin around here, so many armed and wary men, would he have ridden up to this house and found something very different? Something that would have haunted his dreams for the rest of his life? "They were Inquisitors. Black Coats. The Evil One's servants."

Thurston paled. "They were in our village. Why were they in our village?"

"To do exactly what they did," Padrick said. "Plant a seed of fear and suspicion about witches in the people here."

"But . . . why?"

"So that you would stand aside when they returned and not utter so much as a protest when they tortured the witches into confessing to things they never did in order to justify killing them," Liam said.

"If they accuse the witches," Thurston protested, "what's to stop them from accusing other women and killing them?"

"Nothing," Padrick said quietly. "Nothing at all."

Thurston took out a handkerchief, mopped the sweat from his face. "What do we do?"

"Your opinion is respected, Squire Thurston," Liam said. "If you refuse to give in to the fear that was planted, if you stand by what you believe to be right and good, we can stop this before it has a chance to take root."

Thurston studied Liam thoughtfully. "You stand against these . . . Black Coats?"

"I do."

"Then I'll stand with you." Thurston stuffed the handkerchief into his pocket. "I'll talk to the magistrate, if you like. And I'll talk to my tenants, make sure they know to inform me about any strangers." He turned away, then turned back. "Don't you have kin in Pickworth?"

"My mother's cousin and her daughter lived there."

Thurston looked at the ground. "I am sorry, Liam."

"So am I."

"My condolences to your mother. If there's anything my wife and I can do . . ."

Liam smiled stiffly. "Thank you. If there is anything, I'll remember to ask."

He watched Thurston stride across the lawn to where the boy still held his horse. He watched the squire ride through the arch.

"What am I going to tell my mother?"

Padrick sat on the bench beside him. "The truth. You weren't hearing what was under the message the council sent out, Liam. The eastern barons aren't going to want women to know about this. They're sending out riders so the men will smother the truth of what happened. If the women in one village are willing to make that choice, what's to stop others from making the same choice? And if the women who haven't been caged hear about it, it will be far more difficult for any man, even an Inquisitor, to ride into a village and try to turn things to his advantage." He paused. "They must have some kind of magic similar to the Fae's gift of persuasion. That would explain how the ideas get planted."

"And some ability to draw power from an Old Place and turn it into a . . . wrongness," Liam added. "But what does that wrongness become?"

"Let's hope that information is something the Bard passed along to the ladies here."

Liam felt his strength waning. Would Nuala object if he stayed here for a few hours to get some sleep? Would Breanna? "Let's talk to them."

Sitting in the formal dining room, Breanna laid her head down on her crossed arms. She felt exhausted, numb, tangled up in too many feelings.

A whole village of women desperate enough to gather on a night that had always been about life and feeling alive and choose Death as the lover—and angry enough and courageous enough to make that choice for their daughters.

Not a choice she would want to make, and she couldn't say with any honesty that she thought it was the right choice. But she didn't know what it was like to live as those women had lived. She couldn't say if having your life stripped away piece by piece until you were a mind and heart locked in a body someone else controlled could produce a rage that festered until it found the one thing a man couldn't control.

It wouldn't have been violent. She was certain of that. She could picture them slipping away from their houses—some of them probably slipping out of beds while the men who had used them snored contentedly—and gathering in the Old Place. There would be hugs, a few silent tears. Some of them would have had second thoughts, especially those whose husbands or lovers were good men who grieved over what had been done to their wives, their daughters, their sisters and mothers. They would have had second thoughts. And those who held a baby girl to the breast for the last time ... A minute of desperate hope that, perhaps, if the child were spared, by the time she grew up things would be different, someone would find a way to fix the wrongness and the girl would grow up in the same kind of world her mother had before the Inquisitors came to Sylvalan to spread their plague of hatred against women. Then the hope would fade, and the desperation would remain.

It wouldn't have been violent. There were plants that were deadly if picked and distilled the right way. Some of those women were bound to know enough about herbs to make a drink from those plants. Just cook it on the stove, right next to the day's soup. Pour it into jugs and hide everything in the pantry until it was time to go. Then, in the Old Place, a cup someone had hidden in a skirt pocket. The jug passed around. Stretch out on the ground, with your arms around a daughter or a friend, and just slip away from the world, following Death's song.

It wouldn't have been violent. There would have been no pain. But even for the oldest of them, it had been a life that had ended too soon.

Hearing footsteps, Breanna forced herself to lift her head. She jabbed her fingers through her hair, pushing it away from her face.

The dining room door opened. Nuala came in first, followed by Padrick, who carried a tea tray. Liam came in last, shutting the door behind him.

Just the four of them now. The large room had been crammed with the adults while Padrick and Liam had talked about what had happened at the barons' council—and had broken the news about what had happened in Pickworth, while she and Nuala had told them everything they could remember about the things Aiden and Lyrra had said about the Black Coats and the nighthunter creatures that may have been created when the Black Coats who had come to Willowsbrook had drawn power from the Old Place.

He's exhausted, Breanna thought as she watched Liam take a seat at the table. *And he's still far from well.*

"I won't take much more of your time," Padrick said. "There are still a couple more things I need to know."

Breanna accepted the cup of tea Nuala poured for her, then set it on the table untouched. "What do you want to know?"

"Thank you," Padrick said, taking the tea Nuala offered. "I need to return home as quickly as I can."

"Yes," Nuala said. "I suppose you'd like to know how the vote turned out, and the other barons can tell you that."

Padrick shook his head. "It doesn't matter how the vote turned out. The west will never accept what the eastern barons have done. I'm not as concerned about that as I am about my family."

Breanna saw Liam jolt, saw his face become paler.

"You think the barons or the Black Coats might go after your family because you helped me?" Liam said.

"They came here, Liam," Padrick said. "Whether they came here to finish what they'd started in Durham or to do harm to your family and your people doesn't matter. They came here. The Inquisitors aren't stupid men. Once they questioned the men who had been hired to kill you and make it look like a robbery—"

"Wait," Breanna said. "How can being poisoned possibly look like robbery?"

"They sent men after him," Padrick said. "If he'd been beaten to death, the physician who was called to confirm the death wouldn't have looked for anything else."

"Padrick got me away from them," Liam said. "But I was already poisoned. At my club."

"So it wouldn't have taken the Inquisitors long to have someone report on which barons didn't show up the next morning for the vote, question the men for a description of the man who got you away from them, and come to the conclusion that it was me," Padrick said. "If they took a ship, or simply rode hard, there would have been plenty of time for them to get to the west and find my wife and children."

"You've known that all along, haven't you?" Liam said. "You knew that the first night, when you offered to help me get home instead of riding straight for the west."

Padrick didn't answer.

That had taken courage, Breanna decided. To help a man you barely knew, and all during the days of that journey, aware that an enemy might be approaching your own family. "What do you want to know?"

"It's dangerous for me to ride south, and going north will take too long," Padrick said. He hesitated. "Would the ones who rule the Mother's Hills object to my going through their land?"

"The House of Gaian lives in the Mother's Hills," Breanna said, her voice a bit sharp. Did the man know so little about witches that he truly believed he'd come to harm just because he traveled the roads through the Mother's Hills?

"I know that, Mistress Breanna," Padrick said. "That's why I'm asking you, one of the Mother's Daughters, if the House of Gaian would object."

"You're a baron," Liam said, rubbing his forehead as if it pained him. "The baron who rules there wouldn't withhold his consent."

"That's the point, Liam," Padrick said. "The Mother's Hills belong to the House of Gaian. The barons don't rule any part of it. Our decrees don't apply there."

"A part of Sylvalan, yet apart from Sylvalan," Breanna said softly.

"Yes," Padrick agreed. "Just as the Old Places are apart from the human communities. They're the home of the Small Folk and the witches . . . and the Fae."

"The Fae don't make their home here."

"But in the west they do. The Old Places are the wellsprings of the Great Mother's power, and the home of magic. So those are the places the Clans call home. That is the land they defend and allow no humans to encroach upon."

"They didn't do much to defend the Old Places in the east, did they?"

"No, they didn't—and they've paid for it."

Remembering what Lyrra and Aiden had told her, Breanna held her tongue. She wanted to fight with someone because she was tired and scared and her heart hurt for the kin she was certain she had lost, but it wasn't fair to fight with this baron who was also a Fae Lord. He, too, was tired and had family to worry about.

Nuala spoke for the first time. "You'll be welcome in the Mother's Hills. We can send you to kin there. They'll help you on your journey as much as they can."

"My thanks, ladies." Padrick pushed away from the table. "Now I'd better—"

"You'll stay here tonight," Nuala said. "You'll have a good dinner and a good night's sleep. In the morning, Breanna and Rory will escort you to the trail that leads into the hills."

"You've more than enough people to feed, Mistress Nuala," Padrick protested. "I can—"

"That is correct. We've plenty of people who need to be fed," Nuala said. "Two more won't make any difference. You're staying, as well, Liam. Spare yourself the trouble of arguing. The decision has been made."

For the first time since yesterday, when Elinore and Brooke had come racing up to the house, Breanna had to fight a smile as Padrick sank back into his chair and sipped the now-cold tea.

"I daresay you are not accustomed to being spoken to that way," Nuala said.

Padrick choked a little as he swallowed the tea. "You wouldn't say that if you met my wife."

Nuala smiled. "I hope to have the pleasure one day."

Chapter Twenty-two

"Ian? Ian, where are you?"

Ignoring the old woman's confused, almost tearful call, Ubel slipped through the crowd of people on the docks and headed briskly for the posting station to see if there were any horses available for hire. Or, if the mail coach was ready to leave, perhaps he could obtain a seat instead of waiting for one of the passenger coaches. No. A horse. He'd had enough of being crammed in with this Sylvalan filth. And he didn't want to take the chance that the old bitch who was looking for him might be escorted to the posting house before he could leave and try to latch on to him now that she was no longer useful.

Ian. A filthy Sylvalan name. But it had served its purpose, just as the woman had. Just tools to discard now that he was through with them.

He found the posting station. The horses available for hire looked like barely adequate, rough-gaited animals, but he settled for what he thought was the best of them, tied his saddlebags behind the saddle, and made his way through Wellingsford until he reached the road that would take him east to Durham—and to Master Adolfo.

As he kicked the horse into an easy canter, Ubel smiled coldly. He had gotten out of the west, had gotten away from the Fae. Master Adolfo wouldn't be pleased that he'd lost the Inquisitors he'd brought with him, but he thought his report on the Fae's active presence in the west would mollify the Master Inquisitor's displeasure over the loss of the men. After all, even Adolfo hadn't been successful in his confrontation with one of the Fae.

Chapter Twenty-three

S *nort.*
    Stamp.

Aiden looked at the dark horse standing several feet away from him. Sighed. Put the saddle on the ground. Tried to ignore Lyrra's muffled giggles as she saddled her mare.

"All right, Minstrel," he said. "One song—a *short* song—and then we have to go."

Minstrel, the dark horse, tossed his head.

Aiden took a breath.

Minstrel pricked his ears.

Aiden sang the fifth and sixth verses of the tavern song he'd been singing as "a short song" for the past two mornings. When he got to the chorus, he remembered to give it the same hearty enthusiasm as he would have in a crowded tavern to encourage people to sing along.

Minstrel bobbed his head and made odd little sounds, as if he were trying to find a way to sing along.

Aiden finished the last note, gave Lyrra an irritated look when she grinned at him and applauded, and picked up the saddle.

Minstrel walked over to him, a sure indication there would be no sulking this morning. But as Aiden got Minstrel saddled, he also noticed the horse mouthing the bit a little too thoughtfully, and he decided to do the last four verses of the song tomorrow. If Minstrel somehow figured out he'd been given *pieces* of a song every morning instead of a whole song . . .

You couldn't catch a dark horse that didn't want to be caught. You couldn't ride a dark horse that didn't want to be ridden. And a dark horse that was sulking could rattle a man's bones instead of giving a smooth, sweet ride.

But, Mother's mercy, the horse had more passion for music than any wide-eyed apprentice he'd ever worked with. Which was why he'd started calling the horse Minstrel, even though the Fae weren't in the habit of naming animals. At least with an apprentice, he could smile and decline to indulge the child with a song. He rarely declined, but he *could*. Minstrel simply kept trotting out of reach, refusing to be saddled until he got his morning song. In a battle of wills, Aiden was quickly learning he was no match for a stubborn dark horse.

Ah, well. As Lyrra had pointed out yesterday, he was used to singing for his supper. Now he just had to sing for the saddling, too.

After checking the girth once more, Aiden mounted. Gathered the reins. Noticed that Minstrel was still mouthing the bit far too thoughtfully.

Then he looked at Lyrra and saw the smile on her lips, the laughter in her eyes. The little comedy he and Minstrel played out every morning had done her more good than decent meals and restful sleep, and for that he felt grateful. By tomorrow, they would reach the western Clans. Once they crossed the boundary that divided those Clans from the rest of the Fae, he didn't think they'd get much rest.

Chapter Twenty-four

M orag and Ashk studied the two dead trees and the partially eaten bodies around them. Birds. Squirrels. Even a young fox.

"You've seen this before?" Ashk asked quietly. She looked at the surrounding trees—and kept her fingers on the bowstring, ready to draw back the loosely nocked arrow.

"I've seen this before," Morag replied. "Where there were nighthunters."

"So the Black Coats did leave some of their foul magic behind." Ashk went back to studying the dead trees. "Those trees weren't dead a couple of days ago. The Clan has stayed watchful. The hunters have ridden out every day, checking the trails, looking for signs of these creatures. None of them noticed two trees that were suddenly dying or animals killed and then left to rot."

"I think they consume the blood first. That's what they prefer to devour—and the spirit once the body dies. They eat the flesh last, if they're still hungry." But even if the victim managed to escape, the bites would fester and rot the flesh around them. A slower death, but death nonetheless. Remembering the nighthunter attacks she had managed to evade, Morag shuddered. Her gift as Death's Mistress could do little against the creatures since there was nothing in them for her to gather. Releasing her gift would only stun the nighthunters, but it would kill any other living creature that was around them.

"None of those kills are fresh," Ashk said. "But they didn't happen that long ago, either."

"They've moved on," Morag said, turning in a slow circle, listening. Listening. "Once they kill the tree they're nesting in and can't draw anything more from it, they move on, find another tree for the nest. There are a lot of them. Somewhere in the Old Place, there are a lot of them."

Ashk gave her a considering look. "Why do you say that?"

"They killed too much too fast. There was no sign of them yesterday. At least, nothing we could see and recognize. Now, today, there are dead trees and devoured animals. There has to be a lot of nighthunters to consume so much so fast."

"This is close to Ari and Neall's part of the Old Place." Ashk let out a huff of air. "Which direction did they go? Is it possible that enough of them were created that they've formed more than one nest?"

Shivering at the thought, Morag shook her head. "I don't know."

"We're going to have to find out. Let's get back to the Clan house and warn—"

A flutter of wings made Ashk whip around. Before she finished turning, her bow was drawn back, the arrow ready to fly.

The raven that had just perched on a tree branch let out a startled caw.

Ashk lowered the bow and carefully eased the tension on the bowstring. "Report."

The raven fluttered to the ground and changed to a flustered adolescent girl. "I thought you should know that Evan and Caitlin went out riding. Evan said there were a couple of things he wanted to get from the manor house, and Caitlin said she needed some things, too."

Temper blazed in Ashk's eyes. "I didn't give them permission to go out riding, let alone ride to the manor house."

"That's what we told them, but they were mounted and ready to ride out before any of us noticed that they hadn't just gone into the stables to groom their horses. We *told* them not to go, but Evan insisted that they couldn't come to any harm since it was daylight and you'd defeated the Black Coats."

Ashk bared her teeth and snarled.

The sound, coming from a human throat, startled Morag enough to stop thinking. In that moment, when her mind was blank and open, she heard Death's whisper.

"Owen went with them. They said they didn't need an escort, but he rode out with them anyway."

Morag pictured the young Fae male. Death crooned a warning.

"We have to go," she said, pushing past Ashk to reach the place on the trail where her dark horse waited for her. "We have to find them."

They'd left the horses at a place where a game trail crossed the forest trail the Fae rode. Had left them there because the horses had picked up the scent of death even before Ashk, with her keen sense of smell, had.

Now Morag flung herself into the saddle, hearing Ashk, behind her, telling the girl to warn the Clan that signs of the nighthunters had been found. The dark horse turned on his own and trotted up the game trail, waiting for Morag to gather the reins and shove her feet into the stirrups before changing to a canter.

This way, Morag thought. *Yes, this way.* It wasn't the same path the children would have taken, but it was going in the right direction.

She heard the pounding of hooves behind her. Knew that Ashk had caught up.

Foolish children. What made them think they were beyond Death's attention? They *knew* there were dangers in the woods, even at the safest times.

But they were children, and they still believed there were no shadows in the light, just as they probably believed there was no light in the shadows. It would take a few more years before they understood you didn't have one without the other.

Great Mother, let them have those years.

A break in the trees. A narrow clearing.

The dark horse stretched into a gallop.

She heard a male voice scream, broken by fear and pain. She heard other voices scream, young and high pitched.

And Death summoned.

Too late. Too late.

"This way!" Ashk yelled.

They rode hard, weaving through the trees with reckless speed until they burst out into daylight.

And saw.

"No!" Ashk screamed.

A moment caught by the eye, frozen by memory. Morag knew she would see it for a long time whenever she closed her eyes.

A small horse galloping away from the edge of the woods, the rider clinging desperately to the saddle, the horse running for the place it still remembered as *home,* the place that meant safety. Running back to Neall.

Two riderless horses galloping after the small horse.

Owen, still thrashing weakly, covered with winged, black bodies tearing at his flesh, gulping down his blood.

Evan on the ground, the small knife in one hand raised in

an effort to defend himself from the swarm of nighthunters that were almost on him.

And the stag, with nighthunters already covering its haunches, leaping into the swarm, drawing the creatures' attention away from the boy by offering them that big, powerful body.

Then Ashk was gone, her saddle empty, the bow and quiver of arrows on the ground beside her trembling horse.

And a snarling shadow hound raced for the boy.

Morag reined in hard. Tumbled out of the saddle. Ran back a few steps and grabbed the quiver of arrows. The bow wouldn't do her any good, but the arrows . . .

The stag, almost completely covered by nighthunters, tossed its great head, catching two nighthunters on the tines of its antlers as it tried to dislodge the creatures closest to its eyes and throat. It went down, rolling to crush some of the nighthunters under its weight. Got back up on its feet and kept struggling, fighting.

The shadow hound reached Evan. He yelped when her teeth sank into his shoulder, nipping flesh along with the shirt and coat. She pulled him back a few feet, away from the nighthunters still flying around trying to get a piece of the stag who kept pivoting, kept swinging its head, using the antlers as a many-pronged knife. Then the shadow hound changed back to her human form and pulled the large hunting knife out of the sheath in her boot.

There was nothing Morag could do for Ashk and the boy, but there *was* something she could do for Owen. Pulling an arrow from the quiver, she ran toward him. Sensing the moment when his body gratefully yielded to Death's caress, she gathered his spirit and pulled it away from the dead flesh before the nighthunters could begin to feast on it.

Narrowing the focus of her gift, she released it straight at the dead body. The nighthunters rose up, squeaking—and headed right for her.

They were bigger, stronger. Twice the size of others she'd seen. Mother's mercy!

She released her power again.

Two nighthunters veered off, flying erratically for the shadows of the woods. The others fell to the ground, squeaking and flopping around.

Not much time, Morag thought as she ran toward them. She drove the arrow through the body of the first one she came to, pinning it to the ground. Pulling out another arrow, she drove it into the next body, jumping back when it tried to lunge and sink its sharp teeth into her foot. Again and again, she drove an arrow through a black, winged body until all those nighthunters were pinned to the ground.

Glancing at the woods, she quickly moved away from the trees. The nighthunters didn't like daylight, but if prey was close enough, they'd dart out of the shadows to feast.

She turned toward Ashk, not sure what she could do—and saw the remaining nighthunters abandon their prey and fly back toward the safety of the trees; saw the stag stumble for a couple of steps before it bounded away, blood flowing from wounds that were already turning dark and rotten; saw Ashk, her face stark with a kind of brutal beauty, splattered with gore from the nighthunters that had come within reach of her knife, standing over her son; and, with some surprise, saw Neall, mounted bareback on Shadow, releasing an arrow and bringing down another nighthunter before it reached the trees.

The ground was littered with the creatures' bodies—and there were still more of them hiding in the shadows.

Neall swung a leg over Shadow's neck and slid to the ground, an arrow nocked in his bow, his eyes still watching the trees as he sidestepped over to where Ashk stood.

Her legs trembling, Morag walked over to join them.

"Caitlin?" she asked, looking at Neall.

"She's fine," Neall said. "I was bringing the horses in closer to the stables when I saw her. After she told me where Evan was, I sent her to the cottage. Ari will look after her."

"Mother?" Evan said, pushing himself up until he was sitting. His face pinched up with an effort not to cry. Tears spilled over anyway. "Mother, I'm sorry."

Ashk stared at nothing, said nothing.

"What happened?" Neall asked, his tone sharp. "Why were you out riding on your own?"

"I—I wanted to get a couple of things from the manor house," Evan stammered. "It was daylight, and the Black Coats were gone, so I— We weren't going far, and we've gone by ourselves lots of times before. But Caitlin asked if she could ride my horse, and I said she could ride it a little, so we stopped here, just for a minute. But the horse kept acting strange once Caitlin got on his back. Kept trying to pull away and head for your cottage. Then Owen said he thought he saw something in the trees. Told me to hold his horse while he went to take a look. He didn't go very far into the trees before he screamed and ran out and those . . . *things* . . . were on him. And the horse ran away with Caitlin, and I couldn't hold the other two and Owen was on the ground with those things all over him, and I tried to run but I turned my ankle and fell and . . . Mother, I'm *sorry.*"

"It wasn't your fault," Ashk said in an empty voice. "You were wrong to leave the Clan house without permission, wrong to think you knew more than those of us who had warned you there was a new danger in the woods. Those mistakes are yours, and you must answer for them. But what happened here to Owen and—" She pressed her lips together.

Morag watched Ashk fight some inner battle for control.

"What happened here wasn't your fault," Ashk said, finally looking down at her son. "The first person who rode this way would have been attacked."

Evan's lips quivered as tears ran down his face. "But it wouldn't have been Owen . . . or *him*."

Him? Morag wondered, then realized Evan meant the stag.

"Whether you were here or not, he would have been," Ashk said. "He would have sensed their presence in the woods, would have searched for that dark festering until he found its source." She took a deep breath. Let it out slowly. "Neall, it would be a kindness if you'd take Evan back to the cottage with you and keep him and Caitlin tonight. There's something I need to do."

"I can track the stag," Neall said gently. "I'll find him and—"

"No. I know where he's gone. Just . . . look after my children, if you will."

Ashk walked back to her horse, picked up her bow, and mounted.

"Go with her," Neall said, looking at Morag. He slipped the arrow into the quiver on his back, then held out a hand to Evan. "Up you go, laddy-boy. Let's see if you can hobble over to Shadow, or if he has to come to you."

Leaving them, Morag hurried to her dark horse. She slung the quiver over one shoulder and stifled a curse when strands of hair tangled in the straps and pulled. Now she understood why Ashk had started braiding her long hair and wrapping the braids around her head.

She caught up to Ashk easily enough and almost pointed out that this wasn't the direction the stag had headed—and she doubted he would get very far.

But he wasn't always a stag. That had slipped past her in that frozen moment because his leap into the swarm had seemed so terrible and so *right*.

No, he wasn't always a stag, and when they finally reached a meadow, Morag saw that she'd underestimated him. He was there, moving slowly, painfully toward the center of the meadow where wildflowers danced and there were no shadows. When he reached the spot, he stood there, his legs spread and shaking, his head down as if he could no longer hold up the great rack of antlers.

Ashk rode out partway to meet him. She dismounted, then waited for Morag to do the same.

Morag looked at the stag. Blood dripped on the grass beneath him. In the stillness, she could hear his harsh effort to breathe.

Ashk held out a hand.

Morag slipped the quiver off her shoulder and offered it.

Ashk took one arrow, nocked it loosely in the bow.

"Who is he?" Morag asked softly.

Ashk kept her eyes on her bow. "Kernos. He was the Green Lord, the Hunter. He's still the old Lord of the Woods. And he's my grandfather."

"But . . . another took his place as the Hunter years ago."

"Another became the Hunter years ago, but there's no one who could take his place, no one who could be what he was." Ashk looked up at the stag. Her eyes were clear of tears . . . and full of a terrible grief.

Morag placed a hand on Ashk's arm. "You don't have to do this."

"In his own way, he chose a warrior's death. He chose to leave this world as the old Lord of the Woods. So I'll honor him by taking him while he still stands."

Morag's hand tightened on Ashk's arm. "You don't have to do this," she said again—and saw the moment when Ashk understood what she was saying. She could gather his spirit, take it from that dying body without Ashk doing anything.

Ashk stepped aside, pulling away from Morag's hand. "Yes, I do."

She walked out into the meadow until she stood a few yards away from the stag. She took aim, drew back the bow-string, and waited.

The stag slowly, painfully raised his head until he stood straight and tall for the last time, his dark eyes watching Ashk.

"Good-bye, Grandfather. We'll meet again in the Summerland."

The arrow sang Death's song. Pierced the chest. Found the heart.

The stag fell.

Morag closed her eyes. *You could have asked me, Ashk. I would have spared you that pain.* When she opened her eyes, she saw the ghost of an old man, limping slightly, moving toward her. He stopped when he came abreast of Ashk—and he smiled.

"Ashk?" Morag said. "Would you like me to ride back to the Clan house with you?"

Ashk shook her head, her eyes still focused on the stag. "You have your own journey to make now. I'll stay with him and keep watch. But I'd consider it a kindness if you would stop by the Clan house and let them now I'm here—and also ask if someone will go to Ari's cottage. If she's willing, and feels strong enough, I'd like her to turn the earth for him. I'd like him to return to the Great Mother in the spot where he chose to fall."

Morag looped the quiver's strap over the horn of Ashk's saddle. She mounted her dark horse, waited until Kernos's ghost floated up behind her. Then she rode away from the meadow, following a wide forest trail that she was certain led to the Clan house. She hadn't gone far when she met up with

several Fae males, who were scouting that trail for signs of
nighthunters, and delivered her messages.

She rode on until she found another small clearing, bright
with daylight. She could open the road that led to the Shadowed Veil from anywhere she was, but she didn't want to
come back down that road and touch the world again among
the shadows of the woods.

Once she opened it, the dark horse cantered up the road to
the Shadowed Veil. When they reached the Veil, she released
Owen's spirit, saw his ghost form a few feet in front of her.
He bowed to her—or, perhaps, it was to the ghost who rode
behind her—then turned and walked through the Shadowed
Veil to follow the path to the Summerland.

Kernos floated down to stand beside the dark horse.
"Gatherer, is it permissible for you to give a message from
the dead to the living?"

"It's permissible."

"Then tell her I am proud of her courage. I am proud of
her heart."

Morag swallowed the lump in her throat. "I'll tell her."

Kernos studied her for a moment. "You're of a kind, you
and Ashk. It's glad I am to know she has such a friend in this
season of her life. Blessings of the day to you, Gatherer."

"Blessings of the day to you, Kernos."

He walked up to the Shadowed Veil, and through it, without looking back.

Morag stared at the Veil for a long time before she turned
the dark horse and went back down the road to the living
world.

It was late that evening before Morag tapped on Ashk's
door. She didn't wait for an answer before going in, wasn't
sure she would get one.

After returning from the Shadowed Veil, she'd come back

to the Clan house to wait for Ashk and Ari. When they'd finished giving Kernos's body back to the Great Mother, Ari had stayed at the Clan house long enough to have a bite to eat, then had gone home, her pony cart surrounded by armed Fae.

Ashk had said little, had eaten little. She had simply sat at the big outdoor table, her silent grief a wall none of the Fae could breach.

Now that everyone had retired for the night, except those who were standing guard, it was time to see if she could reach the woman behind that wall of grief.

Ashk sat on the bed. She'd put on a nightgown and had taken her hair down so that it flowed in waves down her back. But her eyes still stared at nothing—or at something only she could see.

Morag sat on the bed, close but not touching.

"The meadow was our favorite place," Ashk said softly. "He'd take me there to play, to learn, to talk. He taught me everything I know about the woods, taught me how to use the knife and the bow, taught me about the shadows and the light. And he . . . accepted me when the rest of my family couldn't. Even in the west, many of the Fae are not . . . easy . . . about being around a Fae whose other form is a shadow hound."

"It's a rare form to have," Morag said, keeping her voice as soft and low as Ashk's. *And a dangerous one.*

"I loved him." Ashk's voice broke. The first tear slipped down her cheek. "He had a laugh that— When you heard it, you knew it was the Green Lord, laughing with joy and delight. And after I'd met Padrick . . . after the night of the Summer Moon when I realized I was carrying Padrick's child and he wanted me to wed him in the human way . . . We sat in the meadow, and when I told Grandfather I carried a child, he laughed that laugh. He said my womb had ripened for a fine man, and I should take the man as well as the seed. He said it was the green season of my life and I should honor it, that the other seasons would come soon enough. So I married Padrick in the human way, and the Green Lord stood beside me while I did it."

"Your grandfather sounds like a fine man."

"He taught me. He taught Padrick how to shift to his other form. Padrick had been raised human, and his Fae heritage had been slow to ripen."

Like Neall? Morag wondered.

Tears flowed down Ashk's cheeks. "He taught me everything I know, but it's not enough. It's still not enough. And now h-he's *gone.*"

Morag wrapped her arms around Ashk as the wall finally broke and the grief flowed with the tears.

"He'll be remembered, Ashk," Morag said, rocking the woman in an attempt to give comfort. "He'll be remembered."

"How? He's from the west, and the B-Bard has never troubled himself to come here. Who will remember him for all that he was?"

You will, Morag thought. *And, somehow, I'll find a way to reach Aiden and convince him to come here and listen to the stories about Kernos, the Green Lord, the Hunter, the old Lord of the Woods.*

But she didn't say that, having heard the underlying bitterness in Ashk's voice. Now that she thought of it, it was true there weren't many songs about the Hunter, and the only one she could vaguely recall was the one about a young Lord of the Woods ascending to become the new Hunter and sparing the life of the old Lord.

Kernos. The old Lord had been Kernos, who had been given a reprieve from Death's arrow years ago and had had those years to watch his beloved granddaughter marry and become a mother, to play with his great-grandchildren—and to save one by offering himself.

But she didn't mention that, or make any promises about finding the Bard. Instead, she waited until Ashk had cried herself out for the time being; then she gave her Kernos's message.

"Thank you," Ashk said in a rough whisper. "That means a great deal to me."

There was a quick tap, then Morphia eased the door open.

Morag looked at her sister.

Nodding, Morphia slipped into the room. She brushed her hand lightly over Ashk's head.

"You need to rest now, Ashk," Morag said as she tucked Ashk into bed and arranged the light summer covers. "You need to sleep."

"No," Ashk said, her voice slurred. "I'll see him again. I'll see him leap."

Morphia leaned over, kissed Ashk's forehead, and whispered, "No dreams but gentle ones."

Ashk slept.

Before Morag could move, Morphia turned and kissed her, too. "No dreams but gentle ones," she whispered again. Linking her arm through Morag's, she led them from the room.

Morag's legs got heavy. Her eyelids drooped. If Morphia wasn't leading her to her room, she would have stopped where she was, curled up, and gone to sleep.

"You could have waited until we got to my room," Morag complained sleepily.

"But then you would have realized what I wanted to do, and you would have argued about it."

"Wouldn't have."

Morphia laughed softly. "No, of course not, Morag. You don't argue about anything."

"Iz not nice to laugh at your sister when you've put her to

sleep," Morag grumbled as they reached her room and she just tumbled into the bed. "You get the last word."

"At least until morning," Morphia agreed.

Ashk shifted in her sleep.

It was the meadow, and yet the sunlight touched it differently, softly.

She saw him walking through the grass and flowers, and felt a pang that, even here, he limped a little. He didn't seem to notice. His attention was caught by something else. He began to move faster—and he laughed the laugh that had taught her more about the joy of life than anything else ever had.

She saw him flow from his human form into the shape of the stag. Now he bounded across the meadow, and her eyes could follow him as he headed for the woods.

An old woods. A very old woods. A place where favorite spots would always be found. A place where there would always be a new path to explore. A place where he could wander the trails in the form he'd loved best. A place where there was peace, even in the shadows.

Then he went into the trees where her eyes couldn't follow, but she'd find him again one day, in that old woods.

Ashk shifted in the bed.

One tear trickled from beneath her closed eyelids, but her lips curved in a soft smile.

Chapter Twenty-five

It was a Clan house. In an Old Place.

At first, despite the feel of power rising up from the land, Lyrra hadn't understood what she was seeing because they'd come into the Old Place from a branch of the main road leading west and had ridden past large fields surrounded by stone fences—fields filled with the green of crops. Those fields were interspersed with groves of trees and pastureland that had herds of cows, horses, and sheep grazing in them—which didn't quite fit the way humans farmed, but it seemed too big, too much for a family of witches.

Then they rode through another stretch of trees.

The Clan house sprawled over several acres, looking more like a small village that flowed around and with the land. Some of the buildings were connected through the use of courtyards and gardens, but other buildings were separated from the rest by large stretches of mown grass. It was similar enough to the Clan houses in Tir Alainn to make her certain that was what she was looking at, and yet it felt . . . different.

"Do you suppose something happened to the witches here and the Clan had to come down and live in the human world in order to hold the shining road to Tir Alainn?" Lyrra asked quietly. They'd been noticed—had, no doubt, been noticed long before now—and the Fae men moving toward the road to meet them didn't have any warmth in their eyes.

"They've been here a long time," Aiden said just as quietly. "These buildings are old." As they rode closer to the men now standing between them and the Clan house, he raised a hand in greeting. "A good day to you."

Blessings of the day to you. Lyrra didn't think anyone else had caught the slight hesitation before Aiden spoke, but she knew he'd changed what he'd been about to say. A year ago, that phrase had seemed strange, Other. Something said only by witches. Now that greeting felt so natural, it took conscious thought *not* to say it.

"What's your business here?" one of the men asked.

Lyrra tensed when she noticed the archers who quietly joined the other men, positioning themselves on either side of the road. This wasn't the way the Fae usually greeted each other. Then again, they were in the west now, and everyone who had encountered them said the Fae in the west weren't like the rest of the Fae in Sylvalan.

"I am Lord Aiden, the Bard. This is Lady Lyrra, the Muse. If it's not inconvenient, we'd like to rest and water the horses, and also speak to the minstrel or bard if there's one in your Clan."

"We've both," the man replied. "The minstrel is in Tir Alainn at the moment, but the bard is here." He studied Aiden, studied Minstrel just a bit longer, then said, "Come this way."

They rode the rest of the way to the Clan house between a line of men, the archers falling in last.

To block the way out, Lyrra thought nervously. She glanced at Aiden. His expression held the confident arrogance of a Fae Lord, which was both a relief and a worry. His attitude said plainly enough that he was used to being treated respectfully by the Clans, but that didn't mean *these* Fae would respond in the same way. And, in truth, ever since Aiden began opposing the Lightbringer's attitude about witches, he hadn't received much respect from the Clans in the rest of Sylvalan.

And she had the odd feeling that Aiden riding a dark horse meant more to the Fae here than his being the Bard.

Her nerves danced a little when they dismounted at the Clan house and she watched some of the men lead the horses away. Then she heard children laughing somewhere nearby, and some of the tension inside her eased. Surely she and Aiden could come to no harm if there were children close by.

They followed one of the Fae men through an arch that led to a large, sunny courtyard. The building that surrounded it had several doors on each side. Probably suites of rooms, Lyrra decided. Privacy and yet community. Flowers grew in raised beds of stone, and she saw a couple of birds fly down to drink from a large, shallow stone basin of water.

"It's beautiful," Lyrra said quietly. So easy to imagine the Fae gathering here at the end of the day to talk and laugh. So easy to picture the Clan's bard or minstrel sitting on one of the wooden benches and playing for his own pleasure or to entertain whoever happened to be nearby. So easy to remember the cottage in Brightwood and Fae huddled together in the available beds or on thin mattresses on the floor because there hadn't been room for all of them. So easy to remember the smaller, rougher cottages that Clan had built after so many of them had to come down to the human world in order to keep enough magic in the Old Place to hold the shining road open and their piece of Tir Alainn intact. Given enough time, would they eventually build a Clan house in the human world? Or would they continue to live a mean existence in Brightwood, doing only what they had to do to survive? "You've done so much work here."

The man gave her an odd look. "We live here."

"What about Tir Alainn?" Aiden asked.

"There's a Clan house there, as well. The elders usually

stay there during the winter months since the damp weather can be hard on old bones, and there are others who stay there much of the time to tend to things. The rest of us go there for a few days each season to rest. It's a simpler place. It was meant to be." He hesitated, looked a little puzzled. "I've heard it said that the Fae in other parts of Sylvalan live in Tir Alainn all the time. Is that true?"

"Yes," Aiden said. "It's true. Most of the Fae only come down to the human world to . . . visit."

The man shook his head. "Foolish thing to do, becoming a stranger to your own land."

"If this is the Clan's land, where do the witches live?" Lyrra asked. She saw the man's expression, which had slowly warmed a little toward curious friendliness, change back instantly to wariness and suspicion. She felt the way Aiden suddenly gripped her hand in warning, and realized why he hadn't asked if there were witches living in the Old Place. He'd intended to keep some things between themselves and the bard of this Clan, and she, caught up in comparing this place with memories of the Fae struggling through their first winter in Brightwood, had blurted out their interest in witches.

"That I can't tell you," the man said sharply. "The bard's suite is this way." He led them up a set of stairs to another archway that opened on the second floor of the building. A wide walkway stretched between one building and the next, ending at a rooftop courtyard.

A door at the opposite end of that courtyard took them down into a communal room for that part of the Clan house. The room was empty, which didn't surprise her. If these Fae lived in the Old Place, there was plenty of work to be done in the daylight hours.

A brisk knock on an inner door a few doors down from the communal room. A muffled grumble behind it.

The man opened the door and gestured for them to go inside. "Taihg," he said. "You've got visitors."

She saw a man who looked a little older than Aiden hunched over a slant-top desk, busily scratching notations on a sheet of paper.

"I don't have visitors until I've got this line down," Taihg said irritably.

Before the man could speak again, Aiden just smiled and shook his head.

Lyrra saw a hint of warmth return to the man's eyes. Apparently, he approved of the Bard showing that much courtesy to the Clan bard.

Raising two fingers to his temple in a salute, the man left, closing the door quietly behind him.

Silently, Aiden crossed the room and moved to a place where he could read the notations over Taihg's shoulder.

"Stand back," Taihg snapped. "I said I'd get to you in a moment. Pest."

Aiden obediently returned to a place across the room. He picked up a small harp, settled on a padded bench that stood against one wall, and waited.

Lyrra sat on the bench with him, stifling the urge to wince—or give Aiden a hard poke in the ribs. Those blue eyes of his had that blend of interest and fire that meant something musical now had his full attention. Having seen Aiden when he was intensely focused on music, she felt a little sorry for the hapless bard who was about to be pounced on by the Lord of Song.

Taihg set his quill carefully back in its holder, stretched his back, then turned to his visitors. His mouth fell open when Aiden set his fingers on the harp strings and played the tune Taihg had just written.

"A few chords could be adjusted to give a little more to the song, but it's a lovely piece," Aiden said, quietly playing a few measures of the song again. "The contrast between the melody line and the chords you're using gives it a bittersweet feel. Have you written the lyrics yet?"

"A couple of verses," Taihg said, stammering slightly. "You're—"

"Aiden."

"—the Bard."

"Yes."

Taihg glanced at Lyrra. She gave him a bright smile, and said, "I'm Lyrra, the Muse."

Taihg half rose from the stool he'd been sitting on, then sank back down. "The Bard and the Muse. To what do I owe the pleasure of—?"

Lyrra saw the moment when surprise stopped overpowering Taihg's ability to think. And he was thinking hard now.

"To what do I owe the pleasure of this visit?" Taihg said, but there was no pleasure in his eyes, only wariness.

Aiden continued to quietly pluck chords on the harp. "I'm seeking some information."

Taihg spread his hands. "I'm just a simple bard from a western Clan. I doubt there's anything I can tell you."

"It occurred to me that, when I sent out word last summer that I was looking for information about witches, or the wiccanfae as they're sometimes called, I never heard back from any of the bards or minstrels in the west." Aiden set the harp aside and looked directly at the Clan bard, smiling gently. "I know I didn't hear from you. Why is that?"

"I had nothing to tell you."

Aiden's smile turned sharp and feral. "Which isn't the same thing as not having information. So you'll tell me now."

Taihg's face hardened. "Why should I tell you anything?"

"Because I'm the Lord of Song. I'm the one who commands *everyone* with your gift. And I am commanding now."

Taihg leaped up from the stool, came halfway across the room.

Aiden stood up to meet him.

"Who are you to come here and threaten me?" Taihg demanded. "The *Bard?* When have you, or any of the Bards before you, come to the west to listen to the traditional songs we know or the new ones we've written? When have you shown any interest in *us?* You haven't. Because we're the western Fae, the strange ones who are looked down on and dismissed as having nothing to offer. And now, when *you* want something, you come here and snap your fingers and expect me to dance to your tune? I don't think so, Bard. You have no power here."

"No power?" Aiden said with deadly softness. "I can strip you of your gift, leave you with nothing but an ache to shape a song with no ability to do it. I can strip your gift down so far you'll never do more than fumble through someone else's songs while sounding like a braying ass. *That's* what I can do."

"I can't tell you anything," Taihg said through gritted teeth.

"Won't tell me anything."

"I *can't.*"

Taihg spun away. Took a turn around the room. Came back. "This is my home. These are my people. If I'm no longer welcome here—or anywhere else in the west—because I've given in to your demands, where am I supposed to go? To one of the Clans in the midlands? I've been to a few of them. I know well enough what sort of welcome I could expect from the Fae there. So I won't bend to your demands in order to keep my music when it means giving up everything else. Take my gift, if that's the kind of man you are. When you're done with me, I may fumble through playing a song and sing like a braying ass, but the Fae here will still do me the courtesy of listening because they'll know I lost the gift in order to protect something more important."

Taihg was trembling, almost close to tears. But it was the shock and pain in Aiden's eyes that made Lyrra's heart ache.

"They would shun you for talking to me?" Aiden asked softly. "Truly?"

"Why is this so important?" Taihg cried.

Aiden closed his eyes. "Because the witches are being slaughtered. They're dying, and without the Fae's help, more of them will die. I—" He opened his eyes and looked at her. Haunted eyes now, full of memories of things he'd rather not remember—and would never forget. "We were with one of them when she died. There was nothing we could do for her except give her whatever comfort she found in not being alone at the end. You didn't see what the Black Coats, the Inquisitors, did to her. You didn't hear the screams of her mother's and sister's ghosts when the nighthunters devoured them." He looked at Taihg. "We're here to find help, whatever help we can to stop the slaughter."

"We're trying to find the Hunter," Lyrra said. "The Lightbringer and the Lady of the Moon have refused to acknowledge that the witches are the House of Gaian. They've refused to help. The Hunter is the only one who might be able to persuade the Fae to act before it's too late. We're not only losing the witches, we're losing Tir Alainn. Is there nothing you can say that might help us?"

Taihg turned away, walked to the window, and looked out. After a long moment, he turned back to them. "Go up to Bretonwood. It's northwest of here. Talk to Lady Ashk. No one else will tell you anything about witches or the wiccanfae."

"How far?"

"Since the days are longer now, a couple of days of hard riding would get you there."

A couple more days, Lyrra thought. How much more

might happen in the eastern part of Sylvalan in a couple more days? Who else might die?

"What about the Hunter?" Aiden asked. "Have you heard anything that would indicate he's somewhere in the west?"

Taihg gave them a strange smile. "Bard, if the Hunter wants to meet you, then you'll meet." He walked back to stand close to them. "But don't ask anyone else about the witches or the wiccanfae. And don't use the glamour to create a human mask. Your true face will be safer here."

"Safer?" Lyrra said, alarmed.

"Some of those Inquisitors you spoke of came into the west. Warnings have gone out to be watchful of strangers coming into the west—especially strangers who start asking about witches and wiccanfae."

"What happened to the Black Coats?" Aiden asked.

"One escaped. Might have gotten out of the west by now. That's why it could go hard for anyone who makes the Clans or the barons' guards uneasy. The others . . ." Taihg shrugged. "They didn't escape."

Lyrra shivered, regretting even more her careless remark about witches.

"Go to Bretonwood," Taihg said. "Talk to Ashk."

Aiden nodded, held out a hand to Lyrra. She wondered how he knew her legs were shaking enough that she appreciated the help to stand.

"Thank you for your time, Taihg," Aiden said.

"Bard," Taihg said. "I know you're both anxious to be on your way, but there are times when haste makes for a longer journey. Stay the night with us. Give yourself and your horses some rest. Then you'll be able to start fresh in the morning."

Impatience shimmered around Aiden, but he nodded. "Since we're going to be guesting at this Clan tonight, perhaps you'd be willing to let me hear some of your songs."

"That isn't why I suggested that you stay," Taihg protested.

"I know," Aiden replied. "That's why I offered."

Aiden stared out the window of the guest room he and Lyrra had been given for the night. He hadn't missed the fact that Taihg had shown no surprise when Lyrra had said the witches were the House of Gaian. No surprise at all.

Which confirmed, for him, that the Fae of this Clan, at the very least, weren't ignorant of who the women who lived in the Old Places were. They'd known a year ago, and had said nothing. Would things have happened differently last summer if he, along with Lucian and Dianna, had found out sooner who the witches were? Or would the Lightbringer and the Lady of the Moon have denied it, just as they denied it when Morag discovered what was written in the journals left by the women in Ari's family?

Perhaps it made no difference. Perhaps what happened at Brightwood would have happened anyway.

"At least we know we're looking in the right place for the Hunter," Lyrra said, coming up behind him and wrapping her arms around his waist. "That's something."

"There's a lot of land, and a lot of Clans, in the west," Aiden replied. He turned so that he could wrap his arms around her, giving comfort as well as accepting it. "The longer this takes . . ."

"I know. But there's nothing else we can do." She leaned back enough to look at him. "And we have a direction, a specific place to go and a specific person to ask in order to get some answers." She frowned. "But I did wonder why Taihg thought this Lady Ashk would help us when he was equally certain no one else would."

Aiden had wondered the same thing. But he wasn't going to tell Lyrra that, when he'd taken Taihg aside and asked about it, the reply he'd gotten was, "Ashk doesn't like the Lightbringer."

Opposing Lucian had cost him his ties to his own Clan, had thwarted every effort he had made to convince the Fae to help the witches. He appreciated the irony that his break with the Lightbringer could assist him in winning over the Fae whose help he needed the most now.

And he'd had a moment to feel bitterly angry with himself when he realized his demands for information might have cost another man all the things he, himself, had already lost.

"What do you think?" Lyrra asked.

He didn't want to think about anything for a little while. Brushing his lips against her forehead, he said, "We'll find out in a couple of days."

Chapter Twenty-six

L iam rode through the arch at a gallop, but reined in quickly. Too many people about the Old Place these days to ride into the midst of them so recklessly. But taking care of the people who were his responsibility had taken time, and the day was making that long, soft slide into twilight. Still plenty of daylight left at this time of year, so close to the Solstice, but it wasn't bright, burning sunlight.

"Where are the children?" Liam snapped as soon as Clay approached to take his horse. "Where's Breanna?"

"The children are about here and there, same as they've been for the past few days. Breanna and Keely walked to the far pasture. That stallion of yours has been spooked all day, and he's got all the other horses stirred up. Even I couldn't get close enough to him to do anything. He likes Keely, so she and Breanna went out to see if they could lead him in."

A chill went through Liam, swiftly followed by a shimmer of heat beneath his skin. He'd been fighting that heat all afternoon, ever since one of his tenant farmers had come running to the manor house to report a heavy smell of something rotting near a tree the man swore hadn't been dead a couple of days ago.

"Where's your far pasture?" Liam asked, fairly sure he already knew. He'd noticed some horses grazing when he and Squire Thurston had ridden out to see what his tenant had found.

Clay jerked a thumb in a northerly direction. "Borders your land. We don't use it much—at least, we haven't until now. So if you're worried about your cows straying across the creek to graze—"

"We found signs of nighthunters a little while ago," Liam said abruptly. "On my land, but near that pasture. I'm going after Breanna and Keely. You alert the other men. Make sure the children stay close enough to the house that they can get to shelter quickly if they have to."

"We'll see to it," Clay said, looking pale. "A few of us will follow after you to bring in the horses."

Nodding, Liam urged his gelding forward. He heard Clay shout at someone and saw an adolescent boy dash for the gate that opened into the near pasture, not more than a couple of acres of land that was used for grazing and exercising the horses that were usually here. With all the horses that had come with Breanna's kin, they'd needed to use the other pastures.

But why that one? Liam asked silently as he galloped toward the gate at the other end of the pasture. And why today? Why hadn't anyone paid attention to Oakdancer's uneasiness and brought the horses in sooner? The stallion might have the habit of leaping a fence and going visiting whenever it suited him—which is why, with Nuala's permission, he'd left Oakdancer at the Old Place since trying to keep him at the estate had been pointless—but he was a fairly easy-tempered animal when approached the right way. Clay should have realized there was a reason for the horse being spooked. He shouldn't have allowed Keely and Breanna to go out to that pasture.

Liam smiled wryly as he reined in and maneuvered his gelding so that he could open the pasture gate without dismounting. With the informality and the way everyone at the Old Place worked together, it was easy to forget that Clay actually worked for Breanna's family and wasn't a male relative who was entitled to strongly voice an opinion about what his female relatives did or didn't do. Not that those females would pay any attention, but he would have been entitled to voice an opinion. Which, come to think of it, Clay tended to do anyway.

The earth in the next pasture had been turned and now held planted fields, except for the wide green stretch of grass that served as a road between the fields. Winter feed for the animals, Liam noted as his horse galloped over the grass road. It hadn't been planted that many days ago, but the plants looked as big as the ones in his own fields that his tenants had planted in the spring. Earth magic. A calling to the land to yield what was needed. Were there other witches here now to help Keely draw out that branch of the Mother? Breanna's kin were wary of him because he was a baron, so he hadn't asked many questions. But his mother would know.

The gate to the far pasture was open, and he saw horses trotting toward him. He wondered if he should close the gate to keep the animals from getting into the young fields, then dismissed the thought. Better they trample a bit of the field than to have any of them panicking and trying to jump a wall to escape.

He rode past the horses. The land rolled softly, so it wasn't until his horse took the next low rise that he saw Breanna and Keely. Now that they were in sight, he slowed his horse to a canter.

They'd managed to get a rope attached to Oakdancer's halter. Keely was leading the stallion, who kept tugging on the lead rope, making Keely run a few steps to keep her balance.

Oakdancer wasn't trying to run away, but he seemed determined to keep Keely moving in the direction of the manor house. Liam couldn't make out the words, but he was close enough now to catch the scolding yet cajoling tone of Keely's voice. She sounded like Brooke, and like his little sister would have done, she concentrated on the horse, not really believing there were dangerous, deadly creatures now hiding somewhere on the land she'd known all her life. She probably thought of them as being deliciously scary, like something out of a story. It might frighten, but it couldn't harm.

Mentally, Keely was as much of a child as Brooke. But Breanna was not a child, and as he slowed his horse to a trot, he saw the way she walked a few steps behind Keely and Oakdancer, scanning the sky, looking back over her shoulder at the nearest trees.

And he saw her freeze suddenly as she looked at those trees.

Framed by the rich greens of summer was one tree with several large, dead branches that looked like old bones. Had those branches been dead when the men had brought the horses into this pasture?

The wind shifted, now coming from the direction of those trees.

Liam had a moment to wonder if that had been Breanna's doing before the horses went mad.

Oakdancer reared, pulling Keely off her feet. Liam's horse suddenly swerved to the left, almost throwing him as it made a tight circle to run back toward the manor house. Liam reined in hard, startling the animal just long enough to give himself a chance to dismount and make a quick knot in the reins to shorten them enough to keep the horse from stepping on them. Then he let the horse go.

As he turned back toward Breanna, he saw a black cloud of small, winged bodies pour out of the trees, flying fast toward the two women.

Breanna whirled around, raced to reach Keely. When she

shouted, "Stand!" Oakdancer's front hooves hit the ground. The stallion was trembling but stood firm.

Keely got to her feet, her lips pushed out in a pout. She started to argue, but Breanna cut the argument short by grabbing Keely's shoulders and turning her so that she could clearly see what was heading toward them. Then Breanna spun the mental child who was her mother, grabbed one leg, and gave Keely enough of a boost to mount Oakdancer's bare back.

Breanna glanced back at the trees and slapped Oakdancer's flank, shouting, "Go!"

Liam's heart pounded in his chest as he ran toward Breanna. Oakdancer cantered right toward him, ears pricked, dark eyes focused on the man he trusted.

"Go!" Liam said, pointing in the direction of Breanna's house.

"No!" Keely cried, looking back as if she finally understood what was going to happen. "No! Breanna!"

"Go!" Liam shouted.

The stallion stretched into a smooth gallop and quickly disappeared with Keely.

Liam turned back to look at Breanna. For one long moment, the world held its breath, and he saw her standing there, as strong as the land, the nighthunters filling the sky behind her.

He and Breanna couldn't run fast enough to escape, and they had no weapons. They were going to die in that pasture, and they both knew it.

"You could have mounted the stallion," Breanna said. "Why didn't you go when you had the chance?"

"You're my sister. I won't let you stand alone."

Pleasure. Sorrow. Determination. He saw all those things in her face. Then she said, "The villagers need a strong baron who will stand for them against the Inquisitors and the barons they control. My *family* needs a strong baron to stand for them. None of them will have that if you die here. Run, Liam. Run now."

She turned and moved toward the approaching swarm of nighthunters.

He froze for a moment, unwilling to believe she would stand as bait and sacrifice.

"Breanna, no!"

Heat throbbed under his skin as the distance between Breanna and the nighthunters closed too fast. She was right about the county he ruled needing a strong baron.

He took a step toward her.

She was right.

Took another step.

His heart didn't care if she was right. She was his *sister.*

She glanced back at him, saw him moving toward her. She lifted her skirt, as if preparing to run.

He would never know for sure if she'd intended to run toward the nighthunters to give him more of a chance to escape or if she'd intended to run back toward him. He would never know because, at that moment before she moved, the hawk screamed.

It dove toward the nighthunters, toward Breanna.

Liam felt a stab of jealousy when he saw that same blend of feelings in her face when she looked up at the hawk as she'd had when she'd looked at him.

No. Not quite the same. There was something more there, something a woman wouldn't feel for a brother.

"No!" Breanna shouted.

The hawk had almost reached her. So had the nighthunters.

Wind whipped around her, swirling, gusting, coming from no direction and every direction.

Breanna swung her left hand upward, as if she were tossing a ball into the air.

The hawk screamed again, but it sounded more surprised than angry as the wind Breanna summoned caught it and lifted it straight up into the sky, too high for the nighthunters to attack. Too high to help Breanna.

She made a slashing motion with her right hand, first in one direction, then the other. Wind howled over that part of the pasture, hit the nighthunters, and sent the swarm tumbling in the air.

Liam heard the creatures' squeaking shrieks. Some of them fell to the ground, with one or both wings broken. They flopped and crawled toward Breanna, their mouths open to reveal needle-sharp teeth.

Breanna skipped backward a couple of steps to stay away from the nighthunters on the ground. She made that slashing motion again, and the wind continued to whip around that part of the pasture, keeping the rest of the nighthunters tumbling. Then she turned and ran.

Liam couldn't tell if her foot slipped on a stone or came down wrong in a depression in the land, but she'd run only a few steps when she fell, sprawling full length in the grass.

He ran toward her as the nighthunter swarm fought against the wind to reach its prey. The heat under his skin pulsed like it was alive, feeding on his fear and fury.

"NO!" He flung one hand forward, as if that gesture would stop the nighthunters. Heat roared up from the soles of his feet, up through his legs, through his body, and finally raced down that outstretched arm.

Streams of fire leaped from his fingertips. He spread his fingers. The fire fanned out, following the movement. It hit the nighthunters, consuming them in the flames.

Breanna glanced up, then screamed as charred, still-burning bodies fell and hit her skirt. She crawled forward as fast as she could to get away from the falling bodies.

Fire continued to pour from Liam's fingertips. Terrified, he waved his hand. The fire followed the movement, catching more of the nighthunters, burning them in the fierce heat.

"Liam!" Breanna shouted, continuing to crawl toward him.

Heat continued to flow through his body on its way to his hand. He didn't know what he'd done to cause this, didn't know how to stop it. He started to lower his hand, but the fire streamed out, setting the grass ablaze.

"Ground it, Liam!" Breanna shouted. "Ground the power!"

He didn't understand what she was saying, didn't know what she meant. There was no power, only this heat that, somehow, had become tangible.

Squeaking furiously, the remaining nighthunters fled back to the safety of the trees.

Liam's heart pounded in his chest. His legs shook. His lungs couldn't seem to draw in enough air. The heat was starting to fade, leaving him feeling exhausted and a little ill, but fire continued to spurt from his fingertips, burning more of the grass.

He heard men shouting behind him, heard someone giving orders to bring water and wet blankets—and fetch Nuala.

"Liam!"

Breanna's voice slashed at him. He just looked at her, feeling the panicked desperation of a child who had gotten himself in trouble and now hoped the adults around him could save him from his own folly.

"You have to ground the power now, Liam," Breanna said, her voice strained by the effort to sound calm as she crawled on hands and knees toward him.

"Breanna, I don't—"

"I know, Liam. I know. It will be all right. You drew too much power, that's all. Now you have to ground it, give it back to the Mother. Focus, Liam. Focus on holding on to the fire, of not letting it go."

The heat began building in his hand, started flowing back up his arm. Too hot. Too hot. He had to let it go or burn.

Breanna got to her feet and sprinted to cover the last bit of distance between them. She grabbed his arm, then dropped to her knees, pulling him down with her.

"Put your hands on the ground," Breanna said, her voice firm but quiet.

"It'll burn," Liam protested.

"No, it won't." She tugged at him until his hands were pressed against the earth.

The grass beneath his hands wilted, turned brown, began to crisp.

"What do you feel?" Breanna asked.

"Heat. It's building again." Liam heard the panic in his voice, but couldn't control that any more than he could control the heat.

"Heat is how you feel the power you're drawing from the Mother. You don't need it, so you're going to give it back. Concentrate, Liam. Concentrate on slowly sending that heat into the land. Picture it spreading out under the land, spreading out like a warm, shallow pool of water rather than a basin of boiling water. The heat flows softly out of your hands. Softly. Softly. Can you picture that?"

Closing his eyes, he could picture it quite clearly. He felt the heat spread out under his hands. The ground was already sun-warmed from the day and hadn't begun to cool with the coming twilight. It felt a little warmer now, but not hot. Thank the Great Mother, it didn't feel hot.

Breanna ran her hands down his arms. He felt the heat follow her hands as she guided it to the land. When she finally sat back on her heels, his hands still felt hot but the rest of his body was cold enough that he started shivering.

"That's enough for now," Breanna said. "We'll go back to the house and finish it there."

Liam looked up. The men who had come with Clay to gather the horses and, when they saw the burning pasture, to put out the fire, were standing a few lengths away, just staring at him with a strange expression on their faces.

"The fire," Liam said, his voice rough as he forced it out of a parched throat.

"Rory and some of the others can control it," Breanna said. "It won't spread." She looked at the men. "I need to get him back to the house."

"Take one of the horses," Clay said. "We'll wait here for Nuala."

Rory stepped forward. He took one of Liam's arms while Breanna took the other. "Can you get to your feet, Baron Liam, or do we need to be carrying you?" Rory asked.

"I can stand." He could—barely—but he was grateful for their support as they walked him toward the nervous horses.

Breanna mounted one of the horses. With Rory's help, Liam mounted behind her. She held the horse to a canter, which told Liam she was more confident of his ability not to set them both on fire than he was. He wasn't sure what more she could do at the house to help him, but he wanted to get there as fast as possible.

Then he heard . . . He wasn't sure what he'd heard until he glanced over his right shoulder and saw the hawk flying above them, keeping pace with the horse. He'd never heard a hawk be quite that . . . vocal . . . but if that *was* a Fae Lord, he, being another man, had a good idea what opinions the hawk was expressing about being tossed out of a fight by a witch more determined to protect others than be protected.

"Breanna," Liam said, intending to call her attention to their escort.

Her back stiffened. "I'll deal with him later."

Liam grinned. If he were a betting man, he'd wager on the witch to win. He wondered if the hawk would be following them if it had any idea what it would have to deal with as soon as Breanna got done dealing with *him*.

As they rode through the pasture near the house, his grin faded. There were a lot of unanswered questions about him now, weren't there?

An hour later, Liam watched the steam gently rising from the basin of water. The water had been cold when Breanna poured it over his hands a few minutes ago, but it didn't stay cold long, not with the heat still draining from his hands.

When Breanna led him into the kitchen, shouting for someone to bring a large basin and cold water, several women had hurried to bring what was needed. After observing how fast the water went from cold to steaming, they brought another basin and a couple of pitchers of water. When the water began to steam again, they took that basin and slid the next one into place, pouring more cold water over his hands.

Witches were very practical people, he discovered. They were using all the hot water he was providing to wash the evening dishes.

Practical and strong-willed. Any gentry woman of his acquaintance would have become hysterical after what happened in the pasture. Breanna had remained in control—right up until she'd run her fingers through her hair and combed out a piece of charred nighthunter wing. Her shriek had brought everyone running, and he'd watched that strong will crumble under the fear she'd held at bay.

Now they were both sitting at one of the tables in the

kitchen, wrapped in blankets to fight a coldness that came from within.

He glanced longingly at the kettle of soup simmering on the stove. He wanted something that would help thaw the chill in the rest of his body.

"Almost done," Breanna said, smiling wearily. "I figure another basin of water will absorb enough of the power so that it's back to what you're used to."

Used to? He'd felt that heat under his skin all his life, but nothing like this had ever happened before. "Why did this happen now?"

"I don't know, Liam," Breanna said softly. "I can only guess that whatever wall you'd built inside yourself to protect you from having the gift manifest itself broke because the need to use the gift was stronger than the need to deny it."

"But I—" Liam swallowed hard. He'd been drinking water to ease the fever-dry feeling, but his throat still felt tight. "What am I, Breanna?"

"Nothing more and nothing less than what you've always been. You're still gentry, still the Baron of Willowsbrook. But you're also a Son of the House of Gaian. You always were. The only difference is you know it now."

"Am I a witch?" He held his breath, not sure which answer he wanted from her.

"It's not a word we usually use when a man has a gift from one of the Mother's branches." Breanna shrugged. "Gentry, baron, witch. They're words, Liam. Just words. You'll have to decide which words you'll claim as your own and which ones you'll let go." She slipped her hand into the water, curled her fingers around his. "But I can tell you one thing you're not and never will be."

He looked into her woodland eyes—eyes so like his own—and saw a mischievous sparkle in them. "What's that?" he asked suspiciously.

"You're not one of the Mother's Daughters. You don't have the tits for it."

He didn't think anything could make him laugh after the things that had happened that day, but as his laughter filled the kitchen, he felt the last of the heat in his hands fade away.

Breanna stepped outside. Liam was finally getting the bowl of soup he'd been wanting. Nuala had returned from the pasture and was sitting with him now, having assured both of them that the fire in the pasture was out. The rain she'd drawn from the clouds had quenched the fire better than anything else could have done. Tomorrow Nuala would begin teaching Liam how to ground the power he could channel from the Great Mother. Together, she and Nuala would begin teaching him how to use it safely.

But that was tomorrow. Tonight, all she wanted was a hot, deep bath so that she could scrub her hair and skin clean. A hot bath, a bowl of that soup with some bread and cheese, and settling into bed early with a favorite book that she knew had a happy ending. In real life, one couldn't count on happy endings. Tonight she needed one.

She wasn't going to get any of those things until she dealt with the other male who had wedged his way into her life.

At least he wasn't going to make her look for him, Breanna thought sourly as she spotted the hawk perched on one of the poles that supported the clotheslines.

"*You!*" she shouted, pointing a finger at the hawk. She swung that finger until it pointed to the bench under the tree where they would have a little privacy for this discussion. "Get over there!"

She saw several of the men gathered around the stables take a half step to follow her command before realizing she wasn't talking to them. Deciding to save her temper for dealing with the Fae featherhead, she ignored the men's grins as she strode to the tree.

The hawk fluffed its feathers and stayed where it was.

Breanna's temper soared. The nearby trees bowed to the sudden gust of wind.

"Get over here, or I'll summon a wind that will pluck every feather you've got!"

She clenched her fists and made the effort to ground the power her temper had summoned. The wind eased, releasing the trees.

The hawk turned his head, stared at the trees for a moment, then flew over to the bench, landing as far away from Breanna as he could while still obeying her order.

It was tempting to take the couple of steps between them and smack him right on the top of his feathered head. But the anger and fear that she'd held at bay were now churning nastily in her belly, and since she hadn't smacked Keely or Liam, who had both contributed to those feelings, she couldn't, in all fairness, shovel all of it on a hawk who was staring at his feet, waiting to get yelled at.

So who said she had to be fair?

"Those were nighthunters, you featherhead," she said through clenched teeth. "Did you know that? Do you have any idea what those things could have done to you if they'd bitten you? Just one bite? Mother's tits! What were you thinking of to go flying at them like that?"

Her. He'd been thinking of her. She'd known that the moment she saw him diving toward the swarm. What she didn't understand was *why* he'd do that.

"I can't talk to you like this. I *can*, but the discussion is a little one-sided. I would appreciate it if you would change to your other form." And if he didn't, she'd call up a little wind and knock him right off the bench.

She turned her head to give him some privacy—and

found herself staring at the men who were still gathered near the stables, watching with unfeigned interest. She stared harder. They quickly moved out of sight.

Out of the corner of her eye, she saw movement. When she turned her head, the hawk was gone and a young man dressed in a brown coat and trousers sat on the bench, his shoulders slightly hunched, his eyes focused on his boots. He was about her age—a pleasant-looking young man whose clothes looked as if he'd been living rough for a while.

With effort, Breanna swallowed her temper. He was afraid. No, not quite afraid, but . . . heart-bruised in some way.

"I brought you a rabbit," he said softly.

"And a salmon," she replied just as softly.

He blushed, shifted on the bench as if it had suddenly become uncomfortable.

Breanna sat down on the bench, near enough that she could touch him if she reached out but not so close that she would inadvertently brush against him. "What's your name?"

"Falco."

"You're a Lord of the Hawks?"

"*The* Lord of the Hawks." A touch of arrogance filled his voice—enough to have him raise his head, but not enough for him to look at her.

The Lord of the Hawks had brought her rabbits to pay for a clothes-peg. If someone else had told her that, she would have dismissed it as a funny story.

"Why?"

Frowning, he glanced at her—then looked away just as quickly. "Why am I the Lord of the Hawks?"

Breanna shook her head. She lifted a hand in a gesture that encompassed the Old Place. "Why are you here? The Fae haven't wanted anything to do with us before now."

"You're the Mother's Daughters, the House of Gaian."

"We always were. Why does that make a difference now?"

He shifted again. "Aiden says—" He stopped, his eyes widening.

"I know Aiden and Lyrra are Fae."

The relief on his face made her want to smile, so she pressed her lips together.

"Aiden says the witches need to be protected. There's not much I can do, except . . . maybe if I gave a warning soon enough, you—your family—would be able to escape before the Inquisitors . . ."

He knew someone who wasn't warned in time, Breanna thought. "There are other Fae keeping watch over the Old Place." But none of them had tried to help her against the nighthunters.

"Them."

The anger in his voice surprised her.

"They aren't watching to help *you.* They just want to be sure you don't do anything that might endanger *them."*

"What could we do that would endanger the Fae?"

Falco finally looked at her. "You could leave. You could run away to escape the Black Coats. If a witch doesn't live in an Old Place, the shining road closes, and that piece of Tir Alainn disappears unless enough of the Fae can get down the shining road fast enough to keep the road open. But they have to stay and live in the Old Place."

"I see." Making sure her family stayed so they wouldn't have to fit what she'd heard of the Fae's self-interest—but it didn't fit the Fae she'd actually met. "That explains the Fae skulking about in the woods. It doesn't explain you."

He looked unhappy. "You're interesting." He winced, but pushed on. "I wanted to know how witches lived."

"And how do we live?"

His eyes were too shiny. "You're real, and the world you

live in is real." He shook his head. "Aiden could explain it. The Bard would have the words. And . . . I like you, even when you yell at me."

Breanna felt a tightness in her chest. Curiosity may have brought him that first day, but he had come back for other reasons. She wasn't sure she wanted to examine too closely the reasons why she'd found herself looking for him each day—or why she'd felt so frightened for him when he tried to attack the nighthunters. Maybe, now that she could talk to him, they could find out whether they truly liked each other.

"So," Breanna said, "you come down to the Old Place in the morning and go back to Tir Alainn each night?" His face tightened, and she realized she'd touched the heart-bruise. "Falco?"

"The Clan who lives in this piece of Tir Alainn didn't like me coming here, didn't like that you could see me. Didn't like that I was helping you at all. They got angry over a *rabbit*. Just a rabbit. They said—" He paused. "They told me if I continued to visit you, I wasn't welcome in their Clan's territory."

"You weren't—?" Breanna stared at him. "You haven't been going back to Tir Alainn?"

He shook his head.

"Then . . . where have you been staying?"

"My horse is in a small clearing, and the Small Folk . . . They've been kind. They helped me store my saddle and other gear where it would be safe."

"You've been *staying* out in the woods?"

Falco shrugged. "As a hawk, it isn't difficult."

Breanna continued to stare at him. She felt as if the world had suddenly become one of those toys that Brooke had brought over one day—the tube with colored pieces of glass that shifted and formed a new pattern when you rolled the tube. This moment had shifted unexpectedly, showing her a new pattern.

He's lonely. All these days, shunned by his own kind because he believed we were people who mattered instead of tools the Fae could command and use at their whim. What had he felt, watching us laugh and squabble and work together? He didn't risk his human form, didn't want to be sent away. Who could blame him for that? And now . . . Now he expects to be sent away. Where would he go? Who could he work with, laugh with, squabble with?

She took a deep breath. Let it out slowly. "Have you eaten this evening?"

He shook his head.

"Then come in the house." She tried to smile, but found she was too close to tears and had to fight to keep her voice steady. "After you have something to eat, I'll ask Clay and Rory to go with you to fetch your horse and gear. You shouldn't be out in the woods alone, not with the nighthunters out there."

He shook his head again. "You've got so many people already with all your kin here."

"There's room for one more." She hesitated, then placed a hand on his arm. "There's a place for you here, Falco. There's a place for you here."

She slid her hand down until it brushed his. He turned his hand so that he could hold hers. She stood up, then tugged on his hand until he stood beside her. The mixture of hope and fear in his face made tears sting her eyes. Looking away, she led him to the house.

Chapter Twenty-seven

It was the prettiest village Aiden had ever seen, and just the sight of it lifted his spirits. He could imagine living in one of those tidy cottages, talking with the same people day after day, playing his songs in the tavern or in the square, sharing the joys and sorrows of the community. He could picture Lyrra telling her stories to children gathered around her—and other stories to the adults later in the evening. He could imagine raising their children there.

The village's only flaw was that it had been built in an Old Place. If humans had built a village there, it meant the Old Place was gone. And yet it didn't *feel* gone.

"Maybe it's like the Clan house in that other Old Place," Lyrra said. "Or . . . maybe there's a large enough family of witches living in the Old Place that the magic has spread beyond the borders."

"Maybe," Aiden said. He'd like to believe that. "Shall we ride in and see what the tavern might be offering for a midday meal?"

Lyrra nodded.

Aiden studied her. She looked more tired than she should have, and she'd alternated between snapping at him about anything and turning weepy about nothing. She couldn't, or wouldn't, tell him what was bothering her, and he didn't have the nerve to ask if she was pregnant because, if she was, he was fairly certain whatever response he made to the news would be the wrong one. Instead of asking about something that would create a strain between them, he said, "If the tavern has a room available, we could stay here until morning."

He saw a yearning in her face that changed to hard resolve.

"It's only midday," Lyrra said. "We need to keep going. That bard either lied to us or had never made the journey to Bretonwood and has no idea how long it really takes."

"I figure by taking this road instead of continuing on the main one, we've saved a day's travel."

"That bard didn't mention this road. It's not marked, but it wasn't *that* hard to find."

The sharpness under her words made him uneasy. Her referring to Taihg as "that bard" didn't bode well. But she was right. Taihg *hadn't* mentioned this road, which seemed to head northwest—exactly where they needed to go.

Lyrra sighed. "I'm tired, Aiden."

"I know, love. I know."

"I just want it done. I want the journey to end. I want to find the Hunter and finally know if there's any use in our trying and trying and trying." She sniffled lightly. "And I don't want to stay in that village more than an hour, because if I do, I won't want to leave, and that will make leaving so much harder."

Aiden hesitated. "How would you feel about living among humans?"

She gave the village a long, thoughtful look. "Here, I would be willing to try."

"Then let's find out if it would be possible."

Her mouth dropped open.

Aiden smiled. "Taihg *did* say it was safer to wear our true faces. Let's find out."

The hope and anticipation in her face made him as uneasy

as her sharp tone had a moment ago. All he could do now was hope an hour in the village didn't spoil her pleasure.

They rode down to the village at an easy pace. There were plenty of people around as they rode up the main street. Aiden's heart sank as he watched those people study him and Lyrra with cold eyes before hurrying into the nearest building. So. That answered the question about whether or not Fae might be accepted by these villagers.

As they dismounted in front of the Hunter's Horn, a little girl pulled away from her mother, darted across the street, and stopped in front of Minstrel.

"Pretty horse," she said, raising one small hand.

Minstrel obligingly lowered his head so she could pet his nose.

"Kayla!" the woman said, rushing over to pull her daughter to safety.

"It's all right," Aiden said soothingly. "He's very gentle."

The assurance didn't seem to ease the woman's fear.

"He's pretty, Mama," the little girl said. She looked at Aiden. "Whaz his name?"

"Minstrel."

"Does he sing?"

Aiden grinned. "He would if he could. Since he can't, he just likes to listen."

"I'm gonna be a minstrel when I'm bigger," the girl said. "But I won't be a horse."

Minstrel moved his ears so they stuck out from his head, giving him such a woebegone expression, even the woman smiled.

"Don't be sad," the little girl said. "I'll sing you a song." She began to sing in a sweet, clear voice.

Aiden snapped to attention, his blue eyes intent on the girl. He shouldn't have done it—*knew* he shouldn't have reacted that way—but it was a song he'd never heard, and it pulled at him with a force he couldn't resist.

"*Kayla!*" The woman grabbed her daughter's shoulders and pulled her back a couple of steps. "That's enough!"

"But Mama—"

"What kind of song is that?" Aiden asked, taking a step forward.

"It's a wic—"

"Enough!" the woman shouted. She picked up the little girl, hurried across the street, and went into the nearest shop.

Aiden's shoulders sagged with disappointment. What was so wrong about letting the child sing? What was so wrong about letting him hear the child sing?

"Aiden," Lyrra said softly. "Let's go into the tavern. Now."

There was something wrong in the tone of her voice that pulled his focus away from music. He saw the men who had been on the street slowly walking toward them, a grim expression on every face.

Trying to look relaxed, he loosely tied Minstrel's reins and the packhorse's lead to a post outside the tavern. As soon as Lyrra tied her horse, he took her hand and walked into the tavern with her.

"I'm sorry," he said softly.

"It wasn't you," Lyrra said just as softly.

Aiden smiled at the aproned man who came to greet them—or, perhaps, block them from entering farther into the room.

"What's your business?" the man growled.

"A midday meal, if you're serving," Aiden said politely. "My lady is faint with hunger and could use a good meal."

"*Aiden,*" Lyrra whispered, sounding embarrassed. She smiled weakly when the man stared at her, studying her face.

"We've beef stew today," the man finally said. "It's hearty. Sit yourselves down. I'll fetch it."

"Thank you," Aiden said, leading Lyrra to a table close to the door. The men on the street were drifting into the tavern. If he and Lyrra had to try to run for it, he didn't want to be trapped in the middle of the room.

The tavern owner returned with a large tray. He set down two bowls of stew, a small plate that held hunks of yellow cheese, and two plates that held thick slices of brown bread that were still warm enough to have the curls of butter melting into them. Last, he set down a small tankard of ale for Aiden and a cup of cider for Lyrra.

Lyrra quickly spread the butter over the bread and took a bite. "Mmmm." She chewed slowly. Then she gave the tavern owner a bright smile. "Oh. This is wonderful."

The man's hard expression softened a little. "My wife will be pleased to hear it. She bakes the bread herself."

Wondering if Lyrra was going queer on him or if she really was desperately hungry, Aiden spread the butter on his own piece of bread and took a bite.

Mother's mercy, it *was* wonderful.

Lyrra dug into her stew, gave the spoonful several quick little puffs of breath to cool it, then took the first bite with unfeigned relish.

"You could write a song about this bread," she said. She broke off a piece of cheese, then looked up at the tavern owner, who was still standing near the table watching them. "Aiden is the Bard. I'm the Muse. A poem might do for the bread, but a song would be better. What do you think?" she asked, turning to Aiden.

She'd gone queer on him, that's what he thought. Maybe she *was* pregnant. Women could go a bit strange during that time.

Then he looked into her eyes and realized she'd been trying to send him signals—the same kind of subtle signals they used when they performed together. He'd missed them and didn't have a clue what she was trying to tell him. Worse, her telling these men who they were hadn't eased the tension in the room. If anything, the hostility had increased.

"What would bring the Bard and the Muse to our little village?" one of the men standing near the bar asked.

There was nothing friendly about the question, and the tavern owner continued to stand near their table, watching them instead of serving drinks and food to the other people in the room.

To give himself time, Aiden took a spoonful of stew and chewed slowly. "We're just passing through."

"Not many people pass through this way," the tavern owner said. "Traveling the main road is easier."

"This road headed northwest, so we took the chance that it would join with the road to Breton."

"You've business with the baron there?" the man at the bar asked.

Aiden suppressed a sigh. Why couldn't these men just let them eat in peace and leave? "Actually, we're headed for Bretonwood to talk to Lady Ashk."

A stillness filled the room. Then, as if a held breath was slowly released, some of the tension in the room eased.

"You keep heading up this road, it'll take you in the right direction to reach Breton—and Bretonwood," the tavern owner said. He turned away then, going back to his place behind the bar.

Lyrra let out a quiet, shuddering sigh.

Aiden saw the slight tremor in her hand when she lifted the next spoonful of stew. His belly was knotted with tension, so he ate slowly, resentful that neither of them could enjoy a good meal. And, he thought with bitter honesty, resentful that this village was pretty only on the surface.

"I think they're scared," Lyrra said so quietly he had to lean to one side to hear her.

"Scared of two Fae?" he asked just as quietly.

She lifted a piece of cheese to her mouth. Her hand partially hid her lips. "The little girl . . . She had woodland eyes. So did her mother. So does the tavern owner." She popped the cheese into her mouth.

Woodland eyes. The one physical attribute that seemed common to anyone who had some kinship to the House of Gaian. Of course, not everyone who had woodland eyes was one of the Mother's Daughters. Lyrra was proof of that. But if there were people in this village who had strong ties to the witches in the Old Place, and if they'd been warned about the Black Coats, that would explain why they were wary of strangers.

It didn't make it any easier being on the receiving end of those cold, hard stares.

They finished their meal in silence, and Aiden felt grateful that the price wasn't so dear as he'd expected. If the feel in the room had been different, he might have offered to pay for part of the meal with a few songs, but he didn't think the offer would be welcome—and he didn't trust the temper of these men.

When they left the tavern, the men followed them outside, watched them mount their horses.

Aiden pressed his heels into the dark horse's sides. "Come on, Minstrel, let's go."

Minstrel just planted his feet and shifted his weight in a way that warned Aiden the horse had no intention of going anywhere.

Aiden leaned down, bringing his face closer to the horse's ears. "Not now, Minstrel. We have to go."

Minstrel wig-wagged his ears. His feet didn't move at all.

Aiden felt the weight of all those hard eyes watching him.

He sat up and handed the packhorse's lead rope to Lyrra, who looked at him with wide-eyed apprehension. Twisting around, he unbuckled one of the buckles on a saddlebag and pulled out the whistle he'd taken to carrying there.

Giving the men a weak smile, he said, "He expects a song before we start out." Fitting his fingers over the whistle's holes, he began to play a sprightly tune.

And Minstrel started trotting. In place.

Aiden had no idea why the horse had learned to do that—or why anyone would *teach* the horse to do that, but there they were, with him playing the tune and Minstrel trotting—and going nowhere.

He glanced at Lyrra, who had one hand clamped over her mouth to stifle the laughter. He glanced at the men, who were scratching their heads or rubbing their hands over their mouths. Their mirth filled the air, but they held the laughter in—probably, Aiden thought sourly, so they wouldn't distract the horse.

He reached the last note of the song.

Minstrel planted his feet firmly in the street.

Lyrra was laughing so hard, her face had turned a bright red that was not a complement for her dark red hair.

The men watched him expectantly.

Feeling the heat rising in his face, Aiden stuffed the whistle inside his shirt and cleared his throat. "Uh . . . I guess that was the wrong tune."

Minstrel bobbed his head as if in agreement.

It could have been worse, Aiden thought as he gathered up the reins. *He could have done this at a Clan house and destroyed what little reputation I have left.* Taking a deep breath, he began singing the traveling song.

He got through the first verse and the chorus.

Minstrel refused to move.

When he got through the second verse, he made a "help

me" gesture with one hand. The men were laughing so hard, none of them could hit the right notes, but they sang the chorus with him.

Minstrel bobbed his head and trotted down the street.

Aiden was an embarrassed bard.

Minstrel was a happy horse.

If he hadn't needed a Fae horse, he would have traded the music-obsessed animal for anything that could be saddled and carry a grown man.

But as they trotted down the street, with Lyrra and the packhorse following, he heard two the men call out, "Good luck to you, Bard!" "Hope you run out of road before you run out of songs!"

Aiden just raised one hand and waved to acknowledge he'd heard them—and he kept singing.

They'd gone a couple of miles past the village before Lyrra stopped giggling every time she glanced at him. He'd sung the traveling song—all ten verses with a chorus after every one of them—and a few other songs before he dared quit. Fortunately, by then Minstrel had settled into an easy trot and seemed content to keep going.

While he was singing, he'd had time to think. If they'd left the village easily, they would have left people who were still suspicious of them. Instead, they'd left people laughing—and the village would talk about the Bard and his music-loving horse for weeks to come. And if they had to ride back that way again, they might be greeted with smiles instead of anger.

But he wasn't going to admit to anyone, even Lyrra, that his horse had been the better performer today.

Chapter Twenty-eight

"So," Adolfo said heavily after hearing Ubel's report. "It is unfortunate that the men who went with you were lost."

Stiff-backed, Ubel stared straight ahead. "It was a sound plan, Master, and the men should have been able to carry out their orders—"

"And still they were lost."

You lost all the men you brought with you last summer, Ubel thought resentfully. But nothing would be said about *that.* "The Fae—" He pressed his lips together to keep the words back. The Master Inquisitor wasn't interested in excuses.

"Yes. The Fae." Adolfo drank deeply from the glass of wine that was never far from his hand. "We have dealt with the witches, as we dealt with them in Wolfram and Arktos. They are no match for our righteous anger against female power that keeps men chained, keeps men from being the masters of the own lives and the world that is rightfully theirs. But the Fae . . . The Fae are foul creatures that will devour good men and spit out the bones." His hand shook a little as he raised the wineglass to his mouth. "Good men, turned into nothing more than meat for the maggots and the worms. Because of them. Because of *her.*"

Finally aware of how gray and ill Adolfo looked, Ubel wondered if it had been wise to imply a narrow escape with the Gatherer in pursuit. But he'd had enough time on the journey back to Durham to consider how Adolfo would react to the loss of the men, and he'd gambled that mentioning the Gatherer's presence would soften whatever discipline the Witch's Hammer might decide to inflict. He just hadn't realized how deeply Adolfo's fear of her went.

"I am glad that you were able to escape and return to me unharmed, Ubel," Adolfo said.

Are you?

"Losing those men is a blow to all of us, but losing an Inquisitor with your abilities would have been a harder blow to recover from. Especially now, when we must stand against the vilest enemy we've ever faced."

Adolfo gestured to the chair on the other side of the table. "Sit, Ubel. Sit. You have had a long, hard journey."

The captain's quarters in the borrowed yacht were small but held sufficient luxuries, including the gleaming wooden table where Adolfo usually took his meals alone. Ubel wondered who had been assigned to cut up the Master Inquisitor's meat and butter the bread while he'd been absent. There weren't many Adolfo trusted enough to let them see even that much weakness.

Or had there been some other reason for Adolfo having one of his best Inquisitors doing tasks that were suitable for a woman? Before he'd left on the journey to the west, he'd considered it an honor to help the Master Inquisitor do the things a man with one dead arm couldn't easily do for himself. Now he wondered if it had been a subtle way of reminding him that he wasn't, and never would be, the Master's equal.

Silence thickened around them. Finally, Adolfo said, "You are sure of this? The Fae are actually *living* in the Old Places? They are always present in the world?"

"I am sure, Master," Ubel replied.

Adolfo took a deep breath, let it out in a long sigh. "This is a cursed land, Ubel. The Fae were never so present in

Wolfram or Arktos. That's why we underestimated them as an enemy. Everything I had learned about them has proved false here. We've been able to eliminate many witches in the eastern part of Sylvalan in the past few weeks—and the Fae have disappeared from those places, as well. That much we have done. But that village of bitches choosing to die instead of submit to their proper place in the world has shaken too many of the barons. The news of what happened traveled too far, spread too fast. Subtlety will not win those men now. Even those who would be willing to do what was right are afraid of having the people they rule turn against them if they issue even the smallest decree. Bah. They are not men. They're fools, cowards, little boys still sucking on the teat instead of men who know with certainty that they *own* the teat and it cannot be denied to them."

Adolfo stared into his empty wineglass for a long time. "We cannot walk away, Ubel. We cannot leave this unfinished. The eastern barons are too weak to bring about the changes needed to make Sylvalan a good place for good men. If the other barons are allowed to continue to oppose the right way to live, there will be uprisings. The eastern barons will be overthrown. Even in Wolfram, there continue to be small uprisings. Magic springs up in a place, seducing the common people away, turning females into creatures that can't be trusted. Not that they ever can be trusted. Here, if the other barons continue to defy the good we brought to their land, the eastern barons will fall."

Ubel said nothing, just watched the Master Inquisitor's hand tremble slightly as Adolfo refilled the wineglass.

"I have given it great thought," Adolfo said softly. "Great thought. Witches are the vessels of magic. They are the key. When they are destroyed, magic dies, and the Small Folk and the Fae are driven away from the land. But here, in this accursed country, magic dies as is right and proper—and then it comes back. Pools of it have reappeared in Old Places that were cleansed of magic. Pockets of it have appeared in places where magic hadn't been before. We keep cutting down the weed that blights the garden, but until we dig out the tap root, it will keep coming back. Keep coming back."

Adolfo drank deeply, draining his glass. "I am convinced there is a great wellspring of magic in Sylvalan, a great, filthy nest of witches hidden somewhere in this land, and their power flows underground like hidden springs, rising to the surface when some thing or some place acts as a channel. We must find that nest. Find it . . . and destroy it. We must eliminate the barons who oppose our great work, and we must eliminate the Fae in the west."

Ubel stared at Adolfo. "But . . . all the Inquisitors in Wolfram and Arktos combined wouldn't be enough to do that. It would take an army."

"Yes." Adolfo nodded. "It will take an army. And we'll have an army. From Arktos. From Wolfram. From the eastern barons here. A great army that will roll across this land and wipe out the stain of magic once and for all—*everywhere.* And you, Ubel. You will take the ships and men to the west, and you will exact a fitting punishment on all those who opposed us, who shed Inquisitors' blood."

"Thank you, Master. I will not fail you."

"I know you will not fail me." *Again.*

Ubel felt the sting of the unspoken word.

"Go now," Adolfo said. "Get some rest. We'll sail back to Wolfram in the morning. There is much to do."

Ubel stood, bowed, and left the yacht.

As he walked to the hotel where he had taken a room, he suddenly wondered if being given command of the part of the army that would attack the west was a reward or a punishment.

Chapter Twenty-nine

The village of Breton was just ahead of them. Almost the end of the journey.

Or the beginning of another, Aiden thought wearily. But he wasn't going to think beyond this next task—finding Lady Ashk and trying to convince her the witches were more, far more, than servants for the Fae's convenience.

"Almost there, love," Aiden said. When Lyrra smiled at him, his heart clenched. She wasn't pregnant, and he was grateful for her sake, but the strain of the journey and the lack of quiet privacy she was used to during her moon cycle had made today's traveling difficult for her. He wished he could have stopped at the last traveling post they had passed and let her rest for the day. But his purse was empty, and the only place he could hope to find her a decent meal and a comfortable bed was at the Clan house in Bretonwood.

They were met at the edge of the village by four armed guards who maneuvered their horses to block the road.

"What's your business here?" one of the guards asked harshly.

"Hold your tongue," the guard captain snapped. "You can see just by looking at them that they're two of the Fair Folk." He drew in a breath, blew it out again. "But we still need to be asking who you are and what your business is here."

"You've had trouble?" Aiden asked, pleased that his voice remained calm while his heart pounded wildly.

"Black Coats—and those nighthunter creatures they created."

Lyrra made an small, alarmed sound that had the guard captain slashing a look at her.

"How could they be here? How?" She sounded so frightened and turned so pale Aiden dropped Minstrel's reins and reached out to steady her.

The captain's eyes narrowed. "You've seen these creatures?"

Aiden shuddered. "Yes. And we've . . . seen what they do." At that moment, he wasn't clear in his own mind if he was talking about the Inquisitors or the nighthunters. Maybe it didn't matter. In some ways, they were the same thing. "Was anyone harmed?"

The captain nodded. "Some people have died because of them."

Reason enough to have guards meeting anyone coming into the village. At least these humans didn't seem uncomfortable about dealing with the Fae. "I'm the Bard. My lady is the Muse. We've traveled a long way to talk to Lady Ashk."

"Ashk, is it? Then we'll take you part of the way to Bretonwood." The captain turned his horse. "Sedge, you're with me. You two stay at your post here."

The captain and Sedge led the way through town. As soon as they passed Breton and were traveling through open country, Minstrel started mouthing the bit and snorting softly in a way that made Aiden's stomach sink.

"Not now," he whispered.

Minstrel wig-wagged his ears and continued snorting. His smooth trot suddenly became less smooth, and Aiden felt the jolt of each silent step all the way up his spine.

The captain looked back, frowning. "What's wrong with the horse?"

Aiden unclenched his teeth enough to answer. "He's disappointed that he didn't get a song when we stopped at the village."

Sedge turned in his saddle. "You're the bard with the dancing horse! We heard about you."

"Mother's tits," Aiden muttered as Lyrra started to giggle. "How could you have heard about that?"

The captain pointed skyward. Aiden spotted the two ravens flying toward Bretonwood.

"Roads curve, but news can still travel straight and fast," the captain said, grinning.

"Mother's tits," Aiden muttered again. He could hope Lady Ashk hadn't heard about it. That wasn't likely, but he could still hope.

They rode for a few more minutes. Then the captain said, "There's your Clan escort." He rode ahead to meet the two Fae men who waited near a narrower road that branched off the main one. A falcon perched on the forearm of one of the men. As they approached, the man raised his arm, and the falcon flew away.

No doubt Lady Ashk would know of their arrival long before they reached the Clan house.

The village guards gave him and Lyrra a jaunty salute before riding back to Breton. The Fae escort was uncomfortably silent. They simply turned their horses and led the way up the road that branched off the main road.

Well, Aiden thought, the rest of the Fae had always said those in the west were lacking in some . . . civilities. Or, perhaps, if they knew what was said about them, they saw no reason to be civil to Fae who came in from outside the west.

Their destination was another Clan house in an Old Place. Unlike the other one they visited, this Clan house wasn't in open country surrounded by woods. This one was *in* the woods, a part of the woods.

It made him uneasy, although he wasn't sure why. A glance at Lyrra was sufficient to tell him she wasn't comfortable either.

They're Fae, he told himself. *They may be different from the rest of us, but we've no reason to fear our own kind.*

He didn't believe that, knew from experience it wasn't true. He suddenly wanted open land, fierce sunlight. The old trees were far enough apart that it wasn't dark around the Clan house. There was plenty of dappled sunlight and open ground under the trees, but he wasn't sure anymore that he wanted to meet Ashk. The only reason he rode toward the group of people standing near a large wooden table was that Ashk was the only person who might be able to lead him to the Hunter.

As soon as they dismounted, the Fae men who had escorted them took their horses. A woman with long, ash-brown hair stepped away from the others. She studied him for a long moment. Studied Lyrra's face even longer.

She had woodland eyes. But there was something in those eyes that he hadn't seen in Breanna's eyes, or Nuala's, or any of the wiccanfae he'd met in the Mother's Hills. Something . . . other. Something dangerous.

Then it was gone, making him wonder if it was a trick of the light or if fatigue was making him imagine things.

"Blessings of the day to you," Aiden said, deliberately using a witch's greeting.

She looked mildly surprised, but replied, "Blessings of the day."

"I'm Aiden, the Bard." He reached out, clasped Lyrra's hand. "This is Lyrra, the Muse. We've come to speak to Lady Ashk."

"Have you?" Her smile was slightly feral—and amused. "First you should eat and recover a little from your journey. Then we'll talk."

"You're Ashk?" Aiden couldn't keep the surprise out of his voice. He'd expected someone older, considering how wary everyone seemed to be when her name was mentioned.

Ashk just turned her head to look back at the group of Fae still gathered near the table. A couple of younger males immediately headed for the Clan house.

"Sit," Ashk said, making a gesture toward the benches on either side of the large table.

He would have preferred to stand and stretch his back and legs, but he took a place beside Lyrra. Ashk sat on the opposite bench, across from them, her feet on the bench, her arms loosely clasped around her knees.

The youngsters returned with two wooden serving trays. Plates of sliced bread and cheese, a small bowl of fresh butter, and a plate for each of them that had a generous portion of some kind of white meat. Last, they set down two small cloths and a steaming bowl of water.

Since there was only a dull knife to spread the butter, Aiden decided the cloths and water were to be used to clean fingers that had gotten messy. He swirled his hands in the water, reluctant to pick up food with hands soiled from traveling. He dried his hands on one of the cloths, then buttered a piece of bread for Lyrra while she washed her hands.

Ashk tipped her head. "Do you like chicken? Most of the Fae here find it too bland, but I've acquired a taste for it, and the cooks indulge me on occasion."

"Oh, we've had chicken before," Lyrra said. "But not often since they're mostly kept for the eggs."

"There's only so many eggs that can be used," Ashk said blandly. "And some of those eggs that are laid become little chickens that grow up to be big chickens that lay more eggs. Or they become cocks eager to announce the dawn. And, really, how many cocks does a woman need first thing in the morning?"

Aiden choked on the mouthful of ale he'd just tried to swallow. Lyrra's mouth dropped open before she burst into laughter. Aiden glanced at the men standing near the table. The younger ones were blushing. The older ones just returned his glance and shrugged.

No help there.

"You have a different opinion about cocks in the morning?" Ashk asked.

"Oh, Aiden doesn't— I mean, he— This looks delicious." Lyrra turned her attention to her meal.

Aiden was tempted to give his lover and wife a hard kick under the table, but it wouldn't have done him any good, so he applied himself to his meal.

When they'd eaten their fill and the plates were taken away, Ashk said, "What brings you to Bretonwood?"

"We came to talk to you," Aiden replied.

"Why?"

"We're hoping you can tell us how to find the Hunter."

"Why?"

Irritated by that bland voice that didn't match the *something* almost hidden in her eyes, Aiden got up, walked a few paces to stretch his legs. He turned back to look at her. She just watched him, her expression bland. Too bland.

"Since you know the greeting used by witches, it seems reasonable to assume you've known a witch at some time," Aiden said carefully.

"I know, and have known, several witches," Ashk replied.

"They aren't servants for the Fae to order about."

"Whoever said they were?" Ashk's expression was still bland, but her voice had an edge to it.

Had they finally found an ally, someone who wouldn't dismiss what he'd been trying to tell the Fae for the past year? The edge in her voice lifted his spirits while warning him that he needed to be very careful to explain this in just the right way.

He took a step toward Ashk, held out his hands in appeal, and put everything he had into his words. "Witches are the Mother's Daughters. They are the House of Gaian."

No change in her face. No change in her eyes. Nothing.

"They're being killed, brutally, by men called Inquisitors. And when they die, the shining roads that lead to Tir Alainn die with them, trapping the Fae whose territories were connected to those roads. Maybe destroying those Clans."

"So this is about the Clans."

His temper flared. His hands curled into fists. "This is about the witches. They're *dying*. Can't you understand that? They're gentle people who have a powerful kind of magic, but they're not fighters. The Fae *have* to come down from Tir Alainn and protect the witches and the Old Places. Mother's mercy! *These women are the House of Gaian.* They should be protected for that alone. We've seen what the Inquisitors do to them. We've buried the bodies—and we've listened to the ghosts scream when the nighthunters found them. This isn't about the Fae. This is about the Mother's Daughters. Are the Fae just going to sit back and watch until the last one is slaughtered? If we do, then we deserve whatever happens to us."

Ashk tipped her head to one side. "What is it you want from the Hunter?"

He wanted to grab her, shake her, do *anything* to erase that bland expression. "The Lightbringer and the Lady of the Moon will do nothing to help. They've decided that the witches have a duty to remain in the Old Places to provide the magic that keeps the shining roads open, and most of the Fae agree with them because of who Lucian and Dianna are and because they don't have to do anything more than they've ever done—which is nothing. The Hunter is the only one strong enough to command enough Fae to give the witches some protection from the Inquisitors. Without his help, the slaughter will continue."

He felt movement behind him, saw Lyrra's startled expression. He turned and saw the dark horse—and the woman riding it.

"Morag," he said softly. She'd seen what the Inquisitors did. She was the one who had told *him* before he'd actually seen it for himself. She'd help him convince Ashk. She had to.

She just stared at him for a moment before the dark horse pivoted and raced away.

Confused and, yes, hurt by her reaction to seeing him, he turned back to Ashk.

Her expression was no longer bland, and her woodland eyes held something too dangerous to be called simply feral. His throat tightened until it was hard to breathe. He didn't know what was wrong with Morag, but he and Lyrra needed to get away from this place *now*.

"We thank you for the meal and your time, Lady Ashk," he said formally. "If you would ask someone to bring our horses, we'll be on our way."

"And go where?"

"That is not your concern."

"Bard," Ashk said gently, "do you really think you'll get out of the woods?"

He almost made a stinging reply about the road being easy enough to follow. Then he looked into those eyes and knew what she was telling him: If he and Lyrra tried to leave, she would kill them—or have them killed. They couldn't run fast enough or far enough to get out of the Old Place or away from the Fae Ashk controlled.

She would kill them to prevent them from leaving. He just didn't know why.

"What about the Hunter?" he asked hoarsely.

"The Summer Solstice is a few days away. You'll have your answer about the Hunter after the Solstice." She raised her voice slightly. "Show our guests to a room they can use during their visit with our Clan. I'm sure they're tired after their long journey."

Lyrra got up slowly, moved toward him with fear-stiffened legs. Her hands clamped on his left arm, as if that was the only thing that would keep her standing.

Aiden placed his other hand over hers. They were ice cold.

Several of the men who had remained near the table now came around behind them, blocking any chance to run, if either of them had been so foolish as to try. In front of them Ashk still sat quietly, watching them.

One of the men stepped up beside him. "If you'll follow me."

What choice did they have? Saying nothing, he and Lyrra followed the man to the Clan house.

Ashk waited until she was sure Aiden and Lyrra were in the Clan house before lowering her forehead to rest on her knees.

Mother's mercy. No wonder Aiden had ascended to become the Bard. When his passion rode behind his words, the result could hum in a person's bones until they vibrated to his tune. How had the Fae beyond the west managed to ignore him? Some had heard him and acted. She was sure of that. But not enough. His words had been hamstrung by the Light-bringer and the Lady of the Moon, and from what she knew about the rest of the Fae, she knew he was right—he was telling them a passionate but unpalatable truth while Lucian and Dianna were telling them what they wanted to hear.

The House of Gaian meant something to him. She'd heard the plea under the passion for her to acknowledge that the witches were the Mother's Daughters. How could she deny what she knew to be true?

She would have helped him, had been about to tell him exactly that—until Morag rode up, saw him, and ran.

Morag was from a midland Clan, but she'd been in the eastern part of Sylvalan. She'd been at Brightwood and had helped Ari and Neall escape. She knew Aiden. So what was it about the Bard that would make the *Gatherer* run?

She didn't know, and she didn't like it. She just hoped Aiden was as intelligent as he was eloquent. She'd meant the threat. If he and Lyrra tried to leave, she would kill them.

Great Mother, let Morag's reaction be for some personal or foolish reason. I don't want this man's blood on my hands. I don't want that fine, blazing spirit to leave the world. Let him do the sensible thing and just stay in his room, resting.

"Rider coming!"

Ashk raised her head at the cry. No tension in the voice that had called the warning. No, the voice had sounded almost . . . cheerful.

One glimpse of the horse and rider had her on her feet, running toward them. "Padrick! Padrick!"

He was off his horse and running to meet her. Swept her into his arms and off her feet.

She threw her arms around his neck and held on tight, her eyes filling with tears of relief even while she laughed. "You're home. You're finally home."

He pressed his face against her hair. She felt him tremble as his arms tightened around her.

"Are you well, Ashk? Are you and the children well?"

"We're well, Padrick. Better now that you're home. And you?"

He eased back enough to look at her. His hand shook when he brushed her hair away from her face. "I came as soon as I could. They swore to me you were safe. They swore it. I couldn't have— I had duties, Ashk, but I would have left everything else and come here first if they hadn't sworn to me—"

She pressed her fingers against his mouth. "You had duties to your people, just as I have duties to mine." She frowned. Her fingers lifted away from his mouth. "Who swore to you?"

"Forrester." Padrick looked a little uncomfortable. "After the Black Coats' attack here, he began riding out each morning with a few men to check for signs of those nighthunters."

"Some of my men have been doing the same."

"Yes. Well, your men and mine . . . and Neall . . . would often meet on one of the trails. . . ."

"And Forrester was reassured each morning that the baron's wife and children were safe and well." Well, that explained how her men were able to tell her each day that the people at the manor house and the tenant farms were safe. And it explained why those men had been a bit vague about how they'd come by the information. "If it eased your heart, I'm glad they exchanged news. I wish they had been able to tell me the same about you."

"I was . . . detained. A young baron needed help, and after what I saw on the journey to his home, I'll do whatever it takes to stop the Black Coats and the barons who follow them. But I'm sorry I wasn't here when you needed me. I'm sorry about your grandfather, Ashk. I'm grateful to him for giving his life to save Evan, but I'm sorry you lost him that way."

Ashk shook her head. The grief was still raw, and grief wasn't what she wanted to share with him right now. "There's much we need to talk about, but not yet. Not now."

"What then?"

"A nap."

His expression was uncertain, but his eyes began to twin-
kle. "A nap."

Wrapping arms around each other's waists, they walked
to the Clan house.

"Yes," Ashk said. "You've had a long journey and a difficult morning. A short nap would do you good."

"How short?"

"Oh, an hour or so."

"Will I get any sleep while I'm taking this nap?"

"I don't think so."

He laughed, and she hoped the world, and their duties in
it, would leave them alone for a little while.

Calm, Morag thought as the dark horse galloped along the
wide forest trail. *Stay calm. If you go galloping back to the
cottage, you'll do the very thing you wanted to avoid.*

Light pressure on the reins signaled the dark horse to ease
back to a canter.

It had been foolish to run like that, but she'd reacted without thinking. Or, to be truthful, her thoughts when she'd seen
Aiden had focused on one thing: the Inquisitors' attack and
the worry about the nighthunters still in the woods had been
enough of a shock for Ari. She didn't want the young witch
to have any more surprises right now.

But she shouldn't have run like that. A few minutes to
greet Aiden and Lyrra, a private minute with Ashk, and she
could have left easily enough and talked to Ari before anyone else came by and mentioned the Bard and the Muse were
at the Clan house.

As soon as she reached the open land around the cottage,
she saw Ari sitting on the bench by the kitchen door, spinning
thread for her weavings. Merle lay in front of her, watching
the spindle.

Morag reined in and dismounted. Merle glanced at her,

waved the tip of his tail in greeting, then returned his attention to the spindle.

Ari glanced at Morag, too. "Spinning may be work, but it's sitting down work," she said defensively. Then said, "No," as Merle stretched his neck, his nose—and teeth—close to the spindle.

"Problem?" Morag asked, looking at the two of them as she sat down beside Ari.

"Merle thinks a spindle is a dog toy just because it's made out of wood."

Merle gave Morag a doggy grin, making Morag wonder if the shadow hound really had any interest in the spindle or was simply playing his own version of "tease the witch."

After wrapping the thread around the spindle, Ari put it in the basket beside her. "I thought you were going back to the Clan house for a while."

"I was—and I am. I—" Exasperated with herself, Morag huffed out a breath. If she'd been thinking, she would have talked to Neall first.

"Morag?" Tension tightened Ari's voice. "What's wrong? Has something happened?"

"No," Morag said quickly. She rested a hand on Ari's arm. Felt the muscles quiver. "No," she said again, striving to sound calm. She sighed. "I'm upsetting you, and that's exactly what I didn't want to have happen."

"Just tell me."

"The Bard and the Muse are at the Clan house."

Ari stared blankly at her for a moment. "Aiden and Lyrra? What brings them—?" She paled. "Will they tell Lucian about me?"

Morag shook her head. "They don't know you're here. And they won't know unless you want us to tell them. If you don't want to see them, Ashk and I can make sure they don't come to this part of the Old Place. I wanted to tell you because I didn't want you to drive up to the Clan house and meet them unexpectedly." She paused. "I'm sorry I upset you."

Ari shook her head. "I'm glad you told me." Then she added, "I liked them, Aiden and Lyrra. Sometimes I've wished I could hear them sing again, and I would like to see them. But not if they'll tell Lucian or Dianna that I'm here."

Morag hesitated. Then, remembering the way Lucian almost accepted her bargain, almost traded his life to bring Ari back when he thought the Inquisitors had killed her, she asked the question she'd wanted to ask since she moved into the cottage with Ari and Neall. "If you'd had a choice . . . if you hadn't been bound by the magic in the fancy to accept him, would you have taken Lucian as a lover?"

Ari looked out over the meadow. "I don't know. He was . . . exciting, but I wanted more than trinkets, and that's all he had to give. I think he cared about me, at least a little, and I cared about him. But caring isn't the same as love. There never would have been love. And yet I can't regret what happened because it was one of the things that made it easier to leave Brightwood, and in the end, it brought me here." She rested one hand on her round belly. "With Neall."

Morag stood up. "As long as you're all right about them being here, I need to get back. I left in a bit of a hurry, and I may have some rough edges to smooth over with Ashk."

Ari gave Morag a thoughtful look. "If Neall and I come to dinner at the Clan house tonight, do you think that would help smooth those rough edges?"

"Yes, it would help. But if you come, you'll have to stay overnight. Until we're sure we've destroyed all the night-hunters, it wouldn't be safe for the two of you to drive back through the woods."

"I know. I'll talk to Neall as soon as he gets back."

"I'm glad you want to see them."

"I liked them." Ari made a face. "And I'll like Aiden even better if he doesn't make me sing."

Feeling easier, Morag rode back to the Clan house—and hoped nothing had happened that would make it impossible to smooth those rough edges.

Lyrra stepped out of the women's communal room and tried not to sigh. She would have gladly spent the day in that room, soaking in the deep tub of hot water, sitting by the window and daydreaming, or napping on one of the daybeds and not feeling awkward about the folded towels under her hips. Privacy and rest. She craved it this time with a need that made her want to weep. But she couldn't leave Aiden alone in the room they'd been given, worried and brooding, and until they knew why Ashk had turned on them, she didn't want to leave herself in a position where she and Aiden could be easily separated.

A door a little farther down the corridor opened. Ashk stepped out, hesitated, then approached.

"Do you have everything you need?" Ashk asked politely.

"Yes, thank you," Lyrra replied, equally polite.

She had the sense that Ashk felt awkward around her. She hoped so. If you threatened to kill someone, you shouldn't feel small civilities made up for it.

Why did you turn on us? Maybe she would have asked that question, woman to woman, if she hadn't heard the sound of other women's voices and knew the moment to ask the question had been lost.

Then Morag turned the corner and stopped suddenly when she saw them.

Lyrra noticed the tension building in Ashk. She wanted to get out of that corridor, away from Ashk and Morag. She wanted the reassurance that Aiden was safe.

"You left in a hurry," Ashk said quietly.

"Yes," Morag replied. "For that, I owe you and Aiden an apology, Lyrra."

Morag looked uncertain, and Lyrra discovered it wasn't something she liked seeing in the Gatherer.

"When you saw us, why did you ride away like that?" Lyrra asked.

Morag looked at Ashk while answering the question. "I thought their being here might bring up memories that were . . . distressing . . . especially after the attack by the Black Coats."

"Were the memories distressing?" Ashk asked.

"No."

Lyrra frowned. She'd asked the question, but only Morag and Ashk understood the answer.

Then Morag looked at her. "Ari is here."

"Ari?" Lyrra's heart gave a funny little jump before settling back to a proper rhythm. She took a step toward Morag. "Ari is *here?* She's well? And . . . and Neall? Is he here with her? Is he well?"

"They're both well. She carries their first child."

Lyrra laughed while tears filled her eyes. "Oh, this is wonderful! Aiden will be so pleased. Do you think—?" She looked into Morag's dark eyes and some of the pleasure drained away. Black Coats attacking. Morag galloping away from the Clan house after seeing them, worried about distressing memories.

"You thought our being here would upset her?"

"Yes."

You're here, Morag. Why wouldn't your presence upset her just as much? She knew the answer to that. She and Aiden had come with Dianna to celebrate the Summer Solstice with Ari, and, while they'd meant no harm, they hadn't come honestly. They'd used the glamour to wear a human face and hide that they were Fae. They hadn't known the magic Ari would call up when she did the spiral dance would reveal them for what they were. Their reasons hadn't been cruel, but they had lied to her. They'd all lied to her. Except Morag. Morag had come to Brightwood as who and what she was. And in the end, she was the one who had helped Ari and Neall get away from Brightwood, from the Inquisitors—and from Lucian and Dianna.

Lyrra wiped the tears that dampened her cheeks. "I understand. Is it likely that she'll come to the Clan house? Aiden and I . . . We'll stay out of sight." It hurt more than she expected to say that.

Morag shook her head. "She'd like to see you and Aiden—as long as Aiden doesn't make her sing."

Lyrra opened her mouth to make a hurried assurance, then just sighed. "When it comes to Aiden and hearing a new song, I'm not willing to promise anything. Although, I suppose I could threaten to sing loudly and off-key for the next month if he pesters her."

"That sounds like a suitable punishment," Ashk said dryly.

Lyrra nodded. "For Aiden it would be."

Morag looked at Ashk. "Neall and Ari may be coming for the evening meal."

"They'll have to stay until morning," Ashk said.

"I already told her that."

Lyrra glanced at each of them and realized Morag and Ashk not only understood each other, but they also felt equally protective of Ari and Neall.

"If you'll excuse me," Lyrra said. "I'd better get back to Aiden."

"Ari was hoping you and Aiden would be willing to sing a few songs this evening," Morag said.

"It would be our pleasure." Smiling at both of them, she

hurried through the corridors of that part of the Clan house until she reached the room she and Aiden had been given.

He was still sitting on the window seat, silent. He stood quickly when she rushed across the room. When she threw her arms around his neck, he held her tightly against him.

"Lyrra?" he said worriedly.

She leaned back, and she knew he didn't understand the tears welling up again as she smiled at him. But he would. Oh, he would.

"Aiden, I have wonderful news."

Morag watched Lyrra hurry away before turning back to face Ashk. "I apologize if my hasty departure caused a problem."

Ashk shrugged. "Nothing an apology from me can't mend. And if it can't be mended, so be it."

Morag studied Ashk. "When I got back to the Clan house, I talked to a couple of the hunters standing watch. They told me Aiden and Lyrra would be killed if they tried to leave. Those were your orders."

Ashk met her eyes without flinching, without regret. "Those were my orders. Now that I know why you left so hastily, I'll withdraw that command." She took a deep breath, let it out slowly. "I'm glad they didn't test my sincerity."

"Did you really think the Bard and the Muse were a threat?"

Ashk shook her head. "If they'd truly been a threat to the Clan, or to anyone else in Bretonwood, you wouldn't have run, Morag. You would have killed them yourself."

Ashk settled on one of the benches that formed a half-circle in front of the Clan house. Aiden and Lyrra took the center bench, quietly tuning instruments in preparation for the evening's entertainment.

She'd spent most of the time before and during the evening meal watching them. Especially Aiden. She'd seen the sign of nerves as he'd rubbed his hands on his trousers when Ari and Neall had ridden up to the Clan house. She'd seen the strong emotions in his face and in his eyes when Ari shyly approached him—and realized it was meeting Ari last summer, however briefly, that had begun the journey that brought Aiden here now. She'd seen his delight when Morphia greeted him—and his relief when Morag came up to talk to him. She'd listened as Aiden and Padrick talked about traveling through the Mother's Hills—and laughed together about someone named Skelly and his sweet granny.

And she felt an ache in her heart that he hadn't arrived a month earlier when he could have walked down a forest trail and looked into the wise, dark eyes of an old stag.

Padrick joined her, took her hand in his. He didn't say anything. He didn't have to. The light squeeze of her hand told her he knew where her thoughts had gone.

She looked at Caitlin and Evan, sitting on old blankets with a pile of other children, protected within that half circle of benches filled with adults. The men who formed the outer part of the circle were all armed. They'd found no nighthunter nests close to the Clan house, but she knew there were still some out there. She could still feel a wrongness in the woods. So they would be cautious, careful.

Aiden and Lyrra began with an instrumental piece, followed by a bright little tune. Then Lyrra spent a couple of minutes teaching the children the chorus to another song.

They were all laughing and applauding at the end of that song when a shout of alarm had the adults jumping to their feet.

Ashk's heart pounded in her chest as a dark horse cantered toward them, chased by one of the youths standing watch over the corralled horses. Like the armed hunters, she scanned the trees and the shadows cast by the torchlight for any sign of danger—and sensed nothing.

The horse wove his way between people who prudently stepped aside until he came to a stop at the edge of the blankets filled with children.

"I don't understand how he got out," the youth said, panting from the chase.

"It's all right." Aiden's voice was a blend of embarrassment and resignation. "He just wants to hear the music."

The dark horse tossed his head in what might have been a nod of agreement.

The youth trotted back to the corral. The adults settled back in their seats. The horse pricked his ears.

"Back, Minstrel," Aiden said firmly.

Minstrel hung his head, positioning his ears to create a woeful expression.

Aiden pinched the bridge of his nose. "Two steps back."

One step. Two steps. Still looking woeful.

Aiden picked up his whistle. Minstrel lifted his head.

Like the rest of them, Ashk watched with delight as Minstrel arched his neck and did his trotting-in-place dance to Aiden's tune.

When the applause died down, Aiden said, "Take a bow, Minstrel." His eyes widened and Lyrra sprawled on the bench in gleeful laughter as the horse extended one front leg, curled the other, and lowered his head.

"I don't think the Bard was expecting that," Padrick whispered.

"No, I don't think he was," Ashk whispered back. Aiden's effort to control his expression was as entertaining as anything else so far.

They listened to funny songs and love songs and, finally, at the end, another instrumental piece that was quiet and peaceful.

Padrick slipped an arm around her waist, brought his lips close to her ear. "He's a good man, but he can't win this battle alone."

"I know."

"Will he meet the Hunter?"

She didn't answer until the last notes of the song faded on the air. "He'll meet the Hunter."

Chapter Thirty

Aiden wandered toward the sturdy, makeshift table that held the Solstice feast, curious to see what Ari was doing. She kept glancing around while she held her hands close to the sides of one dish after another. Maybe whatever she was doing meant they'd be eating soon. He hoped so. The scent of the food was making his mouth water and his stomach growl.

He was still a few feet away when Neall stepped out of the cottage's kitchen door, saw Ari, and frowned.

"You're doing too much," Neall said, striding over to Ari.

"It's just a little fire to keep things warm," Ari said defensively, turning to face him.

Neall rested his hands lightly of her upper arms. "If you do too much, you'll be tired by the time you finish the dance and you won't enjoy the entertainment Ashk has planned afterward."

Ari smoothed nonexistent wrinkles on the embroidered shirt she'd made for him. "It's our first Summer Solstice here. I want it to be perfect."

"It won't be perfect, Ari," Neall said with a smile. He kissed her. "But it will be wonderful."

Wondering how to move away without drawing attention to himself and ending their quietly intimate moment, Aiden saw Padrick approaching.

"Neall, I wonder if I can borrow Ari for a few minutes. Ashk has a couple of things she needs to discuss with her."

Ari glanced over to where Ashk was sitting with a few other women, including Lyrra and Morphia. "She just wants me to sit down and rest—like someone else I know."

"That may be so," Padrick agreed. "But I was sent to fetch you, and I, as a dutiful husband, am here to ask you to allow yourself to be fetched." He shifted his face into a comically woeful expression. "If I go back empty-handed, I'll get a pillow and blanket tonight instead of kisses and cuddles."

Ari huffed in an effort not to laugh. Then she noticed Aiden. "Does the Bard have an opinion he wants to express?"

"Indeed I do," Aiden replied. "Your gown is lovely."

Ari blushed a little and grinned. Aiden grinned back at her.

Padrick and Neall just looked at him.

"You're supposed to have a way with words, and that's the best you can do?" Neall said.

"Since Ari isn't arguing with *me,* I'd say I've done very well," Aiden replied.

Padrick and Neall looked so disgruntled, Ari laughed. "Very well, Padrick. I'll not undermine your influence as husband or baron."

Padrick offered his arm to Ari, winked at Neall, and led the young witch to where Ashk waited.

"More ale, Bard?" Neall asked.

Aiden lifted his tankard in a salute. "I'll make do with what I have, thanks. I want a clear head tonight. Do you know what Lady Ashk has planned?"

Neall shook his head. "Well, there's a traditional dance this Clan usually does at Harvest Eve, but Ashk decided to do it tonight as an entertainment for the Clan's guests. That's why she requested a fire pit in the meadow to hold a small bonfire instead of the brazier Ari would normally use tonight."

They both looked back at the table wistfully.

"If I round up the children, they'll become impatient if they aren't fed soon," Neall said.

"Which means the rest of us will get to eat, as well. That sounds like a fine plan."

With a mischievous grin, Neall headed out to the part of the meadow where several children were playing some kind of odd game of tag with Merle.

Aiden drank the last couple of swallows of ale, draining his tankard. A Fae Lord. Oh, the face was certainly human, but there was no denying that Neall was a Fae Lord. A young Lord of the Woods. And a fine young man.

"Blessings of the day to you, Aiden."

Aiden turned. Morag stood a few feet behind him.

"Blessings of the day, Morag." Before she could speak, he shook his head. "You made your apology, and it was accepted."

"I hurt you," Morag said softly.

"Yes, you did. But I can't say I wouldn't have done the same." He looked over to where Ari sat with the other women, laughing about something. "She's different here."

Morag shook her head as she moved to stand beside him. "No, she isn't."

He turned so they both stood facing the meadow, watching Neall and Merle herd laughing children toward a trough where they could wash their hands. "She is. She's bloomed."

"She's accepted here—by the Fae, by the villagers. Here, she's a Daughter of the House of Gaian. Here, she's wanted for herself, not for what she has or what she can do for someone else."

"And she has love's jewels." Aiden sighed. "You made the right choice, Morag, giving them both the chance to get away from Brightwood . . . and the Clan there. Lucian cared for Ari. I'm sure of that. But he wasn't in love with her, and I think he always would have found her . . . wanting . . . in some way, would have wanted her to be something other than who and what she is. He would have cared about her, would have continued to be her lover, probably would have sired a child on her in order to assure that there would continue to be a witch at Brightwood, but he wouldn't have refused an invitation to a Fae lady's bed when he went to Tir Alainn—and he never would have looked at Ari as if she contained all the joy in the world."

"For Neall, she does."

"I know. And she loves him."

"Yes, she does."

He didn't want to talk about Lucian or Brightwood or the past anymore, so he was relieved when he saw Ashk and the other women walking toward the table—and he noticed Neall and the children approaching from the other direction, with Merle tagging along, looking hopeful. Studying the children, Aiden suspected the young shadow hound had good reason to feel hopeful about getting a share of the feast.

"Oh," Morag said. "Ashk said she had the cooks roast a couple of chickens, especially for you, but she wasn't sure if you preferred breasts or thighs. For some reason, Lyrra found that very funny."

Remembering Ashk's last comments about chickens and eggs, and seeing the way she was smiling at him as she approached, Aiden felt his face warm a bit. "Wonderful."

"I'm glad I'm not playing tonight," Aiden said, putting an arm around Lyrra's waist as he watched the musicians check their instruments

"No, you're not," she said, laughing quietly. "If they lent you an instrument, you'd be in the middle of them."

"I don't know the songs."

"When has *that* ever bothered you?"

It did bother him a little. There was music here that had never been heard beyond the western Clans. The fault of those who had been the Bard before him. His fault since he'd become the Lord of Song for never having visited the western Clans until now. "I've played with them for the past few nights. Tonight I'll simply enjoy being entertained."

Oh, a few minutes of hearing the melodies of the songs they were playing tonight was all he would have needed to follow along with them, and play well. He didn't tell Lyrra that he'd asked about playing with them tonight, and the musicians had looked uncomfortable and told him Ashk wanted his full attention on the entertainment.

Lyrra gave him a skeptical look, but didn't have time to say anything before Ashk hurried up to them.

"Come along," she said, looking at Lyrra. "I'll show you your place for the spiral dance."

"My place?" Lyrra said nervously. "I can't participate in the dance. I'm not a witch."

Ashk studied her for a moment. "You have woodland eyes. That means you claim some kinship to the House of Gaian. Tonight, that's all you need." She grabbed Lyrra's hand and pulled her away from Aiden. "Come along. The steps are quite simple. Neall! Come along now!"

"Neall doesn't have woodland eyes," Aiden said to Padrick as the Baron of Breton came to stand beside him.

"No, he doesn't. But his mother, Nora, was a witch. So he'll join the dance." Padrick smiled as he watched Ashk demonstrate the dance steps for Lyrra. "Ashk used to dance with Nora for the Solstice. She's been looking forward to joining this dance again. Having Neall and Ari living here means a great deal to her."

Not because they're useful, Aiden thought as he watched

several of the Fae take their places to form a large, loose circle, *but because they are dear to her. For her, they're like the
favorite nephew and his beloved wife, finally returned home.*

He heard the drums set a slow, measured beat to indicate
the dance was about to begin. His heart pounded a little too
quickly. He'd seen the spiral dance last Solstice, had felt the
magic in Brightwood answer that dance. But Ari had danced
alone that night, and the power they'd felt when she drew all
that magic to herself and released it again had frightened the
Fae who had come to her cottage pretending to be human.

"You've a hungry look about you, Bard," Padrick said.
"Did you have enough to eat?"

There was a hunger in him that had nothing to do with a
full belly. He hadn't realized how much he'd craved seeing
this dance again when he knew what to expect. "Hmm?"
Aiden said, feeling impatient with conversation that was dis-
tracting him. "Yes, I had plenty. Wonderful food. The only
thing I've tasted that was better was some brown bread we'd
had at a village on the way here."

"Brown bread?" Padrick asked sharply. "Where was
this?"

"A village. We took a road off the main one and had a
meal in the village tavern." Aiden frowned. He didn't want to
be impolite, but Ari was walking over to the circle; the actual
dance would start any moment now.

"You stopped in Wiccandale?"

"Didn't have a sign posted anywhere, so I can't tell you
which village it was." Aiden turned his head slowly and
stared at Padrick. "Wiccandale?"

Laughter danced in Padrick's eyes. "You didn't know, did
you?"

"Know?"

"It's a wiccanfae village."

Aiden's mouth fell open. "Are you saying it's *an entire village of witches?*"

Padrick coughed politely. "Only the women are called witches."

"Mother's mercy," Aiden said weakly. An entire village of people who could trace their roots back to the House of Gaian. No wonder the village had the same feel as an Old Place. With the appearance of Black Coats in the west, no wonder they were wary of strangers.

Remembering the woman and the little girl, Kayla, he realized the Black Coats weren't the only danger to those people. Would *anyone* be able to rouse the Clans to protect the witches and the Old Places if they knew there was a place where they could obtain another witch? The Fae might be unwilling to enter the Mother's Hills, but a village in the west? Oh, yes. Dianna wouldn't think twice about ordering the men of her Clan to ride to Wiccandale and take a couple of young witches. She wouldn't care if those women were willing or not, as long as it freed her from being the anchor that held the shining road open at Brightwood. She would justify it as something owed to her because she was the Lady of the Moon.

"Bard."

Something in Padrick's voice pulled Aiden's attention back to the here and now. He wasn't sure if he was looking at a Fae Lord or the Baron of Breton. He suspected the feral heat he saw in Padrick's eyes was one of the reasons the man was obeyed so readily.

"It was wonderful bread," Aiden said softly. "It's unfortunate that I wouldn't be able to find my way back to that village."

Padrick stared at him for a moment before nodding. "If witches were suddenly to go missing, it would displease the Fae in the west—"

Displease the Hunter, you mean.

"—and it would displease me, since Wiccandale is in the county I rule, and I have a responsibility to those people."

"I understand."

"Yes," Padrick said quietly, "I thought you would." He lifted his chin slightly. "The dance is starting."

Aiden turned back to the meadow in time to see Ari take the first steps of the dance. He already felt the eddies and currents of magic in this Old Place start to flow. Ashk took Ari's hand and joined the dance—and the flow became more powerful. One by one, the Fae who had kinship to the House of Gaian joined the dance, and power swirled around the meadow like a contained storm.

Small candles glowed at the edge of the meadow, catching his attention.

Not candles, Aiden realized, feeling his body jolt from the slight shock. The Small Folk had come to watch the dance. It was the magic in them that glowed. He glanced at the musicians. Saw the same misty glow. Last Solstice, that's how Ari had known her guests weren't human. With all the power that came from the Great Mother in motion, the magic inside the Fae and the Small Folk shone like stationary beacons. He hadn't seen it last summer when Ari had danced alone, but here, with so many dancers helping her funnel all that power into the spiral dance, he saw things with a clarity that was almost blinding.

"There," Padrick breathed softly. "There. Can you feel it?"

Feel what? Aiden wondered. His head was spinning, as if he'd had too much to drink. But it was the dance that was intoxicating him, the music that was thrumming in his blood now.

As the music faded, he heard Ari giving thanks to the Great Mother for the branches of earth, air, water, and fire.

Saw flames lick the carefully placed wood of the bonfire. And felt himself lifted up as she released the magic back into the Old Place. The ripples of it flowed through him and traveled on. When she finally lowered her arms, the air smelled sweeter, the land beneath his feet pulsed with life, and passion burned hot inside him.

The dance was done, the dancers rippling out of the spiral in a way that echoed the magic just released. He watched Lyrra walk toward him. The look on her face made him wonder how many other lovers would have an intimate celebration tonight.

He met her. Kissed her in a way that was far too intimate while they were standing in the open with people all around them, but he couldn't stop himself, and the way she leaned into him and answered the kiss told him she wasn't thinking of other people either. But her hands kept his pressed against her waist, a prudent compromise of passion and common sense.

He broke the kiss, wondering a bit desperately how offended Ashk would be if he and Lyrra slipped away without seeing her planned entertainment.

"If you'll excuse me," Padrick said. "I'm wanted for the next dance."

The warning under the amusement was enough to make Aiden struggle to get his libido under control—and finally notice that he and Lyrra had a very interested audience.

"Oh," Lyrra said softly, blushing.

"Well," Ari said.

"My," Morphia said.

Neall and Sheridan, who had recently become Morphia's lover, just grinned at him.

It was the wistful expression on Morag's face before she turned away to watch whatever was happening in the meadow that made Aiden uncomfortable. Had Death's Mistress ever had a real lover? It wasn't something he could ever ask Morag, but the flicker of sadness on Morphia's face before she linked arms with her sister was answer enough.

Sheridan left them, drawing Aiden's attention back to the meadow. The large wicker baskets that had been left near the musicians were now open, and the Fae were carefully unwrapping masks.

Aiden shifted uneasily. Each mask was a work of art, shaped and decorated to represent an animal. The children were squirrels, rabbits, mice, and songbirds. Small creatures. Among the adult masks, he saw hawk, raven, owl, wolf, stag, fox. Watching Padrick fit a hawk mask over the top half of his face, he wondered if the adults wore masks that matched their other forms. He searched for Ashk, wanting to know what her other form was. When he saw her, he wasn't sure what to think.

The mask was female, and feral. Human, but not human. As she passed by one of the torches that had been lit for the musicians, he caught some of the mask's colors—summer greens twining with the oranges and reds of autumn—but she turned away before he could puzzle out the details.

Ashk walked over to the bonfire. The rest of the Fae formed a large circle around her, the elders of the Clan on the outside ring of the circle, the children in the inner ring, the rest of the adults in between.

The music started. Ashk smiled, turned as the Fae in the circle began to move. She skipped a few steps with one child, moved forward to circle with a stag in a way that was highly suggestive of a mating dance, moved on again to do a few steps with a vixen, stepped within the circle to twirl and dance on her own, always moving with the others in a way that was clearly intended to celebrate life.

Then the music changed, becoming darker, deeper—and Ashk changed with it.

Chilled by her slight smile, Aiden watched her raise her arms as if she were drawing an imaginary bow. The masked Fae moved faster now. She loosed the imaginary arrow, and three of them dropped to their hands and knees.

She drew back another arrow. More of the Fae fell. As the arrow pointed at them, the elder Fae moved out of the circle to stand with their heads bowed. A vixen staggered before she fell. A stag leaped high, his back arched, before he crumbled to the ground. Ashk kept pivoting, firing her imaginary arrows as the music filled the meadow. As the last masked Fae fell to the ground, the music suddenly stopped.

Aiden felt Lyrra shivering beside him. A dance that had celebrated life had become a circle of the slain.

A heartbeat of silence. Two.

The music began again, the same part of the tune that had begun the dance, but quieter this time.

Ashk walked the circle, one hand extended. As she passed, the masked Fae got to their feet and began walking the circle with her again. When they passed behind the bonfire, they stepped out of the circle, forming lines beyond the fire.

Once. Twice. Three times. As the last notes faded, Ashk stood behind the bonfire, with the rest of the masked dancers spread out behind her.

Aiden couldn't breathe right. The faces staring back at him were feral and alien, something a part of him recognized—and feared. And Ashk . . .

In the flickering light, he finally made out the details of her mask. Not a human face decorated with vines and leaves, and yet it was. Not an animal face, but it held that quality, too.

The dancers were breaking formation now, helping each other untie the leather straps that held the masks in place. The spell of the dance should have broken with those ordinary movements. It didn't. Instead, Aiden had the sense that those ordinary movements were simply a way of donning a different kind of mask.

"What are they?" Lyrra whispered, her voice shaking.

"They're the Fae," Morag said softly.

Aiden looked at her. Morag's eyes were wide and staring. Her lips were slightly parted to help her breathe. And as she watched Ashk, still masked, walk around the bonfire and move toward them, she looked as if she'd finally seen the answer to something that had puzzled her.

"They are the Fae," Morag said. "And Ashk . . ."

Ashk walked up to Morag, stood close enough that if either of them had extended a hand, they would have touched.

That close, Aiden saw the mask and shivered. It was the woods come alive. Life and death. Shadows and light.

Ashk stood in front of Morag, a strange smile curving her lips.

"And Ashk," Morag said softly, "is the Hunter."

Morag carefully closed the shutters over the window, adjusting the slats to let as much cool air in as possible. Until the nighthunters' appearance in the Old Place, there'd been no reason to shutter the windows at night. Now it was a sensible precaution.

She climbed into bed, pulling the sheet up around her, not relaxed enough to sleep despite the fatigue pulling at her. Perhaps she should have stayed with Neall and Ari. The cottage was her home, after all. But Morphia and Sheridan had stayed at the cottage, and she'd come back with the rest of the Fae to the Clan house.

Who are you, Ashk?

She'd been asking that question in one way or another since she'd arrived at this Old Place. Now she finally had the answer.

Someone tapped softly on her door. Before she could move, Aiden slipped into her room, carrying a small harp. When he reached the bed, he sat near her feet, shifting until he could hold the harp comfortably.

Morag's chest tightened. She pulled her feet up and hugged her knees. There'd been a moment this evening, after the spiral dance, when she'd felt sad and wistful that there wasn't a man like Aiden or Sheridan or Neall who looked at her with the heat of passion in his eyes. But she didn't want a man who was committed to another woman, and she didn't want pity from the Bard. "Aiden—"

"Lyrra knows I'm here," Aiden said quietly. His hands rested on the harp strings for a moment before he began playing idle notes. "We have to talk, and this is the best way to do that privately."

"All right." She shifted a little. "Let me light a few more candles. This one isn't enough."

"Don't," Aiden said, his head bent over the harp. "Sometimes things are said more easily in the dark."

Morag shifted again. One candle made the room too dark, too intimate. Enough light for lovers, but not for friends. Because it was Aiden, she stayed where she was.

He said nothing. Just played idle notes on his harp. It was like listening to the summer leaves stirred by a soft breeze or the trickle of water in a fountain. Her body began to relax into the sound until she was drifting in some easy place where her mind was at rest.

"Tonight," Aiden said softly, "what did you mean when you said, 'They're the Fae'?"

She drifted with the harp's notes. He was right. It was easier to say some things in the dark. "They still are what the rest of us used to be, what we've forgotten how to be. They're the Fae. They've never forgotten their place in the world, never forgotten that there is death as well as life, shad-

ows as well as light. For them, Tir Alainn is a sanctuary, a
place to rest. But they never left the world, and the rest of us
have become a pale reflection of what we used to be."

"You're being too harsh."

"Am I? If the Inquisitors had come to the west instead of
the eastern part of Sylvalan, the first witch they caught still
would have died. But not the second one, not any of the others after that. It wouldn't have mattered what the barons or
the gentry or any other human said, the Fae in the west would
have stopped it. What does that say about the rest of us?"

Aiden sighed. "I don't know, Morag. I don't know if the
rest of the Fae will pay any more attention to Ashk than they
did to you or me."

"Then I pity them."

Aiden stopped playing and looked at her. "Why feel pity
for them?"

"Because the Hunter will have none."

Ashk lay curled against Padrick's side, her head resting on
his shoulder. His lovemaking tonight had ranged from fierce
to tender and back again, demanding enough to make her
forget everything but him. But they needed to talk, and she
couldn't push it aside any longer.

"Padrick . . ."

He turned his head, pressed his lips against her forehead.
"I want to say something first. Then I'll listen to whatever
you have to tell me."

Her heart stuttered. Found its rhythm again. "All right."

He sighed. Shifted a little to draw her closer. "I fell in love
with you the night I met you, and I wanted you in my life in
every way you would let me have you. But I was a gentry
baron, and I needed the legal contract of a human marriage
so that my children could inherit my estate and other property, and my male heir could become the next baron. Because

that was a human need, I followed human custom, which is usually to ask a woman's father for permission to broach the question of marriage. You'd never mentioned your father. Never talked about your family at all. Except for your grandfather.

"I went riding in the woods one afternoon, trying to think of a way to ask you where to find him without telling you why I wanted to find him. Suddenly there was a stag standing in the middle of the trail. He stared at me for a long moment, then turned and walked down the trail. I followed him to a meadow, and he changed into a man."

"Kernos," Ashk said softly.

"Kernos," Padrick agreed. "The old Lord of the Woods. If he'd been an old baron, I would have known exactly what to say, but he looked at me with those eyes that had seen so much, knew so much, and I started stammering like some foolish schoolboy. He cut me off just by raising his hand. And he told me that life has its seasons, just like the woods. He said we would have a green season, a time when life would swell and grow, and he hoped it would be a long season in our lives, one that lasted many years. But the day would come when the world needed the Hunter and the green season of our lives would give way to the next—and when that day came, I would have to let you go. He told me I needed to be sure that I could let you go, and if I couldn't, then he wouldn't interfere with my being your lover but he would never consent to your being my wife."

"But you did ask me to be your wife, and he stood with me when the magistrate spoke the words for the human ceremony." Ashk felt tears welling up. She shut her eyes to hold them back.

"Yes, he stood with you, and he stood by us during the green years. But the season has changed, Ashk, and Sylvalan needs the Hunter. So I have to let you go."

Ashk swallowed the tears. She drew in a breath and choked on a sob.

"No," Padrick murmured, cradling her. "No regrets, Ashk. No tears. We'll get through this. We will. The seasons will turn again, and we'll have more green years ahead of us."

"I don't want to leave you and the children."

"I know. We'll be here, waiting for you."

Ashk wiped her eyes. After a long pause, she said, "I'm going to cut my hair."

Padrick shifted, propping himself on one elbow to look down at her. "Cut your hair?"

He sounded so shocked, she almost smiled. "I can't take the chance of having a braid come loose and the hair tangling with the arrows when I need one."

"I know, but . . . Will you braid it first so that it can be kept?"

Now she did smile. "I doubt Caitlin needs or wants her mother's braided hair."

His voice was rough with emotion. "I'm not asking for Caitlin."

She nodded, afraid she'd end up weeping if she tried to speak. When she thought she had enough control, she took a deep breath, let it out in a sigh. "I'd better get it done."

Padrick rolled, pinning her to the bed. "Not yet. The Hunter will rise from this bed, and that's the way it needs to be. So let me make love to the Green Lady one last time."

Ashk wrapped her arms around him. "One last time."

Chapter Thirty-one

Gritty-eyed and achy from a restless night and too little sleep, Morag stepped out of the Clan house. She shivered in the cool morning air and wished she'd thought to bring a shawl with her. Usually she enjoyed the coolness of morning before the day yielded to summer heat. Now she wanted the heat and bright sunlight of midday. She wanted to sit somewhere open and quiet and let the heat bake the tension out of her body, melt the worry that had chased her through her dreams.

Sylvalan will change, no matter what Ashk decides today. The question is, can we live with how it changes?

Hearing movement behind her, Morag glanced over her shoulder. Aiden and Lyrra stood in the doorway, looking at the Fae who were helping themselves to tea and hot breads from the outdoor stove. Neither of them looked like they'd had an easy night.

"Blessings of the day to you, Morag," Aiden said.

"Blessings of the day," Morag replied. She looked at Lyrra, then at the Fae going about their usual morning tasks. "They're no different from who they were yesterday."

"I know," Lyrra said. "But . . ."

But now you know why they're different from the rest of us.

The rattle of wheels caught Morag's attention. A few moments later, Ari and Neall arrived in the pony cart, followed by Morphia and Sheridan on horseback.

"Come along, then," Morag said briskly. She headed for the large table, sure that Aiden and Lyrra would follow, if for no other reason than because Ari, Neall, and Morphia were familiar faces in a world that had turned strange.

"There was no reason for you to be bringing back all that food," Beitris scolded. "You should have kept it so that you could have a rest day after the dance." She set clean cups on the table while another woman brought over a pot of tea.

"We kept plenty," Ari said. "The cold cellar is stuffed, isn't it?" She turned to Neall as she said it.

"Stuffed," Neall agreed, grinning.

Morag glanced at Morphia, then quickly looked away, biting her lower lip to keep from laughing. Watching Ari deal with this Clan's Lady of the Hearth was always entertaining.

Beitris sniffed. "And I suppose the young Lord bundled you up and had you out the door this morning before you could have so much as a sip of tea."

"No, he didn't," Ari huffed. "I had— Oh. What kind of bread is that?"

"Apple nut," Beitris said. "Would you like to try a piece?"

"Yes, thank you."

"Well," Neall said. "So much for 'I'm too full from last night's meal to finish my porridge.'"

Ari scowled at him. "That was porridge. This isn't."

Nothing has changed, Morag thought fondly, watching Neall pull out the bench to accommodate Ari's belly. *And everything has changed.* Looking at the contentment on Sheridan's face and Morphia's heavy eyes, she didn't think her sister had gotten much sleep last night either—and didn't regret it.

If anyone else noticed that the Bard and the Muse remained strangely silent throughout the meal, no one mentioned it. It couldn't be easy for either of them to be afraid of the person they had searched so hard to find.

Then Morphia said, "Oh, my."

Turning on the bench to see what had caught Morphia's attention, Morag watched Padrick and a slender man walk toward them. The stranger had short, ash-brown hair and woodland eyes, and looked so much like—

"Ashk?" Morag said hesitantly.

The man smiled. "Blessings of the day to you." The timbre was a little lower, but it was still Ashk's voice.

"Mother's mercy," Aiden said. "*That's* how you did it. *That's* why no one ever suspected the Hunter was a woman."

"One can use the glamour for other things besides creating a human mask," Ashk said.

"Did the old Lord of the Woods suspect you were a woman?" Lyrra asked.

Ashk's smile turned feral, but Morag saw the slash of grief in her eyes.

"He was the one who taught me this mask," Ashk said. "He said when the time came for me to take his place, the western Clans would accept me as the Green Lady but the Clans beyond the west never would. He believed the Lords who held the gift of the woods would feel compelled to challenge me over and over because the Hunter had always been the *Lord* of the Woods. Out of respect for him and kindness to me, the Clans here have kept my secret from the rest of the Fae. Now . . ." She shrugged. "That I'm a woman isn't important. The power that I can wield is." She looked at Aiden, who slowly rose to his feet to face her. "Do you still want the Hunter to go with you?"

Aiden swallowed hard. "Yes, I do."

"Then I'll go, and we'll see what can be done about cleansing the Inquisitors from Sylvalan."

"It won't just be the Inquisitors you have to deal with,

Ashk," Morag said quietly. "Even if you use the glamour to look like a Lord, the Fae will resist you too, and the humans outside of the west may not be willing to accept the Fae's presence."

"If the barons command it, the people will accept it," Padrick said. "I can be of some help with that."

"We won't be taking land away from the humans," Ashk said. "We'll simply be taking back the Old Places."

Last summer, I told the Master Inquisitor that the Fae were reclaiming the Old Places, but it never happened, and the slaughter of witches continued, Morag thought. If Ashk can really bring the Fae back to the world, then maybe we will be able to stop this.

"It won't be easy," Morag said.

"No," Ashk agreed, "it won't be easy."

Aiden was looking at her, his expression uneasy. She wasn't even sure why she was resisting, except that Ashk was leaving her home and family without truly knowing how difficult the task ahead of her would be.

"How will you explain to the Small Folk and the witches and all the humans for whom the Fae mean nothing more than a seduction or taking their amusement at another person's expense?" Morag asked. "What words can you say that will keep us from fighting among ourselves instead of fighting the enemy that wants to destroy us?"

"The words aren't difficult." Ashk turned and stared toward the east for a long time, as if she could see beyond the woods, beyond the rolling land, even beyond the Mother's Hills. When she turned back, Morag was glad she had come to know the woman before meeting Ashk as the Hunter.

"This is what we will tell the Small Folk and the humans and the witches," Ashk said softly. "Too long have we been absent. Now we have returned."

The Black Jewels Novels
by Anne Bishop

"Darkly mesmerizing...fascinatingly different."
—Locus

This is the story of the heir to a dark throne, a magic more powerful than that of the High Lord of Hell, and an ancient prophecy. These books tell of a ruthless game of politics and intrigue, magic and betrayal, love and sacrifice, destiny and fulfillment, as the Princess Jaenelle struggles to become that which she was meant to be.

Daughter of the Blood

Heir to the Shadows

Queen of the Darkness

Tangled Webs

The Invisible Ring

The Shadow Queen

Available wherever books are sold or at
penguin.com

THE
TIR ALAINN
TRILOGY

by
Anne Bishop

The Pillars of the World, **Book I:**
"Bishop only adds luster to her reputation for
fine fantasy." —*Booklist*

Shadows and Light, **Book II:**
"Plenty of thrills, faerie magic, human nastiness, and
romance." —*Locus*

The House of Gaian, **Book III:**
"A vivid fantasy world....Beautiful." —*BookBrowser*

Available wherever books are sold or at
penguin.com

P C 000324539